As You Wish

Also by Leesa Cross-Smith

Every Kiss a War
Whiskey & Ribbons
So We Can Glow
This Close to Okay
Half-Blown Rose
Goodbye Earl

As You Wish

A NOVEL

Leesa Cross-Smith

An imprint of Penguin Random House LLC
1745 Broadway, New York, NY 10019
penguinrandomhouse.com

Tiny Reparations and Tiny Reparations Books with colophon
are registered trademarks of YQY, Inc.

Book design by Nancy Resnick
Illustration by Yummyphotos/Shutterstock

LIBRARY OF CONGRESS CATALOGING-IN-PUBLICATION DATA

Names: Cross-Smith, Leesa, 1978– author.
Title: As you wish: a novel / Leesa Cross-Smith. Description: New York:
Tiny Reparations Books, 2025.
Identifiers: LCCN 2024049573 (print) | LCCN 2024049574 (ebook) |
ISBN 9780593476185 (trade paperback) | ISBN 9780593476208 (ebook)
Subjects: LCGFT: Romance fiction. | Novels.
Classification: LCC PS3603.R67945 A93 2025 (print) | LCC PS3603.R67945 (ebook) |
DDC 813/.6—dc23/eng/20241029
LC record available at https://lccn.loc.gov/2024049573
LC ebook record available at https://lccn.loc.gov/2024049574

Printed in the United States of America
1st Printing

The authorized representative in the EU for product safety and compliance is
Penguin Random House Ireland, Morrison Chambers, 32 Nassau Street, Dublin D02 YH68,
Ireland, https://eu-contact.penguin.ie.

For coziness, cuteness, comfort, and healing.
For me, for you. For wishes coming true.

Let other pens dwell on guilt and misery.

—Jane Austen

The Families

THE PARKS

Hye

Minsu

Tae

Eun

Lydia

THE KIM-CRAWFORDS

Rain

Daniel

Fox

Arwen

Haru

Jenny

THE CHOIS

Aera

Geon

Nabi

Selene

As You Wish

PART ONE

Girls

1

Lydia

Lydia was well aware that her au pair host mother, Hye, was a famous actress. She'd googled her plenty of times before arriving in Seoul and had watched her most recent drama, but hadn't expected to see Hye's face plastered *huge* on the side of the taxi next to the car she was in. The air conditioner was on full blast, and instead of asking the driver to turn it down, Lydia buttoned up her brown cardigan. It was mid-August, and she'd known Seoul would be hot, but she was nervous and always got chilly when she was nervous, no matter the actual temperature.

Her hosts, Hye and Minsu, had plenty of money, and although she hadn't officially met them in person yet, Lydia sensed they didn't skimp on anything. They had sent a driver and a big black SUV to pick her up at Incheon Airport because Hye was working late and would barely make it home in time to meet her. Minsu, her husband, was a chef who also worked long hours. He wouldn't be able to leave the special event at the restaurant they owned until well after dinnertime.

There were peach and white roses wrapped in pink paper waiting for Lydia in the back of the SUV, and a card that read *Can't wait to see you* with a picture of the little boys, eight-year-old Tae and six-year-old Eun; their crayon signatures, too. In the middle compartment: a bag of dark chocolates, a can of strawberry milk, a tall glass bottle of sparkling water, and a prepackaged carton of sweetened coffee. Lydia opened the water and took a sip as she continued staring at Hye's beyond-beautiful face. She remained charmed by Hye and her looks, even after they'd video-chatted several times since she'd accepted the position, and they emailed frequently. Hye reminded Lydia of the soft portraits of the ancient, regal women she'd studied in her art history classes. Delicately full cheeks, strong nose, rosebud lips. Hye had a face that *belonged* on a taxi. Pink cartoon hearts were shooting out of her love interest's eyes—Lydia felt like hearts would shoot out of her eyes, too. She pressed her finger against the window as the traffic moved and the taxi pulled ahead.

Lydia checked her phone and responded to her mom back in Kentucky that yes, she was safe in Seoul. She could feel jet lag's long, dark shadow hovering over her, so she traded the water for the carton of coffee, hoping it would keep her alert enough to not have to crash immediately upon meeting Hye and the boys.

Nothing specific had chased her from home, but her day-to-day life had become so monotonous it'd made her feel like being uninteresting was a prison from which she would never escape. Seoul was her chance to begin again, to become a sparkly, important person. Hye's amazingness had to rub off on her somehow; proximity to greatness was always a good plan. Hye was practically perfect, and she'd chosen Lydia out of who knew how many other young women to be her family's au pair. That was a big deal. It had to mean something. Right?

Or maybe it didn't mean anything.

Maybe everything about life was random, even when it didn't seem like it.

"Excuse me? Um . . ." Lydia said in English, searching her brain for how to say what she wanted in Korean. This was easy!

She'd known how to say *excuse me* in Korean for a year, but it'd suddenly escaped her. She opened the Korean door in her mind and flipped through the words for *jump rope, office, lake, dimple,* and *bear.* The only other words she could recall were ones she would probably never need.

When they finally came to her, Lydia pronounced the three syllables carefully, and the driver turned his head, his mouth lifting in a small smile. "I'm sorry . . . I only speak a little Korean," she said. "I *am* studying, though. And practicing! Um . . . they told you where to take me? This is my first time here, and I just realized you didn't ask where I needed to go." Hye had texted her to let her know where the driver would be, describing everything precisely. When the man saw her standing there with her luggage, he hadn't said much. He simply verified her name matched the one on his phone and loaded up the car.

Lydia had goose bumps. She put the coffee carton in the cup holder and rubbed her arms.

"Yes. They've taken care of everything. We will be there in about an hour because of traffic. Sorry," the driver said kindly. *So* kindly, Lydia felt a shard of anxiety inside her soften.

"Oh, that's fine. Thank you," she said in Korean. The driver adjusted the air conditioner, and Lydia felt warmer immediately. To calm her nerves, she put her earbuds in and watched a whole new world whiz by to the sound of "Le Cygne," by Camille Saint-Saëns. Slow, soothing cello like sunlight slipping across water.

Hye was standing in front of the condo building in the bustling Gangnam district in muted chartreuse, her knee-length dress with fluttery layers catching the summer wind. Lydia bowed to her and repeated Hye's *hello* in Korean, smiling. Lydia stood holding the bouquet of roses on the sidewalk as the driver unloaded her things. Both women thanked him again before he drove away.

"Was everything okay? Your flight? Your drive?" Hye asked. "Tae and Eun are *so* excited you're finally here. They could barely sleep last night."

"Everything was lovely, thank you. I'm so excited I'm here. Your boys are *so* cute." The adorable photos of Tae and Eun had immediately caught Lydia's eye while she looked through the list of potential host families.

Hye was rolling one of her suitcases and Lydia was rolling the other. Another bag was slung over her shoulder, her purse across her chest. Hye was wearing black heels with a strap over the top of her foot that looked like it was made of diamonds. Lydia wondered if they were real as she watched them dazzle in the last bit of sunlight before she and Hye entered the building.

"Have you eaten? You'll get used to everyone constantly asking you that here in Korea."

Lydia repeated *have you eaten?* in Korean, so glad she didn't have to search her brain too hard for the phrase: *Bap meogeosseoyo?*

"Exactly. We say it all the time," Hye said as they waited for the elevator. "We're on the twenty-seventh floor. Up, up, up!"

"I had a snack in the car, yes. Thank you."

"There's plenty of real food upstairs. My mother brought some over. She's up there with the boys right now. Oh, here we go," Hye said when the elevator doors opened. Her heels made a satisfying tap on the linoleum as she stepped into the elevator. Lydia followed her.

Tae and Eun—two tiny tornadoes of excitement—tore down the spiral staircase and dashed through the living room to stand in front of Lydia. She'd left her Mary Janes by the door and put on the pretty, cloud-puffy slippers Hye pointed out. The condo was the nicest home Lydia had ever been in. A wall of tall windows sent the sun slanting across the shiny, blond hardwood floor, and the long taupe couch was covered in a panoply of white pillows. Everything smelled lovely—the bright orange of the candle on the bookcase, the sharp tang of the food in the kitchen. The beauty was overwhelming, but there was no time to fawn over her surroundings. She had to focus on the boys. Lydia had met them over video chat, but Hye still took the time to properly introduce her sons.

"Lydia, both Tae and Eun have been so excited to meet you," Hye said.

"*I'm* so excited to meet *you*," Lydia said to them before Hye disappeared into the kitchen with the roses.

Lydia bowed to the boys and bent down to talk to them. She said *annyeonghaseyo, hello* in Korean, and touched the tops of their heads.

"Hi. We're not little babies," Eun said. "My birthday was last week!"

"I know, right? Happy birthday, Eun. You're both big boys," Lydia said.

"He *is* the baby. I'm the oldest," Tae said proudly.

"Wait. You mean, you're not twins?" Lydia did her best fake gasp.

The boys laughed and shook their heads. Tae was a smidgen

taller and bigger than Eun. They had the same haircut and sweet brown eyes, but different demeanors as they looked at Lydia's face. Tae's energy was tender and calm; Eun's was busy and curious. Tae was wearing a Pokémon T-shirt and shorts; Eun, stripes under overalls.

"I will give you a real tour, but right now Tae and Eun can show you their room," Hye said as she stepped out of the kitchen back into the living area.

Lydia stood, held her hands out for the boys. They led her up the staircase.

After both the Tae-and-Eun tour and the grand tour by Hye—which included meeting Hye's mother in the kitchen before she left—Hye and Lydia were alone in Lydia's new bedroom down the hall from the boys' and the primary bedroom. Lydia's cocoa-colored room had its own bathroom and floor-to-ceiling windows. Airy cream curtains skimmed the floor, and the peach and white roses sprayed up from a ceramic vase on the dresser.

"Everything is beautiful. *So* beautiful. Like something from one of your dramas," Lydia said, sitting on the bed after Hye patted the spot for her. Hye's long fingernails were freshly manicured, pale pink.

"Well, thank you. It should feel like *your* home, too. I am very busy, as you know, shooting practically every day, sometimes *all* day, and Minsu is very busy as well, with the restaurant. Often you will be alone here with the boys. Please speak English to them. We want them to be fluent in as many languages as possible." Hye paused as if to check that Lydia was taking it all in properly. Lydia nodded to assure her she would do her best.

Hye continued.

"Tomorrow you can begin helping Tae with his science project. He and Eun are going to science camp, as you know. Eun has been working on his computer, designing a more futuristic subway station, so you can help with that, too. Also, painting! They can paint alongside you while you work on your own things, but as much as you can, speak English to them out loud while you work so they can know what you are doing. Minsu and I like to work side by side with the boys to mimic parallel play as much as possible. It's what they're used to."

As Lydia moved to grab a pen from her bag, find some paper, Hye reminded her that was also taken care of.

"I emailed all of this to you when you were in the boys' bedroom. There's also a copy in your nightstand drawer." Lydia turned to look at the cream nightstand embellished with a small crystal knob. Arranged neatly on top: a rust-colored lamp, a glass water decanter, an unopened lip balm shaped like a peach, a tube of aldehydic flower hand lotion, and a pad of paper with an elegant *L* at the top in fancy script, accompanied by a rose-gold ballpoint pen.

Near tears, Lydia did her best to hold it together. She had everything she needed, all in one place. Hye smiled at her, pulling her hair to one side before twisting it up and knotting it without an elastic band; Lydia's curls had a mind of their own and never stayed put when she tried that. She tucked her hair behind her ear and chewed on her dry bottom lip. She needed the lip balm but didn't want to desperately open the new package in front of Hye. The pause in conversation gave way to an awkward silence. Lydia folded her hands in her lap.

"You're twenty-three, and I know how important it is for young people to get out at night and go on adventures," Hye said. "Yes, believe it or not, I remember!" She touched Lydia's hand.

"I may be fifteen years older, but I *do* understand. You will have time to do that. And, as I said to you when we had our last video call, the other two families we are closest with live in this same building . . . Their au pairs will be arriving this week, too. The three of you are around the same age—I'm sure you'll hit it off. It's so important to socialize with people who are the same age; it helps us to know how we measure up. All of the kids are very close. Their moms are my best friends from childhood. We literally don't remember life before we met, since our mothers are close friends, too." She paused. "It'd be a shame if the au pairs didn't get along. We've all had au pairs before, of course, and those worked out in their own way, but I don't mind hoping for perfection this time." Hye said everything with such confidence, Lydia was inclined to believe anything that came out of her mouth.

The thought of making new friends warmed Lydia. She had one best girlfriend, Vivi, back home, and they'd known each other since middle school, but it'd been so long since she'd made a new, close one. Vivi was busy with a new husband and baby, so they texted regularly but usually had to schedule their calls now. Lydia was an oddball compared to her highly accomplished older sister, and she was an oddball among her friends, too. She simply hadn't outgrown her stubborn awkwardness. Her body noted every bit of it sitting next to her host mother on that bed. She could actually *feel* herself shrinking in Hye's shadow.

"Tomorrow evening we'll have dinner as a family at the restaurant. I'm only slightly smaller than you, and you're welcome to wear one of my dresses, if you'd like. The restaurant is not over-the-top fancy, but I love looking my best and dressing up for dinner, don't you?" Hye stood, looking down at Lydia, who felt every inch of herself wilt under the intense scrutiny. She'd sewn the bottom button of her sweater back on last week after getting it caught in the frame of her apartment door and had scored the tank top underneath it on sale for ten dollars. Could Hye sense this with her likely *I'm Rich and Famous, and Honestly, I've Always Been the Pretty, Popular Girl* powers? Was Hye disappointed she'd hired Lydia to be their au pair? Would Lydia embarrass her as soon as they stepped out into the world together?

Lydia nodded her yes and said *thank you* in English and formal Korean.

"You're more than welcome. The housekeeper comes every Monday, so your bathroom is your responsibility to clean in between if you need to do that. And remember, speak English in front of the children. Thank you so much," Hye said before leaving the room and closing the door behind her. The lavender and rain whispers of her perfume remained.

Once Lydia was alone, she couldn't keep the tears from falling. She was exhausted and overwhelmed and had shown great restraint not crying before now. She needed to get it out, reset. She threw her cardigan on the bed and went to the spotless white bathroom, turned on the water, and watched it pour out of that gorgeous faucet. Flushed the toilet so no one could hear her sniffing.

Lydia wasn't a particularly adventurous person. In fact, she got *Most Likely to Stay Home From a Party* in her high school yearbook. She was well-known for being a homebody in college and unabashedly chose painting alone over hanging out with a large group of people. Her grandmother had left her enough money to go to a private art school without having any debt. Lydia liked the cute apartment she'd lived in before leaving Kentucky and the freelancing work she did. The month before, she'd finished the butterfly murals at the children's hospital and the Noah's Ark mural in the preschool wing of her parents' church. Being alone with a paintbrush allowed her to turn her brain off. No matter what else was going on in her life, no matter what was happening on social media or in the news, Lydia could disappear into gouache and water glasses, the feeling of that first stroke against a new canvas. Painting had been a soothing escape, even in her earliest memories. When she was too shy to speak up about something, or afraid she couldn't put the right words together to say how she felt, her work spoke for itself—she learned she could express her heart through art without ever opening her mouth. Her mom was an elementary school art teacher, and their home had always been fully stocked with supplies. Her parents would set Lydia up in a little smock in the sunshine and let her make the biggest messes she wanted.

But no matter how many people told her how talented she was, or how moving her murals were—and even though she was one of only forty people from all over the world whose entries had been accepted into the art class she would be starting soon in Seoul—Lydia never felt like she was an *exceptional* talent, or that she would ever truly stand out in a crowd.

Seoul was her big emprise, and she'd felt the irresistible push to sign up for au pairing after her mother had made a snitty comment about her being too dependent on their family to travel alone. She was determined to prove her wrong. Lydia loved all she'd previously seen and heard of Seoul and was learning Korean, so she sent her info to the au pair company the next day, having to wait only a week to hear she got the job and would be living in South Korea for a year with her host family.

In the bathroom, Lydia splashed cold water on her face and dried it with the fluffy white towel on the counter. She gave herself a quiet pep talk in the mirror before reapplying her makeup quickly so she could return to the boys.

After eating *banchan*, fish cakes, *mandu*, and rice, and getting so full she let Hye make her a pot of *boricha* for digestion, Lydia sat cross-legged on the floor of the boys' room to read them a bedtime story. With her teacup warm at her feet, she sleepily did the voices of astronauts, farmers, and fish. Tae nodded off quickly, but after the last page, Eun was still wide-awake.

"Time for bed, Eun-*ah*." Lydia stood and went to him, gently pushed his hair back. Hye had gone out for drinks with friends at Minsu's restaurant and wouldn't be home for another hour. Lydia had expected to jump right into au pairing, but maybe not *quite* so quickly. She was anxious about how tired she was, afraid she'd fall asleep and look unprofessional if she didn't stay up until Hye and Minsu returned.

"I'm not sleepy yet," Eun said.

Lydia's phone buzzed and she picked it up from the floor.

Please go to bed once the boys are asleep! Do NOT wait up for us! ☺ Hye texted, reading Lydia's mind.

> Okay, thank you! Tae is sleeping, but Eun says he's not tired yet.

He always says that. Tell him I said it's bedtime, period. Thank you, Lydia.

> Okay!

"Eun-*ah*, your mommy says it's time for bed, period," Lydia said. Tae snorted cutely in his sleep, and she and Eun snickered about it, covering their mouths.

"Do you miss the United States yet?" Eun asked, yawning.

"Not really."

"Do you think you will?"

"Maybe. I'll let you know, okay?"

"What state are you from? I forgot."

"Kentucky. Like Kentucky Fried Chicken."

"I *love* fried chicken. I like Kentucky because you're from there, but I like Disneyland in Tokyo better than the one in Florida. That's what I think, but Tae doesn't agree with me. He likes to disagree with me on everything."

"That's a brother's job. I know because I have a sister," Lydia whispered.

"Younger or older?"

"She's ten years older than me."

"That's a lot," Eun said, turning over onto his side and closing his eyes.

"You're exactly right. It *is* a lot, buddy. Sweet dreams," Lydia said, tucking him in. She turned off the light.

Lydia met her host father, Minsu, in person for the first time in the kitchen a little after seven in the morning. The boys were still sleeping, and Hye was working but would meet them at the restaurant for dinner.

"Hello, Lydia. So nice to see you in the flesh. Welcome to our home. Did you sleep well?" He was handsome and cool enough to match Hye, and while Lydia wasn't one to believe in the myth of the Perfect Couple, Hye and Minsu were pretty dang close to it, at least on sight. He wore a marigold smiley face T-shirt with dark jeans and had a dimple in his right cheek that tempted Lydia to stick her finger into it when he smiled.

"Hello, Minsu. So nice to meet you, too," Lydia said comfortably. Both he and Hye had told her to call them by their first names when they'd met over video. "I did sleep well, but my body clock is upside down right now." She'd fallen asleep around nine thirty the night before, as soon as her head hit the pillow.

"That's to be expected. I fried eggs in chili oil, made toast, and there's fruit. Hye's mother's *banchan*, too." Minsu pointed at the small ceramic bowls on the table, saying some of the Korean names of the food. Lydia recognized most of them from the vocabulary book she used to teach herself *Hangul*, the Korean alphabet. She'd pored over that book obsessively after hearing a K-pop song she loved. That song was the reason she signed up for a year of classes twice a week at her local library, too.

Lydia had eaten plenty of food last night, and Hye's mother had put together a *lot*—kimchi, pickled radish, *jangajji*, seaweed salad, steamed eggplant, *kongnamul muchim*, and stir-fried zucchini. Everything was delicious and Lydia wanted more. Being this jet-lagged always made her ravenous. Once, when she and her family traveled overseas to Europe, Lydia had eaten almost an entire rotisserie chicken by herself upon returning home.

"Oh, and there is coffee, if you're a coffee person. Please say you're a coffee person," Minsu said.

"I am probably one of the coffeeist people you will ever meet."

"We are going to get along fine, I see."

She sat on the stool in front of the kitchen island. He poured dark coffee over ice.

"Cream and sugar?"

"Yes, please."

When it was fixed, he set it in front of her. He put two eggs on her plate alongside two pieces of toast with blackberries and butter.

They talked for a bit. Minsu asked her about her art, and when he talked about the restaurant, she told him she would like to take cooking lessons in Paris one day, like Audrey Hepburn in *Sabrina*. Minsu's favorite Audrey Hepburn movie was *Roman Holiday*. Lydia could see Hye was the one who ran things, but Minsu didn't seem to be one of those husbands who didn't know what went on in his own home. He clearly had full command of the kitchen, which was to be expected, and he was slightly warmer than Hye, but Lydia felt bad for thinking this. Hye had been kind to her, too, but Hye was also *famous*-famous, so Lydia didn't know what to expect. Could *famous*-famous people be especially warm to the *non*-famous people who worked for them? Lydia had learned everything she could about South Korea and Seoul before leaving the United States, but there was no guidebook for *these* intricacies.

"Is *Lydia* a family name?" Minsu asked later as he refilled her coffee, adding cream and sugar again. He refilled his own cup and stood on the other side of the kitchen island, drinking.

"No. Actually, my aunt's favorite book is *Pride and Prejudice*, and my mom couldn't think of what to name my sister or me, so my aunt named us both. My sister's Lizzy and I'm Lydia. When I was a kid, my parents named our dog Puppy. My mom can have her moments, but they aren't especially creative."

"Ha! Maybe not, but *you* are. You're an artist!" Minsu said.

"I guess," she said. "But while Lizzy is the brilliant heroine of *Pride and Prejudice*, Lydia is the silly youngest sister who gets into trouble. So, yes. That's sort of the dynamic between my sister and me, except instead of being silly or making trouble, I'm boring. At least that's what my family thinks. I kind of *am*, I guess . . ." Lydia trailed off.

"Ah," Minsu said, without adding anything else like, *Oh, I'm sure that's not true,* or *Oh, come on, you don't seem boring to me!*

She was immediately embarrassed and hated herself for it. *Get a grip, Lydia.* Why did her wave of insecurities crash through her mouth whenever she got lost in conversation with a new person?

She was thankful when she heard the boys' little feet coming down the stairs.

Before Minsu left for work, he asked Lydia to please collect a box of treats from the café down the street—a surprise for someone's birthday at the restaurant. Lydia hadn't ventured out by herself yet, but Minsu assured her she couldn't miss the place, and that the Korean she knew would be more than enough for what she needed to do.

Lydia's stomach was in knots, but she found the café easily, although it took much longer than it should have to pick up the order because the people working there kept looking past her to other customers. This wasn't entirely new for Lydia. She knew she was forgettable, but when it almost happened the fourth time, she raised her voice and said *hello* in Korean, concentrating on piecing together the syllables to say she was next in line, that she was picking up treats for the owner of Minsu's.

Minsu's restaurant was in a highly posh, hip spot in Gangnam, and focused on modern interpretations of Korean dishes and wines. He had recently opened a restaurant in Busan, and another was planned to open in New Zealand in the new year.

Lydia wanted to wear her own clothes to dinner, but Hye insisted Lydia put on one of her dresses. She went along with it easily when she saw the disappointed expression on Hye's face as she inspected the skirt and collared shirt Lydia had laid out.

So there Lydia sat—next to the children—in Hye's ruffly red dress that was too tight around the middle. Lydia was resigned to not eating much, afraid she'd bust an expensive seam. She ordered the steak but only picked at it, nibbled at her *sangchu-geotjeori* and soy sauce cucumbers. She agreed to a shot of soju since she'd read it was impolite to reject one, but she certainly wasn't going to have more than one around the children. Since she hadn't eaten much, Lydia could instantly detect the soju coursing through her blood. It made her feel like she'd float away if she didn't hold on to her chair tight enough. She planted her chunky Mary Janes firmly on the restaurant floor; her feet were two sizes too big to fit into any of Hye's shoes.

"Well, we're looking forward to an *amazing* year of you being our au pair, Lydia. Excited for the kids to soak up as much of your culture as they can. Let's see, last time our au pair was Brazilian, this year American. Maybe our next au pair will be French, who knows!" Hye said, lifting her wineglass to her lips. "But of course everything could work out and you could stay with us for another year, right? *Anything* could happen." Minsu was next to her but easily distracted. He got up from the table often to speak with the staff and at one point disappeared into the kitchen for at least ten minutes.

"I'm looking forward to it, too," Lydia said, not sure what to make of Hye talking about her next au pair when she hadn't even been in Seoul thirty-six hours. Lydia wondered if she'd done something that made Hye wish she'd chosen someone else. Lydia double-checked her posture and gave her full attention to the boys, who were talking about something in Korean she couldn't quite understand, but she watched and listened anyway, rapt.

Hye called the waiter over for water refills, and he skipped Lydia, even though her glass was empty. No one noticed, and Lydia decided not to say anything. Instead, she refocused on the children and tried to remember that anytime she felt low—anytime she felt ignored, anytime she felt homesick—if she focused on the children, she could handle it. Everything would be okay because the children were her job, and she'd worked enough hours in the nursery and Sunday school rooms at her church growing up to know she could be good at this job.

The boys were still speaking Korean, and Lydia joined them, asking if their food was delicious. Hye shot her a look, and Lydia asked them the same question in English. The soju had made her forget to *speak English in front of the children*. Lydia always got more confident speaking Korean after she'd had alcohol. She made the girls in her Korean class back home laugh whenever she got tipsy, dramatically reciting them passages from her book of Korean short stories by heart.

"I'm sorry. English only," Lydia said, feeling the cool breeze of the air conditioner on her bare arms. She rubbed them.

"Correct. *English* only," Hye said. Minsu returned to the table and put his arm around the back of Hye's chair.

"My dad is a really good chef. He has cookbooks," Tae said. Lydia had seen one of the cookbooks on the shelf in the condo's kitchen, Minsu on the cover in his chef's whites with his arms crossed, smiling next to a shiny industrial oven.

"Our dad didn't make this food! Someone else who works for him did. It's good, though," Eun said.

"I *know* our dad didn't make this, Eun."

"Tae-*yah*, eat your soup," Hye said, adding Korean words at the end that Lydia didn't catch. Hye spoke to Minsu in Korean, and Lydia slammed the brakes on thinking they were talking about her. They knew she was learning Korean when they'd hired her; they wouldn't do that. She attempted to calm her overactive mind. She was still tired, and because she hadn't been able to eat as much as she wanted, she was hungry, too. She focused on Tae and Eun for the rest of dinner.

After putting the boys to bed, Lydia texted Vivi before sitting against the headboard and calling her. She vented about feeling inadequate. Vivi told her what she always did——that she was doing great and would be fine. She encouraged Lydia to enjoy her time. Vivi was the exact opposite of her mom when it came to listening. Her mom always pointed out her flaws, all the things she needed to do better; Vivi always pointed out the positive things about her, all the things she was good at. She missed Vivi and told her so.

"I miss you, too. You'll make friends," Vivi assured her. "I promise. Soon there will be two other American au pairs in your same building."

"Right," Lydia said.

"Then repeat it. Say you'll make friends."

"Sure. I'll . . . make . . . friends."

"Oh, come on . . . You have to *believe* it. Say it like you *believe*, Lydibug."

Vivi would never let her off the phone if she didn't say it with her whole chest, so she did.

"I *will* make friends."

After they hung up, Lydia turned off the lamp and slowly fell asleep in her cocoa-brown bedroom. The colored lights of the city flashed the sky hanging over her, so far from home.

2

Jenny

Jenny put her phone away. She was tired of staring at it, tired of waiting for a message that was never going to come. She'd specifically jetted to Seoul to get away from Ethan, even the *idea* of Ethan, so when had staring at her phone waiting for him to reach out—or listening for anything that sounded remotely like a buzz or a ping, hoping it was him—become her full-time job?

Jenny didn't even know what she was waiting for.

She *hated* her phone. She stepped away from eight-year-old Fox and seven-year-old Arwen for a moment, went to the bathroom, and decided to leave the device facedown on the nightstand.

That lasted one second.

She picked it right back up and debated texting a friend, but knew everyone was sick of her talking about Ethan all the time. Instead, she moved her phone to the top drawer, buried it beneath her underwear, and rejoined the kids.

The Kim-Crawford family had welcomed Jenny with such warmth and kindness, she'd instantly felt at home. Rain Kim had a laid-back presence and only wanted Jenny to hang out and play with the kids while she was at work. She was a dentist with her own practice. Her husband, Daniel Crawford, an American, worked from home a lot as a webcomic illustrator in his sunny, spacious office full of color at the end of the hallway. Jenny,

Rain, and Arwen did hydrating snail-mucin face masks together before bed the night Jenny got to Seoul. Rain told her twice that it was a necessity, since long flights could really dry out the skin.

The Kim-Crawfords had dinner guests this evening.

"Jenny, this is Lydia," Rain said to her, motioning towards the young woman in the foyer sliding her feet into the beige slippers by the door.

"Hi, Lydia," Jenny said, adding *hello* in Korean at the end.

"Lydia, Jenny is from California," Rain said. "You two look like you could be friends. Dan, don't Jenny and Lydia look like they're meant to be friends?"

Daniel was behind the television fiddling with one of the wires trailing from it.

"Oh, hi . . . uh . . . um," he started, popping his head up.

"Lydia," Lydia said, filling in his blank.

"Yes. That's right. *Lydia!* Hi, Lydia. Yes, honey, I completely agree," Daniel said distractedly before turning his attention back to the wires.

"You're even the same height," Rain said, pointing at the tops of their heads. She told them both they had lovely teeth, and Jenny and Lydia took turns saying *thank you* in Korean.

Lydia's host parents, the Parks, were in the kitchen. Their two boys disappeared upstairs to the kids' bedrooms. Arwen popped up out of nowhere, tugging on the fabric of Jenny's dress.

"I was hiding, but Fox wouldn't look for me. I'm gonna hide again." Arwen pouted and blew her bangs off her forehead.

"That's a good idea! Go tell the boys they have to count slowly, okay?" Jenny said.

"Okay!" Arwen said, skipping away and running up the spiral staircase.

"You two want to go hang out with the kids until dinner is ready? Get to know each other?" Rain suggested.

"Of course," Jenny said. She and Lydia followed Arwen up to the bedrooms.

Arwen told the three boys she was going to hide somewhere and that it was their job to find her. The boys obliged, and after learning the Parks' sons' names, Jenny knew it was Tae who started the counting.

"They're all *so* adorable, aren't they? I've nannied for some hella annoying kids before. This is a relief," Jenny said, sitting on the floor of Fox's dark green bedroom. It was as spacious as Arwen's purple bedroom, like all the rooms in the condo. She'd worked for several rich families back home—once for a famous B-list actress a couple years ago—but she liked the Kim-Crawfords better than all of them put together, and she'd only been in Seoul a few days.

Some of that was surely how nice the family was. Some of that was surely how far she was from home.

Five thousand nine hundred fifty-five miles, to be exact.

Jenny's ex Ethan was a voice actor. It used to be reassuring and fun when she heard his familiar cadence play from her laptop or TV—before that reassurance and fun had turned into her biggest nightmare. The day after they broke up, the first thing she heard in the morning was his voice blasting from the TV in the indie movie trailer voice-over he'd been excited to score. She'd cried and started mindlessly flipping through channels.

Five thousand nine hundred fifty-five miles away from Ethan's voice.

Five thousand nine hundred fifty-five miles from Ethan and her apartment and the coffee shop they frequented on summer evenings and the stone bench on Manhattan Beach where they had their first kiss and the farmers' market they went to on Saturday mornings, and and and.

Why Seoul? her mom asked her when she mentioned the au pair opportunity. *I like how it sounds like* soul *and it's blissfully far away* was her answer.

"They *are* adorable," Lydia said.

Lydia was really cute, but Jenny could tell she had no clue how cute she was. She carried herself with the energy of a girl who assumed no one was going to remember her name, so she couldn't have been offended that Daniel had forgotten as soon as Rain said it.

Tae finished his comically slow counting, and he and the boys tore out of the room. Jenny reminded them to be careful finding Arwen, then asked Lydia what brought her to Korea.

"I was bored and stuck back home and thought this would be a good . . . maybe *jump-start* is the right word? I got accepted into an art class, so I'll be doing that, too," Lydia said.

"What kind of art? Painting?"

Lydia nodded, adding that she was also a knitter who tinkered in glass and fiber arts.

"That's awesome. Daniel's an artist, you know that, right? I love his webcomics. I love *any* webcomic, really. That's what I did on the plane over here. Read webcomics and cried my eyes out watching *Crash Landing on You* because it's so perfectly romantic even *before* you know the couple is married in real life. But when it comes to art, I can barely draw a line," Jenny said. Her mom had told her countless times that she was the only child in preschool who hated craft hour.

Lydia asked for the link to Daniel's webcomics. They traded phone numbers and emails before swapping their favorite K-dramas. They sighed over their shared love for Ra Miran, Ji Changwook, Park Seojoon, and Wi Hajoon. When Eun jogged into the bedroom, he snapped them out of their fangirling by asking Lydia if it was time to eat.

"Soon," Lydia said to him. "Did you find Arwen?"

Eun shook his head.

"Well, you better keep looking hard!" she said to him as he walked out.

"Do you know anything about the other au pair? The one for the Chois? I think we're supposed to meet her sometime this week," Jenny asked. Rain hadn't spilled any details about the other au pair besides the fact that she was twenty-five, like her, and from New York. Jenny hadn't met the Chois but knew they lived directly above the Kim-Crawfords.

"No. I don't know anything about her, but it'll be really nice to have other American au pairs in the building. Makes me feel less alone. Although I *came* here to prove to myself I could do this alone . . . in a way, I guess."

Jenny sat there for a moment, considering the paradox of Lydia's personality. She was clearly kind of shy but seemed unable to stop herself from blurting out her true feelings. It made Jenny feel protective, and feeling protective made Jenny want to compliment her. Lydia's clothes were pretty. She was wearing a stylish coral linen short suit, and something about the shape of her face reminded Jenny of Minnie Mouse, which she found extremely endearing.

"I love your suit. I see girls on Instagram wearing them and they always look so stylish!" Jenny said.

"Oh, thank you, but it's Hye's. She was disappointed in the clothes I brought with me, so she's been lending me hers. I guess I'll have to go shopping." Lydia sighed.

"Now *that* I can do. Maybe we can go together."

"I would love that! You clearly know what you're doing. I love your bow," Lydia said. Jenny rarely wore jeans or pants and rarely did her hair without adding a bow. That morning, she'd tied her long ponytail up with a wide pink ribbon, and put on a white slip dress over a little pink T-shirt. She was girly by nature but had turned her Seoul wardrobe up to the *highest* levels of pastels and prettiness. Shortly after the breakup with Ethan, she'd wanted to wear old sweatshirts and jeans, hadn't cared about dressing up anymore, but she refused to let herself fall into that sloppy trap here. Now she dressed up every day no matter what, even if she didn't feel like it. She scoured Pinterest, fashion blogs, and YouTube for ideas, and bought new clothes to complement her new life. The bows and dresses made her look like she was holding it together, even when she knew she wasn't.

Jenny was wearing a pearl necklace and matching earrings. Lydia complimented those, too, and Jenny touched her earlobe as Lydia continued talking. "Ugh. My fashion sense stalled out when I was in high school. I have no clue what I like anymore. I'm an artist, so I *should* be stylish or cool, but I'm not. Like, at all," Lydia said, letting the last part soften so much Jenny had a hard time hearing her.

As soon as Jenny opened her mouth to tell her she seemed cool enough, Rain walked into the bedroom and let them know it was time for dinner.

Daniel had made Korean pizzas from scratch and was excited to show them off. One had shrimp, rice, and *gochujang*; another *bulgogi*, kimchi, and sweet potato. The last was vegetarian, topped with spicy garlic, fried egg, and *jangajji*. In their first conversation over video chat, Daniel had let Jenny know that he was an adventurous cook, and Jenny mentioned she'd learned new dishes after going vegetarian with Ethan three years ago. Once Arwen heard them discussing vegetarianism, she declared she wanted to be one, too.

Arwen was sitting next to Jenny at the table now, looking over at her.

"*We're* vegetarians," Arwen said to her dad as he put a slice of veggie pizza on her plate.

"Of course. How could I forget?" Daniel said, winking at Jenny.

Jenny smiled at both of them and got a slice for herself. The Kim-Crawfords had a huge dining room table, and the ten of them sat at it comfortably, stuffing their faces. The parents were drinking soju and wine; the au pairs and kids, lemon-lime fizzy water. When Fox knocked over his can, Jenny hopped out of her chair and grabbed a dish towel to mop up the mess.

The rest of dinner went smoothly. The pizza was delicious, and Jenny felt like she'd lived with the Kim-Crawfords for much longer than a few days. From what she'd seen, Rain and Daniel seemed to really love each other. Jenny wanted to hold on to any shred of hope that long-term relationships *could* work. The breakup with Ethan had been sudden and absolutely maddening because he'd never given her a reason, and she was far from being healed. She didn't want to wait it out; she wanted to run away, even if she knew in her bones that outrunning her pain was impossible. But she was committed to trying, even as she tortured herself with memories of how happy she and Ethan had been. How intimately they knew each other. How he was the only person in the world who knew exactly where her back was so ticklish it made her toes wiggle.

They'd promised each other forever.

Where did those intense feelings go for him? Jenny was left dizzied, still clutching on to hers.

She wanted to check Ethan's social media so bad it felt like her teeth would chatter from holding back. It was a relief when all the parents stepped out for drinks on the balcony. Rain asked her and Lydia to wrangle the children so they could watch a movie in one of the rooms upstairs before bedtime.

This job will keep me too busy to dwell on things.

Jenny tried to make her mind as blank as possible. She talked and listened to Lydia as she let herself drift away into the colorful, singsongy cartoon projected on the playroom wall.

That night, with the Parks and Lydia gone and everyone else in the condo asleep, the temptation to sneak a peek at Ethan's socials was unbearable. Jenny took a long, lava-hot shower, pinched herself up and down her arms—an attempt to trick her brain into focusing on that instead—before getting the phone from the drawer and turning it all the way off.

It worked.

For about five minutes.

But then she just *had* to turn the phone back on and look.

As soon as she did, she wished she could rewind time and unsee it.

Ethan's ex-turned-girlfriend-again was holding her hand up close, and Ethan was looking at her face. No one on earth could miss the icy rock on her finger.

Jenny felt like she'd been flipped inside out and dipped in alcohol.

Dissolving, she texted him.

> I saw. I just want you to know I saw it. You've
> broken a part of me FOREVER, Ethan, and I
> know I've told you that more than once . . . but
> I'm saying it AGAIN. You replaced me with her,
> threw me away like I was nothing. You continue
> to (try to) make me feel like I'm nothing.

It was around midnight in Seoul, but it was early morning in LA. Ethan would be up by now, showering or having his coffee, while she was on her new bed in Seoul, in her new bedroom in Seoul, with her new door closed in Seoul, waiting for his reply. Finally, it came.

> Jennybelle, I swear I never meant for it to
> happen like this. Please believe me when I say,
> in a way . . . you will be in my heart forever.
> You'll always be a part of my life.

> Fuck you, Ethan. DO NOT call me Jennybelle.
> I'm not your Jennybelle anymore.

> I hope one day we can get past this and be
> friends. I'm truly sorry?

> Not a CHANCE in HELL, but congratulations!!!!

Jenny was crying so hard she couldn't breathe properly. The nerve of him calling her Jennybelle pushed her over the edge.

Most people assumed her full name was Jennifer, but it wasn't. The name had come to her dad in a dream, and although most people called her Jenny, her dad had always called her Jennybelle, which was why it was so special to her.

She'd met Ethan a few months before her dad got sick and died. The night her dad and Ethan had been introduced, her dad had told him the story of how Jenny got her name. Her dad had loved Ethan, even going so far as to tell her that if he could pick a good man for her to spend the rest of her life with, it would be someone like him.

She'd cried, telling Ethan she hated the thought of not hearing her dad say her full name anymore. Ethan asked if it would be okay if *he* called her Jennybelle and she'd swooned.

Now Ethan using her full name felt like being cursed at. She stood and tapped her phone, desperately wanting to delete the messages and his number forever. She blocked him and his ex on socials, then deleted every social media app she had in a fit of rage. She called her mom and could barely get out the words.

"Mama? Ethan's . . . Ethan's *engaged* to his ex now. We dated for *three* years. It's only been *three* months since we broke up, and he's engaged already!"

"Oh, *honey*," her mom said so tenderly it made Jenny cry even harder.

After listening to her mom promise she wouldn't feel this way forever, Jenny put her head on the pillow and made so much noise crying, Rain tapped on her door quickly before coming right in.

"Jenny? Jenny, are you all right? Are you sick? *Home*sick?" Rain asked, sitting on the bed.

"No. Oh, no. I'm so sorry if I woke you. Please don't worry about me. It's about a guy. I'm crying like this about a *guy*, but I promise it'll be the last time. I promise to *God* I will never do this again. It's so unprofessional; I'm *so* sorry. Please don't send me home or anything. I love it here . . . I love this condo. Please give me another chance!" Jenny sobbed out, sitting up. She said *please* and *I'm sorry* in formal Korean. Rain stood and went to the bathroom, came back with a glass of water for Jenny. She drank.

"Stop. You didn't wake me up, and we *love* having you here. Dan and I never considered any other au pairs once we found you. Fox and Arwen are completely in love with you. You're not going anywhere, but please tell me what happened," Rain said, going to the bathroom again, this time returning with a washcloth. Jenny took it and held it to her eyes.

She told Rain everything, and Rain listened, sharing her own story of the brutal, shitty breakup she went through before she met Daniel. Jenny had liked Rain's face from the moment she saw her picture, but in person, her demeanor was even *more* serene. She had an almost supernaturally soothing presence that made Jenny want to tell her everything. Jenny thought about how lucky Fox and Arwen were to have a mother with a face like that—a face that could make them feel like everything was going to be okay. Jenny's mom's kind face was *five thousand nine hundred fifty-five miles* away, but in that moment, Rain's was an excellent substitute.

"I thought I'd never fall in love again, but . . . I did," Rain said.

Jenny saw the way Daniel looked at Rain, how he put his hand on the small of her back in the kitchen. She heard the way Rain said *Dan*—such a common name, but made special by the way she said it, like her mouth was full of light.

"Ethan obviously never loved me the way I loved him."

"If that's true, then he didn't deserve you. It's going to take someone better, and he's out there," Rain reassured her gently.

They hugged tightly, and when Rain left her alone in the bedroom again, Jenny quietly cried herself into a well-deep sleep.

I hate love. I'll never fall in love again. Never ever.

Those were the only thoughts in Jenny's head when she woke the next morning.

Also: *Who is jumping on my bed?*

Fox. It was Fox.

"In an hour, you have to walk me to piano and Arwen to violin, but her class is right down the hallway from mine, so you won't have to go far. Sometimes Daddy lets Arwen walk to violin by herself because she's not a baby anymore, but she's not the oldest, I am!" Fox said, jumping big on the words *I* and *am*. Jenny's half-asleep brain was trying to process everything he was saying. Her cry-headache throbbed when she rubbed her eyes.

"Fox, please don't . . . don't jump, okay? Let me get up and get ready. We'll be right on time, all right?"

"Okay. Mommy just left."

Fox hopped off the bed and out of her room.

When Jenny turned on her phone, she saw a text from Rain.

> Thank you for sharing what's going on with you.
> I'm sorry you've been feeling so sad. I hope
> Seoul is the new beginning you need. See you
> this evening! ☺

> Thank you, Rain. For everything. I'm SO
> embarrassed I broke down in front of you! This
> message makes me feel better. Thank you for
> understanding.

Jenny put on a white baby-doll dress and tied a lilac ribbon in her hair before going downstairs to the sunny kitchen. The kids were heartily gobbling down their eggs and rice. When they were finished, Fox went to find another shirt, since he'd spilled Coco Grape juice on the one he was wearing. Daniel's work meeting was starting soon, but he popped in quickly to say goodbye to Jenny and the kids before they left.

The three of them were on the way to the elevators when Arwen realized she'd forgotten her violin. They went back to the condo to get it. As the group headed out again, Jenny made a joke about how silly it would be if Fox had to bring a piano to class with him every week, earning bubbly giggles from both.

With the kids at their music lessons, Jenny took a walk past cute boutiques and fancy clothiers. Gangnam was flashy, packed full of everything anyone could ever want. Cozy nooks and luxurious showrooms. Bustling cafés and more subdued ones. Salons, skyscrapers, bookstores. She wandered through the mall, window-shopping, pausing to look at anything she found remotely interesting. Her headache had faded, thankfully. When she emerged, she stopped for a cup of coffee and a wedge of violet cream cake that was almost too pretty to eat. She sat by the shop's front window and reread some pages of her comfort book, *Circle of Friends*, by Maeve Binchy. Part of her wished she hadn't deleted her social media apps so she could post a pretty picture. Maybe unblock Ethan, too, and let him see that her life was aesthetically pleasing without him. She'd made sure to throw the book in her bag before leaving the condo, but she couldn't focus. Anger stewed in her heart like tomatoes. She considered calling Ethan one more time, imagining how she'd feel hearing his voice.

She resisted, but barely. What a constant tightwire act this was.

The next day, when all four kids were at science camp, Jenny and Lydia went shopping.

"What do you like? Long dresses, short dresses? T-shirts? Ooh, do you need shorts?" Jenny asked Lydia as she flipped through a rack of clothes in front of a shop.

"I brought a bunch with me, and I like how she's wearing hers," Lydia said as a woman walked past them in cuffed maroon shorts with black tights underneath.

"Okay, tights. Let's do it. What about dresses?" Jenny said, pointing at a buttercup dress in the shop window.

"Hmm. Do you think Hye would like that?"

"On one hand, her opinion matters, but on the other, it doesn't. Do *you* like it?" While she understood Lydia wanted to impress Hye and be liked by her, Jenny also wanted to push back a bit, in case it was what Lydia needed.

"I think I like it?"

"Plus, it's from *this* place," Jenny said, jazzing her hands like a showgirl up at the fancy store sign. "I think Hye will respect that at least."

Lydia decided she wanted it; they went inside, leaving with the dress and two pairs of tights.

They walked past a taxi with Hye's picture on it as they made their way to another shop, where Jenny nudged Lydia to decide for herself if she wanted to buy a plaid blazer or a pair of linen pants. After much deliberation, the blazer won.

"I can wear it with the dress when it gets cooler," Lydia said as they stepped back out into the summer air.

They had just enough time to stop at a café before they had to scoop up the kids.

"Do you have a boyfriend back home?" Lydia asked Jenny, sipping her latte. The café was crowded and cool. A group of college students at the table next to them chatted and worked on their laptops.

Jenny broke her red velvet cookie into two pieces and took a bite before answering.

"I do not. However, there *is* a total asshole back home who ripped my heart out." In that moment, she didn't feel sad; she felt red-hot rage that she'd ever allowed a man to make her feel so low, so unworthy, so everything and nothing all at once.

"I'm sorry, Jenny," Lydia said. It was the first time they were hanging out like this, but Jenny appreciated the intimacy of Lydia's understanding, of how great a listener she was. Shopping, then sitting in a café talking shit about men were the same things Jenny loved doing with her girlfriends back home. Jenny told her so and Lydia laughed. It had been a while since Jenny had hung out with her friends; a few of them had avoided her for about a month before she left because they were so tired of her obsessing over Ethan.

She filled Lydia in on little details about her breakup, as well as being the only child of divorced parents who went on to remarry other people and divorce again.

"So, yeah, my goal is to get over my ex forever and move on with my life . . . whatever that looks like," Jenny ended.

"Being here is a good start, in my opinion." Lydia's curly hair was a deep red-brown, like autumn leaves. She tucked some of it behind her ear.

"I agree. Thanks for saying that."

Jenny imagined Ethan on the other side of the world picking out an engagement ring for his ex-turned-fiancée. Jenny wondered if his proposal had been a surprise, if they had an engagement party, when and where the wedding would be. Maybe his ex was pregnant. No, she would've heard about that, right? But she hadn't heard about the engagement, so maybe not. She stared out the window with her heart on fire, wanting to run, wanting to cry, wanting to scream.

But she stayed still and quiet.

She took a small moment to look at the faces and feet passing outside the café window, until Lydia spoke again.

"I haven't had a boyfriend in forever and can usually distract myself from thinking about it, but now that I see *all* of these hot guys everywhere, I want one again."

"How did it end with your last boyfriend?" Jenny asked.

"We dated back in high school and went to different colleges. Our relationship wasn't strong enough to withstand that."

"Did he break your heart? Ethan was the first guy to ever break mine. It hurts just as bad as it does in maudlin breakup songs. I kind of always thought people were . . . *exaggerating*, you know? They're not."

Lydia shook her head. "I believe you. I've never had my heart broken like that before."

"I need a breakthrough. Something *huge* needs to happen to get me over this emotional turmoil. My dad used to always say, 'A small wound can kill.' My broken heart is *big*, for me, but the sentiment is the same."

Jenny realized she was doing it again. Talking about Ethan and her broken heart too much, because Lydia took charge of the conversation and began telling her about the cool spots they should check out when they had free time in Seoul. Karaoke bars and art installations. Ancient palaces and mountain-high views. They could also rent bikes and ride along the Han River, hit up photo booths they walked past on the way to the café. At first

Jenny was annoyed, but a warm feeling of hope quickly won out. She could have fun in Seoul and leave everything else behind. She, Lydia, and quite possibly the au pair they hadn't met yet could have the time of their lives if they wanted to.

Jenny finished her iced coffee and pulled out her phone. Made a list in her notes app of the places and things Lydia mentioned, and the websites she wanted to look at when she got back to the condo, tucked into her cozy bed for the night.

"Your new clothes are really cute, by the way," Jenny told Lydia on their walk to pick up the kids. "I bet your old ones are, too, though."

"Thank you. I seriously appreciate the encouragement." Lydia paused. "Okay, I'm not quite sure how to say this, but, um, do you think we can try to be *normal*? You try not to obsess over your ex so much, and I'll try not to obsess over how much I fall short next to my perfect host mother. Let's enjoy our time in Seoul the best we possibly can. Deal?" Lydia asked.

"Deal," Jenny said, holding out her pinky. Their thumbs kissed.

3

Selene

"This is Selene. She's an influencer and, like, the most *effortlessly* cool person I've ever met, and I know a lot of cool people!" Selene's host mother, Aera Choi, said to everyone in the kitchen.

Selene's fashion Instagram had 275K followers and Aera had mentioned it the first time they talked after Selene sent over her résumé. Her socials had racked up tons of new followers after her shaggy wolf cut went viral on a popular Brooklyn salon's Instagram, and her Get Ready with Me vlogs and Look Books were mentioned in a popular online magazine's listicle—"Fifteen Fashion Girlies You Should Get to Know Right Meow!" Aera seemed impressed by those things; she wanted her daughter to have a stylish, cool au pair. Aera had been following her socials and loving her posts for a month now, talking to Selene about her favorites.

"Oh, please," Selene replied, a bit embarrassed, "but thank you. Hi, everyone." She waved. Aera finished introducing the Parks, the Kim-Crawfords, and their au pairs, Lydia and Jenny. Everyone bowed, shook hands. The children scattered, including the Chois' nine-year-old daughter, Nabi, the oldest and only *only* child of the three families.

"You do know a lot of cool people," Selene's host dad, Geon, added with a chuckle from his seat at the table. When he stood, he was the tallest person in the room.

"Please call everyone by their first names, although my grandmother would scream about it. There's no need for formalities among our families. Hye and Rain are like sisters to me, and our children have been raised together," Aera said.

Selene tried to remember the family breakdowns: Lydia was the au pair for the Parks. There was Hye; her husband, Minsu; and their children, Tae and Eun. Jenny was the au pair for the Kim-Crawfords: Rain, Daniel, Fox, and Arwen. Selene was only a few weeks older than Jenny; Lydia was the youngest. They quickly discovered all three of them had summer birthdays—two Cancers and a Leo.

Now Selene, Lydia, and Jenny were with the children in Nabi's playroom upstairs. Nabi's white puppy, Gureum—wearing a teeny-tiny yellow T-shirt—yipped as Nabi held the controller to the small butterfly drone she was flying near the ceiling. "*Gureum* means *cloud* in Korean," Nabi had said to her the first time she and Selene met over video. "I also know *nabi* means *butterfly*," Selene had replied. Nabi beamed. Her bedroom and playroom were both fit for a little girl named Butterfly—a kaleidoscope of pink and yellow tulle butterflies hung above them, and long butterfly-wing curtains were pulled back from the windows.

Selene and Nabi had bonded over email before meeting in person. They sent each other pictures of butterflies for weeks, and Selene had impressed Nabi by sending her a video she took of a blue butterfly she came across in Bryant Park that matched the butterfly sticker on Nabi's iPad.

Before everyone else had gotten there that evening, Selene had braided Nabi's long hair as they listened to a BTS track after Nabi mentioned her dad learned to play their song "Butterfly" on his guitar for her. Selene and Nabi both loved BTS and had already spent a considerable amount of time gushing over their videos, flipping through pictures of them, *ooh*ing and sighing over each member's extreme cuteness.

Selene could tell Nabi was the leader of the rest of the kiddos, but she was a kind and gentle ruler. The boys called her *noona*—the word Korean boys used for *older sister*—and Arwen called her *unnie*—the word Korean girls used—with sweetness on their tongues. Selene found Korean honorifics beautiful and loved hearing those words coming from the children's mouths, along with *hyung* and *oppa*—meaning *big brother*, depending on whether a boy or girl was speaking. And although Selene witnessed Tae and Nabi scramble for power when Tae wanted an extra-long turn at flying the butterfly drone, Nabi let him know he had to wait until after Arwen, since that was the order they'd decided upon.

Selene had been in Korea for a few days now, and the transition from NYC to Seoul had been so easy it made her nervous. She was waiting for a dark moment to sneak up, something to let her know this was a mistake, but she hadn't felt it yet. She wished she had someone in her family to call back home. Someone she could let know how comfortable she was feeling, how safe and good. But her parents were in Oregon visiting their friends and she didn't want to disturb them, and her only sibling, Paul, was almost twenty years older than her, busy with his own family. She and Paul had never been super close anyway, since they'd never actually lived in the same house together; he was already off to college on the other side of the country by the time she was born. She'd always known she was adopted and half Korean, had been told the same story her whole life.

Her adoptive mother hadn't thought she wanted any more

children, especially after she and her husband had tried for so long. But one day their church was visited by a Korean missionary who spoke of Korean orphanages. Selene's mother was curious and called, wanting to know if this was God's plan. She saw a picture of Selene wrapped in a red blanket; she'd been put into a box and left on the sidewalk at an intersection one early morning in July.

They found you in the sun with a tiny bee bracelet around your wrist.

Her adoptive parents felt drawn to her, flew to Seoul, and returned to NYC with their new baby. They'd been lovely to Selene all her life; she hadn't lacked anything growing up. They were introverted and kind, both history professors at a university, both in bed with their books by ten thirty every night.

Her parents suspected her biological mother was young and possibly unmarried. It was only in the last year or so, from her small apartment in Brooklyn, that Selene had slowly begun her search, curious to know more. She started by regularly posting on message boards online but found nothing. She'd tried a dozen times to contact the orphanage but never got a response. She gave her DNA to one of those websites and found one *very* distant relative on her father's side who helped her piece together that her father's name was Adam Shelton. He was an American stationed in South Korea for a few years, killed by friendly fire a year after she was born. He was born in Cincinnati in 1977 and had been twenty-four years old when he was killed, a year younger than Selene was now. She found several news articles about his death, and they all used the same photo of him—in it, he was straight-faced, wearing his uniform and a beret. Her birth father was black and handsome, radiating coolness, his full mouth reminding Selene a lot of her own.

Before flying to Seoul, Selene made a stop in Cincinnati to visit her birth father's grave for the first time. Someone had loved him enough to make sure he had a beautiful, unique headstone. The distant relative she'd found could only tell her that her birth father's mother had also passed away years ago. Selene wished so badly she could find another picture of her father so she could see his smile. She wondered if he ever knew he had a daughter. Everything else she searched for was a dead end, and there were no matches for her biological mother or any relatives from her side.

Maybe it was turning twenty-five, a year older than her biological father had ever been, or not knowing exactly what she wanted to do with the rest of her life, but the timing had felt right; Selene decided to come to Seoul herself—armed with the red blanket and the bee bracelet—to see what she could puzzle out about her biological mother. Was she out there somewhere? Could she pass by her on the streets of Seoul and not know it? The thought made Selene buzz with anxious excitement, and it also made her sad.

She didn't even know her mother's name.

As much as wanting to see her face, Selene wanted to know her name. She wanted to say it aloud, see if it sounded like home.

"Surprise!" Aera said, walking into Nabi's playroom. Someone flicked the lights off and on, to get their attention. All six parents were wearing kitschy floral shirts and holding Snoopy plushies for the kids.

Squeals of excitement erupted all around Selene. "Are we going to Jeju?" Nabi asked.

"*Yay!*" Tae jumped up, pumping his fist in the air. The puppy started jumping along with him, and Tae scooped it up, cradling it like a baby.

The au pairs—lounging on the floor with question marks over their heads—looked up at the parents.

"Yes! We're leaving the day after tomorrow, all of us! So, girls, we'll need you to help pack up the kids and get ready. I have matching pajamas for everyone, too, so that's one thing you won't have to remember to bring," Aera said.

Selene, Lydia, and Jenny moved towards their families to get more information.

"We usually try to go together at least once a year, and thought it'd be fun to make it a surprise for the au pairs this year," Jenny's host mother said.

"Do you know where Jeju Island is? Have you ever heard of it?" Hye asked Lydia, pulling out her phone to show her photos.

Aera began telling Selene to allow Nabi to take only two bathing suits, warning her that Nabi usually tried to sneak three into her luggage. "We're a tad *overindulgent* with her, since she's our only child, and I may have gotten her obsessed with fashion a little early." Aera and Geon ran a small fashion design house and shop called Sobok Sweet, which was popular on social media. As soon as Selene learned *sobok* was a Korean ideophone that evoked a gentle *falling*—or the sound light snow made as it piled up—it became one of her favorite words.

Aera liked to talk about how cool Selene was, but Selene thought Aera was the Cool One, with her trendy bangs that stopped right above her full eyebrows and the way she put on dark red lipstick before she came downstairs each morning. Selene had stood frozen in awe of Aera's walk-in closet of leather and lace. The vibe of Sobok Sweet's clothing for women was dark and edgy with a touch of frilly romance—cotton candy tulle skirts with motorcycle jackets and combat boots, long necklaces, cropped unraveling sweaters. All of it right down Selene's fashion alley.

"Nabi's basically an influencer," Selene said.

"*You* would know!" Aera said.

"I watched a documentary on the *haenyeo* last year, the professional diving women of Jeju. It was fascinating. They're my heroes now," Lydia said. When Jenny and Selene looked at Lydia, clearly clueless, Lydia filled them in on the awe-inspiring women who could hold their breath for over three minutes as they harvested seafood and other treasures from the deep ocean.

"What about the Snoopy plushies? Are those connected, too?" Jenny asked her host parents.

"Snoopy Garden!" Fox said.

"What's Snoopy Garden?" Selene asked, completely lost in the muddle of words and descriptions racing around the room.

"A garden with a lot of statues from *Peanuts*. They have yummy pizza there, too. I love going to Jeju. We'll get to feed alpacas at a farm!" Fox's little sister, Arwen, said to the au pairs. Nabi handed the butterfly drone controller to Eun since it was his turn to fly it across the room. The puppy ran around in circles, chasing it.

"Are you excited?" Aera asked Selene as the butterfly fluttered to the curtains.

"I am," Selene said, already imagining herself sunning on the beach in her black bikini and big sunglasses, watching the kids in the water.

Jenny's host mother, Rain, dropped another surprise on the au pairs when they got to the airport. Rain's younger brother, Haru, would be joining them.

"Apparently he's *moving in* with us when we get back," Jenny whispered to Selene and Lydia as they sat at their gate sharing a bag of honey-butter chips, making sure the kids didn't get too wild. Nabi and Arwen were playing a game together on the iPad, but the boys were being loud by the windows, watching the planes take off. Lydia went over and requested they quiet down.

"Wait! Haru is moving *in?*" Lydia asked once she returned.

"Well, *you're* clearly God's favorite," Selene said to Jenny, turning to look at Haru.

He and Lydia's host father, Minsu, had gone to get beers at the bar next to them. Selene learned they worked together at Minsu's restaurant, that Haru had helped Minsu open his second restaurant in Busan, and that early next year, Haru would be moving to New Zealand to open a third. Haru's profile was pretty. His clothes were stylish, too. Selene wanted to take a pic of him for her Instagram. He was wearing a rumpled-on-purpose white linen button-down rolled up to the elbows and mid-thigh navy shorts with a pair of clean, all-white sneakers. An expensive-looking watch with a deep blue face sat on his wrist. A simple outfit, but classic, moneyed.

The families were close friends, but with Rain's brother working with Minsu, everyone was even more tangled up than Selene had realized. "You don't have a boyfriend, do you?" she asked Jenny.

"Me? No. Never. I mean . . . I *had* one . . . but not anymore. I don't want a new one, either. I'm officially anti-romantic," Jenny said before launching into how much of a dick her ex was. She let Selene know she'd told Lydia all about it the other day. Selene listened intensely to the drama, and when Jenny was finished, Selene agreed: Ethan sucked.

"Okay, so I get you don't want a new boyfriend, but even if

he looks like *that*?" Selene said, nodding her head towards Haru. "Girl, don't reject a blessing! But if you're *sure*, tell him to call me. I'm ready and willing if he's single. He's gorgeous."

"Unfortunately, he *is* gorgeous," Jenny said. "But no! Forever single. Leave me out of it!" She made an *X* with her arms.

When the kids got loud again, Selene went over. The host moms disappeared to the wine bar when their one-hour flight was delayed.

Selene saw that the braid she'd put in Nabi's hair that morning was unraveling. She called her over so she could rebraid it. The au pairs waited until Selene was finished, and once Nabi was busy with her device again, they circled back to the Haru conversation.

"He *is* really cute, and, well, let's just say I'm getting desperate. Something like *sexual tension*," Lydia whispered this last part, glancing at the kids, "but more pressing, since it's referring to someone who has only had sex with one guy, and that was in high school."

"Oh," Jenny said, wide-eyed. She looked at Lydia, then Selene.

"Well, that won't last long here, I bet. You're too pretty, and these guys are too good-looking. Hope you're ready for that second virginity ship to sail away, my friend," Selene said wryly.

"I'm *more* than ready, trust me, and if it doesn't happen naturally, I'll hire someone. They have that here, right? World's oldest profession? I'm not above it!" Lydia said, laughing unabashedly. Selene thought she was adorable.

"I'm, like, the total opposite of you two right now. No boys allowed," Jenny said, holding both hands to her heart and shaking her head. The glossy yellow ribbon in her long hair swished.

"I believe you," Lydia said.

"*I* don't!" Selene said.

When they turned to look at Haru and Minsu at the bar again, Haru was sneaking a peek at them with his pretty brown eyes, his smile like a secret.

The first full day on Jeju, the girls took the kids to Snoopy Garden. Eun fell twice before they got to the giant Snoopy on the edge of the dock at Warm Puppy Lake. The au pairs carried Band-Aids in their bags, but Lydia had *Snoopy* Band-Aids, which did the trick. Eun's tearstained face instantly switched to happy mode with the new bandages on his knees. There were a few tiny dramas between Fox and Arwen and Arwen and Tae as they walked through the forest, hunting for Snoopys and Charlie Browns, but the arguments were nearly quashed by the time they got to the café. Jenny had guessed dehydration might've been leading to Arwen's fussiness and suggested they take a break for something yummy to eat and drink. Nabi, Selene had found so far, was practically an angel. She was well-mannered and well-behaved. Selene rarely had to correct her twice about the same thing.

The kids sat at one table eating pizza and fries, drinking tangerine juice. The au pairs were at another, taking in the breathtaking blue views of Jeju.

"You were right, Jenny. Little Miss Arwen needed junk food," Selene said. "Now she's fine."

They watched Arwen giggling with Tae, best friends again.

"I feel so lucky to have the two of you here. Everything is so overwhelming, but in a good way, if that makes sense?" Lydia looked at them, appreciative.

"It makes perfect sense," Jenny said, tapping Lydia's hand.

"I was telling my friend back home the *same* thing the other day," Selene said, spilling more about her friends at the coffee shop / tattoo parlor where she worked.

"I'm too chicken to get a tattoo, I think. Not because of the needle," Lydia clarified. "But because I could never decide what to get."

"I don't have any, either. How many do you have?" Jenny asked Selene.

Selene pointed to the two thin lines on her right ring finger and began counting. She motioned to the tattoos hidden under her clothing—a small strawberry on her hip, a delicate bit of baby's breath on her rib cage, a tiny bee on her foot.

"What did you study in college?" Lydia asked Selene as they dug into the big basket of fries.

"I got a degree in graphic design, but the most remarkable thing I've done with it so far is design the posters for the gigs I've had with the '80s new wave cover band I'm in with my friends from work."

"That's so cool. Do you sing?" Jenny asked.

"Not usually. Background vocals if I'm forced to, but I'm there mostly to play keyboard, piano, whatever. My parents put me in lessons as soon as I could move my fingers."

"I wish I could play an instrument," said Lydia.

"At least you're an artist. Both of you have me beat. I'm not really creative and was a terrible student. Anytime I tried to concentrate really hard on learning something boring, my brain shut down," Jenny said.

"But that doesn't matter because your style is so unique and it seems like you can talk to anyone about anything," Lydia said to her, causing Jenny to blush a bit.

The three of them shared a piece of Earl Grey chiffon cake with their teas as they swapped stories of their lives back in the

States. Selene gave them the shortest possible version about wanting to find her biological mother. She'd let Aera know all about it, too, and she was fully supportive. Lydia was nervous she would be the worst in her art class, and was second-guessing coming to Seoul in general, but was determined to stick it out no matter what. Jenny talked about her ex some more and how thankful she was that she was *five thousand nine hundred fifty-five miles* away from him.

Selene had gone balletcore that morning and thrown a light shrug over her shoulders to match her white tank top and cut-offs. She wore black platform Dr. Martens, even in the heat. She'd always loved being naturally raven-haired, and was letting her shaggy summer layers grow out; she took the elastic band from her wrist and pulled it all back in a loose knot. As they gathered the kids and got ready to leave, she couldn't help but think about how she, Lydia, and Jenny were both completely similar and entirely mismatched. Their lives, their hair, their wardrobes. All three of them running away to Seoul for different reasons, hearts squinting and searching.

The families were staying in spacious art villas with pools. Each had plenty of bedrooms and a large kitchen, plus a massive living room and deck. Selene had grown up with enough money for basically anything she wanted, but her family didn't roll like the Chois. She had never stayed in a place like this before; her family wasn't big on fancy. Her bedroom at the villa was as nice as her bedroom in Seoul—it had a roomy king-sized bed with windows facing the ocean and the blue-blue pool-light glow, plus her own bathroom, which was about the size of her entire apartment in Brooklyn.

That night, Minsu and Haru made dinner in the Parks' villa—soy sauce eggs, steamed perilla leaves, *mul-naengmyeon*, fried chicken, *dubu-jorim*, and *oi muchim*. Everyone ate in the kitchen and on the deck, and when they were almost too full to move, they put on their matching pajamas and went down to watch fireworks on the beach. Fifteen people in light blue pajama pants with little white bunnies on them, striped shirts with fuzzy bunny butts on the pockets. Minsu announced there were watermelon slices in the cooler, and Selene considered them, even though in no way would anything else fit in her stomach right now.

"Hi," Haru said, scooting his chair closer to where Selene, Jenny, and Lydia were sitting. He leaned forward with a green bottle of soju in his hand. His watch strap slid, clinked the glass.

"Hi," Selene and Jenny parroted back. Lydia greeted him in Korean. She'd told them she was basically forbidden to speak Korean around the kids, so she liked speaking it when she could.

After asking, Selene learned Haru was not only fluent in both Korean and English, like his sister, Rain, but also knew a lot of Japanese. Selene threw out two Japanese phrases she'd memorized but had no clue what Haru said when he answered her. He got a kick out of her funny shrugs. All three of the girls practiced their Korean by asking him how he was doing and what he was up to tomorrow.

"My friends from Busan are here and we're going out tomorrow night if you want to join us. Girls and guys . . . most of us have known each other since we were kids. My sister knows them all," Haru said, switching to English again and motioning to Rain, who had Fox in her lap. She was petting his hair.

"You mean real grown-ups and everything?" Selene asked, smiling and leaning over. Not too-too flirty, but his handsome face was *right* next to her. She couldn't help herself. She hadn't been in a committed relationship for years, just a very loose friends-with-benefits arrangement with a guy (Vladimir! soccer player! blue jean eyes!) she met in college, but he'd moved back to Poland a few months ago.

She remembered the last Vladimir kiss in the rain. She imagined kissing Haru in the rain, and wondered if Jenny was into him. Adorable as Lydia was, she wouldn't be competition. She would probably tuck her head into her shell if *any* guy flirted with her.

"Thanks for inviting us, but no thanks . . . we're having girls' night," Jenny said.

"Um, we are?" Selene asked, baffled. They'd made exactly zero plans together for tomorrow night.

"You're so funny, Selene!" Jenny said, lightly smacking her thigh. "Remember Lydia said she was gonna show us that waterfall she's heard so much about? We're hiking there tomorrow, since we have the night off." Jenny looked back and forth between Selene and Lydia. They knew exactly what to do.

"Ha! *Right.* I'm hilarious. *So* hilarious I forget our plans! Thanks for inviting us, Haru, but we're very, *very* strict about girl code," Selene said.

"The waterfall near here is lit up at night, right?" Lydia asked him, adding that she saw it in a brochure.

Haru confirmed.

"Good. I'm excited," Lydia said.

"It's amazing. You'll love it. People call it the Waterfall of God," he said. "The three of you will be missed while you're off on your adventure."

While Jenny was showing Lydia something on her phone, Selene asked Haru more about his friends. Since Jenny was clearly trying her best to ignore him and keep things friendly, Selene didn't mind bringing the extra warmth. As Haru talked, Selene alternated between looking at his face and the sky as the fireworks splashed and sizzled. Each snap and pop was punctuated by *oohs* and *aahs* from the kids. The beach was filled with families, and the weather was cool enough for the long pajama pants they were wearing. The air reminded Selene of the best summer nights back home in New York when she and her friends hung out on rooftops strung with twinkle lights, matching the glitter of the city.

Jenny left and came back with two big blankets, one for Haru and one for the au pairs to share. The night sparkled romantic, and Selene considered going pedal-down on a legitimate crush on Haru but decided not to force anything. Seoul was making her full of love; she adored Lydia and Jenny and had liked Haru immediately. Okay, maybe that *last* bit was horniness, but it didn't make the feeling any less true.

Haru tapped his new bottle of soju against his elbow before he opened it, something Selene had seen so many Koreans do when they drank, she'd started doing it, too. More for good luck than anything else. He handed her the bottle and, in Korean, asked if she wanted some. Selene drank quickly, then leaned back in her chair, warm and sated under the blanket, watching the flashing sky.

The kids were beyond exhausted by the time the fireworks finished. On the way back to the villas, Nabi and Arwen were holding hands in front of them, and Fox hitched a ride on Haru's back with Tae and Eun poking up at him. The parents and the au pairs were bringing up the rear. Sauntering, Lydia mentioned reading that the island was inhabited by countless spirits. Some people believed that if they went to the Waterfall of God and made a wish on a stack of seven stones under a full moon, their wish would come true.

Jenny stopped walking and pulled her phone out of her bag. After tapping and scrolling, she let out a gasp.

"Whoa. I got chills. Tomorrow night is a full moon. Holy shi—" Jenny said. "Girls' Night–slash–Full Moon Wish Night, am I right? Seriously, we have to, even if just for fun. It's meant to be!"

"I'll make a wish," Lydia said quickly, snapping her fingers.

Selene shivered but stayed quiet.

It's meant to be.

Selene heard Jenny say it again as they made their way to the waterfall after sunset.

Jenny's host father, Daniel, gave them a paper map, although the ones on their phones worked fine; he said he didn't trust electronic navigation. They each had a backpack with a flashlight, water, and snacks, just in case. Selene's host father, Geon, kept assuring her he wouldn't allow them to go if he felt it was unsafe to walk alone, but he was okay with it because it was a touristy area and not far. It would only take twenty minutes to get there.

Selene liked how fatherly Geon was about it. She knew he ran six miles almost every day and loved playing guitar, but he was very quiet, though he and Selene had bonded quickly over their shared love of city pop and grunge. Geon taking extra care with her made her feel safe and long for the birth father she never knew. Her adoptive dad had never been overly protective.

"Full Moon Wish Night!" they repeated.

After about fifteen minutes of walking under the streetlamps along the edge of the forest, there was a sign directing them into the trees, leading to the waterfall. The path was half crowded with wide-eyed tourists: solo travelers, couples, and families.

After five more minutes of walking, they could hear it.

Then they could *see* it.

The illuminated waterfall really did ring Selene's God bell. The power and majesty of it! The rush and crash of the glowing water! The girls stood staring in wonder.

Another group was nearby, stacking stones. Jenny walked towards them.

"My sister made a wish here last summer, and the next day her boyfriend asked her to marry him. She *swears* he didn't know," one American woman said. Everyone had to raise their voices to be heard over the water.

"My grandfather wished for a solid week of rain for his farm, and it rained that night. Didn't let up for seven days," a Korean man told those who were close enough to hear the discussion.

"I mean, I can't swear every wish comes true . . . but everyone I know who has come here seems to have at least one mysterious story to share," the American woman said.

Each of the girls chose two small stones to stack. They linked pinkies while Jenny stacked the seventh stone for all of them.

"Are we supposed to say it out loud?" Lydia asked. "Will it work if we don't follow the rules properly?"

"We stacked seven stones, we're here, and there's a full moon," Selene said, pointing up at it. "That's gotta be enough."

"It will be! Why don't we say our wishes aloud?" Jenny said, offering to go first. "Um . . . oh, shit, maybe I shouldn't have started with *um*. What I mean is . . . my wish is . . . to never fall in love again. No matter how hot he is, no matter how much I may *want* to, no matter if he's extremely pretty and smells good and is living in the same condo with me." Selene snorted at her transparency. Jenny paused but quickly became serious again. "I want to be protected from heartbreak. No more romantic love. Not ever," Jenny said, touching her mouth, then touching the stone on top of the stack.

"I wish to be outstandingly special. Like Hye. I'm talking traffic-stopping, hypnotizingly special. So special, everyone notices," Lydia said. Following Jenny's lead, she touched her own mouth before pressing her fingers to the stone.

"I want to find my biological mother. I want to know her name, I want to see a picture of her, I want her to be alive, and I want to meet her in real life," said Selene. She sealed her own wish with a kiss.

A rogue firework popped and shimmered gold zips across the sky.

They looked up, watched them dissolve into a million more stars against the black.

If Selene didn't know better, she could've sworn energy shifted in the atmosphere—the air was sugary and cool, and for one magical moment, the waterfall's gush seemed to hush.

"Amen," Jenny said. She shrugged when Selene and Lydia gave her a look, adding that it just felt like a good time to say it.

Back at the Choi villa, Selene was lying in bed imagining their wishes coming true. She thought of the woman she always pictured as her mom: an older, more Korean version of herself. She imagined the two of them curled up on a couch together with steamy mugs of tea, talking and laughing, as if her birth mother leaving Selene at that intersection were some sort of awful mistake, now instantly forgiven. She imagined Jenny in her dresses and bows, joyful and carefree, with a bulletproof heart. She saw Lydia in the spotlight with undeniable main character energy, all eyes on her.

It was fun to think about and harmless, really. Selene was usually a pretty easy believer but didn't seriously *believe*-believe any of their wishes would come true. So far, her prayers to find her mother hadn't come true, so why would a wish? Prayers and wishes were sisters holding hands in the same aisle of the dream department, but regardless, she believed in prayer. *Prayer with action.* She'd come all the way to South Korea to find her mother; she was doing the work.

Going to the waterfall was just a fun bonding thing, but she was already comforted by revisiting the memory, and it'd only happened a few hours ago. Selene wanted to sleep but couldn't stop thinking about the magic of it all, these new friends she felt connected to so quickly and how Jeju Island had a breezy hum she'd never experienced anywhere else. She'd been to plenty of beaches before, but this? It was different in a way she couldn't explain, not even to herself.

She sat up in bed, body buzzing in the dark. A bright-bulb marquee flashed in her sleepy brain.

But *WHAT IF?*

Ah, the hope boat in her heart had always been wildly stubborn and unsinkable, no matter the waves.

What if?

PART TWO

Wishes

4

Lydia

Lydia sat at the breakfast table with Tae, Eun, and her iced coffee. She hadn't seen Hye or Minsu yet, but knew they'd gone down for a walk on the beach because Hye had texted her. Hye also correctly predicted Lydia would wake up about ten minutes before the boys. Minsu had laid out a bowl of tangerines and rolled omelets with ham, scallions, and carrots. The boys had eaten their fill, and so had she. Now they were both excitedly vying for her attention—they wanted her to decide which one had the best silly animal story. Tae's was about a pair of skinny hippos; Eun's, a zebra in 3D glasses.

"It's a tie! It's a tie! You both win!" she said, putting her hands in the air. The boys looked at each other and high-fived. They were being sweet and attentive this morning, and Lydia hadn't even needed to remind Eun to be careful with his tangerine juice. She watched him drain the bright orange honey of it and wipe his mouth.

The families had plans to hike after breakfast. The boys were on the couch now, content with sharing a device and playing a game with peppy beeps. Lydia rinsed the plates, loading the dishwasher as she wondered if the coastal trails were anything like the trail she'd walked with Jenny and Selene last night on their way to the waterfall. She got goose bumps remembering the gold zips that had flashed across the sky after they made their wishes. She'd remember the night forever. For all that Lydia had imagined South Korea would be—art, work, her host family, all the newness—she'd almost forgotten it was supposed to be fun!

Hye's gasp startled Lydia so much, she screamed and dropped a handful of forks onto the floor. They rattled and flipped over as she accidentally kicked them in a hurried attempt to pick them up.

"Oh! I'm sorry!" Lydia said once she gripped the forks in her fist again, not one hundred percent sure what she was apologizing for, but Hye sounded upset. Lydia's cheeks were hot, and she turned to look at Hye, to apologize for whatever it was. The water was on too high? The dishwasher door was sticking out too far? Maybe one of the boys had spilled something across the table or the couch and she'd missed it?

"Sorry for what? No, you look *fantastic*. I had to have a theatrical gasp about it, that's all. Your eyelet top and those cut-offs are so cute together. Not quite country bumpkin, but country chic. So American. Genius," Hye said with her palms pressed together. She was dressed casually, but her clothes were still ultrastylish and pretty—a pale pink matching top and bottom with her hair in a slick ponytail. Even the island morning-heat blush of her cheeks was in accordance with her outfit. She looked Lydia up and down and smiled bigger when she met her eyes again.

Lydia's brain blurred; Hye had never complimented her clothes before. Hye *never* remarked on her physical appearance, outside of mild, presumably disappointed looks. Lydia managed to stutter out a flabbergasted *thank you*.

"You're welcome. You're beautiful this morning, Lydia. Thanks for doing the dishes. You can stop now, though. It's time to go," Hye said, reaching over to turn off the water.

Minsu came in through the deck door, and Tae and Eun ran

to him as if he'd been gone for days. He opened his arms and Eun jumped into them while Tae playfully punched at his dad's legs.

"Good morning, Lydia," Minsu said, and she said it back. In Korean, he asked the boys if they'd brushed their teeth, and Lydia nodded along with them. She'd stood at the bathroom door and watched them do it, sung the silly toothbrush song twice to make sure they brushed for two minutes.

Fox and Arwen were peeking in through the glass door behind him. Tae and Eun ran out to greet their besties. Lydia could hear Jenny's voice and walked closer to Minsu to see where she was.

"Are you ready?" Hye asked Minsu.

"Yes, let's go. I——" He stopped. "Lydia! I was going to ask if you slept well, but I can tell you did. You look bright-eyed and *in* the world this morning! New day, new you, right?" Minsu smiled at her.

"Oh." It fell from her mouth on its own when nothing else did.

"I'm serious. The Jeju air suits you. We're really glad you're here with us," he added.

"I'm really glad I'm here, too. Thanks . . . thank you, Minsu."

Lydia looked down at her clothes again. They were fine; she was fine. The only possible difference this morning was the waterfall wish, and since that was *im*possible and crazy, she didn't know how to process their praise.

Hye and Minsu stepped out onto the deck with the Kim-Crawfords. Through the glass, in her periphery, Lydia saw Jenny's long dark hair tied with a white ribbon. Lydia opened the door to let her in.

"Hi! Aw, you look pretty," Jenny said after slipping off her sneakers.

"Do I *really*, though?"

Jenny stepped back and gave her a good up-and-down.

Lydia posed—threw up double peace signs, made a heart with her fingers.

"Yes, you really do" was Jenny's answer after careful study.

"Because these are my regular clothes. These aren't 'you helped me buy them because Seoul is one of the most stylish cities in the world' clothes. These are my 'got them in Kentucky, I've had them for years, chill-girl summer' clothes. Hye said I was 'beautiful' and Minsu said 'new day, new you.'" Lydia and Jenny were alone in the villa kitchen with the air conditioner on blast; the tiles were cold-cold beneath Lydia's feet, and she motioned for Jenny to follow her to the bedroom so she could retrieve her socks.

"Well, you *are* beautiful, and it sounds like you're the Chosen One, to get your wish to come true so quickly. It's gonna take longer for mine and Selene's to flesh out, I guess," Jenny said. She sat on the bed. Lydia went into her bag, hunting for her new pair of Snoopy socks.

"I am *not* saying my wish came true. In fact, I'm highly suspicious!"

"Last night was the first night I didn't dream about Ethan since I've been in Korea. Maybe that's how my wish begins. Baby steps, y'know?" Jenny said.

"Good! New day, new you," Lydia said. She pulled on the second Snoopy sock and stood.

Selene appeared at the end of the hallway with "Hi! Ready to head out?"

~

They took a ferry to Gapado, a small island off the coast of Jeju.

The families hiked one short trail through rows and rows of

sunflower fields and another longer one along the rocky coast. Lydia walked slowly, sometimes holding hands with Eun, taking in the beauty of the island, letting herself enjoy the warmth of the breeze on her skin.

When they stopped to picnic near the barley fields, she and the girls found a spot and put a blanket down. Through the blue, they had a dreamlike view of Hallasan, the shield volcano on Jeju Island, the highest point in the country.

"Strawberries. I have them," Haru said, locking eyes with Lydia and crouching next to her. He held out a plastic box.

Lydia had only exchanged polite greetings with Haru so far. She'd probably made eye contact with him only twice. Now he was so close to her she could feel summer heat radiating from his body, smell the soft cotton of his T-shirt.

"Do you want strawberries?" Haru asked her again. She said *ttalgi*, the word for *strawberry*, and *thank you* in Korean as she took one. Every second, Lydia believed more and more that something weird was happening. *Why did Haru ask me about the strawberries first?*

Haru offered the others to Jenny and Selene, and when he left them alone with their fruit, the girls made eyes at one another.

"Did you talk to him last night?" Selene asked Jenny. "You're the one living with him now, so you have to promise to tell us everything." Selene looked at Lydia and nodded so aggressively, Lydia's head automatically moved up and down in agreement, too.

"First of all, I promise. Obviously. Second, he was still out with his friends when I got back. But! He made us *gyeran bap* this morning in his pajamas, and the egg had perfectly crisp edges. Best egg I've ever had. Whatever." Jenny huffed out a breath. "I'm trying to avoid him without being rude. He's great with the kids,

though. They're obsessed with him." Arwen needed help opening her bag of chips, and Jenny hopped up to tend to her.

"Are either of you a little scared about your wishes coming
true?" Selene asked when Jenny returned.

They shook their heads, and Lydia asked Selene to elaborate.

"I just mean that I've built up one version of this epic, mean-
ingful reunion with my birth mother where everything goes
perfectly, and we're both understanding of each other, and everything is so beautiful . . . I know no *real* thing can live up to
my fantasy." She twisted away and looked at the water. "That's *if*
I'm able to find her in the first place," she said, turning back to
them.

Tae and Eun got up and chased after Fox, while Arwen and
Nabi stayed on the blanket, eating. Haru scooped up Fox and
kept running, with the other boys close behind.

"You'll find her. I believe it. Even if the wishes amount to
nothing," Jenny said.

"Selene, I believe it, too," Lydia said with her whole heart.

When it was time for them to pack up their lunch, Lydia stood
and folded the blanket with Selene. She carried it and the picnic
basket over to Hye and Minsu.

"Thank you. Oh, you've folded it so prettily," Hye said, taking
the blanket from her. Lydia looked at the square of it—the most
regular way anyone would fold a large piece of fabric. "Did you
bring your sketchbook? Maybe you and the boys could work on
something together."

"I did," Lydia said. She never went anywhere without it.

"Good. I brought theirs as well," Hye said. She called the boys over and handed them their drawing pads and pencils, told them to go back to their blanket and do whatever Lydia instructed. They both did, without protest.

They sketched the waves together, and the boys drew the secret creatures they imagined were lurking beneath the water—an octopus that ran a small shell shop, a hammerhead shark with his own YouTube channel. After realizing what was happening, the rest of the kids wanted to draw, too, so Lydia tore pages out of her sketchbook for them and made sure everyone had a pen or pencil—her bag was always full of them.

When they were finished and Lydia was putting everything back in her bag, she dropped her sketchbook and bent to pick it up. Jenny's host father, Daniel, got to it first.

"Whoa, Lydia, this is terrific. Jenny told me you were an artist," he said. He looked at her sketch of the ocean closely and held it up to his ear. "It's like you turned the volume up on this. Almost like I can actually *hear* it." The real ocean licked at the stony beach as Daniel handed the book back to her.

"Thank you," Lydia said.

"You're welcome. I look forward to seeing more of your work. Seriously," he said.

The families made their way back to the path an hour before the ferry was set to leave for Jeju.

Lydia called her mom when she was back in her bedroom at the villa.

"I was hoping you'd still be up. Just wanted to say hi. How was your day?"

"Nothing special, but I'm glad you called. It's good to hear your voice. I like checking what time it is over there. Tell me more about island life," her mom said, sounding happy and sleepy. Rarely was her mom in such a sunny mood. Often when Lydia called, her mom wasn't up for talking and had a hard time absorbing anything Lydia said. It wasn't anything specific, just her mom's personality. She usually took a position of deep neutrality. Deep neutrality might've been fine for a lot of things, but not for a mother-daughter relationship. Sometimes Lydia had to wait a bit after getting her on the phone to see if the day was a good one for conversation.

Lydia told her about Snoopy Garden and how cute Tae and Eun were (again). That the boys fought quite a bit but made up fast; Eun respected Tae's big-brother role, and Tae usually got his way because of that. Lydia walked right up to the line of telling her mom about the wish but left that teeny part out when she mentioned going to the waterfall.

"It sounds like everything's going well. Proud of you for setting your mind on something and carrying it out. I know you have a hard time making leaps, but you did it." Huge, high compliments coming from her mother.

Her mom filled her in on happenings at the school where she taught and what Lydia's dad had been up to—work and his pickleball league.

"Love you, Lydia," her mom said before hanging up. She didn't always say it, but this time she did. Lydia put it in her pocket for later, told her mom she loved her, too. The easy conversation felt like an answer to a prayer Lydia didn't have words for yet. She'd fantasized so much about impressing Hye and making a solid connection with her that she'd floated all day from Hye's compliments and the power of positivity. It didn't matter if it made her feel crazy—the idea of the wish had done a real number in the best way on Lydia's brain, and she was going to hold on to it for as long as she could.

Lydia sat on her bed texting with Vivi, grateful her best friend kept raccoon hours because of her new baby and could be reached day or night.

Miss Lydia, didn't I tell you that you'd make friends? Please tell me how right I was!!

You did, Miss Vivi. You were VERY right.

Thank you!! Ok. I have news. Are you ready?

Um . . . yeah. Give it to me.

So get this. I saw Jay tonight and he asked about you.

Jay? Asked about me?

Yep. He said he hadn't seen you in forever. And . . .

And . . . what?

He said he always had a crush on you, but you didn't seem interested.

Are you being serious?

Of course I am! He pouted, saying you don't
follow him on socials.

I figured he wouldn't notice. This is nuts.

Well, he definitely noticed. He looked really cute,
too. Follow him!

I will! :P

Love you.

Love you, too.

Jay was a friend of Vivi's husband who Lydia had known since
college. She'd always thought he was smart and funny, but never
for one second thought he'd be interested in her. He never went
out of his way to talk to her, and he'd never said anything to Vivi.
Until now, apparently.

She tried to configure the possible, practical workings of the
wish again—if it could cover so much time and space. If it had
the sort of power to stretch to Jay all the way in Kentucky and
make him talk to Vivi about her out of the blue.

Lydia went to his socials, scrolled through his posts. She clicked
to follow him, and before she could tap away, he sent her a DM.

Hey! Guess word got to you that I was bummed
we're not connected on here.

Busted :p I talked to Vivi.

Good! 😊 I've missed seeing you around, but no
wonder since you're on the other side of the
world.

> Aw, that's so sweet. I've missed seeing you, too.
> I'm in a villa on Jeju Island right now!

Amazing. But I'll have to wait a little longer to
see you. 😦 Until then, talk anytime and when
you're stateside again, let's make sure we hang
out, please? Bowling rematch!

> LOL. Yes, let's do it.

She posted a pic of her sketch of the beach, and Jay was the
first person to like it.

The families were having dinner at the Chois' tonight, but
before she left the Parks' villa, Lydia texted Jenny and Selene.

> Okay, y'all. I've gotta say it. SOMETHING IS
> HAPPENING. Something magical is DEFINITELY
> HAPPENING. There's NO other explanation!!! I
> promise!!!!

She added a row of gold star emojis to show how serious
this was.

After filling themselves with the *jjolmyeon* and *samgyeopsal* takeout the Chois had delivered, the girls took the kids down to the

beach so they could have sparkler time. Haru tagged along at the last second, peeling a tangerine.

"Want a bite?" he asked Lydia.

Haru held a segment out for her and then another.

More tangerines, and now sparkler light on the beach under the waning moon.

The kids took turns getting their sticks lit by the adults, and Lydia watched, listening to the hard sigh of the ocean. When Haru was down by the water with the kids and the coast was clear, Jenny turned to Lydia and Selene.

"I've been talking to him, just to see if I feel any *feelings*, and honestly? I mean, I like him. What's not to like? I for sure feel *something*, but I don't know what it is, but how could I? I've only known Haru existed for a few days. But also . . . why not test this wish out with the one cute guy who's in my face all the time?" Jenny said, obviously debating the invisible angel and devil sitting on her shoulders.

"Clearly, he's open to it. He's affable, which can be seen as flirty, I guess, but it's not *too* much, or in an f-boy way, so it's chill," Selene said.

"I kind of want it to be in an f-boy way, though. I want to be *tempted* to fall in love, y'know?" Jenny said.

"Careful putting that out into the world," Lydia said. She tried to imagine feeling the desire to be lured into a trap, not knowing if she'd be able to fight her way out. A part of her envied Jenny for being so brave.

As they watched the kids, they told stories of the dickheads they knew once upon a time and wondered which red flags would pop up in Korea. Lydia deferred to their opinions because she didn't have the same amount of experience they had. Her only real, long-term relationship had ended right before she went to college; she was twenty-three now and it felt very far away.

She'd had her fair number of drunken kisses at parties and had fooled around a couple times with the older brother of one of her church friends last summer—nothing special or long-lasting. Lydia refused to sign up for dating apps and wasn't desperate enough to go out howling at the moon, waiting for any old wolf to pop up, but she was more than open to hanging out with a cute guy. More than open to something *more* than that. When she told Jenny and Selene about DMing Jay and showed them his picture, they assured her that she was hot enough to go for him. That he probably meant *hook up* when he said *hang out*, and Lydia believed them, loving how sexy and desirable it made her feel. If, by any chance, the wish took hold, she hoped a byproduct of it would be dating the guys who she imagined, pre-wish, would've looked right through her.

Tae and Eun were fighting over who got to hold the last sparkler, and Lydia walked towards them to clear things up. She split it between them by counting down the seconds until it was time to switch off.

After the girls returned to their respective villas and had gotten the kids cleaned up and put in bed, Haru invited them to join him and his friends from Busan for more beers on the beach.

Lydia practiced flirting with one of Haru's friends when he started chatting her up. He was nerdy in a cool way and had a small yellow flower tucked behind his ear. He pulled out his phone and immediately followed her on Instagram. Selene was laughing and drinking with another guy.

Later, when they were heading inside, Lydia noticed Jenny and Haru fall behind. They were still out there after Lydia had gotten ready for bed. When she looked at her phone, she saw that Haru's friend had sent her a message telling her he had a great time hanging out with her tonight and that he loved her art. She sent him a quick *thank you*.

> You're welcome. You're beautiful! So pretty.

He attached a silly cartoon GIF of a smiling face giving a thumbs-up.

Lydia lay there staring at the ceiling, wondering how corny and weird it would be to send him a pic. She never did things like that. Her friends did, but not Lydia. Sending a photo of herself to a guy she just met wasn't something she'd ever even *imagined* doing, but now, in a daze of confidence, she couldn't talk herself out of it. Maybe she was out of her mind. She didn't care.

She wrote him back.

> You're so sweet! I took this the first day we got
> to Jeju. I never wanna leave!

She attached a pic she'd asked Jenny to take of her. She was standing in her bathing suit in front of the ocean, waving. It was the same one she'd sent in her family group chat with the caption: Me and the ocean, waving hi! As soon as she sent it to Haru's friend she regretted it, but not because it was too much.

Because it wasn't enough.

She attached another that she hadn't shown anyone. She'd taken it of herself yesterday when she was alone on the beach. In it, she was lying on her stomach in her bathing suit, smiling at the camera. Her boobs looked incredible all squished up, and her hair was blowing wild in the sunny ocean breeze.

> I took this yesterday.

Lydia kicked her blankets in glee. She couldn't even remember his name! She put him in her phone under *Haru's friend* and who knew if she'd ever see him again. Who cared? In twenty-four hours, she'd gone from perpetual wallflower to the kind of woman who sent a guy she didn't know pictures of herself. She followed up with a blushing emoji, matching her own cheeks warming in the dark.

> Oh wow. So not only are you beautiful, you're
> (very) sexy, too??

Lydia had no real interest in talking to him again, but the wild-horse thrill of intense flirting galloped through her. She sat up against the headboard and searched for her ex-boyfriend's name in her messages. She and Finn sometimes sent *Happy Birthday* texts and the occasional *Merry Christmas* message every other year or so. Last Christmas was the last time they'd talked. He still lived in Kentucky, but she didn't know what else he was up to.

She wrote:

> Hi Finn! Maybe you heard I'm in Korea? I know
> our parents ran into each other recently. My
> mom told me. It's well after midnight on Jeju
> Island, but I was randomly thinking about you.
> Hope things are good! Xo

She attached the boobs-in-her-bathing-suit pic and sent it. Finn replied immediately.

> Um, whoa. Looking amazing, Lyd. But nothing
> has changed, right? You always look amazing. ☺
> Thanks for thinking of me.

> Send me a pic of you?

He attached one of him in sunglasses, drinking a beer and laughing with his friends. He was still so cute!

> I couldn't sleep and you were on my mind.
> Thanks for not thinking I'm a weirdo.

> You're not a weirdo. Even if you were, it'd be
> okay.

They texted for a couple more minutes before saying their goodbyes, and Lydia scrolled through her contacts wondering who else she could send the picture to.

Jay.

She passed it along to him with no context, just to see his reaction. He sent her five flame emojis and said he would be counting the days until she came back, no matter how long it took. She also sent it to the older brother of her friend from church, the one she'd hooked up with last summer.

> Are you in town? Why don't you come over here right NOW? he sent with a row of laughing emojis. I'm serious! Why didn't we ever have sex? Was it my fault? If so, I'm sorry. Come over so I can fix that?

She kicked her blankets again, giggling to herself. Lydia

explained she was in Korea, thinking of him because she couldn't sleep. He asked if she wanted to call so they could have phone sex; she lied and said the cell connection was unstable. She assured him the reason they didn't have sex was because she was scared and kind of hung up on her ex, but her feelings had changed now. She asked him for a pic, and he sent a hooded selfie he'd taken in his car; he looked dumb and darling. He told her to let him know when she was back in town.

Lydia was a hyper ball of horny excitement. She put her phone away, attempting to calm herself so she could sleep. She kicked her feet again. Outside her bedroom window, Jenny's light laugh rang and rose like a bell.

5

Jenny

Jenny was letting Fox build a sandcastle on top of her feet. She loved going down to the beach as early as possible. She'd grown up on California beaches—morning walks and late-night bonfires, ocean swims after dinner.

Last night, she and Haru had had their longest conversation so far. He talked about his friends, how he went to culinary school in Seoul with one of them and met another working at Minsu's restaurant in Busan. She told him she was a lacto-ovo-vegetarian but had been tempted to eat abalone or some kind of fish since they'd come to Jeju. He said he'd prepare it for her if she wanted to try it, but no pressure. Haru couldn't go five minutes without saying something about food, and Jenny found it so endearing, it made her want to faint. She'd been the same way with Ethan when he dorked out about the *Lord of the Rings* movies or the video games he was doing voicework on. Arwen's name—also the name of a character in *Lord of the Rings*—reminded her of Ethan. She was working on reframing everything related to the franchise because she loved it, too—and it didn't belong to him. Things could exist outside of her relationship with Ethan. He'd broken up with her, yes, but that didn't mean he got *everything*.

Arwen and Nabi were at the water's edge, wiggling their toes. Jenny was helping Fox decide if there should be a taller turret on her left foot—and thinking about *not* thinking about Ethan—when she heard Haru behind her.

"Where's your ribbon?" he asked.

Jenny lifted her sunglasses to look up at him as he stood over her.

She put them back down quickly.

Haru. In swim trunks! *Shirtless*. Slathered in coconutty sunscreen!

He sat in the chair next to her and held out a container of *jumeokbap*, assuring her they were filled only with seaweed, no meat.

"Careful, because now my brain is trained to think of food every time I see you," she said, taking a rice ball and nibbling before telling him how delicious it was.

"I'm okay with that," he said, smiling. "Your ribbon. You always have a ribbon in your hair." Haru touched his own head.

She was wearing her cap-sleeve bathing suit with the zipper—both cute and comfortable enough to wear around the kids all day—and the small gold hoop earrings she'd slept in. No ribbons in her hair for the beach, though. She'd simply pulled it all up in a topknot as soon as she got out of the ocean.

"You've found me out. I don't wear ribbons to the beach. Now you know all my secrets." Her eyes skimmed over Fox, who was humming and building his sandcastle. She waved to Arwen and Nabi when they turned, raising their arms in the air.

"I doubt that. You actually give off a pretty mysterious vibe, aura . . . whatever you want to call it," Haru said.

Jenny wanted to turn her head and look at him, but she couldn't yet; the way he spoke to her felt so comfortable and easy, her eyes burned. She finished her rice ball and drank some water—

her throat was dry all of a sudden. Why was her throat so dry? Why did she feel like she was burning up? She fumbled her phone from her bag and checked the temperature: eighty degrees. She reapplied her sunscreen lip balm, attempting to collect herself.

"I do *not*," she said.

"It's true. But now I feel like you've cracked the door open for me. No ribbons at the beach. Got it," Haru said. Out of the corner of her eye, she saw him use one hand to pretend like he was writing it down. When she turned to him, he looked at her. *Like the cat that got the cream.*

"Fox, I need a break, okay? My legs are going numb," Jenny said. "This sandcastle is *so* cool, though. Let me take a photo of it." She snapped two pictures and slowly slid her feet back.

"No! I want to finish it," Fox said. He shoveled more sand on her legs.

"Why don't you go down by the water with Arwen and Nabi?" she said, pointing.

"I don't want to. I want to play with Tae and Eun, but they're not here yet."

"They'll come out soon. Until then, go down by the water."

"I don't want to."

"Foxie, don't disobey Jenny," Haru said with a deeper voice than he'd used before. He pointed and, in Korean, told Fox to go *now*.

"Okaaay." Fox pouted. He stood, ran towards the girls, and plopped down.

Jenny opened her mouth, but Haru opened his at the same time.

"Wasn't trying to step on your toes there. You're the boss, but my nephew's listening skills aren't the greatest, I know," Haru said.

Jenny thanked him. She added *gwaenchanayo*, meaning *it's okay* in Korean, and watched him get a rice ball out of the container and pop it into his mouth. She watched him chew, watched the honey skin of his bare stomach move in and out with his breath. His (super!) short swim trunks were orange with a thin white stripe down the side. Haru was clearly the test she had asked for, and she had faith she would pass. She remembered the moon's glow—silver, freshwater pearl shimmers—on the waterfall, and the warm, floaty feeling she got on the walk back home. That warm, floaty feeling had returned several times since then. Right now, that warm, floaty feeling was lifting her out of the atmosphere as she watched Haru rub his hands together and ask if she wanted more *jumeokbap*.

In the rainfall shower of the villa, Jenny—lathered in lavender bubbles—gave herself permission to replay the breakup with Ethan. The amber streetlamp flickering through the window when he'd stopped the car. How he'd squinted when he said, *Jennybelle, I love you, but this isn't working—I don't even really know why. I just need to figure some things out on my own.* How the neon-green dashboard lights of his car had blinked off when he pushed the ignition button. How he had put his hand on her knee like he always did, but this time she snatched her leg away. How she had sobbed and said, *Ethan . . . what happened? We were fine! I thought everything was good. I don't understand.* How he'd said, *This is your first big breakup, so it'll be harder for you. I know that, and I'm sorry. I've been through this before, so it's different for me. It hurts, but*

it's different. How it had been the most patronizing, heartless thing she'd ever heard. How small and desperate she'd felt. How embarrassing it all was.

As soon as he'd gotten home, he texted:

> Just because we're not together in the same
> way doesn't mean I don't love you.

She'd stayed in bed for two days, ignoring everything outside of herself, until her mom showed up at her door and coaxed her out onto the couch with takeout and a vanilla cappuccino.

For weeks, Jenny stumbled through her life, confused about how to do basic things. Her usually bright and busy inner world turned gray and sluggish. No mirror or camera could capture her dissociation. Even if she didn't change her pajamas or shower or pull her hair out of her face, she couldn't make her outside appearance match the darkness blanketing her heart. The same thing had happened when she was wholly consumed by the grief of losing her dad so quickly, but at that time, Ethan had been there for her, helping her through it.

Now she was alone.

Amid the abyss of sorrow in her body, she recognized losing Ethan was adjacent to that grief. Ethan had met her dad and her dad had loved him. Now they were both gone from her life. But every sad song she heard, every sad scene in a movie, any mention of *boyfriend* was a trigger, the same way every mention of *dad* had been back then, and sometimes still was.

In the same way she had before, she forgot how to *be*.

She'd put her toothpaste on the wrong end of her toothbrush and vegetable stock in her morning coffee. She accidentally called Ethan when she meant to call her mom. She hung up as soon as

she realized and blocked his number immediately, only to unblock it that night, in case he tried to call. (He didn't.) Once, she
left her mug in the mailbox and looked for it all night, didn't find
it until the next day when she went out to get a package.

Living together was the next big step she and Ethan were
supposed to take, and instead, she was left alone and breathless
in her apartment with the shit he abandoned. The half-empty
stick of deodorant next to his hair gel on the back of the toilet,
his pen and Nordic noir paperback on "his" bedside table. His
blue water bottle underneath it.

One day Jenny tied a pink ribbon in her hair in an effort to
take better care of herself. That same day she stopped accidentally putting the ice cream in the pantry instead of the freezer
and remembered she was the one who had to take the recycling
out; Ethan wasn't going to pop up and do it anymore. They
weren't going to do *anything* together anymore. It didn't matter
how much she wanted to know *why*. What mattered was what
was actually happening. The dreams she had for them—the
small destination wedding; the real, forever marriage; the joy of
having babies with his hazel eyes—weren't happening.

She'd gone through her memories in painstaking slow motion, looking for something out of place or missing from their
relationship; she couldn't find anything. She was tired of driving
herself crazy over that, but the heavy fog she felt hadn't lifted. If
she ever wanted to feel free to be happy again, she needed to be
somewhere else. Somewhere far away so she wouldn't have to
worry about pulling up next to Ethan at a red light.

All the good things that came with loving Ethan and being in
that relationship for three years did *not* outweigh how hard it
was for her to find joy in life after he broke up with her. Anyone
who said it did? They were kidding themselves. *Bullshit*, she said

aloud to herself when she was alone in her apartment, torturing herself by scrolling through Ethan's social media feed. There he was going to the gym and getting beers with his friends like nothing about their breakup had affected him. Her entire world had been upended, and his hadn't tilted one bit. She saw that he'd started eating meat again, too. They'd decided to become vegetarians together, and now he was posting pictures of his squat juicy steaks, pink and leaking.

If she could have all the good parts of love without ever feeling the black-hole suck and sting, she'd be okay with it. The strobing buildup of sexual tension, the violent overflow of mutual orgasms and thunder. Sloppy kisses and rubbing noses. Spooning after too-long afternoon naps. Making nachos at midnight to binge some ridiculous show they would stay up all night analyzing.

She cried in the villa shower, but this time the tears were different. She imagined feeling how she felt before her heart was broken. She imagined the Good Things with someone who wasn't Ethan, somewhere untouchable and new. She thought of Haru's deep voice speaking stern but loving Korean words to Fox, taking up for her when he didn't have to. She thought of which color ribbon she was going to tie in her hair when she got dressed and whether Haru would mention it when he saw her.

She came quickly, surprised—she hadn't even realized she was touching herself. She'd been thinking of shirtless Haru in his wet swim trunks that morning. They'd gone down to the water together, and she'd sat with the kids while he walked into the waves and went under for a second. He popped up, slicking his hair, smooth as a fucking dolphin. She wanted to touch him, to pour herself all over him. Lie down on top of him and undulate, slowly. He dripped like a tree after rain as he sat next to her again, saying nothing, watching the ocean.

The aftershocks of that particular Haru-storm roared through her as she ate a tangerine under the too-hot stream of water raining from above.

Jenny slipped into her peach sundress and braided a peach ribbon through her hair, the closest color she had to match the tangerines they'd be picking on their adventure that afternoon, their last full day on Jeju. After tangerine picking would come the alpaca petting that Arwen had been excitedly talking about all week.

Haru remarked on her ribbon as soon as they stepped out of the villa together with Fox. The rest of the family was inside packing snacks.

She'd thought maybe her time in the shower would lessen the sexual tension she felt when he was near her, but, um, it'd made it worse. There was a flutter between her legs as she looked into Haru's brown eyes—never in a million years would he guess what she'd done, what she'd been fantasizing about.

"It's pretty," Haru said.

"It's pretty," Fox repeated as Haru tousled his hair.

After getting to the tangerine farm, the girls purposely fell behind the group so they could talk.

"Everything's the same? Hye's fawning over you? You do look super cute, by the way," Jenny said to Lydia. Lydia was in a plain white T-shirt and mustard-colored shorts with her Mary Janes. She was wearing brighter lipstick than usual. The thought amused Jenny, imagining Lydia getting ready and deciding to put on more makeup because the wish felt a little real for her. Lydia had texted the girls in the group chat before the shuttle arrived at the villa to pick them up.

Y'all. Believe me, everything is STILL weird!

"I know how nuts this sounds, but she *is*! She said my shirt was 'so cute.' Look at me," Lydia said, stepping back. She pointed at the corner of the small pocket on her shirt. "Eun accidentally flicked raspberry jam on me at breakfast and I couldn't get it out, but I didn't bother changing, because it doesn't matter, because Hye thinks it's 'so cute.'"

"Girl, nobody can see that, and it does look good on you," Selene said, glancing up from her phone for a second. She'd been texting the whole walk up the path to the farm and after saying her piece had started typing again with a fussy expression on her face. "Replying to Instagram DMs," she said before they could ask. "Takes me forever."

"It's not the shirt. It can't be explained any other way . . . It's the wish," Lydia said, lowering her voice on the word *wish*. "Whatever."

"Maybe not *whatever*, though. Look, the wishes are something only the three of us know about and we'll keep checking in with one another. I feel like we should promise not to tell anyone," Jenny said. She lowered her voice on the word *wishes*, too, just in case.

"I'm not telling anyone. That'd be unhinged. I promise," Selene said.

"Promise," Lydia agreed.

"Jenny *unnie*!" Arwen hollered from the front of the group, making her way back to where the girls were. She'd been on a bow kick lately, wanting to wear them all the time like Jenny;

Arwen had picked an orange one today for the tangerines, too. Jenny readjusted it in her hair, and Arwen shook her head in pleasure after Jenny was finished.

After the tangerine farm owners recognized Hye from her dramas and took pictures with her, everyone listened to them talk about the farm's history, describe the different sorts of citrus fruits available, and answer any questions the group had. Next they were instructed to put on gloves, and the adults were handed shears for clipping. Since peak tangerine season was in the fall and winter, they'd be picking inside a greenhouse instead. They were given small baskets, and the kids merrily found their favorite fruits. With help, they snipped and loaded them up.

When they had enough fruit, they decided to visit the gift shop for fifteen tangerine sun hats before shopping for treats in the café. Tangerine sugar cookies, herb crackers, tangerine jam. Icy honey-citron tea and coffee.

The kids wanted to sit together, so Jenny, Lydia, and Selene sat at the table next to them. The café was pleasantly crowded with tourists. An American family of four finished their drinks and filed out, with both children carrying bright orange plushies. Jenny thought of how far away her own family was. Her mom was probably sleeping, since it was so late in California.

Ethan popped into her head, and she stomped him out. Closed her eyes. When she opened them, she saw Haru looking at her from the parents' table.

"Do you like him?" Jenny asked Selene out of the side of her mouth once she and Haru broke eye contact.

"Who?" Selene asked. She looked at the door of the café—a

gray-haired couple was walking in, the man holding the door for his wife.

Jenny sneakily motioned towards Haru. She double-checked to see if he was looking their way, but he was busy talking to his sister.

"What do you mean, do *I* like him? Feels like we're back in the high school cafeteria."

"It does!" Lydia took a bite of her cookie and reminded Eun to be careful with his drink.

"Sorry. I don't mean it like that," Jenny said. She'd gotten too in her head, and now she sounded immature and dumb. Although the word *intimidated* wasn't an exact match for what she was feeling, she did feel intimidated-*ish* by Selene. Probably no guy had ever broken up with Selene, and even if he had, she would most likely have been fine.

"No, it's okay! It's funny," Selene assured her, touching her shoulder. "Don't worry about me, he's all yours. *Fighting!*" The girls said *fighting!* to one another the same way they'd heard everyone else in Korea say it, meaning *good luck*.

"I was only asking because the two of you were flirting—" Jenny started, feeling more embarrassed with every word.

"Right. I mean, yes, I was flirting with him for fun, I guess. There are plenty more where he came from, Jenny. I'm serious. Enjoy," Selene said. She winked at her. Even the way she said *there are plenty more* made Jenny feel silly. Why couldn't she have been like that about Ethan? Why couldn't she just be normal and sad for a short time? Why didn't she believe she'd find another, better person someday who wouldn't leave her in pieces? And where was Selene three months ago when she'd needed her the most? Jenny almost laughed. Ethan had been Jenny's first love and her longest relationship, and here she was on Jeju Island, desperately leaning into the supernatural to help her move on, while Selene oozed the attitude Jenny had been striving for. She wanted that confidence for herself.

"Thank you for listening to me, even though my thoughts are an unfinished mess. My brain is overloaded today," Jenny said.

"I'm right there with you," Selene said. She filled Lydia and Jenny in on her plans to find her birth mother, letting them know she'd picked the day she would go to the orphanage and put it on her calendar so she wouldn't chicken out. "I also made a fun playlist to psych myself up to do it."

"Will you share it with me, please? I need a hype playlist," Jenny said.

"Ooh, me too," Lydia said, leaning over to watch Selene pull the mix up on her phone and send the link to them in their group chat.

Selene's Hype Mix

"Bounce" by JJ Project
"How You Like That" by BLACKPINK
"God's Menu" by Stray Kids
"Eve, Psyche & The Bluebeard's Wife" by LE SSERAFIM
"Super" by SEVENTEEN
"UGH!" by BTS
"Hope World" by j-hope
"Hype Boy" by NewJeans
"10 Minutes" by Lee Hyori
"IDOL" by BTS
"Crazy Form" by ATEEZ
"Bite Me" by ENHYPEN
"Run BTS" by BTS

"Hard Carry" by GOT7
"Daechwita" by Agust D
"Pretty Savage" by BLACKPINK
"I AM" by IVE
"GO CRAZY!" by 2PM
"SEXY NUKIM (feat. RM of BTS)" by Balming Tiger
"ETA" by NewJeans

"Are you going to eat your cookie?" Fox asked as he approached Jenny.

"How many have you had?"

Fox held up two fingers.

"Rain, can Fox have three cookies?" Jenny asked her host mom after getting up and going over to her table.

"He cannot," Rain said, shaking her head.

"Sorry, buddy," Jenny told him over her shoulder. Fox returned to his table, defeated, but seemed to forget all about it when Arwen mentioned the baby alpacas they'd be seeing as soon as they were finished.

"Have a seat, Jenny," Daniel said, pulling the chair out. Aera had been sitting there, but now she was sitting next to her husband, Geon, at the other table.

The controlled chaos of going out in the world as a group of fifteen already felt normal to Jenny. She caught herself daydreaming about what things would look like once they were back in Seoul. How much would Haru be in the condo? Would he be gone with Minsu all day and night at the restaurant? Would he bring friends over to hang out? Would he bring women home? Would she ever be able to deal with how cute his mouth was when he called Rain *noona*? She wanted to properly obsess over all of it, but Daniel was talking to her about the tangerine farm. Haru had gone to the counter for a refill of his coffee, and now he and his navy shorts were back, sitting across from her. Exactly one Superman strand of black hair fell across his forehead, and his T-shirt had a tiny embroidered tangerine on it that Jenny hadn't noticed before. The tangerine had a green stem, a green leaf. Jenny imagined orange hearts in her eyes as she stared.

"You're from California, so you probably have citrus trees in your yard, don't you?" Daniel asked.

"My mom does. Lemons and limes," she said. "My grand-mother has oranges, so we always trade fruit when she visits."

"We only had snow and deep-dish pizza to trade growing up in Chicago," Daniel said, laughing at his own joke. Jenny loved how much he loved being from Chicago. It was a major part of his personality. After unsuccessfully trying to convince Rain to move there, he'd had to let it go, but they still went back to visit every other year or so. "His ex is from Chicago," Daniel said, thumbing at Haru.

"Oh," Jenny said.

"That's true, but it's been over a year since we broke up." Jenny looked at him intently, as he quickly added, "And I've moved on. She was teaching English over here and we met through a friend. We dated off and on a few years ago, before I did my military service, reconnected briefly after, but it didn't work out and that's okay." Haru turned his attention to Daniel and added, "In the end, I think *you* were more heartbroken than I was because she was from your hometown."

"Yeah, maybe. So what?"

"Ah, there it is. I love the truth," Haru said.

"My ex is from California—" Jenny began.

Arwen said Jenny's name and the word *alpacas* three times in a row. She was grateful for the interruption.

She stood. "Okay, let's clean up quickly so we can go!"

The twirl of Jenny's dress got caught in the fence gate, causing her to stumble as the group walked to the alpacas. Haru was behind her and caught her fall, unhooking the fabric from the metal. It happened as though in slow motion, and Jenny was in a total stupor when she looked up and saw Haru's face so close to hers.

Are you okay? he asked in Korean. She nodded, and her tangerine hat slipped down over her eyes. Her heart was beating wildly, like she'd died and been revived in an electric-green Frankenstein burst.

When Jenny was upright again, and Haru had removed his strong hands from her hips, she looked around, expecting everyone to be watching them, but they weren't. The kids were squealing in delight over the animals, and the host parents were trailing behind, doing their own thing. Only Lydia and Selene were witness, wide-eyed and knowing.

The kids were drained and fussy after their busy afternoon, so the families decided to have quiet time in their individual rentals before reconvening, in their matching pajamas, for game night in the Kim-Crawfords' villa. It was technically the wet season—a moody cluster of storms was predicted to brew overnight. Dark clouds were gathering by the time everyone had gotten their fried chicken and beers and sat at the table outside. Jenny was having vegetarian side dishes, as per usual; Minsu had refried a small batch of the sweet, tangy tofu he'd made the night before.

It started raining buckets five minutes after they cleaned up, so they moved the party to the kitchen for *bungeoppang* ice creams. Jenny noticed the pink light click on inside Haru's cheeks after his second beer, and he seemed pleasantly buzzed sitting on the couch with his third. Jenny watched him talk to Lydia about a Korean artist Jenny had never heard of, and he agreed with Selene about how spicy the fried chicken was. The island humidity had fluffed his hair, and it playfully bounced as he nodded.

Jenny felt possessed by a warm, restless energy, and imagined she'd blast up from the floor through the villa roof if she didn't get up and *do* something, so she stood and went to the bathroom. Afterwards, when she opened the door, Arwen and Nabi scared her, waiting on the other side to ask if she'd cut the itchy tags off their pajamas for them. They followed her into the bathroom, where she sat on the toilet lid and used the small crane scissors in the drawer to snip the scritch from the collars of their shirts.

Back in the living room, Aera directed everyone with her arms like a flight attendant. "We've got Uno over here, the gaming system over there, a Go board in the kitchen, and drawing charades–slash–art time with Lydia right here."

"Our brilliant artist," Hye said, looking lovingly at Lydia. Jenny and Selene made eye contact, watching Lydia twinkle under the lamplight glow.

First Jenny ended up at the Go board with Daniel, who was trying his best to teach her how to play with no luck, but she enjoyed listening to him talk about how he learned to play when he first came to Korea. Next she played a round of Uno with Arwen, Nabi, and Selene. For round three, Jenny plopped down next to Lydia with a piece of paper and a pencil in the living room, and Haru sat in front of her with his own supplies.

"I'm sketching you," he announced proudly.

"You're supposed to be sketching that," Jenny corrected him, pointing over his shoulder at the blue-and-white Qinghua vase next to the television. Tae, Eun, and Fox were in deep concentration. They had reached an apparently anxious part of the video game they were playing and were passing the controller back and forth in an attempt to give themselves the best angle to kill some kind of giant mouse monster with fireballs.

"Maybe"—he shrugged—"but I'm sketching you," Haru said, pointing to his own chest and then Jenny's face.

"Not allowed," Jenny replied, eyebrow raised. She was touching shoulders with Lydia and could feel Lydia's eyes on her, but Jenny kept looking at Haru.

A bright bolt of lightning lit up the dark windows, and Jenny turned to see the ocean flash; thunder roared the glass.

"I don't believe in rules," Haru said with a straight face. He was drawing and only occasionally looking up at Jenny. She began sketching him next to the vase.

When Haru was finished, he turned the paper around to show her his creation. A round face with big eyes and extra eyelashes, an oversized bow in her hair with the ribbon tails pouring down over her shoulders. The drawing was cartoonish and cute, making her look like one of Daniel's webcomic characters.

"For you. A gift," Haru said, handing the paper over and motioning for her to keep it.

"This is you." She gave him her sketch—a glorified stick figure with black hair and a mouth full of teeth, now with ridiculously long arms holding the vase behind him.

"Our brilliant artist," he whispered to her as he leaned forward.

The rain was blowing hard against the windows when everyone left the Kim-Crawfords'. The other two dads went to their respective villas and returned with umbrellas to shepherd their families back. They left two by two until they were all gone.

In the kids' bedroom, with Fox and Arwen asleep, Jenny and Rain sat on the floor packing the rest of the suitcases—Arwen's little green sundress with matching bow, Fox's robot T-shirt, tiny socks wrapped into a plum-sized ball.

"Haru said Fox hasn't been listening well lately. He told me how patient you are with him. He also told me about how great you are with the kids when Daniel and I aren't around, but I knew that," Rain said in her extra-calming way. Jenny wondered if Rain knew how comforting her voice was. She'd learned plenty about voice acting when she and Ethan were dating, and although thinking of him gave her a quick sting as she sat on the bedroom floor, she redirected her attention and thought instead about how good Rain would be at narrating audiobooks.

"Thank you. That's very sweet of Haru. Fox has been fine. It's been pretty easy to get him back on track."

"How are you feeling?" Rain asked.

"Good."

"You haven't been crying while we've been here, have you?"

"No. Everything's been amazing."

"I hope it stays that way when we get back to Seoul."

"I hope so, too," Jenny said, tucking the last pair of Arwen's shorts into the packing cube before zipping it closed.

After an hour of lying in bed unable to sleep, Jenny went to the kitchen to refill her water bottle. She discovered Haru—shirtless in the refrigerator light—examining a jar of garlic cloves.

"Oh! I'm sorry. I thought I was the only one up," Jenny said.

"It's still August, right? These aren't expired," he said, holding the jar up to her. She looked closer, shook her head. Her stomach growled loudly enough to be heard over the rain. "*Meokja*," he said. *Let's eat.* He told her he'd be right back and, in a gentleman's move, returned wearing his pajama shirt.

"You don't wear ribbons to bed, either. So, no beach and no bed." He asked her what she wanted to eat, and after only the slightest hesitation, she said tuna and rice. "You're sure?" he asked.

"I'm sure," Jenny said. She'd been craving tuna for days.

"You're *sure*, you're sure?"

"*Yes.*" Her stomach growled again. She held her hand there and apologized.

Haru smiled wide. "Okay, okay, I'm going as fast as I can."

He asked how long she'd been a vegetarian, and she mentioned it was something she and her ex from California had decided to do together. She told Haru that not even a week after they broke up, Ethan had regressed into an oversharing carnivore. It felt good to talk to Haru about Ethan because it wasn't in a wistful way; she wanted Haru to know Ethan was a dumbass and that she was different now, moving on. Haru shared a story about his ex from Chicago, how she couldn't stand anything remotely spicy and got mad at him once for putting mustard on her hot dog because even *non*-spicy yellow mustard was too spicy for her. He said sometimes it was the small things that signaled a relationship was coming to an end, but Jenny's agreeing nod was a lie; Ethan had blindsided her.

When she talked to Haru, he listened attentively, and she did the same. They talked quietly about relationships and food while Haru whisked eggs and chopped kimchi and garlic. It was sexy and soothing, how quick and deliberate he was with the knife. None of his energy was wasted. Every movement was neat and precise, but his hands worked easily, as if he could do it with his eyes closed. He told her he was making tuna-mayo *deopbap*, and that *deopbap* meant *covered rice*. He mixed the tuna with mayo, warmed the rice, cooked the eggs, then put it all together in a bowl for her with kimchi, garlic, and seaweed flakes. He garnished the dish with a bit more mayo and a swirl of chili oil the color of cinnamon candy.

Jenny ate every last bite. It was the best middle-of-the-night snack she'd had in her life, quite possibly the best thing she'd *ever* eaten. The rice was fluffy, and the seaweed flakes added just the right amount of saltiness. The egg was cooked prettily with an oozy but not *too* oozy bright yellow yolk. Glorious. Maybe it was because she hadn't eaten fish in three years. Maybe it was because she could hear the storm rolling out over the ocean, thunder muffled under a new blanket of clouds, moving off to another continent. Maybe it was Haru telling her more about culinary school in Seoul or the best restaurant he worked in before helping Minsu open the new one in Busan a year ago. Maybe it was how he listened to her when she talked about her life and how he said *I'm glad you came to Korea* when she told him she knew she'd had to get out of California to clear her mind.

"Were you drunk earlier? While we were playing games?"

Jenny asked. They were standing at the sink together now. Haru had turned the water on low and was quickly, quietly washing the dishes they'd used. He'd refused her offer to help.

"Drunk from two and a half bottles of beer? No! Absolutely not."

"I don't know how much you can drink!"

"I can drink more than two and a half bottles of beer. That question is almost insulting," Haru said, laughing. "You're asking because I was flirting with you? Sketching you? The truth is, Jenny"—he leaned towards her, letting his face go serious—"I was *disturbingly* sober."

"I was flirting with you, too," Jenny said boldly after weighing the moment. The sky flashed. "You don't have a girlfriend, do you?"

Haru turned off the water and dried his hands. "Do I act like I have a girlfriend?"

Jenny shook her head, giggling.

"I like being around you."

"Same."

"I can't stop looking at you."

"*Same.* But I can't, like . . . not out in the open . . . I mean . . . I'm getting paid to watch the kids, not flirt with their hot uncle while everyone is sleeping."

Haru took her hand, pulling her into the pantry closet. Closed the door with a soft click, leaving them in velvety black nothingness. Jenny wasn't thinking about her waterfall wish, and she *definitely* wasn't thinking about her ex. As he slowly backed her up against the shelves and kissed her, Jenny's only thought was the magic Haru's slow, warm tongue made in her mouth. He let out a small sigh and held her face. She put her hands on his waist, wanting him closer.

6

Selene

Selene promised herself she'd go to the orphanage on Nabi's first day of school in September. She was so nervous, she skipped her morning iced coffee and instead sipped hot peppermint tea with lemon as she walked Nabi to the elementary school all five children attended. Each family had a whiteboard calendar in the kitchen with the children's schedule on it, complete with mentions of the other families' after-school activities. The boys swam on Tuesdays and Thursdays, and on Wednesdays, Arwen and Nabi had tennis. Nabi had private guitar lessons every other Friday, and she and Tae were in the Christmas choir together. The au pairs were planning on walking them to school together most mornings, but Selene wanted to get an early start today since she was going to the orphanage right after.

"You'll have an amazing day, Nabi. Look at this sky, these clouds," Selene said. It'd rained for about a week solid, but they'd had a stretch of divine weather in Seoul the past few days—fat, puffy Studio Ghibli clouds and the kind of cerulean skies that made Selene a little sad, knowing they couldn't last forever. She was so happy to spend her free time outside. The day before yesterday, she, Lydia, and Jenny had taken the kids to picnic and ride bikes along the Han River. Then, yesterday, she, Aera, and Nabi had taken Gureum to Seoul Forest to wander and sniff under the trees.

"I'm not nervous," Nabi said, looking up at her. She swung her hand in Selene's as they joined the crowd of schoolchildren, parents, and au pairs on the sidewalk making their way to school.

"Nabi-*yah*," a little girl in a pearl headband said, waving to her in front of them.

"Yumi-*yah*!" Nabi exclaimed back, letting go of Selene's hand to run into her friend's arms.

It was just the right amount of hope and cuteness to calm Selene's nerves. When she dropped Nabi off, she touched her head and told her she'd see her after school.

Selene had a hard time deciphering the addresses in Seoul and discovered that the easiest way to find something was to get inside the general area and simply walk around until she stumbled upon it. She didn't believe in getting "lost" in Seoul because no matter what, she found something beautiful and interesting to see. Sculptures and surprise gardens, the prettiest roofs and gates, narrow stone pathways over water that led to more shops and restaurants. Signs wrapped in flowers, colorful lanterns strung above entrances. Since the weather was so lovely, Selene decided to skip the bus, and instead strolled towards the neighborhood where the orphanage was located. Nearby, she stopped in front of a café to check how her latest Instagram post was doing. The night before, Aera had asked her to model a cotton candy–pink tulle dress and dark denim jacket from her line with black studded boots, and the post had taken off immediately. She got 15,000 likes before bed, and by morning it was double that.

She was listening to her hype playlist and circled the same two streets three times before she finally found the building where the orphanage was supposed to be. Its almost hidden front door was the same deep red color as the blanket the woman had found her wrapped up in, and Selene felt like that wasn't a *bad* sign. Maybe it wasn't a *good* one, but it wasn't a *bad* one. She purposely hadn't been thinking about her wish too much but liked when it popped into her head. Lydia seemed a blissful believer, and it showed in the way she carried herself now. And Jenny was still being very vocal about her only physical feelings for Haru. She was literally bouncing with joy, recounting how he'd kissed her in the kitchen the night before they left the island. Jenny told the story in such cinematic detail it was like Selene had been there to witness it herself.

Selene stood in front of the orphanage door with her eyes closed, opened them, then tapped the red wood. *I lived and breathed somewhere in here when I was a baby. This was my home when I had nowhere else to go.*

She waited.

No one came, and she didn't hear any movement behind the door. Sheer curtains covered both windows in front. Selene looked up at the dark, decorative roof tiles; she didn't know what they were called and made a mental note to find out. She blinked back tears, imagining the life she could've had if she'd been raised by her Korean mother. If, instead of being a half-Korean woman raised by American parents, she'd grown up knowing *Hangul*, speaking both Korean and English, celebrating Korean holidays and traditions. Things she should've learned from her birth mother and her Korean family, not from books or the internet later in high school and college when she sought them out on her own.

"You can go in," someone said from behind her. Selene turned to see a middle-aged woman holding a shopping bag. "You don't have to knock." The woman touched Selene's arm.

"Oh, thank you," Selene said as the woman continued on her way. Selene watched her round the corner and disappear before she put her thumb on the handle and pushed down, opening the door.

The front office was a cool, dark cove, but the small windows let in just enough light to warm it up. Rows of old books sat on dusty shelves, with stacks of folders and papers on top. A wooden desk sat at the end with a black chair behind it. The older woman inside didn't speak English, and Selene hadn't expected her to. Selene had been studying hard to learn as much Korean as she could before she came to Seoul, and whenever she had time, she still logged in to join the online lessons her Korean teacher provided that supplemented the in-person classes she'd been taking back home.

Selene had worked with her Korean teacher to type out a few phrases that could help her when it came time to speak with someone at the orphanage. She pulled them up on the notes app of her phone and handed it to the woman. The phrases included formal language explaining what she was looking for, her name, where she was from, the date she'd been found and where, and the date she was adopted. She also had the photo of her birth father and a copy of her adoption paperwork with some of the same information on it, including notes about the red blanket and bee bracelet. As the woman was typing her Korean answers into the translation app on Selene's phone, the red door opened again, filling the dark room with welcoming slants of sunlight. The younger woman who walked in spoke English and told Selene she was the older woman's daughter. Selene explained herself and her situation quickly, expressing her gratitude to them for allowing her to share her story.

"My mother used to run the orphanage here, but as you can

see, it hasn't been operational for a long time. Closed down years ago. Now it's used as an auxiliary office and storage space for other orphanages," the younger woman said. She was holding small containers of food stacked, wrapped, and tied in pale purple scarves. She set them down on the desk. "We can look to see if we have your file back here." She spoke to her mother in Korean, and the older woman motioned for Selene to follow them.

After about fifteen minutes of searching, Selene started to worry they wouldn't find anything. She stood by one of the filing cabinets with her puffy black bag on her shoulder, her hands clasped in front of her. *I lived and breathed somewhere in here when I was a baby. This was my home because I had nowhere else to go.* She asked the younger woman if she could do anything to help, and the younger woman kindly said no. She suggested Selene take a seat in the desk chair since it might take them a while, but Selene couldn't keep still. She shifted her weight from one foot to the other, chewed her thumb, thought of pulling out her phone for something to do with her anxiety, but decided against it; she didn't want to seem rude. The women were being so nice. Selene would've been crushed if she'd encountered someone nasty or unhelpful.

"2000. July 2000. The woman who worked here back then had a unique filing system we can't quite crack even now," the younger woman said, pulling a thick khaki folder out of the drawer. She explained that the woman had insisted on keeping paper-only records up until 2001. Selene's hands shook; she fiddled with the wide jade band around her index finger as the older woman opened the folder and flipped through it.

Maybe it was thirty seconds; maybe it was three minutes.

"Lee Bitna. A woman named Lee Bitna found you. Red blanket, bee bracelet. You had a lot of pretty hair. You still do," the younger woman said, looking at Selene after taking the papers out and speaking with her mother in quick snips of Korean.

She handed the papers to Selene.

The one on top was the same one her adoptive mom had given her, the same piece of paper she'd seen her whole life. It listed when and where she was found, what police station she was taken to. The additional papers contained more detailed information about her two months at the orphanage.

The young woman translated it for her.

She'd gotten a mild cold when she was a month old that lasted a week. In neat *Hangul* in the margins, someone had written how much she loved to be held and was *very content after bottle-feeding*. Paper-clipped to that information was a picture of her as a baby—a new one Selene had never seen before. In it, she was asleep in the red blanket with her black hair sticking straight up, like she'd just gotten it scrubbed dry after a bath. In front of her little hands was a tiny white card with a name written in English.

Lee Serin.

Her mom had told her someone at the orphanage named her, and she'd loved the first name so much, she decided to keep it.

Lee Serin.

Serin in Korean sounded like *Selene* in English.

Selene Bee Valentine was her legal name.

Both names belonged to her now.

Selene's tears dripped onto the paper, and she reached into her bag, pulling out the red blanket.

"I brought this with me," she said, clutching the worn fabric.

The women were quiet and patient as she attempted to read the information on the paper. She could only make out some of the words in *Hangul*, but she did see the name Lee Bitna with a phone number and what seemed to be an address under it.

With the older woman's help, the daughter explained that Lee Bitna willingly gave her information and explained that Selene was free to call or visit Bitna if she wanted. She copied the paperwork and the photo for Selene, and Selene took pictures of it with her phone, too.

Thank you, God and Lee Bitna, for this answered prayer. And thank you for this wish I'm slowly beginning to believe in.

Before leaving, Selene thanked the women profusely.

Stepping out of the building into the sunlight felt like emerging from a portal to the beyond. Selene looked at her phone and realized she needed to pick Nabi up from school in an hour and a half. *An hour and a half!* Time had stopped while she was inside with the women and cranked to warp speed as soon as she stepped out. She was hungry, thirsty, and needed to head back. The sun was so bright, and the air had warmed significantly since the morning.

As she walked in the direction of the school, a gentleman in a light blue suit pushed past her. Another clad in black barely missed swiping her shoulder. People in Seoul rarely apologized for bumping into one another—it wasn't unlike NYC in that way. Selene got smashed in between two women at the crosswalk and stepped aside to allow for more room. She stopped at a convenience store for a lemon-lime drink and *samgak gimbap*.

After Selene helped Nabi with her first-day assignment, they took Gureum for a long walk and stopped at a playground so Nabi could get her evening energy out. Aera and Geon would be at Sobok Sweet working through dinner, so Selene and Nabi were having dinner with Lydia, Jenny, and the kids at the Kim-Crawfords'. When they wanted to hang out without leaving the building, the girls had taken to meeting on one of the families' balconies, all three of which were spacious, with tables, candles, cozy chairs, and breathtaking views of the city. It was such a satisfying way to end the day, sharing a bottle of soju with the girls, chatting over everylittlebit of their lives.

The Instagram post Selene had put up for Aera was doing so well, Aera asked Selene if she wanted to do them regularly, and said she'd pay her extra for them. Aera also wanted Selene to help her style some of the mannequins down at the shop on weekends, and Selene happily agreed.

Selene was telling Lydia and Jenny this as they sat on the Kim-Crawfords' balcony. She'd updated them in the group chat about Lee Bitna earlier in the day. Lydia and Jenny were extremely excited about this new development and expressed that in rows and rows of star and full moon emojis.

"I finished three new pieces, and this blew my mind, but . . . Hye says her friend wants to buy one of them," Lydia said. The girls congratulated her, and Jenny poured her a second shot of soju; congrats or not, it was tradition for a person not to pour their own, and polite to hold the shot with both hands. The kids had gone to bed early, and Aera and Geon had popped in to pick up Nabi about an hour ago. Although the girls didn't always have a ton of time to be alone or drink, it was nice to decompress when they could. They had plans to get their hair done together, join a K-pop dance class no matter how embarrassing it was, and go to Hongdae for karaoke on the weekend; they'd gone once and had so much fun they promised to do it again.

"I'm still extremely horny for Haru. Last night I watched him and his big, veiny, manly hands chop for twenty minutes. Sometimes, when he's cooking, he furrows his brow and gets all serious and focused," Jenny said dreamily. She told them he kissed her last night in the kitchen again. "He *loves* kitchen kisses. We have to be sneaky—it's *so* hot. I mean, it's crazy, but it's hot. That's all I care about right now," she said, spilling the last drops of her soju and frowning about it, which made all three of them laugh. Selene lifted her shot glass and looked up at the thumbnail moon before clinking drinks with the girls.

Later, when Selene connected with her parents, she kept the updates vague. Attempting to balance both her emotions and theirs about searching for her birth mother felt like an impossible feat of strength and concentration. They were supportive and offered to meet her in Korea if she needed them, but it was important for Selene to be there on her own. She'd report back when she found her birth mother. Right now, she had nothing but a new name.

Lee Bitna. Bitna Lee.

Another morning, another door. This one was a welcoming light brown wood, the color of honey toast.

Selene had tried calling first, but the number was no longer in service. She prayed Lee Bitna was behind that door, but what were the odds? Bitna could've died, could've moved. Even if she was behind there, what would she know? Would it be enough? Selene closed her eyes again and remembered how she felt stacking the stones. Her body hummed. She took a deep, deliberate breath in and let it out slowly.

Knock, knock.

A small, fiftysomething woman dressed in purple plaid with a cream headband holding her short hair back opened the door.

After Selene told her who she was, Bitna immediately invited her into the forestlike apartment with deep green and purple walls, antique furniture made of zelkova and pine. The pleasing warmth smelled faintly of sandalwood and wet grass, reminding Selene of the Wood Between the Worlds in the *Chronicles of Narnia* books her parents read aloud to her when she was a kid. A sleepy, numinous energy had surrounded her as she stepped inside.

Selene sat at Bitna's kitchen table in her red socks, looking at her boots by the door—the door that felt like a new beginning. She'd stood there and told Bitna everything she knew. When Selene lost her breath and got her water bottle out of her bag to take a drink, Bitna asked when she'd last eaten. Now, over grassy green tea and sweet rice cake balls, she was listening to Bitna tell her the detailed story of finding her.

"I named you and prayed for you. For your mother as well, whoever and wherever she was," Bitna said as she finished, holding her hands to her mouth and shaking her head. "Selene, I never dreamed you would show up here. It's a magical day."

The word *magical* both comforted and frightened Selene. Had the magic of the wish really brought them together? Magic sounded fickle and tenuous. How long would it last? What would be left when it dissipated?

"It feels magical to me, too," Selene said slowly. "Thank you for naming me. I'm sorry I don't speak more Korean, and I'm sorry I showed up without letting you know first—" Selene stopped. She was too nervous to eat, but wanted to be a good guest, so she nibbled again at the rice ball on her plate. She was grateful for Bitna's kindness and how easy she was to talk to.

"Your Korean is so cute! This is a very special occasion that requires no apologies."

They ate, drank, and talked, excited to connect about the

United States and Korea, about food and their families. Selene told her all about her adoptive parents. She loved them well and they loved her well. Selene kept the photo of her birth father open on her phone. She handed Bitna the bracelet and red blanket across the table, and Bitna petted the blanket like a cat.

"I remember this bee catching the sunlight," Bitna said, fingering the metal. Selene had rubbed the gold coloring off after all these years, but it was special seeing Bitna treat the charm so preciously.

The morning she was found, another woman had stopped, but Bitna was the one who took the lead and called for help, reporting she'd found Selene. It had been a sunny morning after a rainy night, and it rained for three full days after she found her—Bitna had thought of Selene so much, thankful it hadn't been raining hard when she was left on the sidewalk.

At first, Bitna thought baby Selene was a box of kittens.

"I guess there are all sorts of reasons why a mother feels like she can't take care of her baby. Pressure from her family—or maybe she'd kept you a secret," Bitna said gently.

Selene didn't even know how old her birth mother was when she'd had her. Layers of unanswered questions, breaking her heart.

"Right. I've considered it from every possible angle. I'm not angry. I want to know her name and see her face, even if it's only a picture. But I do hope to meet her in real life."

"I hope that for you, too."

After an hour or so, the door's keypad beeped and the door opened. Bitna said it was her son and younger sister back from the supermarket. A woman who looked a lot like Bitna and a young man stepped inside. The man was holding two bags of groceries—one overflowing with fluffy green celery leaves and the other with bread and boxes of cereal.

"This is Deiji and Joon. I was pregnant with him when I found you, but I didn't know it yet," Bitna said, lighting up.

The two of them greeted Selene, and Bitna eagerly caught them up on who Selene was, why she was sitting at the kitchen table. Deiji had on winged, dark green eyeliner and wore a chorus of gold and silver bangles on both wrists. In her long skirt and thin cardigan, she radiated the same peaceful hippie warmth Bitna did, with an added splash of whimsy to match her name: *Daisy.* Beaded crustaceans with lemons hung from her ears, an ode to shrimp cocktail.

Joon looked like a quiet, cerebral person in his round glasses and plain white T-shirt—an austere foil to his mother's and aunt's bold, busy colors. Selene had started calling those kinds of frames *slutty boy glasses* in her mind after seeing them on a sultry K-pop idol she loved. She found them sexy. Seeing them on Joon made her want to hide her face and giggle.

"We're going to help you find your mother. A daughter needs her mother so badly," Bitna said.

Bitna had a daughter, too, two years younger than Joon, who was now living in Tokyo. Bitna also told her that she and her husband had been divorced for a few years. Bitna spoke to Joon in Korean as he poked his head in and out of the refrigerator, putting away the produce. He responded, but Selene couldn't understand most of it. Understanding a native speaker was so much harder than reading, but her ears caught certain words no matter who was saying them, like *really* and *right now.* Numbers, and things like *man, woman, family, kitchen*—the first Korean words she'd learned outside of greetings, foods, the days of the week, and a short list of common phrases.

"Joon used to work at the newspaper. He's a photographer," Deiji said like the proud aunt she clearly was.

"That's awesome," Selene said, impressed. She knew she was cool and honestly had always felt that way—no one could make her feel *uncool*, and she wasn't easily intimidated. But she felt like a straight-up dork saying *That's awesome* to an attractive guy around her age. She looked towards Joon again, but most of his face was blocked by the fridge door. All she could see were his light jeans cuffed once at the bottom, the taupe slippers on his feet.

"He's a freelancer now. He took these. Four seasons of Seoul," Bitna said, motioning to the photos hanging on the wall. The statue of King Sejong in heavy snow, cherry blossoms in Seoul Forest, rows and rows of summer lavender, red-orange fall foliage reflected in Cheonggyecheon Stream. Bitna told her the National Museum of Korea had turned the photos into postcards that regularly sold out.

"He just got back from Rwanda last week," Deiji said. "He knows people who work at the newspaper here who could help you. People with access to things." She had an airy way of speaking, as if her thoughts floated down to her through gauzy light and came into focus only a second or two after she opened her mouth.

Joon placed small ceramic bowls frosted from the cold in front of them and tapped a pair of metal chopsticks on the table before digging in. He hadn't said anything directly to Selene except *hello*.

"I could pay you. I don't expect anyone to work for free. I'm

so grateful, I can't put it into words. I'm truly *overwhelmed*," Selene said. She was crying, and Bitna touched her hand.

"We don't care about money. Drink your tea while it's warm,"
she said, refilling her cup. Selene obeyed.

"We're happy to help. Bitna has told this story so many times
over all these years. You're a celebrity to us! The little bee baby
in the red blanket. They could make a movie about you," Deiji
said.

Joon leaned forward. "If you feel comfortable giving me your
number, I'll take photos of this information and make a few
phone calls. I'm leaving for Finland tomorrow, but I'll be back
next week, and I'll contact you." Selene sniffed as she watched
him catch a cube of pickled radish freckled with red pepper between his chopsticks and put it in his mouth. She smiled, and he
returned it with kind eyes before looking away.

"Of course. Thank you!" Selene said. She thanked them again
in Korean, using the highest formality. Her stomach relaxed, and
she finished her sweet rice ball. Deiji stepped out onto the balcony to smoke a slim cigarette as Bitna instructed Selene to eat
everything else on the table. She could see Deiji looking out over
the railing as she smoked, and when she turned, her profile was
pretty and small.

Joon refilled his plate as Selene filled hers. Radish, *hobak bokkeum*, *gaji bokkeum*, and kimchi. Quail eggs and soy sauce beef,
kongnamul muchim and miso soup. When Deiji stubbed out her
cigarette and returned to the kitchen, she and Joon spoke in both
Korean and English, laughing heartily when Joon showed her a
cat video on his phone—long, dramatic meows accompanied by
the clanging of a dish. He held it up so Selene and Bitna could
watch, too.

7

Lydia

After walking Tae and Eun to school in the morning with Jenny, Selene, and the rest of the kids, Lydia made her way to her first art class. She was wearing the baby blue miniskirt she'd finished knitting the night before. She'd also knit a black flower and attached it at the hip with a Jenny-influenced black ribbon; Jenny had wholeheartedly approved when she saw it. Lydia wore the skirt with a plain white T-shirt and ruffly white socks with Mary Janes. She felt like it was good luck to dress like a schoolgirl on her first day of art class. Also, Hye had told her how adorable she looked, which was always a plus.

The night before, Hye had come into Lydia's room and watched her as she was knitting and asked if she'd teach her how to cast on. As soon as Lydia finished her skirt, she helped Hye practice getting the yarn on the needles, and Hye complimented her on how crafty she was. Hye also informed her she would be showing a photo of her latest painting to another one of her actor friends on set because they were interested in buying art for their new place.

Whatever nerves Lydia would've had about the first day of art class settled when she imagined the wish taking hold. All she knew was that she felt confident on the subway in her cute outfit with her cute bag and the cute little Miffy pin she'd clipped in her hair. She felt *extremely* confident as she stepped into the classroom and found a spot towards the front.

The teacher introduced herself as Penelope. Mid-fifties, bouncy black hair with a strip of gray she repeatedly flicked out of her face with her pinky. The way she held her mouth when she smiled reminded Lydia of Cher, which made her like Penelope instantly. She told everyone that although it might seem a little unorthodox, it was okay to call her by either her first name, *Penelope seonsaengnim*, or just *seonsaengnim*, the Korean word for *teacher*. Lydia was used to Tae and Eun calling their teachers *seonsaengnim*. She wrote Penelope's name down in *Hangul* in her notebook as the teacher started going over what they would cover in class and what was expected of them. She congratulated the students for being accepted and listed off countries and cities represented in the room.

"Cadaqués in Spain, Kentucky in the United States, Abuja, Lisbon, Stockholm, and Paris, to name just a few! What a diverse group. Art cannot be contained to one culture, race, or swath of land. Art is free and fluid. Like this," Penelope said, turning on the screen hanging in front of the whiteboard.

Lydia's heart flopped like a fish.

"I went through all of your portfolios and spent a lot of time with them. This piece jumped out to me. This piece by . . . Lydia Shelby," Penelope said after squinting to read the name on the bottom. "Lydia, you're here?"

Lydia's hand shot up.

"Free and fluid! This painting is a wonderful exploration," Penelope said, gesturing towards her. The piece was one Lydia had painted in a flurry last year after a creative dry spell. She'd been working on murals consistently and getting paid well, but the cartoonish drawings had started to bore her. One afternoon, she turned up Camille Saint-Saëns as loud as she could and painted without thinking. She'd lost track of time completely. The moon had risen as Lydia covered the canvas in movements of lavender and orange, sharp black lines, pops of red. It was more abstract than her usual work and inspired an entirely new series. Those were the pieces she'd sent along with the art school application, the ones she wanted to define her painting style going forward. She was already proud of them, but being singled out on the first day of class was beyond her wildest dreams.

Maybe without considering the possibility of the wish being real, Lydia would've been focused on flying under the radar and making sure she didn't embarrass herself. But now she was thanking Penelope both in English and Korean, and her new classmates were agreeing with the teacher that her work was wonderful. An American guy with big green eyes leaned forward to get her attention, told her how much he loved it.

Next Penelope pulled up another abstract painting filled with thick black lines and splotches of bright colors.

"Santi Rivera, where are you?" she asked. Lydia turned to look for him.

A young man with chin-length black curls pushed behind silver-hooped ears raised his hand.

"You are the one from Cadaqués, correct?" Penelope asked.

"*Sí,*" Santi answered.

"*Excelente!* I could tell from your painting. Do you know how?" Santi shook his head.

"Because it is *alive.* This painting grabbed me by the throat and pulled me into the blacks, yellows, reds, and greens of Spain. The deep blue water! I've only been to Spain once, but I was back there immediately when I saw this," Penelope said, pointing at the screen.

"Thank you."

"Those are two examples, but I love everyone's work, and that's why you're here," Penelope said. She clapped her hands together.

Lydia turned away from Santi, but her gaze quickly slid back to him for another good look. When they made eye contact, Lydia smiled; Santi's expression remained neutral as he bent over his sketchbook.

They spent the morning discussing extreme uses of color and expressions of light and dark in famous works of art, and when class was over, Lydia packed up her bag as her classmates filed out. The American guy with the big green eyes was one seat down from her, and when the person in between them left, he introduced himself to Lydia.

"I'm Caleb, from Seattle. Just gonna come right out and ask you if you'd like to get a drink with me tonight. It's forward, I know, but—"

"I'd love to! Nice to meet you, Caleb," Lydia said, holding her hand out to shake his. No way was she turning this opportunity down.

One of her colored pencils rolled to the floor, and she watched it land next to a black suede clog and royal blue sock beneath black pants that stopped a smidgen before the ankle. She looked up to see Santi: He bent and retrieved the pencil, put it back on the table without glancing at her. She said *thanks* but got no response from him. Then he was gone.

She turned to Caleb.

"I promise I've never asked a girl out on the first day of class before, but it's Seoul, we're both American, and these are special circumstances. For example, baby blue is my favorite color," Caleb said, pointing at her skirt. Now that she was standing so close to him, Lydia realized how short it was. She smiled; the skirt alone provided enough flirtation to make an ordinary conversation more interesting.

"All good things!" Lydia said, peeping down at her bare legs. They exchanged contact information, and she agreed to meet him in Hongdae after she got Tae and Eun bathed and tucked into bed.

Minsu made a delicious spread—spicy garlic fried chicken and rice, blanched spinach in sesame oil, *dakgaejang*, and steamed buns filled with red bean paste. Hye was still at work, so it was only Lydia, Minsu, and the boys at the dinner table. Minsu was heading back to the restaurant afterwards but wanted to make sure they ate together. Lydia made the mistake of not being quiet enough when she mentioned to Minsu a guy had asked her out; Tae and Eun overheard, and now they were teasing her mercilessly.

"*Noona*, are you going to marry him?" Eun asked with wide eyes. He took another bite of the steamed bun, and Minsu reminded him to chew with his mouth closed. Minsu was gentle with the boys, but nothing got past him.

"No! She wants to marry a K-pop star! That's why she has a J-Hope photocard hanging from her bag," Tae fussed at his brother.

"You *looove* J-Hope!" Tae said.

"I do! He's sunshine. Honestly, I love everyone in BTS, but I don't think I'm *actually* going to marry one of them. If I bump into someone famous on the street and they ask me out, I'll let you know, but until then, I'm just as excited to be going on a date with a guy in my art class, although I'm not marrying him, either. What I *am* going to do is eat another one of your daddy's yummy steamed buns," Lydia said, reaching over to grab another for herself.

Tae and Eun got into a squabble about whether Tae had a secret girlfriend at school (yes!), and after letting them argue it out for a minute, Minsu said it was time to wash up. Lydia told them she'd be right there, and they disappeared upstairs to pick out their pajamas.

When she got home, Hye seemed thrilled Lydia had an admirer, and was excited to tell her that Jenny's host father, Daniel, wanted to buy a painting, too.

"Three *million* won?" Lydia said. *A little over two thousand dollars.*

"Yes. Does that sound good?" Hye asked. She was on the couch next to Lydia wearing dark jeans and a pink button-down shirt. Like usual, her hair and makeup were immaculate. She looked like she was filming a scene from her drama. Her thick script was open on the table, colorfully marked up.

"That sounds . . . amazing. Thank you! Please tell him thank you, and of course I'll tell him myself next time I see him."

"I will. And, Lydia——" Hye said, pausing to take a good look at her.

Lydia had decided to keep the miniskirt on for tonight since Caleb mentioned it earlier, and she'd traded her top for a buttoned black cardigan to match the black flower on the skirt. She usually wore pink lipstick, but tonight she opted for a bold red-orange. She wondered if she had some on her teeth. She tapped her mouth and rubbed the stain from her fingertips.

"You have *really* turned into something special," Hye finished.

You have really turned into something special.

Lydia kept hearing it in her head as she walked to the bus stop, making her way to Hongdae. She heard it when she was lucky enough to score the last available seat on the bus, and it echoed again when Jenny and Selene texted her in the group chat after she told them about Caleb and sent them a pic of her updated outfit.

> You look so pretty! I LOVE YOUR LIPSTICK.
> Have so much fun. Fighting!

> True beauty! Tell us EVERYTHING later. Text if
> you need us to run interference and rescue you.
> (Just in case!)

They sent star and moon emojis back and forth.

You have really turned into something special.

She heard it when she sent her mom a selfie and her mom wrote back.

> That lipstick makes you look older. (In a good
> way!) ☺

To Lydia, everything was better in Hongdae. The energy and lights made her feel like she was in a pinball machine. It was her favorite place to hang out in Seoul, so full of color—the signs, the sections where the sidewalks and streets were painted red, yellow, orange. And everywhere she turned, music. Hongdae was also brimming with food. The weekend before, she'd gone with Jenny and Selene. They'd eaten their *tteokbokki* with toothpicks while they people-watched and listened to a guy play Stevie Wonder on his guitar before karaoke. Afterwards, they got torched marshmallow ice creams and wandered, looking at all the prettiness. Went to a photo booth and wore silly props on their heads and posed, all three of them leaving with matching picture strips. Lydia tucked hers into the corner of the mirror in her bathroom at the condo, knowing she'd keep it forever.

Caleb showed up on the rainbow concrete steps they'd agreed on, wearing an oldskool Seattle Mariners T-shirt and a perfect-teeth smile with decidedly American confidence and chill. He apologized again for being so bold, asking her out on their first day. She wanted to tell him that maybe it was beyond his control; maybe it was beyond *her* control. That maybe it was something supernatural brewing in his brain that made him want to have a drink with her.

"You look cute," he said as they walked between two noisy rows of shops. Each was blasting its own music, practically overflowing with phone cases, plushies, dresses, and jewelry. "I noticed you immediately, before Penelope *seonsaengnim* singled you out." Caleb was her height exactly and wore a black watch on his right wrist. Lydia looked at it when he pointed which way they should go. He said there was a bar down there he liked, if that sounded good to her.

"Okay! And thank you. You look nice, too . . . I like your watch," Lydia said. It was the first thing she thought of, and he *was* attractive. She'd talked to him for a total of ten minutes so far, including the art class, and she was excited—she hadn't hung out one-on-one with a guy she liked in so long. Maybe she could like Caleb.

You have really turned into something special.

"Wanna get soju? Are you hungry?" he asked once they were standing outside the bar.

"Soju's good. Maybe a snack later. I just had dinner." She told him about Minsu and his restaurant, explained that he was her host father. She also remembered she'd sold another painting and told him that, too. She hadn't remembered to tell Jenny and Selene. Or her mom.

"Oh, shit! Congratulations! Soju was gonna be on me anyway, but yes, soju on me in celebration," Caleb said as he held the door for her. The scruff on his chin had a reddish hue that didn't match the light brown hair on his head, and it made him even cuter. They went inside.

Caleb told her how art had brought him to South Korea. He'd majored in environmental engineering when he was in college but got his master's in visual arts. His last and longest relationship ended about six months ago with a woman he met in Seoul.

They sat outside underneath the colored string lights of the patio, sharing soju. Lydia was mildly tipsy by the time they finished, and she told Caleb it'd been a while since she'd dated anyone.

"Hard to believe that. A *lot* of men look at you. You don't notice?"

"I'm not pretending to be modest!"

"That guy right there looked you up and down when we walked over here. I'll admit I was slightly offended. I mean, how does he know you're not my girlfriend? Is it because we only met, like, ten hours ago?" Caleb smirked.

Lydia glanced at the guy he was talking about—a handsome man in his thirties wearing a green button-down and black pants. She hadn't seen him eyeing her. She watched him for a moment and scanned the rest of the people at the bar before moving to the tables. She loved people-watching everywhere, but she especially loved it in spots like Hongdae, Gangnam, and Myeong-dong, since they were so busy. She was listening to Caleb tell a funny story about some guy hitting on his girlfriend right in front of him last year when she saw Santi from their art class walk up to the bar.

"Ah!" Lydia said, interrupting Caleb. The sound had leapt from her mouth so unexpectedly she was embarrassed. "Sorry, Caleb. I saw a guy from our class . . . at the bar. It surprised me."

"No worries," he said, turning to look.

"That guy, um, Santi."

Lydia watched him get two green bottles of soju and join a mixed group at the table in the corner. It was dark inside. She lost him for a second but spotted him again when the pearlescent blue rose on the back of his black satin bomber jacket flashed in the lights. The jacket was fucking awesome, and coincidently matched her skirt. Lydia imagined herself slipping the jacket on, how it would feel like cool water on her arms, the back of her neck.

Seeing Santi changed her mood in a way she couldn't explain. Now she felt like she had to *pretend* something with Caleb, even though she was having a good time.

After a while, she and Caleb decided to leave the bar to hunt for street food, and on their way out the door, she bumped into Santi—literally. He was heading to the bar again, and she stopped to help a girl pick up some things that had fallen from her purse. When Lydia stood and turned, there was Santi's jacket with a trail of black thorns down the sleeve. There was Santi's shoulder. There was Santi's outrageous hair curling across his forehead and his brown eyes gazing into hers.

"Hi," she said to him.

The bitsy diamond piercing in his nose winked blue in the light. He didn't say anything, just lifted his chin in recognition before turning away. She didn't know why she felt disappointed.

Lydia and Caleb got sticks of candied grapes and strawberries from a street vendor and ate them while they listened to a busker sing two songs by IU. Caleb put ten thousand won in his guitar case.

And.

Their mouths were sticky with sweet candy fruit when they kissed in the dark alley behind the karaoke bar. Lydia had written the bar's name down in her notebook to remember so she, Jenny, and Selene could go back together.

She'd listened with bated breath to Jenny's stories of kissing Haru, so jealous. She'd felt faint, desperately wanting a kiss of her own, and now, *finally*, she was having one. Caleb put his hand flat on the stone of the building and pressed his body against hers, but not too aggressively. She squeezed her eyes shut so tightly she saw sparks.

She also saw the blue rose flash of Santi's jacket; she couldn't stop thinking about it.

"I'm *so* attracted to you," Caleb said between kisses, like it'd kill him to keep it inside. Lydia texted Jenny and Selene about it from the bus.

AHHHHH we kissed for like, half an hour before I left.

GIRL!

!!!! SHE'S BACK, BABY!!!

Santi was wearing The Jacket in their next class, and this time he was sitting right in front of her. Caleb wasn't there yet, but Lydia was excited to see him. First thing that morning, she'd thought about their kisses and gotten so distracted she'd had to ask Tae to repeat the story he'd been telling her on their walk to school. Lydia wanted to fill Jenny and Selene in on more of the date, but they hadn't had any time alone. Wrangling five kids for school together was tough work and didn't always leave room for personal conversations, so they made plans to discuss later.

Penelope *seonsaengnim* explained more about their big assignment for the semester. They would be working in pairs to come up with ideas for several lantern festivals backed by art museums around the world. Two pairs of students would be selected as winners by Kim Chinmae, a world-renowned artist from Seoul. The winners not only would receive fifty thousand dollars each, but also would travel alongside Mr. Kim, all expenses paid, to Paris, Florence, Madrid, and possibly more cities, depending on their success. They needed to propose original, unique ideas to make the festivals in each destination stand out. Penelope showed them different examples on the screen—a row of animal-shaped lanterns floating on a stream in Jakarta, compost-friendly lanterns on the waters of Beijing. Winning was Lydia's ultimate goal. All that money and travel, working with a famous artist. On a more personal level, she was in love with the idea of doing something other than painting. She was ready and willing to grow her artistic mind in Seoul.

Caleb wasn't there by the time they were picking partners. Santi turned to look around the room, and when he made eye contact with Lydia, the words flew out of her.

"Do you want to work together?"

"Sure," he said with a literal shrug.

"Okay, cool," she replied, handing him her phone so he could enter his contact info. She texted him immediately.

Hi Santi! It's Lydia! ☺

He looked down at his screen and said nothing, just put it back in his pocket. *Ouch.* She was acting a damn fool over a guy who literally couldn't bother to crack a smile at how cute she was (trying to be)! By the time Caleb showed up, only one other late arrival was without a partner, so he was paired up with them. Lydia waved and made an empathetic, overly exaggerated sad face at him.

She and Caleb had plans again on Sunday night. So why was she thinking of Cadaqués on Saturday morning while side-by-side painting with Tae and Eun? She'd read about where Santi was from; Dalí and Picasso had lived and vacationed there. She dove into the tangled, rich histories of all sorts of artists nurtured by the beauty and culture of Spain, imagining Santi sketching by the sea. Inspired, she started a new painting awash with blue.

"I want more blue, too," Eun said. He put his paintbrush down and slid his hands into the tiny pockets of his smock.

"He wants to copy you," Tae said, rolling his eyes. He slowly painted a squiggly orange line down the length of his canvas.

"No, I don't! I just like blue. It's my favorite color," Eun said. He and Tae began arguing in Korean, and Lydia let them sort it out on their own before she handed Eun a small tube of cobalt.

The boys had been arguing more and more lately, and Lydia

found that if she intervened or attempted to, they would dig deeper into who did what and why, both of them performing and pleading their case so she would (hopefully) take their side. But if she left them alone to sort it out, only stepping in when necessary, in no time they were happily playing together again.

Tae got testy if he wasn't in charge but was easily placated with the promise of a treat. He was a good listener, and although he could be sneaky—wetting his toothbrush instead of actually brushing like Lydia asked—he wasn't much trouble at all. Eun was more hyper, which was to be expected since he was younger, but he was a well-behaved child, too, and outside the times towards the end of the week when Lydia was sometimes so overstimulated and exhausted she couldn't keep her eyes open, she really enjoyed being around the boys. They were both funny and quick to apologize when she had to scold them. They'd crawl into her lap or put their heads on her shoulder—warm puppies trying to get back into her good graces.

Lydia painted a wide black line across the blue. As she worked on a black-rose-and-thorns idea in the middle, she thought of Caleb's husky laugh and his bright green eyes watching hers, wondering why she couldn't keep herself from swapping his face with the image of Santi taking off his jacket.

When she heard the families arriving at the Parks' for dinner, she told the boys it was time to stop painting and get cleaned up.

After putting the kids to bed, the girls met on the Kim-Crawfords' balcony. Selene caught them up on the latest with Bitna, Deiji, and Joon, and told them she had plans to meet with Joon soon to go over some paperwork about adoption processes, orphanages, and family registries in South Korea. Jenny and

Haru were still stealing kisses as often as they could, and the kid Fox had been having trouble with at school had asked for his forgiveness; they were fine now.

"Well, I have another date with Caleb tomorrow night, but I can't stop thinking about Santi, who is clearly not interested in me at all, not even in a friendly way. I texted him earlier about getting together to talk about our project and he hasn't written me back," Lydia said.

"Have you found his socials?" Selene asked. Lydia had attempted to search for Santi but had no luck, unlike Caleb, who'd followed her immediately. He had a blank page but followed a lot of athletes and art accounts.

Lydia shook her head and told her Santi's last name. "He's probably too cool to have one. He is *literally* the coolest guy I've ever seen in my life. Out of every guy I've ever seen in the flesh, or on TV, or in magazines—I'm dead serious. But it's more than that. He's like . . . *ethereal*. It's not just his looks, though. He has this aura. A mystique. Like Orpheus. Well, Apollo if we're talking god of art, but Orpheus was the one who came to mind. I can't explain it!" Lydia was practically panting.

Selene pulled out her phone and tapped around.

"Look at you! You're in a *love triangle*," Jenny said, laughing. She finished her wine and lifted her shoulders.

"In no way am I in a love triangle. He won't even talk to me! I'm being crazy and I'm fully aware of it, but I can't seem to stop."

Why couldn't she be satisfied with what was going on in her life like Jenny was right now? She needed to chill and have fun with Caleb. Maybe she'd finally sign up for a dating app or two and play the field.

"Found him. Yeah, okay, the dude is beautiful," Selene said, holding her phone out for them to see.

"What?!" Lydia squinted and leaned forward. She took the phone from Selene and looked closely at Santi's face on the screen. She scrolled through his account. It was mostly art and only one or two pics of him. Lydia asked how she discovered it.

"There are only three accounts with *Santiago* in their name following the art store near campus. Easy guess which one was him."

"Santi*ago*. I didn't think of looking for that. Will you do everything for me from here on out?" Lydia asked. She'd only searched widely for *Santi Rivera*. Pretty embarrassing she hadn't thought about the art store or his full name.

"Hey, I may not be able to find my birth mom without a wish, but I *can* find hot guys on social media. Just say the word," Selene said.

Jenny chimed in with her glowing thoughts about how perfect Santi's hair was.

Lydia let out a blissful sigh and changed the subject to the recently announced BTS concerts in November. The girls discussed which day to go so they could take Arwen and Nabi and maybe the host mothers, too, for the best girls' night ever.

In the morning, there was a message from Santi.

> I can do tonight at 7. Only free night this week.
> Growler in Ikseon-dong?

Three sentences at once! Lydia was supposed to meet Caleb in Hongdae at seven for their date, but in a total act of impossible WTF, she wrote Santi back, Perfect. See you then! ☺

8

Jenny

The next week, Jenny and Rain went to a café after dropping Fox and Arwen off at school. Daniel was in Suwon visiting a friend and would return later that night; then he and Rain were going on an overnight spa date to Bucheon. Fox and Arwen would be staying with friends for the weekend, leaving Jenny alone and free to do as she liked until Monday.

She had dinner and shopping plans with Lydia and Selene on Saturday afternoon and was looking forward to that. She hadn't been going to the condo gym as much as she wanted, so she promised herself she'd do an hour-long yoga video on Saturday night and take a bath before bed. She was also looking forward to spending almost all of Sunday alone eating junk and marathoning *Hometown Cha-Cha-Cha*. She was obsessed with the healing, seaside-village vibes of that show, and the pretty lead actress's face reminded her of Rain's—the character was even a dentist like Rain, too.

She also hoped that over the weekend she'd be kissing Haru. A lot.

She was doing better lately, and a large part of that was due to the fun she was having with Rain's younger brother. Plus, Rain was good about checking in with Jenny, and she appreciated that so much. She couldn't have asked for a better or more sensitive host mother. That morning, tucked away in the café,

Rain had asked if Jenny had seen any young men she was interested in since she'd been in Seoul.

"Can you keep a secret?" Rain asked.

Jenny nodded, so curious she wanted to scream but playing it extra cool. She was desperate for gossip; she'd had none since coming to Seoul. The biggest gossip she'd heard in the past six months was about Ethan getting engaged. She hoped Rain had something juicy.

"Haru thinks you're pretty," Rain said. They both had deep-fried honey cookies called *yakgwa* on the plates in front of them. Rain took a bite of hers victoriously, pleased with herself.

Jenny's nervous system gave an itty-bitty shake. She was thinking Haru's name at the same time Rain had said it—*I wonder if Haru is still sleeping?* They'd left him asleep in the condo that morning. He usually got back from the restaurant late at night—sometimes they missed each other completely. One night last week, she purposely waited up for him, and they'd talked for only about ten minutes in the living room before he passed out cold on the couch. One second, he was asking about California earthquakes, telling her he'd wanted to be a seismologist when he was a kid, and the next, he'd fallen asleep. She'd been picturing that sleeping face when Rain said his name.

She debated being completely honest.

Rain, I think your brother is disturbingly handsome and charismatic. He's a peach.

"Wow. Well, if you can find a way to slip him my thanks, please do. He's not hard on my eyes, either. I find him quite pleasant to behold," Jenny said formally, like a Jane Austen heroine. She thought of the last time she and Haru had kissed two days ago, while everyone else was in bed. She took a drink of her iced coffee to cool off.

"I'm debating whether I should set him up. He'll say he's too busy for a girlfriend, I'm sure. Plus, every time I've tried to set someone up, I've failed," Rain said. One attempt was when Rain wasn't fully aware the guy was still married; the second time she tried, the couple fell passionately in love and dated for months until they got in such a big fight the police had to come break it up. Rain was present for it, gave a witness statement and everything.

"You're a fantastic storyteller," Jenny said, clapping. She ate bites of her cookie and sank even deeper into the cozy ambiance of the café. Delicate acoustic music piped from the speakers, and the chairs were extra cushy. Multicolored pastel scarves were draped high across the ceiling, gauzing the lights. It felt like they were inside a warm blanket fort.

"Did I tell you Aera set Daniel and me up? We're a true success story, but she dated him first. Have I not told you this?"

"No! I had no clue." Jenny tried to picture Daniel and Aera together, but her brain refused it. She could only see Daniel with Rain, and Aera with Geon.

Rain told her Daniel and Aera met at a design conference a few months before Rain and Daniel went on their first date; Aera was the first Korean girl Daniel ever dated. Rain was the second.

"I use the word *dated* loosely since they only went on two dates. Obviously, her feelings were so strong for him she decided to set him up with one of her best friends," Rain said, rolling her eyes.

"I love it. Tell me more about the recommitment ceremony, too, please." Rain and Daniel had planned it for New Year's Eve, their tenth anniversary. Jenny saw two short gold dresses she loved the other day and couldn't decide which one to get for the event; she planned on dragging Lydia and Selene back with her tomorrow for their opinions. None of them were going home for the holidays; they'd all agreed to stay and help out with the families. Although Jenny would miss her own family, she was looking forward to keeping her distance from California.

Rain said she used to think recommitment ceremonies were unnecessary and corny, but now she thought they were romantic. "The world is a mess, so recommitting and saying we'd get married all over again is incredibly powerful to me."

The panic Jenny wanted to feel about never being able to love anyone the way Rain and Daniel loved each other was quickly overshadowed by how grateful she was for the protection her wish provided, if she believed hard enough. She felt the butterflies when Haru walked through the door, passion and lust when he kissed her and put his leg between hers, but that was it. *Those* were the things she couldn't live without.

She could definitely deal with having all of the good and none of the bad.

In the morning, after Haru left early for the restaurant, the Kim-Crawfords left Jenny alone in that capacious condo.

She went out with the girls at lunchtime for tornado potatoes and fruity drinks in Nonhyeon-dong, then to Starfield COEX Mall so Jenny could get their opinions on the gold dresses. The one with the bigger bow was the clear favorite, so she got it. Jenny and Selene helped Lydia pick out a dress for the recommitment ceremony, too—sparkly silver with a ruffle skirt. Selene had snatched up a short red velvet dress from Aera's label already and showed the girls a picture of it on her phone.

Before they walked into the condo building, Jenny remembered to send them the new mix she'd made.

Jenny's Pretty Ribbons Mix

"Palette (feat. G-DRAGON)" by IU
"Ditto" by NewJeans
"Confess To You" by LIM KIM
"LOVE FOOL" by STAYC
"LILAC" by IU
"Mikrokosmos" by BTS
"Either Way" by IVE
"Like Crazy" by Jimin
"A.D.T.O.Y." by 2PM
"Dopamine" by Jackson Wang
"Puppy Love" by Erika de Casier
"Look" by GOT7
"Nap of a star" by TOMORROW X TOGETHER
"Cool With You" by NewJeans
"Cotton Candy" by Jinyoung
"FLOWER" by Jisoo
"Butterfly (Prologue Mix)" by BTS
"Our Souls at Night" by Sondia
"nostalgia" by JUNNY, JAY B
"Nightfalling" by John Park

Jenny was alone inside the condo for two minutes before the electricity snapped off and the entire place went dark. The sun had been hidden behind a thick layer of clouds for the past hour, but she did the best she could in the situation, opening all the curtains, lighting the two candles Rain kept on the coffee table, and scrolling through her phone for thirty minutes before deciding to go hang out at one of the other condos. Before she blew the candles out, she went to her bedroom to pack a small bag in case she ended up spending the night.

She stopped in the foyer, double-checking for her phone so she could text the girls in the group chat, but moved back when the keypad beeped. Haru opened the door and stepped in, the emergency hallway lights illuminating half of his handsome, smiling face.

He got the flashlight out of the kitchen drawer, and together, he and Jenny gathered and lit more candles, strategically placing them around the condo until the whole place felt like the inside of a paper lantern. He explained that the electricity sometimes went out in their unit and a few other ones on alternating floors, but said it never lasted more than twenty-four hours. He talked as he pulled dishes from the fridge and put some of them on the table. He was taking the others up to Hye and Minsu's fridge just in case, so they wouldn't spoil.

"Eat," Haru said in such a commanding tone Jenny was left with no room to object. "I'll be right back."

As she waited for him to return, Jenny ate mouthfuls of kimchi and *gamjajeon*, followed those with bites of hard-boiled egg rolled in flaky salt and red pepper. She sipped at a light beer until her mouth tingled. She wondered if Minsu was in the condo upstairs. Was Hye? Would they wonder if she and Haru were alone with no electricity once Haru explained why he was putting the food in their refrigerator? She was suddenly paranoid everyone would know exactly what was going on. Maybe Rain already knew; Daniel, too.

She was so deep in thought the keypad beeps startled her; she sucked in a loud gasp.

"Sorry," Haru said, trading his shoes for slippers again. "Did you eat something?" he asked as he sat at the kitchen table across from her.

"I did. It's delicious."

"Good girl," Haru said, smirking.

"Good *chef*," Jenny teased back, eating two more big bites of sprout salad and black beans.

Dessert was kissing against the kitchen counter, kissing on the couch, kissing on her bed. He'd never stepped foot in her bedroom while it was dark outside until now. He'd never put his hand between her legs until now, had never slipped her bra strap down her shoulder until now. She took her panties off for him and he lost his shirt.

"Do you—" Jenny started.

"Daniel has condoms. I'll—" Haru said, his breath hot against her neck.

Jenny wanted to make sure she gave a clear, verbal affirmation. On the flight over, the flight attendant needed her to give a verbal affirmation about sitting in an exit row; she'd had to say she'd be willing to help in the unlikely event of an emergency. Being naked underneath Haru felt like a life-changing emergency of its own.

"Please," she said.

Ethan came to mind as soon as Haru was inside of her. She couldn't help it. She thought about how Haru felt better. How Haru was gentler. How Haru's sounds were different. Their shadows flickered with the candles—dulcet and dreamy. He clasped her hands above her head, and when he came with a deep groan of pleasure, Jenny vibrated slowly, too. The ribbon in her hair slipped, cool, onto her shoulder.

They talked in the dark until Haru fell asleep, with Jenny's arm underneath him. She lay there, staring up at the ceiling, warm and blissed-out, not wanting to disturb him.

"Just so you know, I have an elaborate escape plan in case I need to use it," Haru whispered when he woke up half an hour later. They were both still naked, and he was behind her now, the big spoon. "I'll go out that window and do a whole Spider-Man thing over to the balcony, come back inside, sneak into my bedroom. I'll do it to protect your honor," he joked.

Jenny thanked him, laughing at the impossibility of his fantasy; her wiggling only made him hold her tighter.

"What *if* they came back right now, though? What would really happen if they caught us?" Jenny asked. She turned around to face him, kissed his mouth. She imagined Rain opening the door to find her brother with his hands all over her in the dark. She loved kissing him, loved being touched by him, loved the warmth of his body next to hers and how he'd asked if she was okay more than once when he was inside of her.

"Probably nothing," Haru said, kissing her neck.

"Nothing? Oh, sure. The au pair sleeping with someone in the house is so cliché, everyone would just let it go?"

"It would be cliché for you to be sleeping with *Daniel*, not me."

"Stop it!" Jenny squealed, covering her face. Although he was a tad too young to be her father, she'd latched onto Daniel as father-figure-*ish* while she was in Seoul, and knew it was because she missed her dad. It felt normal and not like something she needed to stop herself from doing, a fantasy no one else needed to know about. But when she was putting Fox and Arwen to bed and could hear Daniel's deep voice in the other room . . . it reminded her of being a little girl, of the comfort she'd experienced when her dad came home from work, how protected she felt seeing his shoes by the door.

"They're not coming back tonight," Haru said.

"I know. I'm glad."

"Are you?" he asked, smoothing his hand down her side.

"I am."

She slowly spread her legs for him again. What poured from his mouth during and after was a mix of English and Korean, slow syllables melting into one another like warm water and sugar.

On Sunday morning, the electricity returned with the sunrise. Rain texted to let Jenny know they'd all be back by eight that evening. Jenny responded and added that she hoped they were having a great time. She also texted Lydia and Selene in their group chat to let them know she was alive. Barely. She and Haru had hardly slept.

He had plans to hit up the store and replace Daniel's condoms before the Kim-Crawfords returned. Jenny gave herself to him again and again, not knowing the next time they'd be alone. She didn't want to think about it. She just wanted to touch him, wanted him to touch her for as long as possible. When she was with Haru, she felt like a whole new person, not a crumpled piece of paper she was desperately trying to smooth out. Anytime Jenny wanted to second-guess herself about what she and Haru were doing, she remembered that.

She searched her heart often, wondering how they'd end this or where they'd go from here. The convenience of Haru being in the same living space definitely made this whole friends-with-benefits thing a lot easier, and she figured it would just run its course until one of them was done with it. Maybe it'd be Haru. Maybe it'd be her.

It didn't matter.

She was content with their relationship being exactly how it was, and she was thankful for the stones she and the girls had stacked under the moon because, at the very least, the idea of the wish had helped her relax. Every time she and Haru kissed, every time they were together, the rightness of it all was proof.

She stripped the bed and washed the sheets while he made breakfast.

"I have to be at the restaurant at one. You can't keep me around all day to be your sex slave. I'm a working man. An individual with thoughts and feelings! Not some hot-bodied machine built only to pleasure women."

He'd made Jenny a mound of teddy-bear-shaped fried rice—slits of seaweed flakes for his eyes and nose—with a bright yellow egg cooked *just* fluffily enough to look like a teeny blanket on top, covering him. It was almost too precious to eat, but she powered through after taking at least ten pictures. She resisted the urge to lick her plate clean, but it wasn't easy. Haru loved showing off what he could do in the kitchen, and she loved teasing him about it.

He tolerated it briefly before grabbing her, kissing her deeply, then going up to Hye and Minsu's to retrieve the food he'd put in their fridge.

Ok wait, did you send him back up here for RATIONS?! WTF IS GO-ING ON DOWN THERE? You were the one most resistant to hooking up with anyone in Seoul and you're the one getting laid so much you need backup food for energy. JENNYBELLE!! Lydia wrote.

Selene chimed in: We have plenty of food up here too should you need any!

Jenny's body carried the pleasant ache that followed an intense night and morning of being in bed with a man. She imagined Haru chopping in the restaurant kitchen and forced herself to think about him doing the same thing down in New Zealand in January. How he'd probably be doing the same things he did to her last night and this morning to another woman—she consciously thought about the sounds he'd make in her ear, how her body would rise to meet his.

Jenny had tested herself and passed.

Alone for the rest of the afternoon, she made a pot of tea and settled onto the couch to watch the episode of *Hometown Cha-Cha-Cha* where the main character Hye Jin's electricity goes out and her love interest, Du Sik, sneaks a long-lost shoe back into her closet. Later, when Hye Jin steps outside in her sparkly heels (together again!), surprised, all the lights pop back on, like magic; Du Sik rides his bike away with a huge grin on his face.

With her eyes glued to the screen, Jenny felt exactly like both of them in that moment, her smile bright, heart twirling.

That week all three families gathered to have dinner together at the Chois'. Haru had to go back to the restaurant with Minsu, but he was there long enough to make secret flirty eyes at Jenny from across the table, to quickly touch her waist and the ribbon in her hair when they passed in the hallway. If feelings were involved, it would have been *torture*, the way they had to pretend to be nothing more than roommates . . . but it was so sexy, the way he saved certain looks just for her. How they sneakily let the backs of their hands accidentally touch on purpose when they were in the kitchen with the rest of the family. How they casually said *hi* and *bye* to each other like pals in the afternoon but couldn't *not* touch at night while everyone was asleep. The same dress he casually glanced at in the bright morning light was the same dress he slowly slid off in the dark.

Since Jenny was eating meat now, Arwen decided she didn't want to be a strict vegetarian anymore, either. She and Jenny were in the kitchen, sneaking extra bites of mackerel, while Arwen relayed the drama at school—the most popular girl had been accused of bullying, and her parents were angry about it.

"Daeunie said Taeri's mom wanted to smack the teacher, but she didn't," Arwen said, separating the bones of the fish on the plate. Nabi puttered into the kitchen, wanting to know what they were doing. Arwen asked if she wanted some, and Nabi opened her mouth so she could give her a bite.

"Well, good. No smacking allowed," Jenny said. She instructed the girls to put the dishes in the sink once they were done, touched their heads, and excused herself to use the bathroom. Lydia and Selene were busy with the three boys, but soon they'd put the kids to bed and hang out on the balcony like they always did. Jenny couldn't wait.

Daniel's phone lit up on the table, and before he could grab it, Jenny saw that it was a text from Aera. Strange, considering she was sitting in the living room. Jenny wondered what that was all about on her walk to the bathroom.

When she stepped into the hallway afterwards, she saw the

back of Aera's head disappear into the bedroom, Daniel follow-ing her. Jenny couldn't stop herself from taking a quick peek to see what they were up to. Aera got on her tiptoes to whisper in Daniel's ear; his hand was on the small of her back. Aera turned, touching his stomach. Jenny looked away quickly, her heart racing.

She returned to the living room to find their spouses, Geon and Rain, talking about something on the couch, the kids sitting on the floor in front of them. Jenny's face got hot thinking of Daniel possibly betraying Rain. She loved him so much! Did Geon and Rain know what was going on right next to them in that bedroom?

Fuck.

She saw Lydia and Selene through the window talking on the balcony. Jenny asked Rain if it was okay for her to take Fox and Arwen home for their baths, and Rain said yes, thank you. Jenny told Lydia and Selene she'd be back before scooting the kids into the hallway. She had to keep herself from cursing in the elevator, imagining how crushed Rain would be when she found out Dan-iel and Aera were sneaking around together.

Jenny's brain slowly shifted out of control. She remembered an old webcomic of Daniel's that she'd read on the plane. In it, there was a couple in therapy because of a cheating husband. She saw the panels flashing behind her eyes when she closed them—the man on the couch wringing his hands, his wife on the other side, crying.

That was just a webcomic.

In one of the K-dramas she was watching, the husband was cheating, too. Jenny was so invested at one point she screamed into the couch pillow and kicked her feet when it was finally revealed.

That was just a K-drama.

But.

Maybe she hadn't seen anything?

Maybe she was overreacting—she had to be sure. She opened and slammed doors shut in her mind with a new focus.

She needed a plan.

9

Selene

When Joon returned from Finland, he and Selene went back to the orphanage together. Joon spoke to the women there in Korean, making sure nothing had been left out when Selene went there alone. It was surreal, hearing her birth father's name in Joon's mouth. He said it twice, showing them the picture, asking if they recognized him. Again, they said they didn't. Joon was kind and polite, always using the most formal language. Bowing when he introduced himself and when they were finished, thanking them. He apologized to Selene as they left, sorry he couldn't find out anything more for her. They also visited the police station Bitna had taken her to after she found her. No new information.

They walked to a café to put together the rest of their action plan. Joon warned her in advance that the amount of uploaded forms they'd have to go through would be intense. She asked him to teach her the Korean word for *paperwork*, and she repeated it over and over again until she could say it perfectly.

"Oh! What are the roof tiles here called? I meant to look it up but forgot," Selene said, thinking back to standing outside the orphanage, wondering.

"*Kiwa.*"

"*Kiwa,*" she repeated. "It sucks to be half Korean and not know these things."

She was embarrassed as soon as she said it. Not only because it was true, but because it sounded like she was pouting, and she hadn't meant it to. She didn't want to be ungrateful. She had gotten so far already! She'd only been in Seoul since August. It wasn't even the end of September yet, and although she wouldn't dare say she was *close* to finding her birth mother, she was undoubtedly *closer* than she was back in NYC.

Selene added that sometimes she didn't think she looked half Korean anyway. Maybe more like a quarter. She'd grown up with friends from all over the world, but only a few Korean kids had asked her if she was half Korean when she was younger, and only a few more people had since she'd become an adult. Everyone assumed she was black or *kind* of black mixed with something else, but they didn't know what, and that'd never really bothered her. She opened her mouth to explain her complicated feelings and defend her insecurities, but Joon spoke.

"You *definitely* do look half Korean and half black, and that's what you are, so no worrying there. I could tell you were half Korean the first time I saw your face. It's a great face," Joon said as his eyes searched the laptop screen. Her heart purred like a warm kitten. He glanced at her quickly before looking away again.

"Thank you. You have a nice face, too," Selene said.

He gave a small smile and continued. "I'm not saying I know what that's like, to be half Korean or to not grow up over here immersed in this culture, but don't be so hard on yourself. I know plenty of Koreans whose parents raised them in the United States, and they aren't fluent in Korean, either. Some can understand what's spoken to them, but they can't speak it easily themselves. It's much harder if you're not speaking it every day."

She thanked him again as the café's piano music plunked prettily, low. Selene hadn't played piano since she'd been in Seoul and missed it madly. Playing the keyboard in Fox's bedroom wasn't the same. She watched the rain slip down the window, listened. Joon's soft typing on his laptop was also pleasing.

"The guy who used to do investigative work at the newspaper gave me access to this site where we can search by date of entry in the orphanage's filing system," Joon said after tapping some more. He turned his computer so she could see the screen. Together, they entered all the information Selene had, but nothing new came up.

"Feels like a fool's search to think the orphanage would have more information about my birth mother when my birth mother wasn't involved with them. She left me on the sidewalk, not at the orphanage. Is there something I'm missing?" Selene asked. She'd lost her appetite and left half of the piece of matcha cake on the plate in front of her. She finished her coffee, tipping the glass back into her mouth to crunch the ice.

"A lot of times the birth mother will contact the orphanage herself if she has second thoughts. You never know," Joon said, watching her eyes.

"Well, mine didn't. She was very confident in her choice. She hasn't looked for me."

Selene had imagined it in excruciating detail. She'd fantasized about her birth mother frantically searching for her. Imagined her snapping awake in the middle of the night in a panic because she'd left her daughter in a box on the sidewalk. Selene had held out hope that her birth mother wanted to find *her* as much as *she* wanted to find her birth mother, but it'd been over twenty-five years now.

"You don't know that. Often, it's forbidden for the search to work backwards. You're doing the right thing and you're doing it well, Selene," Joon said, his praise like a pillow. He asked if she wanted a refill. He took their glasses to the counter as Selene watched the rain again. From what she knew of him, Joon wasn't particularly verbose, so his words meant a lot, as did his presence.

She'd seen him two other times since meeting him. Once at Bitna's the following day, when Selene went over to have tea and Joon had popped in for a camera before leaving for the airport, and again last week, when she'd bumped into him in front of Bitna's apartment building. Selene had stopped by to bring Bitna a bouquet of cosmos to thank her for her kindness, and as she was leaving, Joon had come home. She'd asked him about his trip, and he didn't have much to say, but he was always kind, even when he was quiet.

Joon clicked around quickly, scrolling through different newspaper archives. She offered him the rest of her cake, and he finished it in two bites, wiping the corners of his mouth with his thumb.

"I don't know the man who wrote the article about my mom finding you that morning, but I know some people who do. The next move is to find him, ask a few questions. Maybe he has extra information he didn't include. Something that can help," Joon said.

He was so organized, and Selene trusted him. He'd come to the café with a notebook and a thick folder with color-coded tabs and copies of news articles for her. She watched his hands as he wrote down names, the ink of his neat *Hangul* on the faint blue lines. His clothes were stylish but unadorned—cuffed jeans and a navy T-shirt, white sneakers. Peanut-butter-colored windbreaker on the back of his chair. A tiny freckle sat on the bridge of his nose that was usually covered by his glasses, but she always noticed it when they slipped down. He had really great ears, and his hair had grown over them a little since the first time she saw him. Why'd she notice that? His hair parted naturally in the middle and always looked a bit tousled, giving it a lite '90s-heartthrob vibe. The length of it covered his eyebrows now, too, and occasionally he pushed it all back off his forehead with both hands; Selene bit into the crisp attraction of that movement like an apple. He did it again when he told her he needed to leave because he was photographing an awards ceremony at the Blue House in an hour.

"I didn't bring my umbrella," Selene said when he went into his bag for his once they were outside.

"I'll walk you to the bus stop," he said, motioning her under. The rain pitter-pattered on the clear plastic. The sound reminded her of how Winnie-the-Pooh books were so good at describing sounds. She'd been romanticizing, reframing the search and her South Korean adventures to cushion the fact she was doing something she shouldn't have to do. A child shouldn't have to go searching all over the world for her mother.

Selene had wondered her entire life why she'd been so easy to leave. She also wondered about the agony her mother might have had to go through to surrender her. But how could the *best* choice have been to leave her in a box for anything to happen? To never see her again? How horrible things must've been. When Selene told Bitna she wasn't angry, she'd meant it. She *wasn't* angry. But. Her birth mother. *Who* was she? *Where* was she? Were Joon's connections *really* going to lead them to her?

"Are you sure?" she asked, standing close to the café door to stay dry for as long as she could.

"Come on," Joon said, tilting his head. Cars whizzed up and down the street next to them and people walked by with their own umbrellas, slipping past, disappearing into the café.

Selene looked up, thanking him. She felt small in the rain, by his side. A crowd of people and umbrellas passed by them so closely on the sidewalk, Selene had to smash herself into Joon. He put his hand on her shoulder, quickly pulling her closer before letting go.

It was . . . something.

Something Selene knew she'd replay over and over again because it was . . . something. A pleasant chime rang through her body.

"Sorry," Joon said.

"Don't be," Selene said with a soft smile. "Thank you."

Once they were at the bus stop, Joon put the umbrella down and held it out for her.

"I've gotta go. Take it."

"Oh, no. It's fine. I'll get one in Hongdae. I'm going there right now to meet my friends." Selene, Lydia, and Jenny had accidentally discovered they were all on their periods at the same time and decided to get their nails done together on the fifth day like it was some sort of ancient ritual. Their host families had given them the night off and they were going out for a drink afterwards.

"I'll see you for Chuseok. You can give it back to me then," Joon said, ignoring her.

"We'll see each other for Chuseok?" Selene was unaware of this.

Chuseok, Korean Thanksgiving, was next week. Some families returned to their ancestral hometowns, which meant the Parks were going back to Gwangju and the Kim-Crawfords were heading to Busan. Lydia and Jenny would be staying in Seoul and were invited to celebrate with the Chois since Selene's host parents didn't have travel plans and would be gathering with their extended family at home to eat and honor their ancestors.

The blue bus was making its way down the street towards the stop where they stood.

"My mom will tell you about it. She'll make you come over, so don't bother trying to fight it. I'll see you then. I'll find the guy who wrote the article and contact you soon. Take this, too, since you didn't finish the cake." He went into his bag and handed her a packaged choco pie with both hands. "Have a good night!" Joon turned and jogged away, covering his head.

The bus was in front of her now with its doors open.

"Thank you!" Selene shouted after him, but he was too far away to hear.

Selene got a new set of matte claret nails with glossy tips. Lydia's were painted powder blue, while Jenny opted for ballerina pink. Selene had nervous energy from her time with Joon, but she couldn't put her finger on why he'd affected her so much today. Maybe it was how he pulled her close so naturally when they were walking together in the rain. Maybe it was the splendor of his high cheekbones. Maybe it was because he was so quiet. Who didn't love those things in a man? Or maybe it was because he was being so helpful.

Maybe it was because she didn't know much about him.

Her brain rolled the dice over and over again, trying to figure out what it was as the girls sat on the rooftop of the bar they'd been to before. It'd stopped raining as they got their nails done, and now the air was rinsed clear; fat gray clouds slid across the moon. There were three green bottles of soju in front of them, and after they all poured shots for one another, Selene took hers.

"You're totally somewhere else right now," Lydia said to her before taking the shot of soju quickly, throwing her head back and letting out a flat *ahh* in pleasure.

"I'm sorry. I know. I just——" Selene started.

"We have to believe that everything is happening the way it should," Jenny said. "Do you believe that? I know you're scared to, and I know it makes absolutely zero sense for any of us to think our happiness or anything in our lives can be impacted by a stack of stones in the moonlight, but even just for, like, *fun* . . . isn't it *fun* to believe something magical is happening for all of us?"

"Hell yes," Lydia said.

"Of course. In some bizarre, nonsensical way, I know you're right. But Joon. There's something about him," Selene said. Maybe when they met him, they'd be able to help her understand what she meant.

"Well, that's simple, Selene. You have a crush on him. It's okay. Maybe you feel weird because of the connection you have with his mom and aunt," Jenny said. They both drank and leaned forward. Lydia lapped them with her third shot.

"*Do* I have a crush on him?"

Selene had had plenty of crushes in her twenty-five years, enough to know what they felt like as soon as they happened. So why didn't she feel that same way with Joon? She was attracted to him. He had the sort of lithe body she loved on a man, and the first time she watched him push his hair back, she'd felt the sting of exactly how long it'd been since she had sex. (Vladimir! Four months and twenty-seven days!) She hadn't been thinking about it too much, being so busy in Seoul, but Joon made her realize how long it had been since the last time she'd been in bed with a man, taken.

Maybe it was primal. What *did* she even know about him?

That he drank his coffee black and was a fast typer? That his mom and aunt were unique, sharp dressers, that he had a stash of cameras? That he probably studied the Stoics? He seemed to favor olive green above other colors, and she saw that his lock screen was a photo of the sun setting into the ocean, but she didn't know if he'd taken it, and if he had, where? Did she think she had a crush because Lydia and Jenny had huge crushes and she didn't want to feel left out? Wasn't she too old for that? She made a note to herself to google *puppy love* because maybe that was how she felt.

Joon was becoming an itch she couldn't scratch because she didn't know where it was. Everywhere she tried made the itching worse.

"It *sounds* like you have a crush on him," Lydia said.

"Does it?" Selene asked, scrunching her nose up at her friend.

"Makes sense if you don't want to mix business with pleasure with Joon, but the harder you try to fight these sorts of things, the harder it gets. Joon is the first male lead in the K-drama of your life. Santi is Lydia's, and Haru is mine. Those are the facts," Jenny said. She segued easily into a discussion of how amazing Haru was in bed and the specific tongue flick he did that could send her to the moon. "Is this what it's like for men? Is this why they're such assholes and can't be bothered to admit that they, like . . . *feel*? Because this no-strings-attached thing is a *dream*. I mean, no offense to you two, you know I love you. I just mean that, for me, this lack of deep feelings and meaning is perfect." She finished her soju and looked up at the sky.

Lydia was leaning in, aggressively asking for more details about Haru's tongue trick, when Selene noticed Hye's face on a magazine on the table next to them. A lipstick ad.

"Look! It's Hye," Selene said, pointing.

"It's Santi," Lydia said after she turned away from them and back again.

"No, it's Hye! Here," Selene said, getting up to retrieve the magazine to show it to her.

"No. Santi*ago*. He's walking this way. That's him right there in the jacket. Remember I told you about the jacket?" Lydia said through gritted teeth.

"*That's* Santi?" Jenny said.

"You saw pictures of him!" Lydia said.

"Yeah, but . . . he *really* looks like that?" Selene said.

He was as ethereal in real life as Lydia had described him. His dark, curly hair was blowing in the night wind as he sat at another table with a group of friends. He turned his back to the girls, and Selene knew what Lydia meant about The Jacket now, too. It was like the fabric was threaded with soft light. She couldn't look away.

"The Jacket," Selene whispered.

"The Fucking Jacket," Lydia whispered.

"Are you gonna say something to him?" Jenny whispered.

"If he sees me, I'll say hi. Otherwise, I'll just talk to him in class tomorrow morning," Lydia said in a more normal voice.

They agreed on one more round of soju before calling it a night.

Friday morning, after walking Nabi to school, Selene went to Aera's shop to work with her assistant on a front-window display. Summer had melted into fall and Aera wanted more leaves and cozy autumn vibes. Aera left the condo so early Selene hadn't seen her yet, not until she walked into her office and found her dressed in all black, standing with her cup of coffee in her hand and her head tilted, eyeing an undressed mannequin.

Selene greeted her in Korean; Aera's face brightened saying it back.

Aera offered her a coffee, and they went to the kitchen area to get it, taking their time to pick over the twisted cinnamon doughnuts Geon had dropped off earlier after his run. He was out at a meeting now but would return soon. Aera asked Selene how things were going with Joon; she only asked Selene about the search for her birth mother occasionally, letting her know she was available to listen anytime she wanted to talk, but that she wouldn't press. Selene filled her in on the latest.

"How about I pay you more and you help me out here a couple days a week? Well, technically you'd be helping my assistant, too," Aera said, shaking cinnamon sugar off her fingers.

"Oh, wow. Easy yes," Selene said. She'd helped out at the shop a few times over the past couple weeks. Mostly refreshing displays and occasionally giving Aera and her assistant input on dressing the mannequins. Once standing in for a model who couldn't make it to the fitting. All very cool opportunities she was thrilled about. Being Aera's assistant's assistant sounded like something she wouldn't want to pass up.

"Trust me, I know how busy you are, getting Nabi to and from school, and her extracurriculars, and, in between, your own life! Spending time with Bitna and the searching you're doing with Joon, not to mention the friendships you have with Lydia and Jenny. It's a *lot*."

Hearing her list it off like that made Selene want to cry. Her heart was an ocean sloshing with so many feelings, and when she stopped long enough to think about everything she was doing on top of the emotionally taxing work of searching for her birth mom, that ocean came close to crashing in on her. Even with the sliver of faith she had in the wish. Her mind immediately reached for Joon, a beacon of light in her stirring sea of emotions. She wondered if he'd learned anything else. She wondered what he was doing.

"It *is* a lot, but I want to do this. It feels right" was all Selene said.

Aera explained that Selene would be helping with errands and occasionally styling the models, handling the displays when necessary, and social media. A magazine was coming to shoot in the store after Chuseok, and Aera asked if she could be available for that.

"Nabi will be going home with Fox and Arwen after school that day, so that works," Aera said after looking at her planner and snapping it closed.

"Right," Selene said, remembering.

"Promise to let me know if it's too much?"

"I promise."

"Okay. Come help me decide between purples for the *hanbok* fashion show, please. Oh, and think about what you want for lunch, too. I'll get Geon to bring it back." Aera stood, motioning for Selene to follow.

On Saturday, the girls took the kids to the zoo. Tae and Nabi had been getting along well lately but were fussing at each other again. Nabi let it go on for a little bit before she pulled rank. She loved being the oldest of the kids and couldn't wait to turn ten in January so she would seem even older to Tae's and Fox's single-digit age of eight. Selene kept Nabi and Arwen busy so they wouldn't be bothered by the boys. She took them to see the black crested gibbon and the sun bears before meeting everyone else over by the zebras for lunch.

"Are you excited for Chuseok?" Selene asked the kids as they ate.

They launched into what they were specifically ready to eat, see, and do.

Joon had been right. The day after she met him at the café, Bitna had called and invited Selene to spend Chuseok with them, which was so exceedingly kind of her, Selene wanted to squeal into the phone, but she let her formal *thank you* suffice. Chuseok lasted three days, and she would spend half the time with the Chois and their family and the other half with Bitna, Deiji, Joon, and their family.

Selene's stomach did a deep swoosh when Joon's name flashed across her phone. She excused herself to go over by the flamingos and talk to him.

"Selene, is now a good time?"

"Sure. Yes. I'm at the zoo with Jenny, Lydia, and the kids." She watched the variegated flamboyance of flamingos shake and preen as she asked him what was up.

"Not too much, unfortunately. I found the guy who wrote the article, but he didn't have any more information. But let's not lose hope. Someone else he used to work with was the one who got the story initially and passed it on to him when he was set on another project. That guy also wrote at least two articles on adoption and orphanages, so I'm going to track him down next. He may have information we need to hear. Any sort of gossip or inside scoop would be beneficial . . . a story that wasn't originally reported," Joon said.

She felt flutters again as she thanked him.

"I'm going to visit my sister and shoot film in Tokyo for a few days, but I'll be back for Chuseok. We'll talk then. If something comes up beforehand, though, I'll text you, or call."

"Oh. Okay. Wow, I really appreciate it."

"I've got a good feeling we'll find your mom, Selene. Feels like fate that you're here right now. And every time a door closes, another one opens up a crack, doesn't it?"

"It does. I just wish I could repay you for your help."

"You're going to have to let that go," Joon said sternly. "You *have* to stop saying that; I'm serious."

Whoa, she liked him telling her what to do. Selene generally walked through the world confident and independent, not needing much from anyone, but Joon taking charge was the hottest thing he could've possibly done in that moment.

"Yes, *sir*," Selene said. She imagined him in his military uniform. Able-bodied Korean men had to serve a mandatory eighteen to twenty-one months in the military, and Bitna had mentioned that Joon did his time after he left the newspaper, returning home a year ago. She pictured him saluting, the impeccable slope of his beret. She thought of the picture of her birth father, and an overwhelming fondness for Joon washed over her, heavy and fragrant.

"Excellent," he said with a soft chuckle.

She also remembered the choco pie he'd given her. She'd sat on her bed and eaten it slowly in the dark with the city lights flashing like fireflies outside the window.

Selene asked Joon if he was eating well, and he said he was on his way to get *bibimbap* with a friend; he asked her the same. She told him about the tasty pollack soup she and Aera had for lunch the day before.

In Korean, Selene said she'd see him soon.

Chuseok with the Chois was making beet *songpyeon* with Aera and her mother while a wild mess of children ran, ate, screamed, laughed, and played in the condo. Selene loved the whir of busyness around her as she folded the cool, wet dough over sweet sesame seed filling, and crimped the edges to keep them closed.

"You're good," Aera's mother said to Selene as she watched her scoop more filling into the dough.

"Only because *you* taught me."

"Your mother is Korean?" Aera's mother asked.

Selene said *yes* in formal Korean. Aera was back in the fridge again, putting things away. One of her aunts popped in, speaking in Korean about the food. Geon came in next, explaining to Selene that he *would* help, but that it was tradition for the women in the family to make everything. He shrugged and told her to look it up if she didn't believe him and winked at her before stealing a plate of *japchae*.

"I hope you find her. She will teach you how to make *songpyeon* and *gujeolpan*," Aera's mother said, pointing to the big plate on the table sectioned off into nine spots. Earlier, Selene had helped Aera fill it with mushrooms and matchstick carrots, shrimp and beef, eggs, cucumbers, garlic, nuts, and sauces.

Aera's mother shared stories about learning to make the Chuseok dishes from watching her mother and grandmother in the kitchen when she was little. Selene had made *songpyeon* with her Korean class a year before in the basement of a Korean church back in NYC, but she'd never been in a Korean kitchen with Korean women making traditional Korean foods like this. It was overwhelming, and she needed a moment alone to calm down about it.

"Pretty," Aera's mother said in Korean, motioning to the dark red *songpyeon* sticky in Selene's hand. She'd forgotten to put it down, and Aera's mother took it from her palm. Selene thanked her, excusing herself to the bathroom.

Selene texted her parents hi and sent a selfie, since they'd asked for one. She scrolled through Instagram as she leaned against the bathroom counter. Earlier she'd posted a pic of herself in one of the modern *hanbok* dresses Aera designed for Sobok Sweet, and the likes were blowing up, as per usual. Selene was hearting a few comments when she got a text from Joon.

> Happy Chuseok! Your first in Korea. I hope you
> are enjoying it with your host family. ☺

> I am! Thank you for thinking of me. I'm looking
> forward to seeing you all soon.

> Mom and Deiji keep telling everyone about you.
> It's very cute.

> That IS cute. Thanks for sharing that with me.

Selene wanted to write *YOU'RE very cute* as she sat there staring at the gray bubbles Joon was making.

> The guy who wrote the articles on adoption
> and the orphanages told me he is going through
> his notes. He is supposed to contact me when
> he gets back in town. He's traveling for
> Chuseok.

Okay! Thank you and please thank him for me.

He was happy to do it. I enjoyed working with
him and I'm enjoying working with you.

Selene turned the bathroom light off and became one with
the blue glow of her phone. She was sweating, but it wasn't hot.

You're making all of this so much easier on me. I
BELIEVE IN US.

I believe in us, too.

He wrote *see you soon* and *have a good night* in Korean, and
Selene wrote them back, adding a black heart at the end.

Joon started typing again, and in a moment of weakness, Selene second-guessed the heart. Maybe the black threw him off.
Maybe just a smiley face would've sufficed. She didn't see the
point in playing coy with him, though. Didn't want to. He'd
opened the door to them getting more personal, and she was
determined to kick it down with her stompy black boots.

BTW I saw this in Tokyo and thought of you.

He attached a photo, and Selene clicked to make it bigger. It
was a Tears for Fears T-shirt with kittens instead of the real band
members. She'd been so anxious about everything the first time
they talked in detail about finding her birth mother that she'd
rambled on for a while about her band back home. She'd mentioned Tears for Fears, and he remembered.

He remembered.

> I LOVE IT. So much. I must be doing something
> right if this made you think of me.

Ha! You must.

Lydia and Jenny joined the evening festivities at the Chois',
and for the rest of the night, as Selene ate and watched and listened to everyone celebrate Chuseok, her mind spun with Joon.
She pictured him in one of his outfits she loved—the olive-green
sweatshirt that said *small winter night* on it and light jeans, his
boyish backwards ball cap and those round glasses. He'd been all
the way in Tokyo thinking of her; she was on this peninsula
miles away, thinking of him, too.

Joon texted again as she was getting ready for bed.

> Sleep well.

Selene gifted both the Chois and Bitna and Deiji a box of pears,
apple mangoes, and grapes for the holiday. Chuseok with Bitna,
Deiji, and Joon began in the morning with *charye*, the memorial
service for the ancestors. Everyone was dressed in traditional
Korean clothing, and Deiji brought a lilac-and-white *hanbok* for
Selene and helped her put it on. The *hanbok* had the faint smell
of her cigarettes and the earthy, peppery perfume she wore. She
held Selene's face in her hands and told her how pretty she
looked. Deiji had a strong, nurturing energy about her, and Selene wondered if she had children, although no one had mentioned any. She imagined if Deiji did have children, how warm

of a mother she'd be. Selene's adoptive mother was kind and understanding but not overly affectionate, and Selene hadn't realized that until she'd had experiences with her friends' moms and a few teachers at church and school. Both Bitna and Deiji were huggers, and so was Selene. Their visits were punctuated with tight embraces upon arrival and departure.

Selene got to Bitna's very early in the morning, and the women spent hours making the food, preparing the table. The meats, drinks, rice, and soup faced specific cardinal directions, and although Selene had read about it, learning from Bitna and Deiji in the kitchen was beyond special for her. After quiet bowing and more eating, they drank *makgeolli* together with the rest of Bitna's family.

A lively array of people were in Bitna's apartment, and Selene was so happy to be there with them, even when she imagined her birth mother celebrating Chuseok without her, wherever she was. Selene wondered if she was thinking of her. If she had other children she'd kept. Selene wondered if those children were helping her birth mother in the kitchen today, if they were as warm and content as she was getting buzzy on rice wine in the flickering candlelight.

Deiji acted out animated stories in Korean and English about her life as a dancer. She and Selene bonded over their love of playing piano, and she offered hers up to Selene anytime she wanted. Selene loved how Deiji would randomly break into song but hadn't known Deiji had been in musicals in her twenties and thirties, and a few in her forties, too, traveling the world. Now she was forty-five and taught dance. She remembered most of the moves from the musicals, and at one point stood in the middle of the room, performing the opening choreography to the last show she'd been in. Selene couldn't keep up with everything

Deiji said in quick Korean, but she repeated a lot of it in English so Selene could understand.

Selene also met Bitna's daughter, who came home from Tokyo for the holiday; she sweetly translated for Selene whenever the conversations got carried away. Joon was chattier with his sister than Selene had seen him be with anyone else. It was adorably clear she brought out his more playful, extroverted side.

Selene was a wee bit drunksy when Joon asked her if she wanted to step outside for some fresh air. He'd changed out of his traditional clothing and stood in front of her wearing a plaid flannel over a black turtleneck with his jeans. She said *yes* and went to Bitna's bedroom to change her clothes as well.

The leaves were on fire—red and orange in the sunset light.

Seoul was noticeably emptier during Chuseok. The evening was quiet, and Joon was quiet, too, as they strolled up the street, turning down an alley full of mostly closed restaurants and shops.

"I got that T-shirt for you. The one from Japan," Joon confessed, walking slowly next to her. She loved how he moved so unhurriedly. His posture was perfect, and Selene took it upon herself to memorize the exact way his shoulders moved. She'd described it to Lydia and Jenny as his Disney Prince walk without regret.

"You did *not*," Selene said.

"I did. It's in my bedroom. It was supposed to be a surprise for later, but the liquor has loosened my lips."

"I'm going to put it on as soon as we're back. I promise."

Her feet stopped and started again, tripping over absolutely nothing. Joon reached out to steady her and teased her about it. Over the past few weeks, he'd gone from stoic to proper at best, but now he was *teasing* her. The way he'd opened up so slowly without her even noticing until it was done had made everything about their relationship feel easy. They'd been thrown together in an unusual way, but their slow-growing friendship felt beyond natural. She wanted to trip again just so he'd catch her.

"Being with you is a gift. I'm working all the time. I like hanging out with you."

"Me too." Selene wanted to tell him there was a chance they had a special helper—a waterfall wish on a stack of moonlit stones.

"Nope," she said aloud, except she'd only meant to say it in her brain, to herself.

"*Nope*, what?"

"*Pshh*, I was talking to myself, wondering if that was the noodle restaurant I thought it was. It's not," Selene lied clumsily, pointing at the sign across from them covered in enormous fake pink flowers.

"Helping you find your birth mother isn't work for me, by the way," Joon said.

"All I do is thank you. All day and night, it's 'thank you, Joon, thank you so much, Joon.'" Selene said it again in Korean, letting her tongue linger and snake out the *s* in *gamsahamnida*. "Don't you get tired of hearing it?"

He told her it meant she was a grateful person and he appreciated that. He assured her that he was only doing exactly what he wanted to be doing.

They walked in a long, wide circle around the apartment building, chatting and zigzagging their way back by ducking down empty alleyways, past more cafés and clothing boutiques. There was a holiness about everything being shut down that made her feel even more detached from reality than the rice wine had. She leaned into that feeling, looking up at Joon, wondering what he was thinking.

"Selene, you've been here before? I'm assuming, but I wanted to say something just in case," Joon said softly as they stopped at a crosswalk.

"Been where? Here?" Selene looked at the café next to them and told him she hadn't.

"No. I mean, this. This is the intersection where my mom found you that morning."

Joon pointed at the sidewalk across from them, a small patch of autumn grass at the bottom of the streetlight pole. A white sign hawking cell phones shot up next to a plastic orange-and-yellow flower spinning in the wind.

Selene shook her head. She was planning on visiting but hadn't yet.

"I'm sorry you didn't know. I wasn't paying that much attention to where we were walking. I was . . . distracted," Joon said. "Would you have preferred if I hadn't said anything? I'm sorry." He looked at her with sad eyes that got even sadder when he saw she was crying.

"No. Please don't apologize. Thank you for telling me. I'm okay, really. I just wasn't . . . prepared."

She looked around, attempting to memorize everything, attempting to imagine the same spot twenty-five years earlier surrounded by the colors of summer, not early autumn. She envisioned her mother leaving home before sunrise that morning with her in a box. Or maybe she only carried Selene in the blanket, picking up the box along the way. Selene imagined her birth mother setting the box down carefully and walking away. Or maybe she ran. What had the rest of her day looked like? Did she have lunch? A shower or a bath? Did she stand across the street and watch Bitna find her? Where did she go? Where was she now?

A car's horn jarred Selene out of her thoughts. Startled, she grabbed Joon's sleeve. His warm hand touched hers for a second, and he asked if she wanted to be alone.

"No. I don't want you to leave," she said. They stood there quietly together for a few more minutes.

When they returned to Bitna's, in a quick moment of tenderness that made Selene's holiday heart fold into a paper bird and soar, she felt Joon's hand press to the small of her back as they walked inside.

10

Lydia

Lydia had been honest with Caleb when she canceled on him last-minute before their second date, explaining it was the only time she and Santi could meet up to discuss their project. Caleb was so kind and forgiving about the whole thing, Lydia couldn't wait to see him again, and offered to take him to her favorite pizza spot in Hongdae as soon as possible.

Their third date was a campy comedy in an ice-cold movie theater and a romantic, leafy walk to a nearby Korean BBQ restaurant. She didn't know what she'd say if he invited her back to his place, but he didn't. On the bus ride home, she realized she was *relieved*. Not because they weren't making that leap yet, but because he'd seemed to make the decision for her, so she didn't have to. Not yet. She liked Caleb's hands and how he had an affinity for plain white T-shirts and dark jeans, which had become his date uniform. His hair smelled like apples.

In early October, on the night of their fourth date, they met at a small, candlelit restaurant in Seongsu-dong for spring rolls and light white wine. He told her about his dad's veterinary business, that his mom was the receptionist. How when he was little and his dad's practice was just getting started, they used to live in the apartment above the office, so Caleb would hear all sorts of barks and meows throughout the day—it only bugged him sometimes. Mostly, he found it comforting. Being in Seoul was the first time in his life he didn't have a pet. He was considering tracking one down soon because he'd discovered a fostering program specifically for foreign students who wanted the comfort of caring for an older pet while they were away from home. He was split between getting a cat or a dog. He guessed correctly that Lydia was a cat person. On their way out of the restaurant, he squeezed her hand and called her Lyd.

"Did you know they call Seongsu-dong the Brooklyn of Seoul?" Lydia asked as they wandered down the street with full bellies.

"Ah, maybe I read that somewhere? Have you been to Brooklyn?"

"No. My friend Selene is from there, though."

"You have to ask her if it's exactly like Seongsu-dong and get back to me."

"I guess I do," Lydia said, smiling over at him, holding his hand.

"So, this is going well, don't you think?" he asked. They slowed in front of the big Dior boutique, shining like a diamond. Caleb turned to her, eyes green in the light.

"What is? Us?"

Caleb nodded.

"I think so," she said. Dating Caleb was a lot like she'd imagined dating anyone at this point would be. It wasn't serious but felt like enough. They'd kissed a lot, and the last time, in the park after the movie, he'd pressed his entire body against hers in a way that made her ache for more, although she wasn't sure she was ready for it. Still, she ached.

"Good. That's all I wanted to ask." A boyish, husky laugh escaped his mouth, and Lydia kissed him.

They walked and walked. As they approached the subway station that would take her back home, she wondered again if this was the big moment when they'd decide to make the night last longer. They stepped into a dark alley and kissed. She wrapped her arms around his neck and pulled him closer. After forever, she looked at her phone and said she'd better catch the train since it was the last one until morning.

But the next time she and Caleb were supposed to go out for dinner, Santi unknowingly interrupted again, asking if Lydia could meet to work on their project. She didn't want to tell him no, since he'd been busy and they needed to get together. Again, she told Caleb the truth, assuming he'd understand, but his text response had been coldish. Lydia had a knot in her stomach when she left the condo to meet Santi instead. It took an hour or so for that knot to undo itself.

Near the end of October, Lydia and Santi were meeting more consistently, at least once a week (sometimes twice) outside of art class, and diligently working while they were in the classroom, too. Caleb had taken her canceling their date to mean she wasn't interested in him at all anymore, but that wasn't true. She tried to explain that to him, but he said no to meeting her for drinks so they could talk about it. She wanted to tell him that Selene said Seongsu-dong really *did* feel a lot like her favorite parts of Brooklyn. Now he sat on the other side of the classroom and avoided eye contact with her, which did bum her out a little since she hadn't meant to hurt him. She still liked how he walked and noticed when he got a new pair of sneakers. She learned he'd found a pet one day when she overheard him saying something about his dog to another guy as they walked into class together.

Santi hadn't warmed up to her much more, but Lydia happily went on a date with a French guy from class who everyone called

Godzilla because it was his favorite movie, and because he wore a vintage Godzilla T-shirt at least twice a week. He was *also* a good kisser. They grabbed sushi on the rooftop of a restaurant and had a superb view of the fireworks festival, then ended up at karaoke with another couple from class, which included a girl Lydia had made friends with. As they were leaving, when Lydia saw Santi disappear into the bar next door, her heart let out a red-hot scream.

One other guy from class—the one she started calling *Not Godzilla* in her head, simply because she was talking to both him and Godzilla at the same time—had asked her out as well, but they hadn't locked down the date yet. They were texting, attempting to coordinate their schedules, and he'd sent her a few songs he liked. Lydia didn't like them but thought it was a nice gesture.

But Santi.

So many guys in class found Lydia charming. They laughed when she made a joke and agreed with Penelope when she praised Lydia's work. Even the ones who hadn't approached her were friendly when they saw her, offering to open the door or smiling when they crossed paths in the hallway.

Lydia practically levitated with an iridescent glow from the attention.

Jay, from back home, had been texting her frequently, and her ex, Finn, wrote saying she could send him pictures of herself anytime she wanted. Haru's friend from Jeju pestered her so much for another pic, she took one for him in her lacy bra in the condo bathroom late one night. He sent one of himself back. In it, he was in his bed in his underwear with his hand on his stomach. He said he wanted to see her again.

But Santi.

When they were together, Santi would hyper-focus on their project. They were putting together a portfolio of lantern mock-ups and ways to incorporate sounds and textures into the festival experience. Santi had ideas for using sustainable paint that would clean the water, and Lydia was working on knitting lantern covers to demonstrate how museums could store and display them when they weren't in use.

They met at cafés and bars, sometimes in Hongdae or Itaewon. One night they found each other in the golden lights of Hanyangdoseong—the Fortress Wall of Seoul—and walked to an art exhibit at Dongdaemun Design Plaza, a spaceship of a building that took Lydia's breath away no matter how many times she passed it. Once they wandered a few of the art galleries in Songhyeon-dong; another time they searched for brutalist-style architecture and ended up walking along the mural-filled streets of Hapjeong, where she convinced him to stop for *bingsu*—sweet shaved ice with fruit. Mango and melon. He opened up the tiniest bit that day, telling her about his early life in Spain, and that this was his sixth trip to Seoul. When he closed himself off again, Lydia attributed his temporary volubility to sugar rush.

One of her favorite things about hanging out with Santi outside of his beautiful face, hair, hands, speaking voice, and jacket? Being with him meant she always saw something she'd never seen before. Santi's Seoul was filled with underground art and narrow streets lined with ivy and potted plants. Sexy, nocturnal Korean hip-hop spilled from the speakers of a gallery Lydia wouldn't have known was there if someone hadn't shown it to her. Galleries with winding pathways through urban gardens and wide stepping-stones over skinny streams lit with colored lights. She followed him up the hills where red neon crosses glowed spookily through the fog, to a small gallery in Itaewon in the back of a café Lydia had walked past plenty of times, unaware. It wasn't far from the pub where they filmed one of her favorite K-dramas, *Itaewon Class*.

Lydia *knew* Seoul. She'd taken it upon herself to do proper research before arriving and didn't mind getting lost on her walks. Occasionally, when she had the time, she'd take a bus or the subway and get off at a new stop, try to make her way back home without using her phone. But some of the places Santi knew weren't even listed on maps. He knew how and where to find them because he had connections. He seemed to know people wherever they went—Koreans who had lived in Seoul their whole lives, Korean Americans who were visiting, other people from Spain, Australia. Once, he introduced her to a flock of bros he knew from Florida. She didn't even know *how* he knew them—it just all seemed magical when she was with Santi. He was the one who seemed to remain untouched by her newfound charm, but everywhere they went together, people showed up who were glad to see him, and her in turn.

Last time, they met in Mullae-dong and took a long walk, scoping out metal art sculptures for inspiration. There were plenty to discover, some hidden down alleyways Lydia would never have considered exploring alone. While on the hunt, they followed the sound of screeching tools and metalwork and came across a class full of people learning to make their own sculptures. The glass windows of the building were pushed open; she and Santi stood in the cool night air watching the hot sparks fly.

Tonight, they were meeting in Ikseon-dong again. Lydia had sold two more small pieces to Hye and her friend, and another to Aera to hang in the dressing room at Sobok Sweet. She'd been mostly painting and hadn't had as much time as she'd wanted to work on the lantern project, but the other night, she'd gone for a bus ride and meandering walk after getting Tae and Eun ready for bed, sat in between streets lined with skyscrapers, and sketched as the lights shimmered on Cheonggyecheon Stream, gathering fresh ideas she was excited to share with Santi.

He showed up in The Jacket, and it was the first time he'd worn it to meet her. She wanted to scream about it, but instead told him calmly how cool it was.

"Thanks," he said.

He clinked two green bottles of soju down on the table. Poured a shot and pushed it towards her before she poured one for him. His hair was unbelievable tonight, and she wondered when he'd washed it last. Was this his one-day dirty hair, or had it been a few days? Maybe he'd washed it that morning? When he leaned over and sat back up, his hair did this absurdly attractive flip that made Lydia turn into a cartoon damsel. She wanted him to throw her over his shoulder and whisk her off to wherever. She restrained herself from clutching her heart and sighing, from dissolving into a million billion tiny bits of stardust and blowing away.

"Where'd you get it? Your jacket," Lydia asked, pretending to be normal. A group of guys walked past their table. One of them looked down at her and they exchanged smiles.

"You should go talk to him," Santi said when his eyes met hers again.

"Who?"

"That guy who just walked past and looked at you. I don't mind. I need to finish the rest of this design I started earlier," Santi said, pulling his sketchbook out of his bag.

Lydia turned to see if the guy was still looking at her, and he was, sitting at a table with his friends now. She refocused on Santi, watched him get out his pencil and begin shading the water and light he was working on.

"I don't want to go talk to him. I want to sit here with you and talk about our project. Well, first I want you to tell me where you got your jacket," Lydia fussed. She downed her soju quickly and Santi did the same.

"The guy at the door was looking at you, too," he said, pouring her another shot. Lydia mirrored him and they drank.

"I don't care. All I care about is your jacket."

"I got it in Kyoto."

"I've never been."

"You should go."

"Maybe I will."

"Good," Santi said. He leaned back and drank. Lydia finished the rest of her soju quickly and got another bottle after she pulled her own sketchbook from her bag.

Now she was dangerously close to drunk.

She hadn't been paying attention, forgot to eat. They were outside the bar, and it was cold. When did it get cold? She was wearing a thin dress with long sleeves that she got on discount at Sobok Sweet, but she might as well have been wearing nothing, because it was late October in Seoul, and why hadn't she thought about that? Probably because she was only thinking about looking cute since she was meeting Santi, and maybe any second now the wish would start working on him.

The ground was whirling.

She and Santi were walking together, but Lydia had to stop and lean against the building for a moment.

"Do you need to sit?" he asked with a crinkle of concern in his voice that Lydia hadn't heard before. She melted again.

"No. No, I'm okay. I'm just cold and need to eat something," she said, pushing off the wall and stumbling away from it. She stood up straight, trying to steady herself. Santi moved close to her, then closer. She felt his jacket pour over her shoulders; he stepped around her and zipped it up.

"Get on," he said, standing in front of her.

"Thank you. I can't believe I get to wear The Jacket. No, no, you should be the one wearing it," Lydia slurred, unzipping it. "Oh, wow, I'm drunk. Earlier I thought maybe I wasn't drunk, just tipsy, but now I know I'm *actually* drunk, so let me go home and sleep and try this *aaaall* over again tomorrow."

"Nope. Hop on. I'll carry you to my place not far from here and get you some proper food and water . . . sober you up a bit before we get you home," Santi said.

"You want me to . . . A piggyback ride?" Lydia managed to get out.

Santi bent over for her, and she climbed on.

The colored lights took on a bokeh effect, bouncing as Santi walked up the street with her legs wrapped around his waist, his hands holding her thighs. Seoul was incredibly hilly, and even in her drunken state, she took the time to appreciate his strength. His jacket was *just* long enough to cover the hem of her dress, so she wasn't being carried around the city with her ass hanging out. She thought of this and laughed, rubbing her face against Santi's nape.

Lydia narrated their walk and occasionally Santi would react with his head, but he didn't open his mouth to say anything. They passed a wall covered in posters of Hye and her K-drama co-star hugging; Hye was holding a rose. She mentioned again that Hye was her host mother.

"Santiago," she said, sighing, letting her head rest on his shoulder. His hair smelled like minty wood, a sharp difference from Caleb's apples. Caleb, who was really great, but was not Santiago. "Santi*ago*," she said again.

He carried her up one flight of red stone stairs lined with terra-cotta pots and white lights. A glowing red lantern hung next to Santi's door, and at first, Lydia thought it was moving, but alas, it was only her head spinning. He managed to put in his key code and open the door with her on his back. Once they were inside, he let her down onto the bed and left for a moment, returning with a glass of water.

"Drink," he said. And she did.

"This is your bed? I'm on *your* bed?" she asked, adding that she didn't know if he had a roommate.

"I don't have a roommate."

"I do. I have *four* roommates because I'm an au pair, which is French for *on par . . . equal to . . .* but we're in Korea and I don't know how to say it in Korean. Two parents and two kids," Lydia said before gasping. "Hye! I have to text Hye and let her know where I am and that maybe I won't be home tonight, if me staying here is okay with you?"

She had Santi proofread for drunken errors before she sent it.

> Hye, I'm so sorry I didn't let you or Minsu know in advance, but I'll be staying out tonight. I will be home first thing in the morning before the kids need to get ready for school, though, I promise. Thank you!

In Santi's bathroom, the mirror covered the entire wall above the sink and toilet. After peeing, Lydia stared at her reflection as she splashed her hands with soap and water, surprised she looked decent. Her lipstick wasn't smudged, and her hair hadn't entirely frizzed out. Her creamy blush had rubbed off, but the soju and the piggyback ride had given her cheeks a natural coral glimmer.

By the time she emerged, Hye had texted Lydia back, and she read it in Santi's bedroom as he clinked around in the kitchen.

> Okay, Lydia, thanks for letting us know! We
> would have worried. Be safe and see you in the
> morning. ☺

She sent Hye another *thank you* and smiley face emoji and lay back on Santi's (!) bed, letting the ceiling spin slowly. She closed her eyes.

Santi returned to the bedroom and woke Lydia up, handing her a cup of noodles.

"I let them cool down. Sit up and eat so you won't be sick in the morning. You have to eat some carbs and drink more water."

"*Maybe* I'll be able to go home tonight."

"You should stay here. I'll sleep on the couch."

Santi sat in the chair across from her as she crossed her legs on his bed and took a bite of noodles using the pair of chopsticks he'd given her. When she realized she was still wearing his jacket, she started to take it off as she ate. He put his cup of noodles down, took hers from her hands, and patiently helped her shrug it off. He hung it up in his closet and sat in the chair again. Both of them resumed eating.

"I get on your nerves," Lydia said, sticking her bottom lip out.

She imagined Jenny's and Selene's wide eyes if she told them she accidentally let anything slip about the wish to Santi. *The wish works on other people, but it doesn't work on you, Santiago. Please tell me why.*

"Do you need to text your boyfriend, too?"

"I don't have a boyfriend! You think I'd *want* to talk to the guy at the bar *and* have a boyfriend?" Lydia took one last slurp of her noodles and put the cup on Santi's bedside table. Drank more water. Her stomach was too full, and she didn't want to puke. She hadn't meant to get so drunk; she just wanted to relax so Santi would like her. Here she was, finally coasting because of the wish, or at least *believing* in the wish, finally getting exactly what she wanted, but she couldn't stop obsessing over the One Person the wish had no effect on.

"I thought the guy you talked to in class was your boyfriend now . . . or used to be."

"Caleb?"

Santi shook his head and shrugged.

"Godzilla? *Not* Godzilla?"

"Yeah. That dude. One of those," Santi said, half laughing and rubbing his eyes. "No judgment on my part. Everyone should do as they please. I just don't want some guy showing up here in a few hours, beating down my door." He pushed his hair from his face and stood, scooping up his noodle cup and hers before leaving the bedroom.

"I don't have a boyfriend," Lydia said again, loud enough for him to hear from the kitchen. She got under the covers of Santi's bed and curled up on her side, closing her eyes.

"I would never let you stay here if you got on my nerves," she heard Santi say softly before she fell off the sleepy cliff into the dark.

Lydia felt better than she'd thought she would as she walked Tae, Eun, and the other kids to school in the cool gray morning air with Jenny and Selene. Her alarm had buzzed her awake at Santi's, although she hadn't remembered setting it. Maybe he set it? He had a bowl of warm *haejang-guk*—hangover soup—waiting for her. She ate it as he curled up on the couch again and went back to sleep, made a quick cup of coffee in his kitchen before leaving. Being quiet and easy with him in the morning like that was a dream. She was mortified at having to crash at his place, but also felt as if they'd finally rounded a sharp corner in their relationship.

"But *nothing* happened, and you just came home?" Jenny asked as they walked away together after dropping the kids off.

"I wish I had more to tell. He was beyond adorable sleeping on the couch, though. He had his hoodie on, curled up with his blanket," Lydia said, miming Santi pulling the throw to his chin.

Selene checked her phone as they walked, only looking up for quick moments when they were at crosswalks. In Seoul, a lot of the streets had a strip of electric light at the edges that turned red or green, letting walkers know when it was time to stop or move, so sometimes Selene didn't even have to look up. She occasionally *mmhm*-ed but was clearly in her own world.

It wasn't until they were standing in front of Lydia's art school that Selene put her phone away.

"Sorry. Joon wants me to meet another guy at the newspaper, but it'll probably be a dead end, too." Selene sighed. She'd been keeping them posted on everything about the search for her birth mother, but the biggest development so far was that Selene wasn't attempting to analyze her crush on Joon anymore. She'd leaned in and accepted it.

"The wish is working—maybe it's just slow so you don't miss any magic along the way," Jenny said.

"It's impossible *not* to believe when you say things like that."

"Don't stop believing! We'll talk more tonight," Lydia said, hugging them both before hurrying inside.

In class, Lydia said hi to Santi, like always, and, like always, he gave her only a small chin-lift of recognition. She thanked him (again) for letting her sleep in his bed and . . . nothing. Even awkwardness would've pleased Lydia, *some* show that last night had been different. She'd slept in his bed! But Santi just dove into talking about the colors of the organic cotton yarn she was using for the lantern covers.

She felt pretty in her shorts and the tights she'd bought with Jenny, and she was wearing her plaid blazer, too. She spent extra time thinking about her outfits now, wanting to wear something stylish and cute every day, never phoning it in.

Penelope *seonsaengnim* was making her way around the classroom. When she got to Lydia and Santi, she praised their work, specifically telling Lydia how much she liked her sketches.

"I love the curves. They elevate the piece," Penelope said, touching the corner of the paper. It was a photo of the last painting Lydia had sold to one of Hye's friends. After the sale, Hye had offered up half her home office for Lydia to store her paintings in, said Lydia could work in there if she wanted to. Lydia was grateful—it was much bigger than the boys' playroom.

Lydia let Penelope know the piece had found a buyer.

"Congratulations. I can see why," Penelope said, flicking the gray strip of hair out of her face.

Not Godzilla came over after Penelope walked away and

asked Lydia if Saturday night was okay for their date. Santi had one earbud in and was erasing lines on the paper, his hair falling in his face. Lydia stared at him, wanting to frame the moment. That was the picture she wished Santi would send to her or post online, the sext that would push her over the edge—a photo of him concentrating on his work, ignoring the world.

"Okay!" Lydia said to Not Godzilla, telling him she'd meet him at a bar in Hongdae.

 ～

The city twinkled like a star.

The girls were on the Kim-Crawfords' balcony and Lydia was abstaining from alcohol. She nursed her sparkling raspberry water as she listened to Jenny whisper about accidentally spying on Daniel. She'd told them all about her suspicions and filled them in whenever she had a new revelation.

"He said he was going to the café up the street. Arwen and I went out for ice cream, and there he was, sitting in the café window on his laptop," Jenny said, leaning in. "You haven't seen him at Sobok Sweet, have you?" she asked Selene.

Selene shook her head.

"He goes out without Rain or the kids, but I don't always hear where. Trust me, I know it's none of my business, but I need to know if I'm right about Daniel and Aera having an affair," Jenny said. She drank more of her wine and looked out at the sky. She was wrapped in a blanket she'd taken from the couch, and Lydia and Selene were in light jackets. A pumpkin-scented candle burned on the table between them, and Lydia imagined they were the three witches from *Macbeth*, terrible at spells and almost satisfied with their own wishes, gossiping about everyone else's business.

Lydia was torn on whether to believe Jenny. She tried to keep an open mind, but Selene wasn't having it.

"You're one hundred percent sure you saw what you saw?" Lydia asked.

"*Yes*," Jenny said, explaining again how weird it had been, seeing Daniel and Aera in the bedroom in secret that night at the Chois'. Lydia and Jenny went back and forth for a bit about what non-affair reasons they could have for doing that.

"I'll keep my eyes open at the shop, but I doubt he'll be there," Selene said, a bit dismissively. "Speaking of, I'll bring our school-girl costumes home with me tomorrow and text you."

All three families were going together to Lotte World for the Halloween festivities soon, and wearing school uniforms and animal-ear headbands to Lotte World was tradition, no matter the season. Aera had a few uniforms from the shop to give them, and Lydia planned to accessorize with a pair of gray mouse ears.

When Selene's phone lit up with a text from Joon, she excused herself to go home to call him back.

For the next few days, Lydia sketched lanterns and painted at home. After her art classes, she came right back to her studio / Hye's office and worked. She painted with Tae and Eun after school on days they weren't busy with extracurriculars. When she was alone, she put her earbuds in, turned on a classical music playlist, and created for hours. Recently she'd been shutting her brain off from the world and listening to music with frenetic violins like "Flight of the Bumblebee." Music that made her feel as though she could run a mile at warp speed. The pieces of hers that had sold in Hye's friend group were the ones she painted when she used her anxious energy as rocket fuel, covering the canvas in fat glops of color, then threading them together with thin black or white lines. The last piece she sold was focused on shades of purple. The current one she was painting was yellow— sunny egg yolks to faint morning light. Another of Hye's friends had commissioned it.

She was also consistently working on her lanterns. A small section of Hye's office and most of Lydia's bedroom floor were covered with parchment paper and tubes of watercolor paint, glue, paper plates, boxes of wire. As closemouthed and undecipherable as he could be, Santi was always on top of anything related to the project. He'd done more work than she had so far. She was grateful for that. She didn't want to let Penelope down and wanted to have a real shot at being selected to work and travel with Kim Chinmae. She and Santi had plans to go to the lantern festival on Cheonggyecheon Stream in November for inspiration, and every time Lydia thought about it, she felt like a lantern herself—glowy and floating.

On Saturday, Lydia helped Hye make *sundubu-jjigae* for dinner. Hye said Minsu usually got nervous when she did the cooking because although she was neat everywhere else, she was messy in the kitchen, and he was a control freak about that, but since he was at the restaurant, she was free to do as she pleased. Tae and Eun were on the couch in the living room watching Disney. The cooking sounds met cartoony noises in the air, and the boys' laughter popped up like bubbles.

"You've still been going on quite a few dates, right?" Hye asked as she chopped kimchi. Lydia was on scallion duty; she stood down the counter from Hye with a green and white confetti of onions on the cutting board in front of her.

"I have. Nothing too exciting, though."

"No one particularly special?" Hye raised an eyebrow, and Lydia shook her head before she let it out.

"Well, there was the first one I went on a date with and liked. We had a good time together, but it didn't work out. Then a couple in between. The date I'm going on tonight is no big deal. There is a *particularly* special one, but we haven't been on a date yet and probably never will. He doesn't seem interested in me."

"That's hard to believe."

"It's true."

"Dating can feel impossible, I know. Minsu and I have known each other practically our whole lives. We were childhood sweethearts, so it wasn't hard for us to get romantically involved later on. Aera and Geon met in school. But Rain and Daniel—they met through Aera," Hye said. Lydia listened without saying Jenny had already told her this. "It's so funny, too, because Aera and Daniel would've never worked out. It *had* to be Rain and Daniel. They love each other so much." She slipped the kimchi into the *ttukbaegi* on the stove when the broth had a satisfying cauldron bubble to it.

Lydia hoped what Hye said was true, that Jenny was wrong about the affair. "The six of you make me believe in real love. My parents are married, but I don't think it's particularly romantic. Maybe it never was," Lydia confessed. Her parents barely slept in the same bed anymore. Sometimes her dad would fall asleep watching whatever sporting event or documentary was playing on PBS and stay in his recliner or on the couch all night. She hadn't lived with them for any extended period of time since she graduated high school, but that was how it'd always been. She had no reason to think anything had changed.

"Have any of your dates been very romantic?" Hye asked.

Lydia scanned through them, and besides some sweet moments with Caleb, she came up empty. There had been some great kisses and plenty of fun—Godzilla even won her a white kitten plushie in the claw machine on their first date, which she'd been sleeping with ever since.

But.

Her brain whizzed and stopped at Santi slipping his jacket over her shoulders in the cool autumn air, giving her a piggyback ride to his place, putting her to sleep in his bed after feeding her and making sure she drank enough water. Those were the most romantic things a guy had done for her maybe ever, and they hadn't even been on a date.

"A little," Lydia replied.

"If you want romance, don't settle until you get it." Hye stirred the soup and set the spoon down. She leaned against the counter in her peach dress and apron, telling Lydia about a time when Minsu sneakily hired a babysitter and brought calla lilies to set in the middle of the night just because he wanted to do something special for her. She talked about how they'd been married for twelve years, but he still did things like that for her all the time. Earlier, before Minsu left for the restaurant, he was helping Hye run through her lines on the couch, and when he got up to go to another room, he took her script with him, speaking louder so she was sure to hear him. "There's a quote in my drama that goes, 'Anyone romantic enough to want romance in their life deserves it.' Don't you agree?"

Lydia kept thinking about romance when she was out with Not Godzilla that night. He was nice and they had fun but zero spark.

When he kissed her lightly on the lips at the bus stop, she felt nothing.

Later that night, she wrote Santi.

> Hi! What are you doing tonight?

She was about to put her phone away when he messaged back.

> Hi. I was just thinking of you. Weird. I'm painting and I sketched a little earlier, but that's it.

I was just thinking of you.

> Why were you thinking of me?

> Because I ran out of white paint so I couldn't make light blue. Light blue reminds me of you.

> It does? Why?

> Maybe because of the skirt you wear sometimes? I don't know. It just does.

> Honestly? Never in a zillion years would I have guessed you've noticed anything I wear. ☺

> This is a color combo I love.

He attached a photo of a clear blue autumn sky and two long rows of gold-leaf ginkgo trees. Lydia kissed the screen.

11

Jenny

Haru told Jenny that November was for making kimchi, so that was what they did. *Gimjang* was the word for when families got together to make enough kimchi to last through the winter, and making it was a satisfying cycle that turned with the wheel of the seasons. Anchovies and shrimp collected in the spring plus sea salt and red chili flakes harvested in the summer made late autumn and early winter the perfect time to combine them with crunchy green cabbage. Jenny had seen Haru make kimchi with summer vegetables like cucumbers and radishes; now the condo was filled with the scrumptious funk of cabbage. She was in-between Rain and Rain's mother, who was visiting from Busan.

They put Jenny to work chopping carrots, and Haru showed her how small to cut them. He was on massage duty; massaging the vegetables by hand released the juices that made the kimchi taste so complex. He was next to them in the kitchen in his plastic gloves, making eyes at her whenever they were alone.

Last night he'd gotten home late from the restaurant and texted that he was going to sneak into her room after he took a shower. She'd had a busy week of getting Fox and Arwen to and from school, to and from their piano and violin lessons, Fox's swimming on Tuesday and Thursday, Arwen's tennis lessons, followed by late-night hangs with Lydia and Selene talking about anything and everything, bundled up in their jackets and blankets out on the balcony. She kept falling asleep even though she desperately wanted to stay awake for Haru. Jenny felt (as) comfortable (as she possibly could) with Haru coming to her room because it was on the other side of the condo and not next to Rain and Daniel's bedroom like his, and it wasn't next to the kids' bedrooms, either. It was, however, down from Daniel's office, which Jenny worried about—what if Daniel needed to go to his office in the middle of the night and accidentally bumped into Haru pulling his shirt on, tiptoeing away from Jenny's door?

He came into her room while she was sleeping, got into bed, and woke her up with a whisper. When she checked in with herself about what they were doing and who they were to each other, what rose to the surface immediately was how much she enjoyed the steamy, mind-blowing sex they had. Her sex life with Ethan had been fine—she'd been so obsessed with him, maybe she wouldn't have even noticed if it was bad? She would've never complained because she wanted everything with Ethan to stay how it was, and an easy way to do that was to ignore anything that bothered her. But with Haru, she could let him know *exactly* what she needed. He told her what he liked and how much he liked it, in English, in Korean. Sometimes she couldn't stop talking when they were intimate, and they laughed about how much they whispered in bed, how much they loved hearing what turned each other on. Jenny loved spreading her legs for Haru in the dark; he loved it when she wore nothing but a ribbon in her hair. He loved it when she was on top and poured herself all over him when they finished together. She loved how he got up to double-check the lock on her bedroom door (again) before he'd put the condom on. It was meticulous and sexy, the same energy he brought to the kitchen.

I love the way you taste, he always said to her with his face between her legs.

Once, he asked her to make herself come in his bedroom while he was at the restaurant and to text him a photo afterwards. She got a blinding rush from it. She double-checked a trillion times to make sure she was completely alone in the condo and that his door was locked. She buried her face in his pillow, covering herself with his scent under his sheets. She dared him to do the same thing the next time he was home alone, and he sent her the photo afterwards of him shirtless in her bed, making a finger heart. He also took a pic of her pink-and-white panties after the housekeeper accidentally put them in with his T-shirts, saying he was keeping them and sleeping with them under his pillow.

"You smell delicious," Haru said to her in the kitchen after he kissed her neck and poked at the vegetables.

Who was Haru to her?

She liked Haru. They lived together and saw each other first thing in the morning and last thing at night. They watched movies together and read Fox and Arwen bedtime stories. They took the kids to the playground and for walks, stopping for coffees and *chal oksusu*, wandering the long way so they didn't miss the sunset.

He was by far the best kisser who'd ever put his tongue in her mouth. Someone whose lips formed a fetching pout when he was focused and fussing in Korean. Someone with the kind of strong, hard, honey body she hadn't seen in person, only on her TV.

"Stop trying to seduce me. Your mother is right outside," Jenny whispered, repeating the last part in Korean. She couldn't see the entire balcony from the kitchen, but all Jenny would have to do was turn around and lean over, and she'd be looking right at her.

She got on her toes to kiss him quickly, boosted by the rush of knowing they could get caught. She heard Fox's and Arwen's footsteps upstairs, moving from one room to the next.

Haru leaned back and took off his gloves. "I want to take you out soon. We can meet somewhere. A restaurant or wherever you want to go."

"You're asking me out on a date?" He stuck his tongue out of the corner of his mouth like a puppy. She could go on a date with Haru because a date with Haru would only be cute and fun—no big deal.

"Yes, Jennybelle, will you go out with me?" he asked with teasingly earnest eyes. "I also want to take you to Busan and Sokcho. I think you'd like them."

Who was Haru to her?

Haru had started to call her Jennybelle sometimes after she told him it was her real name. At first, she thought it would upset her, remind her too much of Ethan and her dad. Instead, coming out of Haru's mouth, her full name felt fresh again, hers. Like a reclamation. Her dad would've loved Haru, too.

Was that why her eyes stung when she said yes?

"I thought it over, and I want to set Haru up on a blind date with her. What do you think?" Rain sat on the end of Jenny's bed, holding out her phone for Jenny to see a young woman on the screen. She was sitting at a restaurant table with a glass of red wine, her long black hair pulled over her shoulder. Jenny imagined another girl having dinner with Haru. Maybe she'd be eating a meal he made especially for her. Maybe even a little mound of rice in the shape of a teddy bear with a blanket of fluffy yellow egg on top.

As long as he didn't make *exactly* that for the blind date girl, whatever. Who cared?

"She's pretty," Jenny said.

Haru could go on a blind date with a pretty girl if he wanted.

"She's one of my hygienists, and she wants a new boyfriend to get over her last one. I know you know what that's like," Rain said, waiting for Jenny's response as a cue to continue. "It was actually my mother's idea."

Jenny again tried to imagine Haru with someone else, but she thought about the wish—she couldn't fall in love with him even if she wanted to. They'd spent so much time together, both alone and with the rest of the family. She knew Haru smelled like coffee and fresh laundry in the morning; that he usually took his quick showers at night after returning home from the restaurant, his longer ones on lazy afternoons spent at home. He wouldn't wear dark purple because he hated how it looked on him, and avocado made his mouth itch. He loved Frank Ocean and Snoop Dogg and doing the dishes when he was thinking over an important decision. When he was tired, he got quiet and a little grumpy, like a toddler, and he definitely milked his younger-brother status around Rain whenever he could—making puppy eyes when she scolded him for forgetting to pick up her face masks from the store. But also, Jenny and Haru had been sleeping together for months, and had only decided to go out on a real date together next week. Rain looked at her, sitting on Jenny's bed, where Haru did unspeakable things to her in the dark.

"Do you think he wants a serious relationship?" Jenny asked.

"Probably? He'd have to deliberately make time for it. But also, if a girl only wanted to keep it casual, he'd be okay with that, too, I'm sure. He's a romantic, though. When he's in love, he jumps in with both feet." Rain paused. "Speaking of romantic, Dan's been having to go into the office a lot lately, and we keep missing each other. We're planning a date soon, and I'll keep you posted on that because we may do another overnight and Fox and Arwen will stay here with you and Haru."

"Okay," Jenny said, wondering if Daniel was really at the office or hanging out with Aera.

"I'll keep you posted on Haru's blind date, too. He has to say yes first!" Rain said, standing.

"*Noona*, will you play with us?" Fox hollered to Jenny from the hallway. Rain stepped out and reminded him not to yell quite so loudly. "*Noona*, will you play with us?" he whispered.

"Let's do it," Jenny said, walking to him and taking his hand. They found Arwen waiting for them, giddy and grinning cutely with her missing front tooth.

In the end, the plan Jenny came up with to catch Daniel and Aera in the act of cheating—*if* that was what they were doing—was pretty simple: catch Daniel and Aera in the act of cheating. One night, after she, Lydia, and Selene fulfilled their au pair duties and made sure the kids were bathed and put in bed, they decided to see where Daniel went after he left work.

"Here, wear these," Jenny said to Lydia as the subway lurched forward. She handed her a pair of bright green sunglasses.

"Girl, the sun has been down for hours," Selene said.

"Daniel will spot us if we don't wear disguises!" Jenny insisted. She was wearing a vintage trench coat she'd gotten a few years ago after falling down a rabbit hole of French fashion. Stripes, red lips—Jenny loved how classic and easy they were to incorporate into her wardrobe. She was wearing them sans bow tonight, and she'd traded in her dresses for a pair of slim, dark jeans. Not wearing a dress or a bow in her hair was her disguise, and she'd left her hair down, when she usually pulled it up.

"You think he won't know it's me?" Lydia asked, putting the huge sunglasses on and pointing at her head. Her pretty curls stuck up and out just the same.

The girls laughed so much on the usually mouse-quiet subway they reined it in faster than usual, so as not to annoy everyone with their silliness. Lydia kept the glasses on the entire time, which made everything that much funnier.

"I'm assuming that's for me?" Selene said, motioning to the blue ball cap in Jenny's bag. She'd swiped it from Haru's bedroom when no one was home.

"Please?" Jenny said, making big, adoring eyes at her.

Selene pulled it on her head, tucked her hair behind her ears.

"Only for you, Jenny Foster. I mean it," Selene said with a grumpy face before digging into her bag and reapplying her lip gloss. She passed the fruity tube to Jenny when she held her hand out for it so she could do the same; Lydia was next. When Selene put it away again, she continued. "If you're right about this, I'll give you all the money I have on me, which is like forty thousand won, but I *will* give it to you. I see Aera and Geon every day, and they're *actually* happy. I accidentally walked in on them making out in Aera's office the other day. Plus, they work together! When would she even have the time?"

"I don't know! I just need to be sure it's not true. I love Rain and Daniel together, and I love Aera and Geon. But I need to see. Consider it research. We're David Attenborough and we're simply going to *observe* what we see."

Jenny asked Selene again if Aera was supposed to be at work right now.

"Yes. And Geon's at home with Nabi. I saw them with my own eyes," Selene said as the subway voice announced the stop right before theirs.

Lydia was in her own world, texting and smiling.

"Santi," she said to them in a moony voice. Lydia had said he'd been texting more regularly, even when it wasn't about their project, but disappointingly, he hadn't done anything to suggest he thought of her as more than a friend.

"It's time to focus. This is us," Jenny said, pointing at the digital sign when it announced their subway stop.

The girls found a bench across from the building where Daniel's publisher was located. If he was inside, he would come out in about ten minutes in order to get home when he said he would. Jenny reminded Lydia and Selene of this as she got a Korean newspaper out of her bag and held it in front of her face.

"Are you serious?" Selene asked. She pulled her ball cap down and giggled so hard her shoulders shook.

"Shh!" Jenny said as the three of them watched the building, pretending *not* to watch the building.

She got an adrenaline rush anytime a white guy with light hair walked out, but none of them were Daniel. After an hour of waiting with no luck, Lydia and Selene walked to get warm *bungeoppang* and sweet potatoes from the food stalls on the corner, leaving Jenny alone on the bench, watching the building. They returned just as Jenny spotted Daniel walking out.

"There he is, there he is. So, he *was* in there. Now where's he going? We have to follow him," Jenny whispered.

"What are we supposed to do with all of this?" Lydia said,

holding a box of three steamy-hot sweet potatoes. Selene held the *bungeoppang* down by her side.

"Shh. Just follow me."

Jenny made her way down the sidewalk across the street with the girls behind her in a single-file line. Daniel walked away from the building towards the café on the corner, and Jenny wanted to do a fake-out of walking one way, then turning back, careful not to lose him. When he crossed the street, they waited, watching. He ducked into the café, and they crossed the street again, finding a spot to sit and eat in peace where they were hidden but could still see inside.

"What is this proving?" Selene asked.

"That he's not with Aera somewhere! That he's dorking out on his computer with a coffee instead of ruining his family," Jenny said, sighing.

"So, is this all you needed to know? Do you feel better?" Lydia asked.

"I don't know. It still doesn't explain what I saw but . . . it solves the question for tonight," she said with a mouthful of potato. Daniel took a seat near the window and opened his laptop, sipped at his iced coffee. When he finally left, the girls headed back home, too.

When Jenny returned to the condo, Daniel, with his short strawberry blond hair, was in the kitchen making himself a mug of tea. He explained he'd started mixing chamomile, Earl Grey, and ginger, and while he admitted they weren't *great* together, he liked surprising his taste buds from time to time.

"Would you like me to make you one?" he asked after inquiring if she'd had a good night. She felt silly seeing him in the kitchen; she stood in the doorway with her bag on her shoulder.

"No, but thank you, Daniel."

"Of course. Sweet jacket," he said, pointing at her trench. She thanked him again. Dammit, cover blown. Mental note not to wear it next time she was spying on him.

"Good night."

"Oh, and you may hear Haru coming in really late tonight. He popped in for a sec, but he just left. Good night, Jenny."

Jenny turned on the light in her bedroom and closed her door. On the bed was a long wine-dark ribbon, a color she didn't have. Next to it, a small piece of card stock with a hand-drawn heart and a lowercase *h*.

Jenny and Haru had planned their secret date over text and tonight was the night. She put on the pink dress that made her feel like a fondant rose blossom on a cake. She tied the new ribbon in her hair, too. Haru had picked out a restaurant in the Four Seasons Hotel near Gwanghwamun Square that Jenny had seen a bunch of times, so she knew exactly where it was. He texted her when he was leaving work at the restaurant, and after Jenny let Rain know she was going out for the night, she left the condo and made her way to the subway station.

Haru was dressed in a black turtleneck sweater and black pants with a gorgeous, long camel-colored coat that looked like it cost a million dollars. Jenny remarked on his clothes immediately because although she'd seen him in a lot of things—from pajamas, to his relaxed but still a bit preppy everyday wardrobe, to the nice clothes he wore for special events at the restaurant—

she'd never seen him in clothes *this* nice. He looked like he'd stepped right out of *Guardian: The Lonely and Great God*, her latest K-drama obsession, and she imagined Gong Yoo and his umbrella in the slow-motion rain, heard the main song from the soundtrack in her head when she took Haru's hand and walked with him down the spiral steps to the restaurant.

Jenny got the truffle ravioli and Haru, the sea bass *cartoccio*. Before they dug in, they both said *jal meokkesseumnida*, which meant they would eat well.

For dessert, they shared the pear sorbet.

He talked about work and his upcoming move to New Zealand in the new year. They discussed the places they'd been, the places they wanted to go. Jenny had noticed soon after meeting Haru that whenever he got deep into discussing something he was excited about, his body couldn't hold it in. It ran counter to her first impression of him—so cool and put-together, like it'd be hard to get him worked up. But now the layers had been pulled back and she knew better. Noticed how he'd bounce his leg or tap his fingers, lighting up when he encountered something he loved, and he loved a lot of things. Big dogs they passed on the street and small groups of old men with their hands clasped behind their backs, watching construction. Soccer and the NBA. Letting his hair air-dry with a beer on the balcony and watching the dumbest, silliest videos he could find on YouTube with Daniel. Helping Fox get past the hardest video game levels and turning on Arwen's favorite songs when she was upset, coaxing her out of her bedroom. His bright energy around the kids was infectious.

Haru was a good listener and a sexy, proper flirt. He leaned his chin on his hand and looked into Jenny's eyes intensely when he asked if she was truly over her ex.

"I mean, *totally* ready to move on. You don't talk to him anymore, do you? Not at all?"

"No. Not at all. I don't want to."

"I hope you feel good about that."

"I do. I feel great," Jenny said. The candlelight danced in his eyes; she watched his dark lashes blink. He took her hand in his and kissed it.

"Do you want to unblock him and take a pic of me and post it with a caption about your hot new man? Because I'm not above being objectified by you."

"Trust me, I've considered that multiple times!" She told him she'd thought about it on Jeju Island when she saw him come out of the ocean. She'd wanted to post a pic of him dripping salt water in the sunlight but had restrained herself.

"Do you know my sister is trying to set me up on a blind date with a woman she works with?"

"Yeah, she told me."

"I figured. I'm not going, by the way."

"Why not?"

"Because I don't want to," Haru said, shaking his head. He held out the spoon, offered her the last bite of sorbet.

"Even if your mother wants you to?"

"Even if."

"Maybe you should. Maybe it could lead to something incredible—you never know."

"I doubt that."

The marble and candlelight made the restaurant feel underwater, like they were floating in an enormous, twinkling rectangle of dark blue and bright gray. Jenny had always loved restaurant ambiance—the sparkly *plink clink* of dishes, the effervescent rise and fall of countless conversations. A man behind them laughed like a papa bear; a couple at the next table animatedly swapped stories. The night was as light and ebullient as the bubbles in the champagne glass the waiter was carrying as he made his way through the tables.

"Why not? Why don't you want to go on a date with a beautiful young woman who's interested in you?"

"You mean, why don't I want to go on a date with *another* beautiful young woman who's interested in me? This is me assuming you're interested in me, right? To be completely honest, I'm not thinking about other women at all," Haru said. The waiter stopped by their table to collect their dish. Haru spoke to him in Korean, asked for the check.

"You're not wrong about me being interested in you," she said, wondering if that was too much. They hadn't talked about their feelings, hadn't needed to. "I *do* enjoy sleeping with you quite a bit."

She imagined them stealing away to the bathroom, or maybe even getting a room upstairs. She imagined him taking off her flower cake of a dress, how she'd step out of it. He'd fold his expensive coat over the back of a chair and pick her up.

"Is that all, though? You just enjoy sleeping with me?"

"Of course not." Jenny laughed it off.

"Good." He said *I like it* in Korean—an easy phrase for Jenny to catch every time—and she repeated it.

"You like what?" she asked him.

He leaned back slowly, smiling at her. "Everything."

Jenny got the idea to go to Namsan Tower as soon as she saw it shooting up like a bright wand in the distance. Haru suggested they stop in a convenience store for a red heart-shaped lock and fine-line marker.

They taxied to the tower and rode the spacey, neon-lit cable car all the way up to the top, admiring the blinking colored glass of the city's lights below. He stood there in his K-drama coat holding the lock in one hand and the marker in the other, looking down at her. "I'll write your name and you write mine?" he said with his ears and the tip of his nose pinking in the chill.

Jenny wrote *Haru* in *Hangul* and English before giving him the marker. He wrote *Jennybelle* the same way. She slipped the lock on the railing, and they both clicked it closed. She took a picture of it hanging there in a rainbow sea of other locks, each a wish of its own.

"You look so beautiful," Haru said, pulling the collar of her coat closed. "Don't get cold." He put his arms around her waist and warmed her with kisses.

Jenny and Haru were happy to ride the bus halfway home and hop off again so they could take their time and wander through the November chill the rest of the way. They stopped in a café for hot *kokoa* and drank them by the window, with Haru assuring her Daniel was at work and Rain was home with the kids, so there was nothing to worry about.

"I don't care if they know, but I am respecting what you want," Haru said, turning to her. "Can I come to your bedroom when we're back home, once I'm sure everyone else is sleeping?"

"If you *don't* do that, I'll never speak to you again."

Under the table, he put his hand on her leg. Squeezed.

Wandering, Jenny didn't know they were walking towards the publishing company where Daniel worked until Haru pointed it out.

"But we're going that way," he said, motioning with his head. They'd be taking a sharp turn right before they got to it.

"Ah. We—" Jenny said, stopping herself from spilling the fact that she, Lydia, and Selene had followed Daniel the other night. "I didn't recognize it, walking this way. I've only seen it when I come from that way." She pointed.

They were holding hands, and Haru tugged at hers, pulling her into an alley with him.

"There's Daniel walking out. If you don't want him to see us, we'll stay here until he's gone. He'll go around there to the parking lot," Haru said with his face close to hers.

Again, the proof she was looking for. Daniel was at work and not prowling the city touching the small of Aera's back. Jenny peeked around the corner so she could see Daniel herself. When she did, she pulled her head back quickly and kissed Haru, sighing into his mouth. If they were on Jeju Island again at the Waterfall of God, Jenny would've specifically wished for an eternity of nights like this, kisses like this.

They stopped at a playground to sit on the swings and talk. It was the same thing the couples always did in K-dramas, and Jenny let Haru know how big the moment was for her.

"Look at me, making all of your dreams come true." He smirked.

The plan was to stagger their entrances, until Jenny stepped in a sticky wad of gum on the sidewalk in front of the condo. She sat on the bench, attempting to scrape it off the bottom of her shoe. When that didn't work, she took the shoe off and started hobbling inside.

"Come here," Haru said, moving closer. He scooped her up into his arms. Her breath caught in her throat, and she giggled when she told him to put her down. He walked towards the elevators with her hugging his neck, her sticky ballet flat hooked on her finger.

"*Haru*," Jenny said as he pushed the up button.

"Can't let your little foot get cold on the floor."

"I'm wearing tights!" She wiggled her toes, but he ignored her.

Inside the elevator, Haru asked Jenny to push the button for the twenty-first floor since his hands were preoccupied and to punch in the keypad code when they got to the door. He didn't put her down until they were inside where she could put on her slippers. She didn't know what Haru would say if Rain and Daniel were in the living room when they walked in, but they weren't. Jenny thanked Haru for the ride in Korean, and he kissed her forehead before walking to his bedroom.

Haru came to her hours later, when she was sleeping. Jenny liked thinking of him, sexually frustrated, awake, waiting until *just* the right time. Afterwards, she wanted to fall asleep in his arms, but he had to go back to his bedroom. She closed her eyes anyway, listening to his breathing.

"I really, *really* like you," Haru whispered, a brush of light coloring the indigo night.

Like he didn't expect her to respond. Like he assumed she wasn't awake to hear it.

Getting amazing seats at the BTS concert was no easy feat, but Aera made it happen through a stylist who had recently gotten some Sobok Sweet pieces and used them in a photo shoot with a new K-pop girl group.

Jenny, Lydia, Selene, Arwen, Nabi, and the host moms piled out of the limo Hye had rented for them, clutching their stadium-approved clear bags and ARMY bomb light sticks, and breathlessly entered the venue, where they were met with a glorious adrenaline-tinged, confetti-filled affair of chaotic screams and organized fan chants from the crowd of seventy thousand. Jenny had on a purple dress and Park Jimin's yellow dog plushie character on her headband, in his honor. Lydia's bias was J-Hope, and she was wearing a colorful smiley face Jung Hoseok T-shirt with a pair of baggy cuffed jeans she'd borrowed from Selene, who was dressed head to toe in black with her stomper boots for Jeon Jungkook. The rest of the boys—Kim Namjoon, Kim Seokjin, Min Yoongi, Kim Taehyung—were represented in glittery accessories they'd planned weeks ahead of time.

All seven members of BTS looked perfect and beautiful in their perfect, beautiful costumes, singing their songs with the crowd singing along to every word. ARMY bomb light sticks synced up with the music, and the arena sparkled and shook with color. Arwen and Nabi were wild, zoomy balls of energy. BTS hadn't held a concert as a group in two years because they'd all been away fulfilling their mandatory military service. The crowd let them know how much they were missed; the radiating energy in that stadium was strong enough to power its own universe. The scope of the show was both out of this world *and* intimate, and by the end, it felt like all seventy thousand ARMYs were holding hands in a mess of tears, firework-hearted and giddy to have taken part in the experience, sad it couldn't last forever.

The first day of December was Jenny's first snow in Seoul. Magic. It was also the first time she, Lydia, and Selene were all going out together with the new guys in their lives. The girls had joined a K-pop dance class the night before and laughed through the awkwardness of how hard it was to keep up. Even though the teenagers next to them ate them alive, they had tons of fun. Jenny's arms were so sore she washed her hair as quickly as she could because *ouch*. She spent the morning and afternoon Face-Timing her mom and looking after Fox and Arwen and, in the evening, dropped the kids off at a birthday party.

When Jenny arrived at karaoke, everyone else was already there. Lydia squealed, putting her arms around her before pulling her into the room. She introduced Jenny to Santi, and Selene introduced Jenny to Joon. Haru wrapped Jenny in a hug, lifting her up off the floor. He knew Jenny told the girls practically everything, and she loved how comfortable he was with her friends. She was tickled for the six of them to be together like this.

"We weren't gonna start without you," Selene said, picking up the karaoke controller and tapping around.

"Thank you." Jenny waited until Selene was finished selecting a song to hug her tightly.

Lydia had mentioned she was nervous to ask Santi to come with them to karaoke, afraid it sounded too *couple-y*, but he seemed happy enough as the walls rumbled with music from the other rooms, and he was dressed sharply in a loose, modern black *hanbok* and black clogs. His ears were pierced with pretty silver hoops, and he had one stubborn corkscrew curl of dark hair he kept tucking behind his ear, only to have it pop out again. Joon's face was as refined as Selene had said it was. He had soft, caring eyes, as if his kindness couldn't be contained, even when he wasn't saying anything. She could easily see why Lydia and Selene were so smitten. Joon and Santi were both taller than the girls, but Haru was the tallest. He was also the most extroverted of the guys and sat in between them as the colored lights slowly faded from red to blue, engaging them both in conversation while the girls hogged the karaoke controller. They stacked a killer list of songs, starting with two classic sing-alongs guaranteed to get everyone on their feet: "What Makes You Beautiful," by One Direction, and "No Scrubs," by TLC.

After karaoke, the six of them went to a photo booth and put on animal ears, bows, and sunglasses in front of the camera, taking tons of pictures. They stopped in a *pojangmacha* for soju afterwards. Jenny felt safe in Hongdae knowing Daniel was probably working late at his publisher and Rain was at home alone since the kids were at sleepovers; no one could spot Jenny and Haru rubbing noses, holding hands, or stopping in a dark alley to kiss. Like always, Lydia got a little drunk a little fast, and she and Selene called it a night after sharing one more bottle of soju; Santi and Joon escorted them to the bus stop.

Jenny wanted to keep walking, so she and Haru wandered until they were across the street from Daniel's building again. As they stood catty-corner to it, she wondered what she would do if Daniel came out.

Haru looked at his phone and said, "Ah, it's Minsu. I need to answer this. Won't take long." He stepped away from the street so he could hear better, and Jenny moved with him. She was facing Daniel's building. Haru was turned away from her, talking to Minsu in Korean.

Jenny stared at the building's revolving door for a minute, slightly tipsy on soju, with a couple of the karaoke songs mashed up in her head on a loop. She pulled out the photo booth strip she and Haru took by themselves—Haru in a plushie Doraemon hat, Jenny in pink bunny ears. In one of them, he was kissing her cheek and Jenny had her eyes closed in bliss.

When she looked at the building again, she saw Daniel in front of it.

She saw Aera, too.

Jenny knew it was Aera because she'd recognize the coat Aera was wearing anywhere; she'd told Jenny about it when she asked. It was white with a rainbow of fake fur and a splatter of black paint—a design Aera said came to her in a flu fever dream.

Daniel was next to Aera now with her hood up, and he pulled it up some more. The snow was falling, they were kissing, and Jenny was crying. Poor Rain. Poor Geon. Poor everyone. Love was a joke. Why couldn't anyone stay together? Why did Ethan have to break her heart? Why'd her parents even try to get re-married after their divorce? Why was she in Seoul, crying over someone else's marriage?

What the *fuck*?

By the time Haru was off the phone, Daniel and Aera were gone. Haru hadn't seen them, but he saw the expression on Jenny's face.

"Is everything okay?"

"Yeah. Of course. Maybe I just had too much soju," Jenny said, shaking her head.

"Need some food?"

Jenny nodded.

They walked to a churro cart for one to share.

She tried to keep up with Haru's conversation, but she was getting more and more depressed the closer they got to home. She was sickened by what she had seen.

"Jenny . . . hey," Haru said softly as they were standing outside the condo door. They'd decided to walk in at the same time. No rule saying they couldn't go to karaoke together.

Haru tugged on the sleeve of her coat.

"I want to talk to you about something, but I don't want you to think it's coming out of nowhere because it isn't. I've been thinking about this for a while, waiting . . . Jenny, I love you, I really do." He said the last part quickly, wet ghosts of snowflakes in his hair.

She'd been too late to stop him. She would've stopped him. She didn't want this. Why was he saying this? *I really, really like you* had been a lot on its own, the other night he'd whispered it to her in the dark.

A door in Jenny's heart swung closed, locked itself tight.

She watched his eyes searching hers. He was holding her hands now, a connecting current as he confessed his feelings. She had no choice but to confess hers, too.

"Haru—"

"I *love* you," he said again. "I want to be your man. I want you to *want* me to be your man. I know we haven't talked about our feelings in depth, and I can't read your mind, but this is real for me, Jennybelle."

Jenny slowly pulled her hands away and stared down at her feet, spiraling.

"I'm sorry, Haru. I can't do this right now . . . at all. We haven't . . . I don't . . . I need some time. I can't. I'm so sorry."

She turned away and, in a blur, punched in the key code. Once inside, she took off her shoes and walked quickly to her bedroom. Closed the door. Haru had been right behind her the whole time, but she shut him out. He tapped, then knocked louder.

"Jenny, wh . . . what are you doing? Come out here and talk to me, *please*," Haru said loud enough for her to hear. If he did it again, he'd wake everyone. He said a paragraph in Korean she didn't understand. He never said things in Korean without translating for her. "Jennybelle. Jenny. You can't just walk away. Talk to me."

"Haru, not now. I mean it. Please stop."

She stood back, staring at the strip of shadows and light at the bottom of the door, painfully, patiently, waiting for him to leave. When he finally did, her body moved to the bed.

She wasn't crying because she loved him. She didn't. She couldn't!

She was crying because life was stupid and disappointing, even when wishes came true.

12

Selene

Selene always had a lovely time when she was with Bitna and Deiji. Sometimes, when Selene went to Bitna's apartment, it would be only the two of them for a bit, but Deiji usually showed up, and Selene was always glad to see her. Bitna liked to wear the same color from head to toe; Deiji's wardrobe was more of a surprise. One day, she'd be in a fitted dark green military-style jacket with a black top and jeans, and another day, she'd wear a long, bright yellow sweater made of feathers with paisley leggings. She always wore at least one piece of statement jewelry, but usually more. The last time Selene saw her, she was wearing one egg earring and, hanging from the other lobe, a frying pan. When Selene mentioned them, Deiji pulled a mac and cheese ring from her bag and confessed she had a whole collection of food trinkets. Kept them in a little fridge-shaped jewelry box on her dresser. And Selene rarely left Bitna's without treats to take home; she liked to hand her at least three boxes of *banchan* wrapped with *bojagi* fabric before saying goodbye.

This morning, Selene, Bitna, and Deiji were in Bitna's kitchen having coffee. Selene had taken the bus over after dropping Nabi off at school. She wasn't staying long because she needed to go to Sobok Sweet to help out, but it was important to her to see Bitna and Deiji at least once a week.

Selene updated them on the meeting she and Joon had with a guy from the newspaper before Joon went to Vietnam for work. He had given her a new list of names of people who worked at orphanages near Seoul, saying they might be able to provide information about adoptees who were successful in their search for their birth parents. Most of the information could probably be found online, but pounding pavement and talking to people face-to-face could make a big difference.

"I've been asking everyone I know about your mother, your father, too. I haven't stopped," Deiji said in her airy way. Her bracelets jingled as she added two heaping spoonfuls of sugar to her mug and stirred. Her eyes were lined with orange with a wing flick at the corners.

"I have as well. I usually hate gossip, but in this case, it would help," Bitna said.

Deiji stood to go smoke on the balcony. She tapped her cigarette on the case and moved towards the door.

"Good news about our Joonie—it seems he'll be staying in Seoul for a while. He'll always be a wanderer, but he's content here. He may be in Vietnam right now, but I believe he'll make Seoul his home," Deiji said. She'd told Selene she learned English in school but perfected it in Australia when she lived there for five years, so her English had the slightest wavy twinge of an Aussie accent.

Selene loved the way Deiji talked about Joon as if he were her own son, the closeness the three of them had. Selene felt as if nothing bad could ever happen to Joon, so long as he had Bitna and Deiji in his corner. Here Selene was, searching for her birth mother, and Joon had *two* mothers who were crazy about him. She wondered what Joon was doing right this moment in Hội An.

Was he working early mornings? Late nights? Both? Did he like taking photos of rice farmers all day? They were friends on Instagram now, and she loved seeing the pics he posted. Last night, he'd uploaded one of the sunset, but the best thing about it was that he'd sent the picture to Selene first via text, just saying hi.

"Yes, Joon is very happy here now," Bitna said as Deiji stepped out onto the balcony. "He's guarded with his feelings and they're hard to interpret, but I'm always aware when he's happy. You can see the peace on his face."

"I love hearing the two of you talk about him. He's so loved."

"So are you, Selene," Bitna said, tapping her hand.

Joon texted from Vietnam at least once a day, but Selene wanted to see him. She wanted to be in his presence. His absence loomed large. Bitna's kitchen was so much bigger and emptier without him in it. Selene had stood in the doorway of Joon's dark blue bedroom, imagining him in there sleeping and working. She touched his scarf on the hook by the light switch, got close and put her nose to it.

She loved hearing Bitna and Deiji tell stories about him when he was little. *Our Joonie.* How he liked lining up his little toy trucks by color against the wall of the kitchen while Bitna cooked, and how he'd been afraid of dragons when he was four, worried one day he'd look out his bedroom window and see a glowing green eye as big as a bike wheel staring back at him. When Bitna and Deiji talked about Korean culture and growing up in the '80s, she wanted to hear Joon's take on how different their generation was, growing up Gen Z in Seoul. Selene longed to hear his deep voice chiming in with his opinions. To watch him gently lift his mug with his strong hands. To see his mouth when he spoke Korean, his full peachy lips pouting *opsoyo.*

Selene helped Aera's assistant book models and refresh the window displays the whole week Joon was gone and worked behind the register a few days when one of the employees was sick. She also officially ran the Sobok Sweet social media account while the woman who usually ran it was on maternity leave. It was a good week for Joon to be gone because Selene would've been distracted if he were physically in Seoul, but her mind wandered thinking of him *not* being there, too.

Nabi had a two-night guitar recital coming up, and Selene helped Aera make *galbijjim* for the host families' dinner. It was Geon's birthday, and braised short ribs were his favorite. His mother dropped off seaweed soup in the morning and, per tradition, he ate it for breakfast to honor her.

Selene connected with Lydia and Jenny at a bar that night because it was too cold to sit outside on the balconies. They drank too much, mostly in an attempt to cheer Jenny up about basically ending things with Haru. Jenny had filled them in on what she'd seen go down between Daniel and Aera and why she was feeling what she was feeling, but Selene brushed it off, even though it annoyed Jenny to no end. She desperately tried to pull Selene to her side, but Selene was extremely resistant. Lydia leaned more towards Jenny's view of things, but Selene wasn't sure if Lydia *truly* believed or just wanted to placate Jenny. Selene believed Jenny when she said she'd seen Aera and Daniel together but thought Jenny had interpreted the interaction all wrong. They were close friends! It was probably just an innocent hug—Aera's hood had been up, so that was why Jenny was confused. Jenny wouldn't budge on anything and let them know that, silly as it might be, her feelings hadn't changed about the wish just because she was sad Haru wouldn't be warming her bed anymore. She still believed *something* magical had happened on Jeju, and her being able to have only a physical relationship with Haru was proof of that. In her opinion, even a thimble's worth of magic or belief could do some good.

Once Joon was back in Seoul, Selene tried to hire him to take more photos for Sobok Sweet's socials, but he wouldn't accept money, so she took him out for *jjajangmyeon* instead. They ate and drank *boricha*, talking about anything and everything except searches, adoption, and orphanages. Joon loved horror and made a list of his favorites for Selene, and she told him he had to promise to watch some with her.

"As if that wasn't my plan all along?" Joon asked, teasing.

"As if that wasn't *my* plan all along," Selene said without shame.

He had the sort of beauty that grew the more she looked at him, the more she fell for him, and that was Selene's favorite kind. She found instantly-handsome-to-her men a bit boring. Joon was also the kind of good-looking that would only get better as he got older. She imagined his brown eyes with smile crinkles, his head with gray hair instead of black. She imagined both of them older, still friends, together, and wondered if that was too much, too ridiculous. She allowed it for a moment, then forced it away.

"Good to know we make an excellent team," Joon said.

"Yeah, but we already knew that."

"Right again. No surprises there."

A caterpillar line of small children in neon yellow vests walked past the window on a field trip, and after taking the time to remark upon their unbelievable cuteness, Selene and Joon made a plan to start with a zombie K-drama she was too scared to watch on her own. Leaving the restaurant, they headed to Eunpyeong Hanok Village, near Bukhansan Mountain.

Hanoks were traditional Korean homes, and Selene never got tired of wandering the streets of the villages or taking in the alluring views of the roofs in the foreground, the mountains in the background. When she had time alone and wanted to walk and think, she often found herself in one of the *hanok* villages for the atmosphere and quiet. They were living, breathing neighborhoods, and although they often teemed with tourists, everyone was kindly asked to keep as quiet as possible. A sign read *Promises We Make to One Another* before it listed the rules of the village, and Selene thought of the sentiment often, of the unspoken promises family members, friends, and lovers made to one another. From silly ones, like *I promise not to watch any more episodes without you*, to faithfulness and love until death and beyond.

Eunpyeong was less hilly than some of the other *hanok* villages, and Selene and Joon sauntered under the sunshine. Stepping back in time like that reminded her of the afternoon she, Lydia, and Jenny got Korean BBQ for lunch, rented traditional *hanbok*, and took pretty pictures at Gyeongbokgung Palace for their socials. The palace was crowded with tourists posing like characters from the past in front of the water and trees. They watched the changing of the guard, which felt like being in one of the *sageuk*, the historical K-dramas Selene loved so much, especially because of the costumes. *The Red Sleeve* and *Hwarang* were next on her to-watch list. Giant flags of yellow, red, and blue waved, and what seemed like hundreds of people observed about a hundred men in red, teal, and dark blue regalia march down the path towards the palace entrance as delightfully noisy drumming and traditional Korean instruments filled the air. The autumn leaves had also put on a show—bright, wine-colored fires against the blue sky, framing the wide array of displayed colors on the ground.

Today Selene was wearing the same sort of tulle skirt she'd been seeing on well-styled women all over Seoul ever since the summer, and she admired that, instead of pushing back against the trend or jumping off onto a new one, Aera sank into it further, making more tulle skirts in more colors and experimenting with lengths and ruffles. Selene's was bright candy apple red. She was wearing it with a Jackson Wang T-shirt, her leather jacket, big hoop earrings, and stomper boots. She stood in front of one of the walls in full sun while Joon snapped pics of her for Sobok Sweet's socials. The wind was blowing prettily against the fabric, sending it flying when Selene swished it around.

"These are really good," Joon said, taking a moment to flip through them. "I photograph people and things all day long, and you've made this extremely easy for me."

Joon asked her to move to the other side so he could take close photos of her face in the half-light and shadows. He showed them to her.

"You're beautiful," he said as they stepped closer to each other to let a line of tourists walk past.

"Thank you, Joon."

When their eyes met, he made a closed-mouth sound of affirmation and suggested they take a few extra in the field so he could capture more mountains in the background. Afterwards, they went to a cozy teahouse nearby to drink flowers and eat soft, sweet *injeolmi*.

The next night, after staying late to help Aera's assistant do inventory at Sobok Sweet, Selene bumped into Joon on her way out. He stepped back, breathing hard.

"Hi! Were you just walking past?"

Joon shook his head.

"Did you run here?"

Joon nodded.

"All the way up the hill?"

Joon nodded again.

"Is everything okay?" Selene asked, suddenly concerned. She searched his face and looked around for anything out of place. Anything to explain what was going on. Aera's assistant had just closed the door of her car and driven off. The traffic was normal, the streetlights on. Two women with shopping bags walked down the sidewalk arm in arm. From Selene's side of things, nothing was weird or different besides Joon swapping out his round glasses for black frames; both made her feral.

"I read an article about an assault in the area earlier and the police haven't caught the guy yet, so I wanted to get here before you left so I could walk you home. I didn't want to be late," Joon said after catching his breath. His coat was zipped, buttoned to his chin. His glasses were fogging, and he took them off, inspected them quickly before putting them back on.

"Are you serious?"

Joon nodded.

She hugged him for the first time, getting on her tiptoes to put her chin on his shoulder. Her body buzzed.

"Thank you for being so thoughtful."

"I wanted to make sure you were okay," he said, wrapping his arms around her even tighter.

Joon took her bag and threw it across his chest. They walked through the cold, in and out of warm watery light spilling from the cafés, bars, clothing boutiques, restaurants, bookstores. When they were outside the condo building, Selene readjusted his snow hat for him, pulling it snug over his ears. They hugged again before she went inside.

A few days later, Deiji left on a short trip to Jeju with her new boyfriend, so Selene and Joon had her place to themselves. She'd greeted Joon with another tight hug when she saw him standing in the cold in front of Deiji's traditional Korean house that evening; Selene had never been there before. Deiji's home was cozy and cushy, with minimal overhead lighting. The living room lamps gave off a peaceful, golden glow, and a gently buzzing red neon sign on the wall read *heart* in cursive. There was an upright piano in the dining room with a bouquet of baby's breath on the bench, wrapped in marigold paper.

Selene thanked him for the flowers and warmed up with Bach. Once her fingers were loose, it was Mozart and Chopin. Joon sat at the table, watching and listening in his dark green sweater, drinking his black coffee. She played a Ryo Fukui song she knew he loved. When he demanded an encore, she played "Butterfly," by BTS, for him under a messy pile of thoughts, getting emotional thinking of Nabi and her approaching birthday. Time was flying by so quickly! Joon gave her a standing ovation when she finished before sitting next to her, their thighs pressing together. She helped him plunk out what little he could remember of the two weeks of piano lessons he'd taken as a kid.

Later they sat close on the couch and watched two episodes of the zombie show, with Selene jumping out of her seat whenever something scary happened and Joon playfully laughing about it, patting her leg. Once, she screamed so loudly, she apologized, and he said it was fine because at least he still had hearing in his other ear. They took a break and put four red bean steam buns in Deiji's rice cooker, shared a hoppy beer waiting for them to warm up.

She listened to him talk about Vietnam until the rice cooker jingled and they took the buns out. Selene let one cool on the plate, then took her time tearing off pieces and putting them in her mouth. Steamed buns tasted like love.

"You eat prettily," Joon said, biting right into his. He made a funny face to show her the filling was too hot inside.

As he continued talking about Hội An, he told her that, wildly, he'd bumped into an old friend there, and given him a rundown of Selene's search. The old friend had a contact at Busan's newspaper and had tried to reach him but couldn't. Joon said he'd keep trying because the guy in Busan had written several stories about orphanages in Korea and adoptees searching for their birth parents.

"I didn't want to mention it because it may be another dead end, and I don't want to disappoint you. Shit, you came all the way here to do this, and I'm so sorry I can't help more," Joon said, leaning over and putting his forehead in his hand.

Selene scooted closer to him, touched his face.

The kiss was initiated by both of them at the same time, a volcanic release that had been slowly building for months. It wasn't long until Joon took off his glasses and put them on the table. His arms were around her—so strong, so warm—and Selene allowed herself to think that maybe, just maybe, the wish's magical power had detoured and led her here, to these tenderly intense, intensely tender kisses with a man she'd gotten to know in this way, at a time when she needed him most. She'd had to make herself so vulnerable to ask for help, to allow it to be given. Joon pulled back and hooked his finger under her chin, bringing her close again.

She wanted to say something. She had to.

"Joonie—" she started and stopped. She'd called him Joonie in her head a million times, but never to his face. She asked if it was okay to call him that, and he just smiled slightly, nodding his head yes before bending to press a slow kiss to her neck. "I care about you so much," she whispered as he trailed his lips up to her ear.

"I feel exactly the same. I didn't want to overstep—" Joon said in a low tone before Selene kissed him again, moving her hands over the slope of his shoulders.

"I didn't want to make a mistake and ruin things because you've been so kind to me . . . and your mom and aunt and— I adore them."

They took a long break to kiss, to tug on clothes, to get as close as they possibly could.

"My mom and aunt adore *you*. So do I," Joon said after some time, her cheeks in his hands.

He pulled her closer, and now they were lying on the mossy velvet of Deiji's dark couch. Selene was on top of him, making up for all those lost nights without his kisses.

The next time they paused to talk, they both confessed how attracted they were to each other, how long they'd felt that way. Joon expressed himself so calmly and clearly, it turned Selene on to no end. His mouth tasted like a beery steamed bun and everything he'd held back since they met in September. He moved his tongue slowly against hers, and his patience was so sexy it was starting to stress Selene out.

Time screeched to a halt at Deiji's. Selene didn't know how long they'd been kissing on the couch—the almost-winter sun had set long before they met at the house, and there were no clocks in the living room, only small, framed pictures and post-cards on the walls. Hooks adorned with beaded necklaces. On one table next to the lamp sat an elephant statue made of jade. On the other, a stack of poetry books in Korean, plus two books in French. The Christmas tree twinkled in the corner, sur-rounded by a menagerie of fake plants in colorful baskets. The lights, the falling snow, the softness of the space—Deiji's house was a den of seduction, and Selene laughed in Joon's mouth think-ing about it.

She compared the unrelentingly romantic lighting to a Wong Kar-wai film. Joon covered his face with his hands before push-ing his hair back and slowly, reluctantly agreeing, assuring her he'd definitely never thought of his aunt's house that way and didn't bring Selene there with that purpose in mind. "Although I've been wanting to kiss you for months now," he confessed, "I promise there was no elaborate lure with the piano. I really en-joyed hearing you play, and I know how much you've missed it."

"You've been wanting to kiss me for months and I had no idea."

"I didn't know you were feeling the same way. I'm admittedly terrible at this, and I was anxious about confessing, so I'm glad we figured it out," Joon said, turning his head and kissing her again. She made a home on his shoulder and nuzzled into it when they stopped to talk. His sweater smelled like fresh soap—a mix of his laundry and morning shower. Selene imagined the hot water raining over his naked body. She moved to kiss him again and softly bit his bottom lip, letting her body sink completely between his legs. A low moan entered her mouth from his as he adjusted his grip on her hips.

"Should we, um . . . take a break? Stop this from happening right here, right now? Not that I don't want it to, but just to make sure it's not too fast? I wanna do this right," Selene said a bit breathlessly, but she was proud of herself for taking a moment to assess the situation. She didn't want them to blow right past talking all the way through their feelings and go straight to sex, no matter how hot she was for him. This connection mattered to her: learning more about Korean culture with him and through him, Bitna, and Deiji; continuing to search for her mother even when all she had to go on was a blanket and a wish.

"Like, go out for fresh air and food and then kiss more later. Talk, too?" Joon asked close to her face, a bit breathless himself.

Selene pushed herself back from him, sat against the couch. "Maybe we should?"

"Are you hungry?"

Selene bit her thumb and nodded.

"Okay." Joon put his glasses back on. He stood, adjusting himself.

They decided to go out for *gamja* hot dogs from the shop down the road before it closed. Selene had to wake before sunrise to get Nabi to school extra early for tennis—she couldn't stay out all night, so taking a break was the right thing.

She kept telling herself this.

Before they made it to the door, Joon remembered something he wanted to show her.

"You'll get a kick out of this," he said, taking her hand and leading her into Deiji's spare bedroom. After getting under the bed and pulling out two boxes, he rooted around in one until he found what he was looking for: a picture. A younger Bitna and

Deiji dressed up like Elvis and Michael Jackson, and Joon dressed like Dolly Parton with a blond wig and balloons under his sweater.

Selene sat on the bed, cracking up.

"It's a blackmail photo that Deiji keeps around to make sure I stay in line. I think I look *extremely* sexy," Joon said. He sat next to her, leaning back on his elbows.

"Oh, you *do*. Even Dolly herself would appreciate this." Selene moved closer to him, pointing out every hilarious detail before he refused to take her playful jabs any longer. In an uncharacteristically bold move, he secured both her wrists in one of his hands and plucked the photo from her with the other, tossing it next to them. He leaned over to kiss her again.

"If we don't leave now, I never will," Joon warned.

"Okay. All right. Let's go." Selene sat up in a daze, smoothing her hair. He excused himself to the bathroom, and she watched him walk down the hallway, fantasizing about more.

Selene looked at the dresser, inspecting the jewelry box shaped like a fridge that held the food-shaped accessories. So kitschy, so Deiji.

She sat on the floor and put the photo back into the box after looking and laughing at it one more time. Then she moved to push the first box under the bed. The lid of the second box wasn't on all the way, and when Selene lifted it to readjust, the red blanket inside practically jumped into her hands, she snatched it so fast.

When she unfolded it, a little bee necklace fell out.

The blanket was bigger than the one Selene had, but it was the same fabric—scratchy on one side, smooth on the other, with red satin edging. The bee charm was an exact match with the one on the bee bracelet Selene always carried with her. Her hands started to shake. The blankets were obviously a set. The bee charms, a pair for mother and baby. *Together.* Of course Selene's birth mother would have the match.

Deiji.

Deiji.

It was Deiji this whole time.

Deiji was her mother.

That was why every lead was a dead end, why Bitna was the one who found her that morning.

Deiji is my mother.

Deiji played piano like Selene, had an affinity for fashion. They both loved ketchup on their eggs, were allergic to bananas.

Deiji is my mother.

They had the same big brown eyes, a penchant for olives and deep red lipstick.

Deiji must not have wanted to take care of a baby because it would've ended her dancing career. She'd abandoned Selene on that sidewalk so she could continue performing, do everything she wanted without the burden of a child.

Selene put the blanket back, let the bee necklace fall from her hand. She put both boxes underneath the bed again before moving to sit on the edge. She didn't need to see any more. She knew.

Joon startled her when he stepped back into the bedroom; Selene was looking away from him.

Joon was her cousin.

Joon is my cousin.

He couldn't have known about this. There was no way.

She'd almost had sex with her cousin.

Selene's stomach lurched, and she put her hand over her mouth.

"Okay, hear me out. What if we *don't* leave right now, Selene? What if we stay here? We can order food and stay the night.

Deiji won't be back until tomorrow evening, and I tried—I really did—but I can't stop kissing you. I don't want to," Joon said from behind her. She turned slowly to see his fingers laced atop his head. His face, open and sweet.

You can see the peace on his face.

Selene's heart splatted hard. She couldn't be in that room for one more second. When she didn't say anything, she heard her name coming from Joon's mouth with a question mark floating after it.

"Joon, ah . . . this . . . was a mistake. I can't . . . I mean . . . I have to go. Fuck! I'm *so* sorry. I'm freaking out and I'm sorry. I have to leave . . . right now. I have to go," Selene said with her hands in front of her, careful not to touch him, adding in formal Korean that she was sorry.

She felt him move behind her as she got her bag from the floor. He was apologizing and asking if he did something wrong, but she couldn't bring herself to turn around and look into his eyes again. She saw them in her mind and even that was too much. He grabbed her wrist, but she wiggled it away from him. She had to get out. That was all that mattered. The sliding glass door was open now, the sound of wind chimes singing through the dark.

"I'll . . . text you. I have to go," she said again, her breath puffing white against the night. Joon followed her out into the cold, calling *Selene-ah! Selene-ah!* as her boots tattooed the freshly fallen snow.

13

Lydia

By early December, Lydia had unloaded two more paintings and had made around six thousand dollars. She'd finished Christmas shopping for everyone back home, and it felt good to be able to send presents that were more expensive and special than what she usually got her friends and family. She ordered a cashmere blanket for her mother and a matching one for her sister, sent her dad a nice travel mug and three bags of fancy organic coffee beans.

Lydia was enjoying every bit of Christmastime in Seoul, and when she wasn't looking after Tae and Eun, hanging with the girls, in art class, or working on the project with Santi, she was shopping. She'd been picking up things for her host family here and there, secreting them away in her bedroom—a sunny pair of smiley face socks for Minsu, a pale pink coffee mug for Hye, new Pokémon shirts for Tae and Eun. She'd knitted both boys matching winter pom-pom hats and simple, thick scarves for Jenny and Selene, too, pink and red.

She also sent the girls a Christmas playlist she'd put together a month ago.

Lydia's Christmas in Seoul Mix

"Crystal Snow" by BTS
"Winter Bear" by V

"Winter Wonderland" by SHINee
"Christmas Love" by Jimin
"Candy" by NCT DREAM
"Snow Flower (feat. Peakboy)" by V
"Miracle" by GOT7
"Merry & Happy" by TWICE
"Winter Sleep" by IU
"Christmas Tree" by V
"Confession Song" by GOT7
"Poppin' Star" by TOMORROW X TOGETHER
"Merry Christmas ahead (feat. Chundung)" by IU
"Warm Winter" by JOY
"Christmassy!" by THE BOYZ
"snowy night" by Billlie
"Fairy of Shampoo" by TOMORROW X TOGETHER
"Christmas Paradise" by BoA
"Christmas Day" by EXO
"Love you on Christmas" by Yerin Baek

Matching beaded bracelets for the three of them were in the works as well. And she couldn't help herself when she picked up a gift for Santi—a small blue rose enamel pin; she'd gotten it the night they went to the lantern festival together. After being lost in the beauty of the glowing lights on the water, he'd bought them cotton candy, and she'd seen the pin winking in the window of a little shop. She'd snuck in and bought it before he got back.

Santi was sitting across from her in the swooping lights of the club. Jenny and Selene were there, too, but neither was much in the mood to dance or drink. Lydia thought it was awesome of them to show up, even though they didn't feel like it. They'd had this fun Christmassy night planned for weeks, and Haru and Joon were supposed to join, too, but Jenny and Haru weren't talking right now. And although Selene hadn't spilled what had happened with her and Joon, she wasn't talking to him right now, either.

"Joon is texting me, still," Selene said when Santi disappeared to the bar. She took a look at her phone again before tossing it in her bag.

"You should talk to him," Jenny said.

"You should talk to Haru," Selene snapped.

The DJ turned on "Lovesick Girls," by Blackpink, which the girls had dubbed *their* song. It always felt good when they randomly heard it out in the world; they'd usually squeal and dance to it together. Lydia smiled at them when she realized, but Jenny and Selene were focused completely on their conversation.

"He's in Busan, so——" Jenny said.

"It's not like his phone doesn't work there," Selene interrupted.

"I understand why both of you are taking breaks," Lydia said. "Well, Jenny, I understand you and Haru. Selene, whenever you feel ready to talk to us about what happened, I know you will."

"We kissed," Selene said.

Lydia and Jenny gasped.

"A lot. Like, a *lot*. We were extremely close to sleeping together. That's what I wanted to do. Basically ever since watching him pour green tea into his mug at Bitna's the first day I met him. He put the teapot down so carefully, picked up his mug so carefully. He does everything deliberately. So many men are sloppy, but Joon——"

Lydia leaned her head over the railing to see if she could spy Santi in line at the bar, hoping he wasn't coming back already, and there he was, waiting and talking to a guy he knew, thank God.

"Joon is thoughtful and tender—he's literally everything I've ever wanted. Everything I've tried to find back home or in college or wherever. He's right there." Selene put her hands out in front of her as if Joon were sitting with them.

"So, what's the problem?" Jenny asked.

"Is it because you're so close to Bitna and Deiji? Do you feel like it'd be too weird?" Lydia asked.

"You could say that," Selene said. She finished her drink and sat back. She took her time looking around at everyone, at a scrum of people walking past, drinking and talking.

"I don't get it," Jenny said. Lydia was similarly confused.

"I found the match to my red blanket at Deiji's. Deiji is my birth mother—Joon's *aunt*. Joon is my first cousin. I made out with my first cousin. For *so* long," Selene said with such an expression of bewildered incredulity on her face, Lydia would've laughed if she weren't in total shock.

"No. She's not, he's not," Jenny said, shaking her head.

"What do you mean, Jenny? I made a wish like both of you, and it actually came true. I found my birth mother." She explained exactly how and where she'd found the blanket, told them about the matching bee charm and everything that happened after. Joon had been frantically trying to contact her and even came to the condo building looking for her, but she wouldn't go down. After that, he'd sent her another bouquet of baby's breath. "I told him I needed time and I'd come over to Bitna's sometime before Christmas. He's convinced he hurt me in some way or was too aggressive, but he wasn't! I loved everything we did. That's not the point. The point is . . . he's my fucking *cousin*!"

Santi was making his way to the staircase now, and Lydia

warned Selene this wasn't going to be a private conversation for much longer.

"I'm a wish believer, you know this, but Selene, are you sure? Completely *sure*?" Jenny asked. "I mean, the odds——"

"I am. I'm sure."

"I'm so sorry it happened this way, but I'm glad you found your birth mom," Lydia said softly, after a few moments had passed.

"Selene, that's *huge*. It's what you came here for," Jenny added.

"Thanks. So why do I feel so bad?" Selene asked. Her voice cracked like glass. She told them she didn't know exactly when or how she was going to confront Bitna and Deiji about it. She had no clue how to tell Joon. She guessed she was still in shock, still trying to stop the bleeding.

They stopped talking about it when Santi returned, and shortly afterwards, Jenny and Selene decided to go home. Lydia hugged them both and they promised to talk tomorrow. She felt a little black cloud hovering over her with how sad and disappointed the other girls were with their lives right now. Lydia drank, listening to the loud music, staring off into space until Santi asked her if something was wrong.

"I'm in a weird mood. Maybe it's the music."

"We can go back to my place if you want to hang out in a significantly less noisy environment."

Lydia was tipsy again at Santi's. Nothing new. On the way to his apartment, they had a smart, detailed conversation about lanterns, and the use of light and dark in John Singer Sargent's *Carnation, Lily, Lily, Rose* and Luther Emerson Van Gorder's *Japanese Lanterns*. But by the time she was in Santi's living room, and he'd shown her the latest lantern he'd made—a mosaic of red dragons on parchment paper that he'd covered with one of the pieces she'd knitted—the drinks she'd drunk in the club had sloshed her proper brain cells out. They were on the couch together now, and in a moment of drunken silliness, tempted by an intrusive thought she hadn't bothered fighting off, she was showing him how she'd been texting the guys from back home and Haru's friend on a pretty regular basis.

"So, these guys give you attention and that makes you happy?"

"I know I'm supposed to say no. To act like I'm above that, right? I'm an independent woman *dot dot dot* fourth-wave feminism." Lydia gave her fist a tiny shake. "But the answer is yes, Santi. It does make me happy—it makes me feel good for these guys to compliment me. I haven't always been like this, but I guess I am now. I know how shallow I must seem."

Santi took the phone from her and scrolled through some of the texts, at times holding it closer.

"You get plenty of attention from guys in real life, though. It's easy for women to get attention from men."

"It's not easy for me!"

"How are you texting three or four different guys and dating a few others from class right now if it's not *easy* for you?"

Lydia took her phone back from Santi and put it away. She was wearing a tiny, sparkly red dress and white tights; she tucked her feet underneath her on the couch and sat against the armrest. Santi was leaning away from her.

"I don't know," Lydia said. *Probably because I made a wish.*

"You do just fine," Santi said, shaking his head.

"What about you? Do you do 'just fine'?"

Not once had Santi ever mentioned an ex or a girlfriend. She'd never even heard him say he thought anyone was pretty. It was like he'd taken a vow of secrecy about those things.

"I broke up with my girlfriend back in Spain before I came here this time." Santi took his thumb and scratched the middle of his forehead, a move that made Lydia believe he didn't want to talk about this.

"Are you upset about it?"

"Not at all."

A light laugh flew from Lydia's mouth.

"What's funny?"

"I cannot read you! It's hilarious how off I am."

"I'm not trying to be mysterious," Santi said, pushing his hair behind his ear. He was in his modern black *hanbok* and royal blue socks again. He stretched out and crossed his ankles. His small Christmas tree glowed in the corner; the lights gave a soft click when they changed colors. Santi had turned on music as soon as they walked in, and while Lydia didn't recognize any of the songs, she liked them all—lo-fi, cyberpunk beats and beeps, songs using rain and thunder as instruments.

"Maybe not, but you *are*."

Lydia confessed to Santi that she hadn't had sex since high school.

"That won't last for much longer, I'm sure," he said, amused.

Lydia gasped. "What's that supposed to mean?"

"I hope you don't think I'm shaming you for anything because I'm honestly not. What you do isn't my business. I'm only saying you're texting guys and going on dates, and guys are interested in you, so you *probably* won't be celibate for much longer *if* you don't want to be," Santi said.

"I don't feel shamed." A little stupid but not shamed.

"*Fighting!*" Santi said. He made a celebratory fist.

"Are you drunk?"

"Kind of," he said. She could never tell that with him, either.

He didn't act much differently when he was drunk. Sometimes he talked more, but that was it.

"Okay, look, I was thinking *maybe* tonight was the night, y'know. *Maybe* we would . . . kiss." Lydia said it quickly so she didn't have time to stop herself. She'd been obsessively fantasizing about this night all week. Her red dress, the club, the drinks, the walk back to his place. The red lantern hanging by his apartment door. His hair, his couch, The Jacket in his closet. All that was missing was The Kiss.

"Ah, your nose is bleeding," Santi said, pointing at her before hopping up.

Lydia took two fingertips and pressed them above her lips. She pulled them away, stained with bright red blood. Her body was literally pumping out her desire for Santi's strong danseur body and the deep dip of his philtrum. The way he moved through the room. Her eyes were on him as he returned from the bathroom with a wet washcloth and some toilet paper.

"Are you okay?" he asked.

Lydia thanked him, said she was fine, completely mortified.

They waited in awkward silence for her nosebleed to stop, but she was determined to finish their conversation. She pulled her compact from her purse and double-checked her face to make sure it was clean before wrapping the bloody toilet paper up in the washcloth. She cupped it carefully in her hands.

"You're not just another guy on my list. I don't care about them like that. Everything is different with you. No matter who I went out with, I always ended up thinking about you," Lydia confessed.

"You're drunk. And we're friends. I like that we're friends," he said. So sexy and soft, Lydia wanted to die. He'd used his charm to turn her down. "You should drink water and sleep. I should, too."

"Okay," she said.

Santi used his thumbs to wipe away her tears.

Lydia texted Vivi.

> Santi TOTALLY AND DEFINITELY rejected me. I
> think. I was drunk . . . it's a long story.

She'd debriefed "nosebleed night" with Jenny and Selene, but also didn't want to put too much on them since they were dealing with stuff of their own. Vivi was a better listener for this right now.

> THIS IS SO FREAKY BECAUSE I JUST PICKED
> UP MY PHONE TO TEXT YOU. FINN AND JAY
> RAN INTO EACH OTHER AND THEY TALKED
> ABOUT YOU AND THEY KNOW YOU'RE
> FLIRTING WITH THEM BOTH.

Lydia couldn't help but laugh.

> Okay well, so what? I've also been texting
> Haru's friend and the guy I made out with last
> summer. I guess you can let them in on all of
> that, too!

> They weren't mad, Lyd. Like, they think it's hot
> or whatever. They were talking about how cool
> you are now and how much you've changed. I

couldn't WAIT to text you about it, but I never
know what time it is over there!

I had to fly to the other side of the world to get
the guys back home to pay attention to me.

They're the dumb ones, not you. Love you,
Lydibug. FaceTime soon.

Yes! Love you too!

Lydia was making an early batch of Christmas cookies with Tae and Eun, so she invited Jenny and Selene to bring the kids to join in. There were only a few days left of school, and Lydia worked it out with Jenny and Selene to watch Tae and Eun for the few days when her art class overlapped the break. Lydia and Santi would be presenting their lantern project next week, nine days before Christmas.

"It's my turn to sprinkle!" Arwen said, literally stomping her tiny foot on the kitchen floor.

"Arwen-*ah*, you'll get to in just a minute. Patience, please," Jenny said as she helped Fox readjust his cookies so the sprinkles would land on them and not all over the baking sheet.

"I want to eat *those*," Eun said, bending down and pointing to the cookies in the oven.

"You will, once they're done," Lydia assured him.

"Can I watch a movie?" Nabi asked, tugging on Selene's sweater.

"You don't want to do more sprinkles?" Selene asked. She touched Nabi's long braid.

Nabi shook her head, and Tae decided he wanted to ditch the cookies for the movie as well. They ran out of the kitchen together.

"Don't——" They were gone before Lydia could remind them not to run. "Whatever."

"I miss *you-know-who* being here," Jenny said carefully once Fox was out of the kitchen. She put Arwen in a prime sprinkle position before looking back at Lydia.

"You haven't talked to him at all?" Lydia asked. She eyed Eun and Arwen to see if either of them was paying attention to the conversation, but they weren't. Eun was singing a song he'd made up about cookies, and Arwen was decorating hers so meticulously, Lydia was mesmerized, watching as Arwen separated the colors and added them in rainbow order around the edges, then repeated the process backwards as she worked her way inside.

"He texted me," Jenny whispered.

"And?" Selene asked.

"I haven't responded. He'll be back soon, I know. But I miss him right now. I *really* didn't expect to miss him this much," Jenny said.

Both Lydia and Selene looked at her, waiting for her to say more. When she didn't, they got back to work. Lydia loaded the dishwasher; Selene swept up the mess the kids had made on the floor. Jenny shooed Eun and Arwen out of the kitchen with a platter of finished cookies and yogurt drinks to take to the others.

"I feel . . . *something* for Haru. I can admit that now," Jenny said, answering a question neither Lydia nor Selene had asked. "As stupid as it may sound, Daniel stepping out on Rain has made me question everything and everyone. It's not like I can talk to Haru about that—it feels like I can't talk to him about anything! But I do miss him. He's been a gigantic part of my life here, and

I . . . miss him. I know I'll miss him in January when he's all the way in New Zealand, too. I just . . . I don't know. I don't dream about Ethan at *all* anymore, and I stopped thinking about him completely when Haru and I were together. I've *finally* moved on, and now I have *this* to deal with." Jenny huffed. She paced as she talked, managing to scoot out of Selene's way anytime she came near her with the broom. Jenny was the only one not cleaning; Lydia handed her a dish towel so she could dry the baking sheet.

"I hear you. And for what it's worth, maybe you can just focus on sorting out your feelings . . . whatever they are . . . and drop the Daniel-and-Aera thing, Jenny. It's confirmation bias—you saw what you expected to see," Selene said carefully.

"It was Aera's coat, Selene! There's only one like it. You know this!" Jenny said.

"You *thought* you saw them kissing, but they weren't," Selene said so confidently, Lydia knew it would make Jenny pause. She didn't argue. Selene finished sweeping and put the broom back in the closet.

"I feel stupid talking about Daniel and Aera when you have a much bigger burden on your mind," Jenny said to Selene.

"Thanks, but like, when you think about it . . . and I know you both have . . . all our wishes really did come true. Lydia, you're the star of your own show, and Jenny, I mean, who knows what could happen in the future, but for now you're not *completely* destroyed by whatever's happening with Haru. And I . . . No matter how unbelievably cruel and impossible it is to fathom right now, I found my mom, I guess . . . even if she doesn't want me to know it."

"Right. Maybe. But I'm still not satisfied. I want Santi," Lydia groused after giving Selene extra space to breathe about her awful situation, wishing for Santi without the help of stones or the full moon. Just three girls and some holiday hope in a kitchen.

"You'll get Santi," Jenny said, touching her head.

Lydia heard Jenny's *You'll get Santi* voice in her head as she stood outside Santi's apartment door. She'd seen him in art class earlier that day, but they were so busy working on their project that she didn't get a chance to talk to him about how sorry she was if she'd crossed a line by telling him she wanted to kiss him. She asked if he could meet up tonight, but he didn't write back. She couldn't stand the thought of things being weird between them or having to wait until tomorrow to see him again. Showing up at his apartment unannounced didn't seem entirely irrational until she did it.

She tapped and he answered quickly. His face looked the way it always did when he saw her—like he registered who she was and that was fine, but with no other emotion. The same way she looked at a box of cereal or grass.

"I'm sorry for coming here out of the blue. I don't necessarily think that's a good thing to do. I texted you but got no response, and I didn't want things to be—"

"Hi," a woman said, stepping up behind him and peeking under Santi's arm.

"Hi," Lydia said. *Oh, hell no.* This really had been dumb.

"Come in," Santi said, motioning for her to step inside.

Really dumb.

She took off her coat and boots and stood close to the door, awkwardly clutching her bag to her chest like a shield. She would always remember that moment in Santi's small, warm living room when she met his girlfriend and felt like the stupidest person alive.

The young woman stood in front of her.

"I'm Rosa, Santi's sister," she said as they shook hands.

Sister.

Lydia's stomach shimmied back into place.

"Oh. I'm Lydia, Santi's friend from art class. We're working on a project together, and—"

"You're so pretty. Santi, your friend is so pretty," Rosa said, turning away from her and plopping onto the couch. Santi was in the kitchen making a surprising amount of noise with the dishes.

"Thank you. *You're* so pretty," Lydia said, smoothing down her hair. Now that she didn't feel like she was going to throw up, Lydia could see Rosa and Santi had the same nose and eyes, the same dark curls. Rosa's were longer and assembled on top of her head. She wore dark cherry-red lipstick and had a nose piercing, but instead of a teeny diamond like Santi's, she had a small silver hoop.

"Did you know we're twins?" Rosa asked.

Twins.

"No, I didn't," Lydia said, shaking her head. This was the most sober she'd ever been at Santi's place, and the apartment had a much brighter feeling when her head was on straight. Usually, it was two in the morning with at least three candles burning. Now it was after nine p.m., and the only candlelight was being thrown from a squat one on the coffee table. A lamp was on that Lydia had never noticed before. She felt almost vampiric, like she wanted to hiss and cover her eyes.

"Come, sit," Rosa commanded, patting the couch.

Santi came back into the living room with warm *hotteok*, a bottle of Garnacha, and three glasses. No way was Lydia drinking tonight, but she watched Santi pour, and she took the glass from him when he handed it to her. Held it as he and Rosa returned to the conversation they must've been in the middle of when Lydia showed up. Santi had only made direct eye contact with her twice, and she still felt like she was intruding, but Rosa asked her more than once if she was going to eat and asked if she wanted anything other than wine, since she'd noticed Lydia wasn't drinking hers. Lydia said she was fine.

"I'll get you some water," Santi said, leaving the room for the kitchen again.

Rosa spoke to Santi in Spanish, and Santi's Spanish voice floated back. Lydia had never heard Santi speak so much Spanish. His voice was a little deeper than when he spoke English or Korean. When Lydia first started taking Korean lessons, she and her classmates talked about their "Korean voices," and whether they sounded like their "English voices." Lydia's Korean voice was slightly higher than her English voice, and she tried to match the tone of the Korean words with how native Korean speakers said them. She liked that the voice she used for Korean was different, if only just. It surprised her, revealing a part of herself that she hadn't known was there. Her Korean teacher said her Korean was very cute, and Lydia held on to that when she got frustrated. *My Korean is very cute*, she reminded herself when she wanted to quit.

Before Lydia could wonder whether Rosa or Santi was going to translate the Spanish for her, Rosa started talking.

"I told him I would never stop calling him *pollito*. It's what our parents called us when we were babies, but since I'm seven minutes older, he'll be my baby brother forever."

Santi came back and handed Lydia a bottle of water. He took the wineglass from her, giving it to Rosa, who had finished hers.

"She came early to visit for Christmas, but only for a few days," he said.

"Then off to Beijing again. I teach there," Rosa said.

Lydia learned Rosa was engaged to a Chinese man and that she loved Beijing but planned on moving back to Spain in two years and hopefully having a baby.

"I'm a serial monogamist, but Santi dates on the wind, fluttering around like a butterfly, not letting any woman pin him down," Rosa said. She put her hands in the air like graceful butterflies—up, then swooping down again. She asked him if he'd gone on a date yet, and Santi shook his head no. Lydia got the feeling that they'd had this same conversation recently. "Look at this face—and never been in love!" His sister grabbed his chin and pointed, as if Lydia hadn't been obsessed with it since the moment she saw him.

She distinctly remembered turning around and getting her first glimpse of him in class. If Lydia had the power to ask God to give her a dream man who was the *exact* sort of handsome she wanted, God would've made Santi's face and presented it to her just like Rosa was doing.

"This is what it's like being her little brother," he said.

"Look at this beautiful girl right in front of you!" Rosa said. She asked if Lydia had a boyfriend, and she told her no. "This beautiful girl without a boyfriend!" Rosa said, louder. She called him *pollito* and kissed his cheek.

"She *is* beautiful," Santi agreed, looking at Lydia again. She'd never come right out and told him that he was the most beautiful person she'd ever seen, and he'd never told her she was beautiful, either. They were not the kind of friends who said those sorts of things to each other. She'd been trying so hard to dodge being *only friends* with Santi. She didn't want to remove herself from being a potential romantic partner for him, but he'd given her absolutely nothing to go on. Hearing he thought she was beautiful helped soften the embarrassment of the kiss conversation, and Lydia would have to snuggle up with that crumb for who knew how long.

"Thank you," she said to him.

She'd come over to his apartment to apologize, but now she had to wait. Rosa was off to another subject in a blink, and she and Lydia squealed when they realized they were both horse girls.

After an hour, Lydia had filled her stomach with Japanese rice crackers and water, and Rosa had put herself to sleep in Santi's bed. Lydia considered bringing up the kiss conversation now that they were alone, but Santi was wine-sleepy.

"Now it's my turn to take care of you," she said, fluffing the pillow he had out on the couch, pulling the blanket up to his chin. "I'm sorry I showed up unannounced tonight. I shouldn't have done that. I'll talk to you tomorrow."

"No. It's fine," Santi said, repeating it in Korean. "My phone died, and I plugged it in and forgot about it once Rosa showed up. That's why I didn't text you back. I'm glad you got to meet her. She's a good-luck charm."

"She is?"

Santi nodded, half asleep. He opened his eyes one more time to tell her good night, this time in Spanish. Lydia replied the same in Korean.

"*You're* beautiful, too," she said to him before putting her boots on and quietly closing the door on her way out.

14

Jenny

Rain and Daniel went on their overnight date, and Jenny's dream of her and Haru hanging with the kids during the day and being alone together at night was obviously a bust. Haru was two hundred miles away in Busan with his end of the string that tied them together, and Jenny was in Seoul, a mess of tangled yarn.

Before Haru left for Busan, he went on the blind date. Jenny hadn't let that slip to Lydia and Selene because she didn't want to talk about it. She'd found out only because Rain had excitedly gushed about the date, adding that Haru had been vehemently against it at first, but then, for whatever reason, had acquiesced. Their mother was ecstatic. Rain said the woman liked Haru a *lot*, and even threw out what they could name their babies to her, but Rain didn't know how he felt.

"But Haru is leaving for New Zealand soon, would that work for them?" Jenny couldn't stop herself from asking. "And baby names, really?" Jenny forced a laugh. She waited for Rain to laugh with her, but she didn't. She just made a cute face and kept talking.

"Maybe not right now, but who knows?" Rain crossed her fingers, and Jenny used every ounce of energy she had to keep smiling.

Jenny texted Haru and asked if he had a nice time on his blind date. He wrote back six hours later.

It was fine. Are you talking to me now? What do
you want me to say?

I don't want you to say anything. I was just
wondering if you had a nice time on your date,
that's all.

I didn't want to go on it. I thought you and I were
heading somewhere real together . . . I guess I
was wrong.

Maybe you WEREN'T wrong, though.

I told you I loved you and you stopped talking to
me. I wasn't trying to pressure you into saying it
back. You wouldn't even look at me before I left.
You're very smart, so I'm assuming you can
imagine how that made me feel. Fucking
crushed, if I need to get more specific.

I didn't think you were trying to pressure me. I
do love what we have together, Haru. It's special
to me.

You really hurt me, and I don't understand why.

I'm sorry. I mean it. I want to talk about this face
to face.

I still don't know what you want me to say. I
guess I'll see you when I'm back.

> Please eat well and dress warmly. Don't get
> sick. Looking forward to you being home safe.

Jenny longed to hear the pouty inflection in his voice when he was angry or frustrated. She wanted to go to her bedroom and close the door, cry herself to sleep just to purge these feelings. But she couldn't. She had to make sure Fox and Arwen finished their homework, were fed and bathed. She thought of asking Lydia and Selene if they wanted to bring the kids and make a slumber party out of it, but Tae and Nabi had a Christmas choir concert that night. It was just Jenny alone in the condo with her kids. Haru's absence was so weighty that, after getting Fox and Arwen ready, Jenny went to his bedroom and smelled his pillows while the kids watched an episode of *Bread Barbershop* before bed.

Rain FaceTimed, checking in, and Jenny assured her that everything was fine, that the kids had eaten and taken their showers. They both got on the phone with their parents and told them a few stories about their day. Daniel showed them the hotel pool, explaining how it was warmed up in the winter.

Jenny was filled with rage thinking of Rain so delighted to be on a romantic getaway with Daniel when he was doing what he was doing. Aera was supposed to be Rain's best friend! Jenny hadn't even let her anger overflow to include Aera yet, she was so focused on Daniel.

Last week, when they'd gone up to dinner at the Chois', Aera had complimented Jenny's ribbons in the kitchen. Talked about how she'd started using even more ribbons and bows in her designs. Jenny had been polite, but the whole time Aera talked,

Jenny was imagining her and Daniel kissing in the snow. She wondered if Daniel snuck upstairs to their condo while Geon was gone. If the only reason Aera had asked Selene to be her assistant's assistant was to get her out of the way more so she and Daniel could have the condo to themselves for however many extra hours a day. When the truth finally came out—and of course it would come out—their cozy pod of families would implode, and everything would be ruined. Maybe Jenny would lose her au pair job in the mess and have to go back to California. Have to hear Ethan's voice all the time, see him and his fiancée in line at the coffee shop. *Fuck!*

Fox fell asleep quickly, but Arwen stayed awake wondering if their mom and dad were swimming in the warm water of the hotel pool or out to dinner. She asked Jenny if it was their anniversary because she couldn't remember.

"Almost. It's on New Year's Eve, and that's why we're all gonna get dressed up and go to the hotel that night," Jenny said. Arwen had a red dress for the occasion to match Fox's bow tie. "That's when you'll wear your sparkly silver shoes."

"I love my shoes." Arwen's long lashes flicked her bangs before she closed her eyes.

Jenny said good night to her in Korean and, when both kids were sleeping, went to Haru's bedroom and put her face in his pillows again. Enchantment. His sheets smelled like the thunderstorm on Jeju Island the night they'd kissed. They also held the faint scent of the woodsy cologne he didn't wear very often, but when he did, Jenny couldn't get enough. She wanted to roll around on his bed like a dog. She just missed him and the black half-moon lashes of his eyes when they were closed. She missed how he'd use his chopsticks to hold one perilla leaf for her so she could peel the other one off. She missed his thighs in his striped boxer shorts and his arms when he opened the jars that were screwed on too tight for her. She missed seeing him be more obviously gentle with Arwen than he was with Fox when they play-wrestled, and how he'd scoop them both over his shoulders at the same time, spinning until they begged for mercy. Their small, bright voices calling him uncle as they smacked his back.

She fell asleep in his bed and woke up in the middle of the night, returning to her own room.

At four a.m., she texted Haru *I miss you* in Korean. *Bogoshipo.* She heard BTS singing *I miss you* over and over again in its un-conjugated form in her favorite song of theirs, "Spring Day." I want to see you.

When she checked her phone in the morning before getting the kids out the door to school, she saw that he'd read it without responding.

Jenny was in the condo alone when Rain came home at lunch to pick up a gift for a friend she'd forgotten that morning.

She sat on the couch with the pink box in her lap.

"Jenny, I don't want to make this awkward, so I'm just going to come right out and say it, okay?" Rain said. She placed the gift box next to her and leaned towards Jenny, putting both hands on her knees. Jenny paused *Yumi's Cells*; Kim Goeun's pretty face froze on the screen.

Rain must've known that Jenny had caught on to Daniel and Aera. She probably wanted to know why Jenny hadn't told her about it. Maybe she was firing her. Jenny's hands shook as she thought of leaving Seoul before Christmas and not being able to say goodbye to Haru. She'd miss Lydia and Selene so much. Fox and Arwen, too; all of the kids. She opened her mouth to say something, but Rain kept talking.

"Daniel saw Haru leaving your bedroom. He only mentioned it to me after I told him about the blind date. He figured Haru would tell me himself soon enough, but he didn't, and now that I know, I wanted to talk to you about it directly."

"Oh."

Jenny didn't think she and Haru could sneak around unde-tected forever, but she hadn't expected to talk about this with Rain today. It would have been better if this had happened two weeks ago when everything was fine with Haru. He would've been there next to Jenny, talking to his sister, explaining things. But no, Jenny was alone with Rain, and Haru was in Busan. He'd left because of her. Was that why she was crying? Because he was gone?

"Rain, I'm so sorry I didn't tell you about it. I didn't know how to handle it. I know I crossed a line, but I love being your au pair. I was scared you wouldn't let me stay," Jenny said, sniffing.

"Why'd you let me set him up on a blind date without saying anything? I never would've suggested it if I'd known. Why'd he go? Was it to try to keep your relationship a secret?"

There was no angry energy coming from Rain, only confu-sion. Jenny would've felt stupid if Rain were being aggressive, but she wasn't. She asked the questions delicately. She was still being Rain, which was such a relief, it made Jenny cry even harder. How could she begin to explain everything?

Jenny snatched a tissue from the box on the table and wiped her nose.

"I didn't know what to say," Jenny said after taking a deep breath.

"Looking back, it's so obvious and I *should've* known, since you're around the same age and get along so well. You're beautiful . . . I mean, of course Haru is in love with you. Is that why he left? Did the two of you call it off? What's going on?" Rain asked, moving closer to Jenny. She patted her knee. "Did he do something? I don't always trust men."

Jenny wanted to open her mouth and tell her that she *shouldn't* trust men, certainly not her husband. But she could trust Haru. Her heart had been whispering that. Wow, she missed him *so* much.

"He didn't do anything, no. He told me he was going to check on Minsu's restaurant and then visit your parents."

"Well, when it's warm, he loves going to Busan to play golf with our dad. That or fishing. Those are the things they love to do together the most. When it's cold, they just like to drink and eat."

Haru had told Jenny that, too. She loved it when Rain told her something she already knew about him. It proved Haru was open and honest, confirming her belief that he was the man she thought he was.

Jenny gave Rain background information on her relationship with Haru. That she'd thought he was gorgeous the moment she laid eyes on him at the airport as they'd waited to board their plane for Jeju Island. That Haru would do *anything* to make her laugh and how much she loved that he was the one who made fish for her after she'd spent three years as a strict vegetarian. Jenny shared that he had made *yuja* tea and *dakjuk* for her on the first day of her period not long after that, and how comforting and healing it was when she finally decided to eat a big warm bowl of his chicken and slow-cooked rice. That Haru made her *pajeon* one evening as a storm rolled through because the skillet's scallion-sizzle sounded like the rain. No one had cooked like that for her—purposely and with so much love—since she was a child. When she thought about it hard enough, the way he cared for her . . . Haru was beyond her wildest dreams of what a man could and *should* be. She didn't want to curl up and cry herself to death when she thought about Ethan anymore because she'd properly grieved that loss now and moved on, found a true partner. Being in Seoul with the Kim-Crawfords, her close friendships with Lydia and Selene, the physical and friendly relationship with Haru—it had made all the difference.

Rain hugged Jenny on the couch, pulling her closer.

"I'm proud of you, Jenny. Putting yourself in a position to have feelings for someone again takes a lot of faith. You've been working on yourself, and it shows. You should be proud of *you*."

When Rain went back to work, Jenny texted Haru.

> I know you're not talking to me right now, but Rain and Daniel know about us.

> I know.

> What do you mean, you know??

> I mean, I know Daniel saw me leaving your bedroom.

> Why didn't you say anything??

> Because it didn't matter to me if they knew. I told you that. I'm a grown man, you're a grown woman.

Are you going to talk to Rain about us?

Is there an "us" to talk about, Jenny?

You KNOW there is, Haru. You know that.

Haru typed but stopped, leaving her the last to respond.

After dropping the kids off at school, Jenny expected to have the condo to herself for a few hours, but Daniel was there when she got back. He announced himself as soon as Jenny walked in.

"I need to get some work done in my office, and I didn't want to startle you," he said. He was standing in the doorway in a white button-down and khakis and bright orange socks.

She wished she could feel warmth towards him. She wished she didn't know what she knew. A prism sticker on the window of his office made the colors slip across the walls and the floor when the sunlight hit it; the sides of Daniel's face glowed with rainbows. Jenny stood down the hallway in front of her bedroom, listening to him.

"Has Fox been any trouble lately? I know he's doing better when it comes to listening. Haru was keeping me updated as well, but he's MIA," Daniel said. The two syllables of Haru's name swung out of his mouth as though in slow motion, and Jenny felt like she was sinking. She wanted the condo to herself so she could zombie out and finish *Yumi's Cells*. Watching the little animated cells inside Yumi's body observe her every move and make sure she was well loved and taking care of herself was causing Jenny to be gentler with her brain, too, imagining her own cells doing the same. She was exhausted from all her crying yesterday and didn't want to listen to Daniel say Haru's name any more this morning.

"No. Fox has been great. Arwen, too. They can be real angels sometimes, but you know that."

"Well, they love you and that makes a difference."

"And I love them," Jenny said, turning to go inside her bedroom. Polite conversation managed.

"Oh, Jenny! I've been meaning to tell you. It's a surprise, so please don't say anything, but check it out," Daniel said, walking towards her with his phone in his hand. He showed her a picture of Rain in an intricately laced and beaded dress on her wedding day, then swiped to show another picture of that dress ruined and un-beaded by flooding and water stains, then showed the same dress pristine and pressed on a mannequin. "Aera helped find someone who got Rain's wedding dress back to brand-new, so she'll be able to wear it at our recommitment ceremony." Daniel explained that Rain had accepted it was ruined, and never went to any lengths to fix it after it was accidentally destroyed years ago.

"That's awesome! It's *so* pretty," Jenny said, telling the truth but pretending to be more interested than she really was so it wouldn't be weird. She took his phone and flicked through the pictures again, taking her time to give off the full effect.

"I can't wait to see her in it again."

"It's *so* exciting! I'm looking forward to it," Jenny lied. She was looking forward to dressing up, dancing, eating delicious foods and drinking delicious drinks, but a recommitment ceremony when you were cheating on your wife was a *supreme* dick move.

Jenny was in the primary bedroom with Rain and Arwen, who was sitting on the floor of the walk-in closet with her feet in a pair of Rain's black heels.

"How do you walk in these things?" Arwen said. She stood and put her hands on her hips, took one step forward, and fell sideways.

"Be careful, Arwen-baby," Jenny said. She helped her up and told her to go to her own bedroom and get changed for dinner at the Parks'. When Jenny first started working for the Kim-Crawfords, she used to feel slightly weird telling Fox and Arwen what to do when Rain and Daniel were around, but not anymore. She reminded Arwen that her clothes were laid out on her bed.

"One last thing I wanted to add to our conversation yesterday is that I hope you know you can be completely honest with me about things. About Haru, or if you're not content working with our family. If you need anything, you can ask for it," Rain said from the closet.

It was foolish for Jenny to think she could tell Rain about what she saw between Daniel and Aera in the snow. Maybe Daniel and Aera had been working together so closely on getting Rain's wedding dress fixed that their sparks had reignited. She couldn't tell Rain about the dress, couldn't tell Rain about the kiss. She wanted to promise Rain that she would be honest with her about everything in the future, but Jenny couldn't do that, either.

She had her mouth open—not fully knowing what was going to come out of it—when Rain pulled a garment bag off the hook and unzipped it to reveal Aera's coat. Jenny would know it anywhere; she'd recognized it from across the street.

"*Aera's* coat," Jenny said, pointing.

"Yes. It's strange and pretty, isn't it?" Rain said, sighing and petting the fake fur. "I've had it for weeks because I borrowed it after spilling coffee all over my jacket when I stopped in to visit her at work. It's so warm I don't want to give it back, but I will because I'm a good friend."

"So pretty," Jenny said, floating away from her voice.

Aera's coat had been in Rain's closet for weeks. Rain had been wearing Aera's coat that night in the snow.

Daniel was kissing Rain, not Aera.

That couldn't be true. Was it?

"You wore it the first night it snowed, right? I can't remember. I think I went out that night, too?" Jenny asked, as if the evening in question weren't seared in her memory.

"I did! Yes, it was when the kids were at sleepovers. Right before Haru left for Busan. Did I tell you Daniel and I snuck away for dinner after I surprised him outside of work?" Rain was using the moonstruck voice she saved for talking about her husband.

Jenny shook her head no.

"It was like a movie, really. So romantic, with the snow falling down, and this coat has an enormous hood, look at it." Rain slipped the coat out of the bag and put it on, pulling the hood up. The top of it fell over her eyes. She pushed it back. "It's so deep it covers my whole face. I can tuck up in here and go to sleep." She giggled and let the hood fall down again before taking the coat off, putting it back on the hanger.

Jenny thought she faked a laugh when it was appropriate, but didn't know for sure. She was dissociating.

She'd been wrong about Daniel and Aera.

When she'd seen them together in the bedroom, they'd only been whispering about Rain's wedding dress. Jenny had been hunting for cracks so desperately she'd gotten everything wrong. Rain and Daniel's relationship was the real deal, not an example of love soured.

If Jenny could love, she'd want a love like Rain and Daniel's. But she couldn't.

Right?

For the first time, she wanted the wish undone. Even if she'd only *imagined* its power, she'd somehow manifested these real, blocked-up emotions for herself, and she wanted to rewind time and never make the wish at all. Who would Haru have been to her without it? Who could they be to each other now?

Jenny told Rain she'd be a little late coming up to the Parks' before bolting into her bedroom, closing the door, and turning on her laptop, frantically searching Jeju Island boards about the Waterfall of God. Had anyone posted anything about undoing their wishes? Jenny couldn't find exactly what she was looking for in English or the Korean she knew, so she used a translator for the other key-words. After searching for twenty minutes to no avail, she considered giving up until after dinner. But right before she closed the browser, her eyes landed on a post in English from two years ago.

Anyone ever have a change of heart?

Hey everyone. Long story short, a year ago I made a wish on the stones under the full moon @ the Waterfall of God. I wished to stop being so ambitious because I was obsessing over wanting to get a new job, better salary, more more more, and it worked! I relaxed and enjoyed my life, but I think I

worded my wish wrong or it worked too well, because I can't
get motivated to do anything. I liked it for a while, but now I'm
really frustrated. I'd like to know if there's any way to UNDO a
wish? Like, if I go back to the waterfall under another full
moon and wish for my wish to undo itself . . . will that work?
Has anyone ever heard of anything like this or experienced it
for themselves?

UPDATED I did it! I went back and undid the wish and
started feeling more motivated almost immediately!!! It's been
two months now and it really did work, I swear! Thanks so
much to everyone for your stories, and I will leave this up in
case it helps someone else!

Jenny's chin trembled as she read through the comments. Loads of people had returned to the waterfall and unwished their wishes, big and small. Just as many people chimed in about how absurd it was to shape your life around a wish "coming true" on a stack of stones. But Jenny ignored these—after everything she'd seen and experienced, no part of her was willing to take the chance the wish wasn't real.

She checked her moon app to see when it was full next.

Tomorrow night.

Tomorrow night was her last chance to undo the wish before the new year, her last chance before Haru left for New Zealand.

She scrolled through more responses and saw one that gave her chills.

My friend and I made our wish together and we went back to
unwish together, too. I'm not saying that's what has to
happen, but that's what worked for us!

Jenny waded through pages and pages of responses calling bullshit but was left unmoved. Lydia and Selene needed to go with her. It shouldn't be a problem for Selene because she'd found her birth mother already, and Lydia was doing fine! She'd sold some paintings and was close friends with Santi now. The timing was perfect. They'd go back together and undo the wishes so Jenny could have her brain and heart free for whatever happened next with Haru, because he was worth it. The girl he went on a blind date with? Please. Haru loved Jenny. Of course he was more to her than just a beautiful body in her bed. He'd fallen in love with her even though she hadn't said a word to him about her feelings. That alone was magic. Maybe *that* unexpected magic was what was giving her strength, in this moment. She owed it to herself and to their relationship to do all she could to free them from any wish weirdness. She wanted it gone.

She checked her phone again, hoping Haru could somehow feel her heart reaching out. Jenny texted him again.

Haru, please talk to me. Please?

She waited for his response but got nothing. She went upstairs to join everyone at the Parks'.

Jenny was ravenous, and although she really missed Haru's cooking, eating Minsu's food eased her pain. She scarfed down braised quail eggs, *saeng sun jun* with rice, and a small bowl of *doenjang-jjigae*—a soothing fermented soybean paste stew that Haru had cooked for her once, explaining that his mom always made it for him when he came back home after being gone for a long time.

She was giddy with the thought that the girls had accomplished what they set out to do with the wishes, and confident that they'd all agree to go back to the waterfall tomorrow night. When she had a moment alone with Lydia and Selene, she teased that she had big, big things to discuss with them after the kids went to bed and asked them to meet her on the Kim-Crawfords' balcony.

"It's freezing," Lydia said in shock, looking out the window.

"Wear your coat," Jenny instructed. "You have that coat I helped you pick out. Put it on!"

"Why can't you tell us now?" Selene whispered.

"Because it's a special conversation and we need to be completely alone," Jenny said as Arwen came back down the stairs asking her to help her and Nabi put on the pirate costumes they'd found. "See?" She followed Arwen upstairs, Lydia and Selene right behind them.

Later, on the balcony, it was so cold, Jenny was surprised the frosty fog of their breath didn't solidify into ice.

"Rain borrowed Aera's coat. It was Daniel and *Rain* kissing in the snow, not Daniel and *Aera*," Jenny said. It was such a relief, getting that out. Jenny took another sip of soju to warm herself up and convinced the girls to do the same.

"Girl, I told you they weren't cheating. I knew it!" Selene said.

"Yes, you did, and I'm an idiot, but all that matters now is that it's not true and they really do love each other so much and love isn't dead for everyone!" Jenny said.

"Good. Yay! Let's go inside now," Lydia said.

"No! I have one more thing."

"What?" Lydia and Selene said at the same time, exasperated.

"We have to go back to the waterfall tomorrow night and undo our wishes. I want to be open to having deeper feelings for Haru. I *need* to. I need to get everything back to zero so we can start fresh." She stopped to drink, letting that settle for a moment before filling them in on what she'd read online. "Both of you need to come with me because there's a better chance everything will work properly if we re-create that night in August. It has to be tomorrow night because it's the full moon. We can't wait. If we wait, it'll be too late. Haru's leaving for New Zealand soon and I need to fix this before he goes."

Lydia and Selene said nothing.

"Come *on*! Selene, you found your birth mother. Lydia, you're so much more confident now—you don't need the wish anymore. You both got what you wanted. I'm the one who needs this, and I need you both to come with me so we can do it right." Jenny had to focus on her breathing because she was too excited, too out of her mind about this.

"I still need my wish, Jenny," Lydia said firmly. "I don't want to undo it. Santi just started opening up to me and we have our lantern presentation *very* soon—I don't want to blow it. All that money and free travel . . . we've worked too hard. I'm keeping my wish. *Something's* different. *Something's* working!"

"I feel sort of neutral," Selene said. "I mean, um, sure, I found my birth mother and I'll handle the *mess* of all that somehow, so I don't need my wish anymore . . . but, Jenny, it's not fair to try and make Lydia undo hers if she doesn't want to."

"I didn't know this was going to happen. I made a wish to never fall in love again, and my connection with Haru is so strong, *something* broke through somehow, but I need to make sure the wish isn't bad luck or something. I don't know! I haven't been able to unravel every thought about it yet, but I'm trying.

Lydia, please come with me. Your presentation will be fine, and Santi obviously likes you—you two spend so much time together. That'll all work out, I know it will."

Jenny wasn't cold anymore; her aggravation was keeping her warm. Lydia's wish was the most trivial of all of them. All she'd needed were better clothes and confidence.

"No, Jenny. I'm sorry, but I won't do it. I won't go." Lydia's tone was final.

15

Selene

"It's too cold to have this conversation out here. I'm serious. None of us can think straight," Selene said. She racked her brain for where else they could go and suggested a bar not too far from the condo building. They'd never been before, but it looked warm and cozy whenever Selene walked past, and maybe the change of scenery would make everyone behave more rationally.

Selene and Lydia stood in the hallway in front of the Kim-Crawfords' door while Jenny was inside, explaining to Rain that they were leaving.

"I won't do it, Selene. Jenny doesn't get to tell me how to feel. I love the wish, or the *idea* of the wish . . . whatever you wanna call it. It's working for me, and I never want to go back to how I felt before," Lydia said quietly.

"I know, and you're allowed your own feelings. Let's talk to her about it without getting overly emotional," Selene said. She missed Joon's calm presence in that moment. Selene's life in Seoul was full of excitement and surprises at every turn, but when she was with Joon, her anxiety quelled. Receiving disappointing news from him about her search for her birth mother always had the added cushion of Joon being Joon, giving her a soft place to land. Everything had changed now, but she remembered that.

She *had* to stop thinking about him like this.

Selene also couldn't seem to process the fact that she'd been hanging out with her birth mother since September without knowing. She was so angry, and was trying like hell to block it out, feign normalcy. She didn't care about the wish at all anymore, but Lydia and Jenny didn't need to eat each other alive about it, either.

The girls caught the bus to keep warm, taking it to the bar. They were silent together, on their phones, staring out the windows. When they arrived, they took off their coats and sat, ordering a round of soju in the blue bottles this time. Selene poured three shots and commanded they take them at the same time before getting back to the conversation. She counted to three in Korean for them—*hana, dul, set*—before they downed their drinks. Selene was grateful the music wasn't too loud; the vibe was chill, the bar festively decorated for Christmas.

"If we don't do this tomorrow, it's too late for me," Jenny said resolutely after wiping her mouth.

"I think you're overreacting, Jenny," said Lydia. "The same way you overreacted about Rain and Daniel's marriage. Just because Haru is going to New Zealand doesn't mean you can't talk to him or that it'll change his feelings for you."

"I'm not talking about his feelings for me. I'm talking about *my* feelings for *him*. I need to do this. I have to fix things. I'm not going to let him go without doing everything I can to unblock myself so I can feel my truest feelings."

Selene didn't care which decision they made and didn't feel like they needed to make it together. Lydia wanted to keep her wish and Jenny wanted to undo hers. Fine! They should both do whatever they wanted.

"You don't get to say that it's time for the wishes to be over. You don't have that right. Your wish isn't more important to me than mine is, Jenny. You can't tell me how to feel." Lydia looked right at Jenny and shook her head.

"You're only saying this *because* of the wish! Because it makes you confident and able to speak your mind so freely. You wanna know what's not fair? It's not fair that you get to use the wish to try to charm me into not undoing it. Lydia, your wish was *not* as important as mine and Selene's, and you know it." Jenny crossed her arms and leaned back in her chair.

"Jenny, you wished to never fall in love again because *one* guy broke your heart. One! Be serious." Lydia held up one finger, and now it was Jenny's turn at headshaking.

"Really, Lydia? Your last boyfriend was in high school—what would you know? You said yourself you've never had your heart broken. Selene, you should be more on my side about this!"

"What? Why? Why should I be on your side over hers?" Selene asked. Lydia and Jenny glared at each other again.

"You just should," Jenny said, finishing her soju and standing.

"I can't go tomorrow anyway because I need to talk to Bitna, Deiji, and Joon."

"Okay. Look. Whatthe*fuck*ever! I'm leaving. I want to be alone right now. Tomorrow I'm going to Jeju alone, and I'm going to the waterfall to undo my wish alone. If that means both of your wishes are undone, too, oh well. But I want to say—" Jenny stopped.

She looked up at the ceiling and started to cry. Her shoulders shook, and she wiped her nose with the back of her hand. The people at the table next to them stared, but Jenny didn't seem to care.

"You two have more of a life outside of the house, I know.

Your art class and Sobok Sweet," she said, pointing at them. "You have Santi, and you have Joon, and you've both made friends outside of me, but I haven't made friends outside of you. *All* I have is Haru. I thought the two of you would understand, but I was wrong. I'm always so wrong about who I give my heart to. I was wrong about Ethan, and I was wrong about the two of you, but I'm gonna be right about Haru. This time I know I am."

"Jenny, wait—" Selene said, standing.

"No. I don't want to talk to either of you. I really don't."

"*Jenny.*" Selene watched her dark ponytail and bow swish out of the bar, around the corner towards the bus stop. She sat back down across from Lydia, who was quietly sniffling, and finished her soju slowly, not saying anything.

Selene had bought Christmas gifts for Bitna, Deiji, and Joon—a bright purple Sobok Sweet silk scarf for Bitna, a pair of earrings for Deiji (a teeny bottle of soju and a shot glass), and a gray wool cardigan for Joon—but she left them in her bedroom, wrapped on the floor. All of them now without a home. What was the point of giving gifts to people who had been lying to her for months?

When Selene arrived at Bitna's, she didn't feel the same nervousness she felt when she stood in front of her door for the first time. Now she was angry. She didn't hesitate to knock. She'd texted Joon first thing in the morning and let him know that today was the day she was coming, and he answered the door quickly.

"I'm so glad you're here, Selene. I'm so happy to see you," he said, surprising her with a hug. She wanted to melt in his arms but couldn't. One certainly shouldn't melt in their cousin's arms the same way they would a lover's.

Selene was glad she and Joon weren't alone so he couldn't ask the questions she knew he wanted to ask. Bitna was in the kitchen, and Deiji was out on the balcony, smoking. Selene stood there staring at her birth mother, noticing every small thing she'd missed before. Deiji held her mug with both hands, close to her chest the same way Selene did when she was cold. She crossed her ankles when she leaned forward in a chair, and so did Selene. Even the way Deiji's hair flicked out over her ear was the same as Selene's. She watched her smoke for so long, Joon must've had to say her name more than once to get her attention.

"Selene? Have you eaten?" Joon asked. She shook her head and sat as he loaded up the table with side dishes. His hair was tousled down over his eyebrows, and he was wearing a red sweater. Her favorite color. Selene had never seen him in red before. Why today? He looked fluffy, handsome, and a bit tired. She imagined he'd been having trouble sleeping, just like her, and she hated thinking about it. She turned away from him as Bitna asked her what her host family was doing for Christmas. Selene gave short, canned answers with as much warmth as she could muster and used her chopsticks to take one bite of spicy tofu before putting them back down. Joon sat and took a piece of flatfish from his bowl before gently placing it on top of the rice in Selene's. She forced herself to eat it since he'd shared his food so kindly, like he always did. Eating together had become an important part of their relationship, and she loved Bitna's cooking. She hated having to associate the tastes on her tongue with these roiling emotions.

"Just this morning at the café on the corner, I bumped into someone who worked at the newspaper. He knows a man he's confident would recognize your father's name. He's written about military deaths quite extensively and worked at the paper when your father was killed. We can try to make a connection that way. If we can find anyone who knew him, knew who he dated while he was stationed here . . ." Joon trailed off with that sweet, open-sky expression on his face. His words drifted to Selene slowly, through a thick, stormy fog.

Deiji opened the door and walked into the kitchen, smiling. Selene couldn't keep it in any longer.

"Joon, stop. Deiji is my birth mother. I found the red blanket at her house. The bee necklace to match my bracelet. I'm assuming you don't know this because why would you be pretending? But, Bitna, you know 'finding' me was part of this whole plan. I wanted to know my birth mother more than anything, and the two of you have been playing this game with me and I want to know why. I deserve that. Don't you think I deserve that?" Selene was crying hard now, her hands folded under her chin.

"What? Oh, *no*, Selene. That's not true. Selene, none of that is true," Bitna said slowly with pleading eyes. Selene's blood fizzed cool.

"Selene—" Deiji interrupted.

"I don't want to hear more lies. I can't stand it! It's so cruel!" Selene wiped at the tears on her cheeks. "Joon, you're my cousin. That's the reason I acted the way I did the other night . . . when I realized." She was sweating with embarrassment. She felt so stupid being there and wanted to leave, but she was crying too much and couldn't move from her chair.

"Selene—" Joon said softly. She looked right into his sad, dark eyes.

"Selene, Joon is *not* your cousin. I am *not* your mother. We would never do that to you. It's horrible you think that," Deiji said with a high, angry voice. Selene watched Deiji's face crumple in confusion as she shook her head.

"Nothing else makes sense. Why do you have the matching blanket, the matching bee necklace? I saw it at your house! You knew about the red blanket—why wouldn't you tell me you had one exactly like it?" Selene snatched her blanket from her bag. Shook it in her fist. She went back in for the bee bracelet and waved it over the table.

"Deiji-*yah*, I know what blanket she means. Selene, I know the blankets you're talking about, and I understand why you're confused. It never crossed my mind before, to tell you. I thought you knew it was just a blanket," Bitna said from the other side of the kitchen. She spoke to Deiji in quick Korean; Selene couldn't keep up.

"My mom is telling Deiji that it must've been in her ex-husband's things. His parents used to own a convenience store in the late '90s, early '00s, and their house was filled with all sorts of stuff they sold there. Pretty much every store sold sets of blankets and charms like that. They were really common back then. My mom has a better memory than Deiji," Joon translated. "Selene, I'm not your cousin. I *know* why you would've freaked out about that—I would've done the same thing. I just wish you would've told me because I could've explained to you that Deiji isn't your birth mother. It's *impossible*. She can't be. She—"

"Can't have children. I can't. It's why Joonie and his sister are like my own children. It's why my ex-husband left me and why his family considered me worthless. We tried for so long. It's very painful for me to talk about. Oh, how I wish you were mine, Selene. I would've kept you. I never would've let you go," Deiji said, holding her hand to her heart. She was crying now, too, as was Bitna.

Was it true?

Selene was so used to imagining what meeting her birth

mother would be like, so used to feeling rejected because she'd abandoned her, that she had also forced herself to consider being rejected *again* by her birth mother when she finally found her. *If* she found her. Maybe this was another way for Deiji to reject her again.

"I'm sorry, Deiji. I'm so sorry about that, I truly am. But I just don't know what to believe. I don't understand why you wouldn't tell me you had a red blanket and a charm just like mine!"

"I didn't know it was in my house! I haven't gone through any storage boxes since I moved in, which was not that long ago. Joon-*ah*, where were they?" Deiji said, asking the question again in Korean.

He guessed aloud where Selene had seen the box, and when Selene confirmed it, Joon responded to Deiji in Korean.

"Under the bed in the spare bedroom, under the box of pictures," he said, repeating it in English for Selene.

"I've never looked under there! You two put the boxes away for me," Deiji said, gesturing to Bitna.

"It's awful you think we've been lying to you this whole time—after everything, you're like family to us. Selene, I remember the first moment I laid eyes on you. Nothing like that had ever happened to me, and I felt so connected to you, especially when I found out I was pregnant with Joon at around the same time." Bitna paused, choosing her words carefully. "I was sad for any mother who felt like abandoning her baby was her only choice. I've thought of you often. There were times I couldn't get you off my mind. I wondered where you were and if you were okay. If you were warm and well-fed. It was so special how you found your way back to us. What you think we're doing . . . we would *never* do that to you."

The fat chunk of ice in Selene's heart melted upon hearing

the emotion in Bitna's voice, but still she pushed back, insisting there were too many coincidences, not just the blanket and charm. She went through the list she'd been writing in her mind since that night: She and Deiji both loved loud colors, quirky accessories, and pairing leather with lace. Fujii Kaze and 2PM albums. They both preferred sherbet over ice cream, hated parsley, and neither of them could keep a houseplant alive. Selene told them she'd felt an immediate connection to both her and Bitna, and that mattered to her in such a colossal way she hadn't even attempted to overthink it or explain it to herself. She didn't need to. She *felt* it.

"I feel connected to you, too, Selene, but I don't have to be your mother for that to be true!" Deiji snapped.

Selene cried harder after being scolded by Deiji. She hated the expression on her face when Deiji did it, like she was severely disappointed in Selene for getting everything so wrong. Joon met Selene's eyes and put his forearms on the table, leaning closer to her. She couldn't believe that even in her snotty, crying embarrassment, he could comfort her with such a small movement.

Bitna stood next to Selene and put her arm around her.

"Not only would we never do that to you, we would never do that to Joon, either. We would never have him meeting with people and searching the country for your birth mother when she was right here. That's evil. We are not *evil*, Selene," Bitna said.

"I'm sorry. I have to go. I have to go and think. I can't stay here. I'm sorry," Selene said, looking right at Joon when she apologized in formal Korean. *Joesonghamnida.*

She got up to put her boots back on, and Joon stood, like she'd known he would. He grabbed her wrist in the hallway, and she turned to him.

"If this guy recognizes your birth father's name, that's *huge,*

Selene. All we'd have to do after that is find *one* person who knew who his girlfriend was . . . what her name is . . . we can find her easily once we know her name."

"I thought I'd already found her!" Selene cried, imagining Jenny taking the trek to the waterfall by herself in the cold.

Joon took both of her hands and held them. "Please let me keep helping you. I have a good feeling about this, and I have a good feeling about us." He let go only to wipe away her tears with his thumbs.

"Joon, I have to go," Selene said as kindly as she could.

As soon as she stepped outside Bitna's building, Selene called Jenny.

"Jenny! Deiji isn't my birth mother. I was wrong! Please don't undo the wishes. Not until I find her. I need to find her. Please, Jenny," Selene said as soon as she picked up.

"What? What do you mean?"

Selene sat at the bus stop and explained everything as quickly as she could, letting the heated bench slowly warm her butt and legs.

"Please don't undo the wishes," Selene begged.

"I'm going."

"Please don't!"

"You claimed to be neutral, but you're not. You're on Lydia's side! How do I even know what you're saying is true?" Jenny screeched.

"You really think I'd *lie* to you about not knowing who my birth mother is? Jenny, that's messed up. You're not making any sense."

"Selene, how am I supposed to know? Maybe you don't want me to do this because you have a crush on Haru."

"What? What the hell are you talking about! I don't have a

crush on Haru. I never did. I just thought he was cute for, like, a minute. I've always been supportive of you two. You know how I feel about Joon. Not everything is about *you*!"

"I'm going to the waterfall. I'm already on Jeju. I'm sorry, but I'm doing this tonight, no matter what."

"Fuck you, Jenny."

Selene was still crying when she hung up the phone. She stood when she saw the bus coming but decided to walk in the cold.

PART THREE

Inyeon

16

Lydia

Lydia was going to bomb the project presentation with Santi, she just knew it, but not because they hadn't been working hard. They'd spent the past few days on the floor of his living room making lantern after lantern based on their sketches and carefully packing them up in boxes. But did any of the preparation matter anymore if Lydia felt like the power of the wish had disappeared?

Selene came to the Parks' condo to see Lydia last night and told her that she'd tried to convince Jenny again not to go ahead with undoing the wishes, but she wouldn't budge. Lydia wasn't surprised. Jenny had been so angry she practically had green smoke pouring from her ears, and Lydia was still hurt from how Jenny had talked to her. It was clear Jenny thought she could run right over her, and that she'd bend to her every whim, but she wouldn't. Never.

Selene also filled Lydia in on all things Bitna, Deiji, and Joon. She really was so relieved Joon wasn't her cousin, but she seemed even more desperate to find her birth mother now. She felt like Jenny undoing the wishes was opening the floor beneath her.

The two of them sat on Lydia's bed listening to the Sad and Pretty playlist the three girls had made together, picking at bags of shrimp crackers and candy for hours until Selene almost fell asleep and went home to go to bed.

Sad and Pretty Mix

"Spring Day" by BTS
"Ending Scene" by IU
"My You" by Jungkook
"Closer (with Paul Blanco, Mahalia)" by RM
"i hate to admit (Bang Chan)" by Stray Kids
"Abyss" by Jin
"Say Yes" by SEVENTEEN
"The Truth Untold" by BTS, Steve Aoki
"Hope Not" by BLACKPINK
"Blue & Grey" by BTS
"When The Wind Blows" by YOONA
"You, Clouds, Rain" by Heize, Shin Yong Jae
"Gone" by ROSÉ
"Take Me To You" by GOT7
"Sweet Night" by V
"Beautiful" by Crush
"If you're with me" by Sung Si Kyung
"Here I Am Again" by Yerin Baek
"Breath" by Sam Kim
"We Could Still Be Happy" by Rachael Yamagata

It felt so weird to be hanging out, listening to their playlist and eating snacks in one of their bedrooms without Jenny, and it made Lydia sad even though she didn't want to talk to her right now. Lydia wanted to *want* to talk to Jenny, and she hated thinking about the three families getting together for Christmas and Jenny having to isolate herself from her and Selene. The awkwardness if anyone asked them what was going on. What could they say?

She expected Hye and Minsu to treat her differently immediately, if what Jenny did had erased Lydia's wish, too, so she was
on high alert. At first, everything seemed okay, but then Hye had
to remind her twice that the dishwasher was broken and the
repairman was coming to fix it later that afternoon. The second
time, Hye had seemed exasperated at having to repeat herself.

"Lydia, you have to leave it in the sink to wash by hand," Hye
said as she was bending over to tie Eun's shoe by the door, which
was something Lydia had just done, but it had untied itself.

Not a *You have really turned into something special* to be found.

Lydia would've felt better if Hye complimented her clothes.
She was wearing a short, cream turtleneck dress with pink tights
and pink ballet flats like the pair Hye had in her closet, but with
a much lighter price tag. Hye looked her up and down without
saying anything, but she did wish Lydia a perky *fighting*.

It was going to suck having Hye unimpressed with everything she did from here on out. Lydia apologized again for the
dishwasher and the shoelace in formal Korean and left the condo
to drop Tae and Eun off with Selene at the Chois'. Hye would be
busy on set all day, and Minsu would come pick them up later.
Lydia had asked for the day off so she wouldn't have to worry
about getting back home at a certain time; she was hoping to
spend the whole day with Santi.

Lydia got a table at the café and waited for Santi. They were
meeting before class, to go over everything one more time. She
had to order their drinks twice because the barista forgot to
make them. Not the best sign she wasn't invisible again. She was
grateful Santi saw her as soon as he walked in, sat across from
her in a puffy black coat, and smiled. A Santi smile was a precious

thing—the scrunch of his nose and how his face seemed to explode into it never failed to make Lydia smile, too. She told him the other coffee on the table was for him and refused when he tried to pay her for it. He liked his coffee with two quick splashes of cream and one and a half raw sugar packets; Lydia had been proud of herself months ago when she gleaned this information simply from watching him carefully as he made it.

"We're more than ready, don't you think?" Santi said.

She was relieved he seemed to be acting normal towards her. She'd obsess over the possible fallout from the undone wish after their project presentation, once she could free up brain space. She really hoped Jenny was okay on Jeju. Lydia was furious with her, but she didn't want anything bad to happen to her.

Lydia searched Santi's eyes for disappointment that she wasn't quite as special or sparkly today but found none. Outside of his smile, that was the best luck she'd had all morning.

"We've done all we can, that's for sure. I have my laptop with the slideshow ready to go, the color booklets of our sketches, and the knit lantern covers." Lydia patted her bag for him.

"I double-checked to make sure the lanterns still have working LED tealights. I went over there before I came here." Santi motioned across the street to the art school.

Lydia bowed her head and thanked him in formal Korean.

"Why do you use formalities with me? We're basically the same age." Santi chuckled.

"I want to be respectful. You've seen me so drunk you had to give me a piggyback ride home, and I've embarrassed myself in front of you in so many different ways—I'm trying to make up for it, I guess," Lydia said. She was too nervous to lie. She'd ordered decaf so she wouldn't get too cranked up from the caffeine. She finished her coffee and waited to see what Santi would say next.

He drank, stealing glances around the crowded café and through the window next to them, letting his eyes drift to Lydia in between.

"My sister wanted me to tell you that it was really nice meeting you. She left this morning."

"It was really nice meeting her, too. I'm sure you miss her already."

"We have plans to meet my parents in Spain in March."

"I'd love to go back to Spain soon, too. The other day, my mom emailed me some old travel photos, and a few of them are from when we went to Europe in 2014." Lydia hadn't gone through all the pictures but loved that her mom had sent them. And although she cringed at the awkward clothes and hairstyles she'd been dumb enough to try, she mostly felt empathy and kindness towards her younger self.

Santi said *daebak*, which meant *awesome* in Korean, and added that he'd like to see them. Lydia warmed thinking of her and Santi making a night of going through their old pictures—she wanted to see his, too. Looking at him across from her, she imagined him as a cool, confident teenager—an artist with a sketchbook in his back pocket, a rainbow of paints smudging his fingers. She had an almost irresistible urge to draw and photograph Santi's details. The hair falling in his face, how the morning sunlight glinted off the small silver hoops in his ears when he turned his head.

"We should go," Santi said after more quiet.

Lydia checked her phone to see if she had a text from Selene or Jenny. Nothing.

"Let's do it," Lydia said, standing.

Lydia was shaky at first, and feeling chilly like she always did when she was nervous, standing in front of the classroom. The plan was for her to lead, but she dropped her note cards and asked Santi to start while she picked them up. He was calm and prepared. When she attempted to chime in, she stumbled over her words, looking to Penelope with an apology written all over her face. She also noticed Caleb's big green eyes and full smile and couldn't tell if he was being supportive or a jerk. Godzilla sat there in his Godzilla shirt, and Not Godzilla was in the back, talking to the guy next to him. Her cheeks got hot, and she needed to pee again. She cursed Jenny in her mind for fucking everything up.

"The slideshow will, um, show our ideas for the lantern festivals, including how we aim to create a multisensory experience, cover the lanterns with knits when they're not in use, and incorporate wind chimes to add sounds on the water. Of course the lanterns we've made aren't all true to size—most will be much bigger—but we want to show the assortment of shapes, styles, and colors that have inspired us," Lydia said, regaining scraps of confidence with every syllable that came out correctly. She and Santi had made a mock-up of a stream with foam and blue tissue paper in the giant galvanized tub they'd borrowed from the supply room; the bubble machine Santi had procured sent pops of water into the air.

As Lydia clicked on the LED tealights in the lanterns, Santi turned off the overhead lights and started the fan for the wind chimes. Lydia pulled up the lantern festival playlist—a mix of jazz and K-pop—on her phone and turned it down low. They let their classmates soak their senses in the moody ambiance for a little bit.

They turned the overhead lights on again, and Santi described the photos in the slideshow. When the sketches appeared, it was Lydia's turn, and their classmates flipped along in their color pamphlets. After the slideshow was finished, Santi held the lanterns up over the tub, describing them while Lydia fielded questions.

Santi ended by telling the class their ideas for on-site lantern-shaped photo booths and DIY-lantern vending machines, since the smaller lanterns were simple enough to be constructed on-site. They would make paint available as well—the same things they had at larger festivals, but with more focus on sustainability. He mentioned the magical feeling of the lantern festival on Cheonggyecheon Stream that he and Lydia had gone to together in November, saying things he hadn't told her about that night. Like how he'd never been to one before, and it'd made him feel like a kid again.

"So how will you adapt this to every city's festival?" Penelope asked with her arms crossed from the side of the room. She was wearing an icy-gray suit that matched the strip in her hair, and the combination made her seem downright villainous, although Lydia knew better.

But was her voice different? Colder? Was this the same teacher who had singled her out on the first day of class? Clearly, Lydia didn't have the same effect on people anymore, but she took a deep breath and steeled herself anyway.

"Thank you. Great question. Here you will see that Santi has sketched different flowers on the sides of the lanterns, representing each city's flower and colors. Since the paint is eco-friendly and some changes colors depending on sun or rain, we have options when it comes to decorations. A major bonus is that if it rains for a really long time during any of the festivals, the paint will wash away and dissolve into the same sort of products the city uses to keep the water clean, and the bottoms of the lanterns will release safe treats for the fish. The lanterns can also be re-painted and reused at a later date." After elaborating some more, Lydia finished by saying, "Some cultures believe that lighting a lantern and letting it float into the sky or setting it on the water to drift away is akin to a wish. We want our lantern festivals to feel like dreams . . . like wishes come true." Lydia got goose bumps, but she wasn't chilly anymore.

The satisfied look on Penelope's face let Lydia know that her and Santi's months of hard work had seriously paid off.

Lydia and Santi went out for food and drinks to celebrate. She felt confident their ideas would at least make it to the final round delivered to Kim Chinmae.

She checked in with Selene, who still hadn't heard anything from Jenny. Selene asked how the presentation went, and Lydia sincerely thanked her for that because Selene had so much going on, and remembering to ask was kind of her. They decided that if Selene didn't hear that Jenny was back in the Kim-Crawfords' condo by six o'clock, she was going to get Haru's number and text him to see if he knew anything.

"You look different. You *seem* different. I can't put my finger on it," Santi said after the waitress put two bottles of soju and two shot glasses on the table.

It's called charisma, buddy. I used to have it and now it's gone, never to be found again. A dark, lantern-less river of sadness rushed through her. *I hope you're safe, but fuck you, Jenny.* The river turned to bright red fire, burning.

"Do I? I wonder." They poured shots for each other. Lydia took hers and waited for him to take his.

"You look really pretty. You always look pretty, but something's different today. I'll let you know if I figure out what it is."

"Sounds like a plan," she said, smiling at him, pleasantly surprised and pouring him another shot immediately.

They were at an eatery in Mullae-dong, an art village where Santi had taken her on one of their first adventures to hunt for sculptures, and again a month later to visit the art store for supplies and an exhibit at one of the new galleries. The tiny streets of the village were lined with cafés and boutiques, and when the weather was warmer, the storefronts overflowed with green, flanked by carts filled with rainbows of flowers and round pops of fruit in front of the market.

Santi put the thinly sliced meat on the grill, and they drank as the pink turned dark, then darker on the heat. Lydia had grown emotionally attached to the hiss and smoke of it; now it only meant good things in her heart. It reminded her of long, fun dinners with Jenny and Selene and of getting to know Santi. Of entering restaurants before the sun went down and emerging to moonlight. She imagined that whenever she was back home in the United States and heard the sizzle of a grill, she'd want to look around for the friends she made in Seoul, expecting to see Santi's nose and the tiny diamond in it right in front of her like it was now.

They talked and talked, eating the steak along with kimchi, *sukju namul*, and rice—sometimes rolling it all up in bright, frilly lettuce to make *ssam* and gobbling it in one bite. They ordered another round of soju, mixing their leftovers with the kimchi fried rice they made at the end, devouring every last bit.

As they walked up the red stone steps of Santi's apartment building, Lydia's phone vibrated.

A chunk of text from Selene.

> Jenny's back. Rain came to the condo, brought
> Fox and Arwen to hang with the kids and I heard
> her mention to Aera that Jenny had just gotten
> back from Busan? I don't know whether she
> actually went there, or if it's just where she told
> them she was going. I haven't talked to her. I'm
> glad she's home safe, but I'm not going to text
> her or anything. Are you?

Lydia responded quickly.

> I'm glad she's home safe, too. Thank you for
> letting me know. I'm not going to text her either,
> but we can only avoid each other for so long,
> right? If we act weird with her, everyone else will
> pick up on it immediately. Guess we'll see what
> happens. But honestly? It really is SO
> DEPRESSING to think about the wishes being
> real . . . and now over.

> Agree. IDK what else to say. Enjoy your Santi
> time! Talk tomorrow. Love.

> Love.

What a relief that Jenny was back home from Jeju Island, no matter how mad Lydia was at her. Lydia was so happy about it, she blurted it out to Santi without thinking he might ask questions about why Jenny went to Jeju alone, but Santi only listened, adding a cheerful *glad to hear it*. He turned on sleepy music and they sat on his couch talking, still bubbling about their successful morning.

Santi's Sleepy Mix

"Indigo Night" by Tamino
"blossoms" by frad, bloom.
"Lover, You Should've Come Over" by Jeff Buckley
"WHY?" by Def.
"Okinawa" by 92914
"Vanilla Baby" by Billie Marten
"Numb" by Men I Trust
"Vete" by Biig Piig, Mac Wetha
"For Lovers" by Lamp
"FALL IN LUST" by EDEN, Jiselle
"Parfum d'étoiles" by Ichiko Aoba
"Mexican Dream" by Piero Piccioni
"Merry Christmas Mr. Lawrence" by Ryuichi Sakamoto
"3:00 AM" by Finding Hope
"magnolia" by keshi
"The Longing" by Tamino
"Present Tense" by Radiohead
"In A Good Way" by Faye Webster
"In a Sentimental Mood" by Duke Ellington, John Coltrane
"Sleep Well" by Jinyoung

Time was warm and pliant when Lydia was with Santi. She was surprised when she realized the sun had gone down without them noticing and surprised again when her stomach growled, since it seemed like they'd just eaten.

"Okay, say no more. Let's order something," Santi said.

"I really don't want to overstay my welcome. We already ate together once today." Lydia put her hand on her middle.

"So what? It's been hours and it's time to eat again," Santi said, scrolling through his phone. "*Chimaek?*" he asked cutely, using the portmanteau of the first syllables of the Korean words for *chicken* and *beer*, one of Lydia and South Korea's favorite combos. She also had a soft spot in her heart for *pimaek*, pizza and beer.

Lydia nodded as he was ordering, asking him to please make hers extra spicy.

"Tea while we wait?" Santi asked when he was finished, heading towards the kitchen.

Lydia nodded again and thanked him. As she heard him filling up the kettle, she checked her phone, wondering if Jenny had popped up in their group chat, but no. None of the guys she'd been casually texting had written, either. They usually didn't unless she reached out first, and why would they now that they were untethered from the wish? Lydia hated thinking about the rest of her time in Seoul not being as exciting and fun as the beginning. Whenever she imagined it, her mind turned into a disaster zone she couldn't sort out. She just stood there, staring at the rubble.

She got out her laptop and was opening her email when she remembered her mom had sent those old digital camera pictures. In London—there was a photo of Lydia and her dad next to a guard clad in red and black in front of Buckingham Palace, and another of Lydia alone, doing a dorky salute. There was one of her and her sister—both in overalls—in front of the Eiffel Tower. Her family made quite a few stops that summer. They'd taken the train to Spain, trading the Tate museum and the Louvre for the Museo del Prado in Madrid. Lydia had vivid memories of being overwhelmed by the blue of the ocean in Paul-Jacques-Aimé Baudry's *The Pearl and the Wave*. The museum had a class on color Lydia was allowed to join, and a small batch of students sat in front of the painting, re-creating that blue, sketching and painting their own versions. Afterwards, Lydia and her family went to a restaurant with a yellow door to get big, juicy cheeseburgers and fries, and when Lydia looked in the bathroom mirror, she saw tiny blue freckles on her nose and left them there.

She was overwhelmed with gratitude and nostalgia on Santi's couch—it'd been so long since she looked through these pictures. Her heart softened towards her mom, who'd been the one to suggest Lydia take the class. Her parents were always supportive of her art; it was the one part of her life her mom didn't criticize. Her mom had been the first person to recognize Lydia had artistic talent, and she never said no to Lydia when it came to art supplies. Lydia knew not every kid who was interested in art had parents like that or got to go to museums in London, Paris, and Madrid over the summer.

"Santi, I have those pictures my mom sent me, and you have to see how bad my hair was," Lydia said from the couch, laughing. She was looking at one photo of her on a tour bus in Paris where she'd clipped the front of her curls up with tiny glittery butterflies. She zoomed in and laughed, wishing she could tell the Lydia in the memory that one day she'd be hotter with much better hairstyles, in a pretty dress in Seoul, on a very cute boy's couch while he made her tea.

"Sweet. Just a sec," Santi said from the kitchen as the electric kettle thundered with bubbles.

Lydia enlarged the photos from Madrid. In one, she was sitting on a bench, and on the ground in front of her, there was a girl she remembered talking to about her shirt because Lydia was wearing a turquoise Hello Kitty shirt and the girl was wearing a green Keroppi shirt, another Sanrio character. They'd been amused by it. Behind them under the spotlights was a giant marble statue of two naked men mid-swordfight. Lydia zoomed in to see if she could read the artist's name but couldn't. She zoomed in on everyone, everything.

"I've gotta show you one kid in this picture from Madrid, specifically. He's wearing black clogs and royal blue socks just like you do." The kid in the picture even had one clog on its side and the other perched on top, the way Santi arranged his feet when he was sketching. Lydia zoomed in on the kid's dark, curly hair, which was covering most of his face.

She felt as if a swarm of bees were bumbling from side to side in her stomach, making their way through her body and blood to her chest. The kid in the picture had a small cloud-shaped birthmark splotch on his forearm, also like Santi.

The kid in the picture *was* Santi.

Lydia gasped so hard her throat closed up. She jumped from the couch and opened her mouth, but nothing came out, her entire body prickling with excitement until Santi poked his head out of the kitchen to see what was going on.

"What? What is it?" Santi asked, looking around the room for clues.

"Holy*yyy* shit, Santi! Look at this! You're in my picture. This is you! Isn't this you? June 2014 in Madrid at Museo del Prado?

This is me and this is you. Holy shit!" She shoved her laptop into Santi's hands.

"What?" he asked again, looking at it.

"That's you. That's *me* and that's *you*. You and me, look!" Lydia said, pointing to herself in the picture and then to him, doing it back and forth three more times.

"I—"

"Is that you?"

"Yes. Yes! It's me, but . . . I don't understand. What is this? How . . . did—"

"We were meant to meet. This is *proof*. It's why we kept bumping into each other outside of class, too. We took the same color class when we were both in Madrid, and we're both in Seoul in the same class right now. It's fate. It's *inyeon*! We were going to find our way to each other, no matter what," Lydia said to him, her heart beating like she was runningrunningrunning.

Inyeon was a Korean word referring to relationships, meaning a human connection was fated. The wish was the wish and *inyeon* was *inyeon*. She'd heard about it in a movie and read about it online before coming to Korea, fascinated by the idea. She remembered it again after falling in love with Jenny and Selene and how quickly they'd felt like sisters, like they were meant to be. Hye, Rain, and Aera had grown up together and stayed close, deciding to use the same au pair company so that Lydia, Jenny, and Selene could meet, become friends, and make their wishes. And now, after seeing this photo, Lydia was sure she and Santi had been destined to meet, too. They were *connected*. It'd happened the moment she saw him, this unstoppable desire to know him intensely, intimately, completely.

No wonder she'd fallen so hard so fast. *Providence*.

Lydia searched Santi's face, and for once, she knew exactly what was on his mind before he said it.

"Holy shit," they both said at the same time.

The deliveryman rang Santi's door as he and Lydia sat on the couch, letting their tea go cold, talking about that summer in 2014. They cracked open the beers immediately and left the chicken in the bag. Lydia was hungry but too overexcited to eat.

She'd never seen Santi so animated before. She was getting to experience a whole new collection of facial expressions and lifts in his voice. Sometimes he switched to Spanish when they were talking about Spain, then back to English. Occasionally he spoke in shocked Korean, like when he took Lydia's laptop so he could zoom in on the photo again. He said he used to go to Madrid every summer to visit his maternal grandmother; she was an artist as well. She always took him and his sister to the Museo del Prado, although his sister wasn't interested in art, and museums bored her to death. Santi's grandmother had passed away two years ago, but he still liked to go to the Museo del Prado during the summer. He had gone earlier that year, about a month before Lydia came to Seoul. He met his parents there the last time he visited Spain.

When Santi dug into the bag for the chicken, Lydia ate, too. It was the best chicken she'd ever had, and of course it was, because it was the best night she'd ever had.

"Now I know what's so different about you today," Santi said after licking sauce from his thumb. Lydia took great pleasure in watching him do it.

"What?" Lydia asked in Korean. Her lips tingled hot, and the bright bubbles of the beer kicked the heat into overdrive.

"All of this. The picture, the *inyeon*—you looking so beautiful. Like everything has been working up through the end of summer and fall, until now, to this moment." He looked at her intently, focused, like he was about to say something important, when the window caught his attention. "Ah, *and* it's snowing. See? Everything," Santi said, pointing over her shoulder. Lydia turned to see a bliss of snowflakes caught in the red-lanterned air. She smiled, entranced, but when she twisted back, the drumstick she was holding slipped onto her cream dress and slid into her lap, leaving behind a viscid orange skid mark. Lydia rolled her eyes as far back as they'd go, *pbbbpt*-ed her tongue out, cracking up at how violently the chicken had stained the fabric.

"Wait," Santi said, disappearing into his room. Lydia kept perfectly still, only turning her head so she could continue watching the snow fall outside the window. From where she was sitting, she could see it glow in a flurry across the slanted spaceship beam of the streetlight.

Santi pinched the drumstick between his fingers and put it on a napkin on the coffee table before handing Lydia a wet wipe from the bag. Once she'd cleaned her hands, he told her that he'd left some clean clothes on the bed for her.

"I can take your dress to the laundromat for you in the morning if you want me to," Santi said. She didn't need him to do that, but the thought of him putting her dress in a bag and waiting while it was washed and dried made her want to lie down. So domestic and couple-y! She had to sit on his bed in silence for a moment after closing the door.

Lydia stood in Santi's bedroom in her underwear, imagining being there for a sexier reason. She put on the oversized, ketchup-colored *España* sweatshirt that Santi had left out for her, and the matching sweatpants she had to cinch tightly at the waist. She asked him for a plastic bag, and she put her stained dress in it, shoved her tights into her purse. Santi handed her another beer, and Lydia wormed her arm out of the long sweatshirt sleeve to grab it.

"It's still snowing," Santi said with his nose-scrunch smile after another hour of beers and conversation. Lydia lit the candle on the table, and now the living room smelled faintly of tobacco and vanilla. His sister had given him that candle for Christmas, which prompted Lydia to ask him about his favorite Christmas presents growing up. They shared stories of Barbies and art sets, a synthesizer and stacks of books. He also showed Lydia a sketch he did of her when they were out at a bar together one night. Lydia hadn't known he was drawing her; she was busy sketching the vending machine, trying to capture the lantern-like glow of the fruit juices. Santi's sketch was of her profile, her hair falling across her face.

Lydia wondered what he thought of her back then, as he put his feelings onto paper. It was hard to believe, but finally, Lydia knew. She could see the proof of it in her hands. The way he'd captured the exact deep brown-red color of her hair, the near invisible freckle she had under her bottom lip.

He'd drawn her like she was the most special person in his life.

She touched the paper and told him how much she loved it, too overwhelmed to say more. Lydia leaned on the armrest of the couch, watching the snow fall harder. She was trying to figure out what this all meant when Santi said her name.

"Yes?" she said. Not drunk-drunk but floating on that fluffy pink cloud she liked to get on when she had a few drinks. He was looking at her again, gaze intense, and she held her breath a bit when he shifted closer to her.

Like everything has been working up through the end of summer and fall, until now, to this moment.

"I really want to kiss you. Can I? Please?" Santi asked. "I know I said that whole thing about us being friends, but what I meant is that I wanted to be sure, and I wanted *you* to be sure . . . I don't know if you still—"

They moved towards each other at the same time, and Lydia didn't say anything, just wrapped her arms around him and kissed him like it was the only thing that had ever mattered. Opened her mouth and let his tongue brush hers before pulling away quickly.

"What's wrong?" he asked with his eyes half closed.

"So are you *sure*? Because I'm sure."

"I mean . . . you had a ton of dates, you were texting a bunch of other guys—I didn't know if you were seriously interested in me, and . . . it takes me a long time to process things sometimes. But yes." He pushed her hair back from her face gently, looked straight into her eyes. "I'm absolutely sure."

"What about when I got a nosebleed? You didn't know I was seriously interested then, either?"

"That didn't count because you were drunk. Or *we* were drunk."

"What about every time we were together after that?"

"Sometimes I feel shy with you. I can't explain it . . . but today is different," Santi said, pressing his hands to her back and kissing her again.

"Can we go to your bed?" Lydia said as his mouth moved down her neck.

She was awed she didn't need a wish for this. Empty thoughts, tingly lips, slowly slipping fingers. Vanilla air as the snow fell softly outside the window. Santi making her come with his tongue before finally pressing himself inside her, until he *mmm*-ed and *mmm*-ed, his mouth against her ear. Hot together, cooling, then sleep. Her heart beating *Santi, Santi, Santi.*

17

Jenny

On Jeju Island, Jenny spent a good chunk of money for a room close to the villas where they'd stayed back in August. Last time she was on Jeju, she was with fourteen other people, feeling so safe and cared for. The spite that had driven her to book her flight, the revenge she wanted to enact on Lydia and Selene for not coming with her, the anger she felt at this being her last resort—those things crumbled to nothing once she sat on the hotel bed alone.

She'd told Rain that she was going to Busan to talk to Haru but to please keep it a secret and not say anything to him about it if he called. Jenny explained she wanted it to be a surprise, and Rain swore herself to secrecy, adding that she wasn't expecting to talk to Haru anyway, since he'd been so busy. She felt awful lying to Rain because she loved her, and even more terrible for keeping her relationship with Haru a secret in the first place. Jenny imagined a day in the near future when all of this would be over, when she and Haru could be out in the open about whatever relationship they had, when she wouldn't have to lie about anything because the wish would be a distant memory, merely a launching pad for the goodness to come.

Fuck you, Jenny, Selene had said the last time they talked. Jenny had cried out of anger then. Now, sitting on the bed in the room of that hotel, Jenny was crying out of loneliness.

The room was small, with a wide window facing the ocean; the linens smelled like Christmas—piney woods and sugar cookie snow. She arrived in the afternoon and let Rain know she was in "Busan" safe and sound. She sat in her room for a while and texted with her mom, letting her do most of the talking, not mentioning a word about what was going on, but sinking into the warmth she provided.

She texted Haru again, too.

> You're still not talking to me, but I miss you.
> There is an "us." You know there is. I came to
> Jeju alone to get a breather, but I told Rain I was
> going to Busan to find you. I didn't want to tell
> her you don't want to talk to me. I'm here for just
> one night and it's so cold, but the moonlight on
> the water will be worth it. I wish we could talk
> right now, but I'm looking forward to talking to
> you when you're back in Seoul. I'll be back
> tomorrow afternoon. I hope you're staying
> warm. I hope you're eating well, too. (I know you
> are.)

Jenny sent him the picture she took of their love lock at Nam-san Tower. Her stomach hurt; she'd barely eaten all day. She put on her warmest clothes and walked to the doughnut café ten minutes away.

Daniel and Haru had taken Fox and Arwen to the same café for milk crème doughnuts when they were there over the summer. That wintry afternoon on her own, Jenny ordered one milk crème doughnut and a hot coffee and sat at a table by the window. While packing for Jeju, she'd grabbed *Circle of Friends* by instinct, since she always threw it in her bag, but today the title was too painful. Jenny's circle of friends was fractured, and she was going to try to block it out for twenty-four hours the same way she'd had to train herself to block out thoughts of Ethan. Instead, she had brought a copy of *Kitchen*, by Banana Yoshimoto— a slim, cozy novel with a calming seafoam green cover that matched the thin bows clipped on the sides of her head. She'd forgotten she'd put Haru's sketch of her in the book for safekeeping. The one of her with big cartoony eyes and a bow. Jenny felt happy and sad remembering that game night and looked at the drawing for a long time before turning it facedown.

Jenny was able to focus on the book for about five minutes before a trio of girlfriends swished into the café in their winter coats and fuzzy hats. They sat two tables over from her and she heard *Fuck you, Jenny* in her head along with her own voice saying, *I don't want to talk to either of you.* Of course that wasn't true. She hated that she'd said it. She wanted to text Lydia and Selene and ask them to forgive her. She'd admit she'd been out of her mind and panicked—that part of her still was—but that she could've gotten her feelings across in a better way. Jenny just felt so stupid now, so embarrassed but committed to finishing what she'd started.

She wondered how long the three girls in the café had been friends. They filled the air with infectious energy that zapped across the room. It made her miss her own friends so much. The old ones, and Lydia and Selene, too. She'd reconnected some with her friends back home, texting them occasionally and liking their posts on socials. And it hadn't been that long since she last talked to Lydia and Selene, but it was still the longest they'd gone without checking in since they met. Now she heard Selene's voice saying *Fuck you, Jenny* on a high-speed loop.

Lydia and Selene were a gigantic part of her everyday life. Not only did they see one another at the families' condos and for their dinners, but they never missed their meetups on the balcony, or at the bar when it was too cold. If it wasn't karaoke, it was wandering and shopping. On top of that, they texted all day about the kids and their K-dramas and K-pop idols. About random memes and celebrity gossip they found. Selene was so good about making playlists and sharing them every week. Lydia would send pictures of her art in progress, and whenever Jenny found something adorable online or Haru made her something delicious, she'd share that, too. They talked fashion, their host families, their families back home. Anytime there was a new BTS, Seventeen, or Ateez photo shoot, they raced to see who could send the photos to the group chat the quickest.

She hated the thought of Lydia and Selene texting about her now. They were probably hanging out the same way the three of them always did, but without her.

Jenny promised herself she would apologize to both of them when she got back to Seoul. After she undid the wish, she'd tell them how sorry she was for acting how she had. Now, on Jeju, she had renewed faith that maybe Lydia's and Selene's wishes would stay intact, but even if they didn't, she believed, with Joon's help, Selene would find her real birth mother, and Lydia would continue to feel amazing about herself. In spite of her lingering sadness, Jenny forced herself to find new bursts of hope.

Back at the hotel, she decided to take a nap to help the time pass, then rewatched a comforting episode of Hye's K-drama on her laptop. When it was over, she looked out the window at the full moonlight on the water—milk spilling on ink.

She bundled up and put on her boots. Loaded up her backpack with a flashlight, water bottle, and her phone, along with the blanket she brought for the airplane. Then she left the hotel, stepping out into the clear night.

The path was easy to find on her own, and she was surprised to see small groups of people out in the cold like her, a few of them alone, too. The night would have been terrifying if not for the other people, armed with their own flashlights. If she thought about how scary it would be to walk into the darkness alone, she would've been able to talk herself out of coming, but like everything, she didn't want to deal with it until it was time, so she blocked it out. She willed herself to put one foot in front of the other until she heard the rushing water.

Until she could see the Waterfall of God.

The breezy warmth of that night in August was replaced with the wet island cold of December. Jenny shone her flashlight down at the stones, unstacked and waiting. A French-speaking couple nearby bent over and collected their own. Jenny wanted to warn them to be *careful, careful.*

Maybe if she was careful and stacked only three stones—two for herself and one more for good measure—the only wish undone would be hers. She really cared about Selene finding her birth mother and would never want to do anything to hinder that, and it was so selfish of her to consider Lydia's wish unimportant since Lydia could say the same about Jenny's.

It hit her all at once. This was stupid. She didn't have to do this. She'd had a lot of time alone to unravel her thoughts, and no matter how much she rolled everything around in her mind, she couldn't get over how ridiculous this all was. Breaking what she had with Lydia and Selene because she was afraid she wouldn't be able to love Haru was nonsense, right? All in her head. She refused to fracture her girlfriendships over a guy.

My wish was overdramatic and ridiculous. All of this is overdramatic and ridiculous.

Jenny was instantly overwhelmed with relief as she flirted with the idea of just walking away.

There has to be another way. Wishes, bad luck. I don't have to believe in any of this if I don't want to. I know my heart, I do. I can trust myself. The waterfall roared, and that same warm, floaty feeling she got last time she was on Jeju rang through her body.

Under the moonlight, with the cold-cold air wrapping around her, she looked at the unstacked stones one last time before turning and walking back the way she came.

Jenny's first flight was delayed, so she didn't get to Seoul until early evening. She thought she saw Haru standing there holding a sign with her name on it as she walked through the terminal and then laughed at herself for being so delusional.

Until she heard him say her name.

"What?" Jenny said, looking at him, the *JENNY* sign in his hand.

"What, what?" Haru said, taking the handle of her carry-on suitcase.

She blinked at him once, twice. "How long have you been here?"

"I came earlier, but your flight was delayed, so I went to my car and slept until you arrived."

"But why are you here? You haven't been responding to my texts."

"*Because* it was crazy for you to go to Jeju by yourself and lie about it to my sister. I wanted to get here before you did anything else because apparently you can't be left alone."

Jenny swatted at his arm, but he caught her hand and scooped her into a hug, lifting her off the ground.

"I can't believe you're really here," Jenny said, shaking her head. She never dreamed Haru would do something like this. He'd gotten his hair trimmed, and she put her hand on the back of his neck where his hair was much shorter now, kissed his cheek. She didn't know how soon or even if they'd return to kissing again like nothing had happened, so she didn't want to push it, but her entire body felt like a puppy's violently wagging tail when she looked into those brown eyes she knew so well.

"Well, like I said, I had no choice. Can't have you out here getting yourself lost or kidnapped or killed, can I? Come on," he said. He took her hand, leading her to the exit.

The trip from Busan to Seoul was over four hours; Haru had spent a big chunk of his day driving and waiting for Jenny to get back from Jeju Island. Even if it had taken a bit of time for her to relax into her decision to not undo the wishes, she'd made the right choice—she knew that. It might also take time for this new heart-trusting thing to make its way to her brain. She wanted to stop being in a rush to have everything all figured out.

Looking out the window as the city whooshed by, she prayed for patience.

She'd never been in the passenger seat with Haru driving, never been alone with him in a car like this. Occasionally he would put his hand on her thigh and squeeze. Sometimes she reached over and touched his hair again, let her fingertips linger on the lobe of his ear.

"I hated not talking to you," she said as they got closer to Gangnam. Haru stopped at a red light and looked over at her.

"I was really upset. I'm still upset. I don't understand why you did what you did," he said after some quiet, moving forward when the light turned green again.

"Do you want to talk about it?"

She did. She didn't know what she wanted to say, but she didn't want him going silent again. She loved the noise of him, the sound of him saying her name and knowing he was in the condo because he was laughing too loud with Rain about something in the kitchen. His trot music and hip-hop blasting on the other side of the bathroom door when he was in the shower.

"No," he said, patting her leg but not squeezing.

Three more minutes of silence until he pulled into the condo's parking garage.

Jenny and Haru showing up at the condo together made Jenny's lie about going to Busan look true, which was a nice bonus. Rain and Daniel didn't pry, and Jenny kept herself busy with the kids, making a dramatic fuss about missing them so much she *had* to come back as soon as possible.

"What did you do in Busan? Mommy was born in Busan," Arwen said as she got underneath the blankets in her bed.

"Oh, I just wandered around and saw some pretty things. I also saw your uncle." Jenny took extra time fluffing Arwen's pillow, telling her again how much she had missed her.

"We had fun with Nabi and Selene, too. Selene's good at video games. Did you know that?" Fox asked from the corner as he rooted through their manga collection, hunting for the one he wanted to read before bed.

Jenny's heart pinched at hearing Selene's name, thinking of Fox and Arwen spending time with her. She was nervous to see

Lydia and Selene. She wondered if they all really were as close as Jenny once thought. If they were, they'd be able to get over this, right? It didn't have to be a big deal. Jenny especially regretted accusing Selene of lying about finding out Deiji wasn't her birth mother after all. She knew Selene would never do that—she'd only said it because she was mad and wanted them to be her sisters in this, a trio with an unbreakable bond.

She imagined Selene cross-legged on the floor next to Fox, playing video games with him. "She *is* good at them, isn't she? She beats me every time," Jenny said, pointing to herself.

"Maybe all of us can play together when we go up there for dinner tomorrow," Fox said.

Shit. Jenny had forgotten the families' dinner tomorrow night, and although she was planning on talking to Lydia and Selene tomorrow-ish and letting them know she didn't undo the wishes, she didn't want the first time she saw them to be in front of everyone. She wanted to meet with them alone. She considered texting the group chat, asking if they would be available in the morning, but she knew she couldn't handle any potential excuses they might come up with for avoiding her.

"Such a good idea," Jenny said after Fox got into bed in his room with his book. She let him know he had fifteen minutes to read, then lights-out.

Haru caught Jenny looking in the fridge, and whenever Haru caught Jenny looking in the fridge, an unrelenting quiz show of when and what she'd last eaten ensued.

"Basically nothing since yesterday, okay? Busted," she said, holding her hands up.

"Nothing except what I had in the car?" Haru asked. He'd

picked her up from the airport fully stocked with snacks—banana milk, fizzy strawberry juice, buttercream bread, Pepero, spicy dried squid strips—but no, she hadn't eaten properly in days. She hadn't eaten *super* properly since before he left for Busan. Between her fight with him and her fight with the girls, her stomach was having a battle of its own, and while she could snack here and there and pick at her dinner, it'd been a bit since she'd deliberately sat at a table and eaten anything substantial.

Jenny shook her head as Haru clicked his tongue in disappointment.

He made them both bowls of shrimp ramen with eggs—kimchi and rice on the side. They ate it with the *oi muchim* and *dubu-jorim* Rain had made earlier in the week. And they were both pleasantly surprised Daniel's latest pomegranate "salad" kitchen experiment wasn't so bad.

"I eat too much when I'm with you. I get overfull," Jenny said across the table to Haru when they were finished. It was late, and Rain and Daniel were in bed. The condo lights were dim and the Christmas tree in the living room sparkled with white twinkles and colored, mirrored ornaments.

Nighttime had always been *their* time, and being in the condo with him in the dark again—when last night she had been alone in the cold moonlight—made her brain wobble with happiness. She leaned forward, blinking pretty eyes.

"Ah, don't look at me like that," Haru said, leaning back, not snared by her trap so easily. "We still have a lot to discuss."

She made the cutest face she possibly could and widened her eyes some more. "Look at you like what?" She was so tired of overthinking everything. She wanted Haru to swipe the dishes off the table and hook his arm around her waist. Kiss her because it'd been so long. Too long. How would she deal with him being all the way in New Zealand? She let those thoughts pour out of her mouth, desperate for the intimacy she'd missed when he was gone.

"Jenny, I told you I loved you."

"I know, and that means so much to me. I can't explain to you why I was so scared—"

"Well, I wish you would've tried."

"I *will* try. You stopped responding to my texts."

"I was too upset."

"And now?"

"I want to know why you can't tell me how you feel about me in real words. Why's it so hard for you?"

"I promise I will. I'm still catching my breath," she said. *My heart is slowly settling, and I am learning to trust it. Please, just wait a little longer.*

A soft sigh escaped his mouth.

"What about the blind date?" she asked.

"You're not allowed to care about things like that, right? We're not a couple, we're not exclusive, so I can go on a date, and you can go on a date," Haru said, standing. He cleared off the table. Jenny stood, too, helping him with the rest.

"Haru, I don't want to go on a date with anyone else."

"So, what *do* you want?" He rinsed a bowl and put it in the dishwasher.

"*You*," she said, handing him a spoon.

She both did and didn't want to know if he'd kissed the dental hygienist, but since Haru was being so honest with her and it was nighttime and she'd missed him so much, she had to ask.

"I did not," Haru answered.

"Apparently, she's thinking about what she wants the two of you to name your babies. I know I said maybe the date would lead to something incredible, but . . . you know I would've been so jealous if you'd kissed her," Jenny said, relieved.

"*Do* I know that?"

"Yes." She hugged him tightly from behind. When he turned, she got on her tiptoes and kissed him as the water ran hard into the sink. "Please, can you let me show you how sorry I am? Will you come to my bedroom?" she whispered. Her hands were under his T-shirt, palms spread across the warm skin of his back.

"For what?"

"Stop it."

"Stop what?"

He leaned back against the counter.

"You're serious? You won't come to my bedroom?" Jenny put her hand on his chest, not *really* worried he was turning her down, but willing to play this game with him.

"Is that what you want? For me to come to your bedroom?" Haru said with his eyes on hers and an even deeper voice than usual. Jenny's legs felt light. She nodded slowly.

"Gimme a sec," he said after a painfully long pause. He kissed her neck, slowly squeezed her ass, and then gently pushed her towards her room.

Jenny was naked under her blankets when Haru opened the door, but he didn't get under with her. He sat on top of the comforter and turned on the lamp. His face was solemn, like he was half a second away from bursting into tears. What the hell had happened between the kitchen and her bedroom?

"Jenny, are you pregnant? Is that what's going on?" There was a dark zap in his voice—a shock felt through a fluffy pillow.

"What? No! Why would you ask that?"

"So the positive pregnancy test in the other bathroom isn't yours?"

"No, Haru. It's not mine. I haven't taken a pregnancy test. I don't need to. My period just ended a few days ago. Plus, you know how careful we've been! It must be . . . Rain's," Jenny said, opening her mouth in surprise. Oh, wow, Rain was pregnant! Fox and Arwen were going to have another sibling, and Jenny felt nothing but absolute joy at the thought of this. Slowly, Haru's expression relaxed.

"Okay. *Whew.* My mind was like—" Haru said, miming a head explosion. He relaxed his posture, finally letting it sink in that she was naked underneath the covers. He lifted them and took a peek before smiling at her.

"I'm so excited for everyone!" Jenny said, sitting up, suddenly distracted.

Rain and Daniel's love was real and growing. She wanted to say this aloud, but she didn't want to say the word *love* to Haru because she didn't want to argue. Instead, she put her hand between her naked breasts, on her heart.

"I am, too. But . . . you don't think it's our fault, do you? Like, because I used Daniel's condoms?"

Jenny covered her mouth. "We haven't had to do that lately, and you put them back, right? You never left the box empty."

"There may have been a couple days when I swiped one or two, and *maybe* there wasn't a box on a couple nights. I don't know." Haru kissed her, finally. "No one's mentioned it. No one's counting them."

"Haru!" she said.

"It's definitely not our fault. We don't know their business," he said, shaking the thoughts from his head, moving to kiss her again, more deeply this time.

Jenny pulled back slightly. "Do you have your *own* tonight?"

"Yes. I have my own." He touched his pocket so she could hear the crinkle.

"You didn't buy them for someone else? Someone in Busan?" She hated thinking it and hated asking it even more.

Haru removed his shirt and turned the lamp off, checked to make sure the door was locked just like he used to.

"I bought them for us. If there *is* an us," he said, walking back towards her.

"There is an us, Haru," Jenny whispered, pulling him to her. All she wanted were his lips and hands and teeth.

Still, he held back, and Jenny felt like she would scream. "Our baby would be really cute, though," he said after a moment, laughing lightly.

"*So* cute," she agreed, but she'd been patient enough. She took his hand and directed it exactly where she wanted him to touch her in the dark. He didn't have it in him to resist her anymore after that.

The next evening, Jenny and Rain were in Rain's bedroom as she decided what to change into for dinner. She'd invited in Jenny for advice, saying she wanted to turn her brain off completely after a long day of root canals, dental implants, and convincing children who hated the dentist that she wasn't a monster. Jenny eyed her for any signs of pregnancy but found none.

"I hate my clothes today," Rain said, standing in her closet with her hands on her hips.

"It's all in your head—your wardrobe is killer, and you always look cute. What about this sweater and a pair of comfy jeans?"

Jenny said, pointing to a pretty Kermit-colored sweater on the bed. Rain popped out to look at it.

"*You* always look cute," Rain said to her. Jenny was wearing a wine-red velvet turtleneck with a pair of dark jeans. She'd pulled her hair up in a ponytail and wrapped the ribbon Haru had given her around it. She thought of how Haru had tenderly tied that ribbon around her wrists one night last month and wouldn't untie her until he made her come three times.

She crossed her legs and told Rain *thank you* in formal Korean, hoping she wasn't blushing too much.

"Green is so pretty on you. Don't overthink it."

"Can I tell you something and have you promise not to say anything to the kids?"

"Of course."

"I'm pregnant," Rain said, covering her mouth with both hands. "Barely," she said after letting her arms fall back to her sides. She explained that she took the test yesterday and hadn't made a doctor's appointment yet.

Jenny hugged her tightly and congratulated her over and over again, giving an Oscar-worthy performance of happy astonishment.

"We wondered what would happen if we tried one more time, and surprise! Daniel knows already, and I'll tell Haru tonight." Jenny beamed as Rain continued. "We're excited but not telling the kids yet. We'll wait until after Christmas and the recommitment ceremony. *Too* much excitement, you know what I mean?" She held a long black skirt up to her waist, and Jenny gave her a double thumbs-up. "You're okay with taking care of *three* kids? Obviously, I'll pay you more. I'd love for you to stay on for at least one more year if you can. Honestly? Probably two."

"Absolutely," Jenny said gleefully. The thought of staying with the Kim-Crawfords, of being in Seoul as long as they wanted her, warmed Jenny up so much, she was certain she was blushing now.

Jenny slid off her shoes in the Chois' foyer after waiting for the Kim-Crawfords to take theirs off. Gureum popped over, wagging his tail in a tiny striped sweater, sniffing at her feet. Jenny scooped him up to pet him, let him lick her cheek. She straggled on purpose, deeply dreading the moment she would see Lydia and Selene. Letting them know she didn't take back the wishes should solve 90 percent of the problems they had with her. It was the other 10 percent that worried her.

She saw Lydia in the living room first and smiled at her; Lydia barely gave a slight smile back. Eun had spilled red juice down the front of his sweater, and Lydia was helping him get it off. Arwen's tights were twisted, so Jenny lifted the hem of her dress and fixed them.

"Lyd, have you seen Nabi's iPad?" Selene asked. She stopped when she saw Jenny but looked away quickly to talk to Lydia again. "It was on the couch earlier. It's in the pink case. Please let me know if you see it. I'll be upstairs in her room until it's time to eat," Selene said, turning and going back up the staircase.

"Will do," Lydia said to her before getting on her hands and knees to search under the couch.

Selene had looked at Jenny so coldly, she wanted to cry. She deserved it, but it still hurt. She fought back tears, not wanting to have a breakdown in the Chois' living room.

Arwen and Eun disappeared with Selene upstairs, and after Lydia exhausted every possible iPad hiding spot in the living room, she went upstairs, too. The host parents filled the kitchen with chatter and laughter. Since Daniel was American, Jenny's ears could catch the Korean he spoke. She knew they were talking about the *ganjang-gejang* Minsu made last month and how Hye didn't enjoy raw crab, no matter how fresh it was.

Tonight dinner was spicy beef-and-vegetable soup, and Jenny only sipped at it until Haru surprisingly showed up, which made her feel both hungrier and less alone. The December cold made her crave meat and warmth, hot bowls of vegetables in broth to fill her up, make her feel cared for. She looked at Haru standing by the oven with a spoon, talking to Minsu and Geon about how delicious everything was.

Wasn't love wanting to be near someone as much as possible and making sure they were safe, warm, and well-fed? Wasn't love wanting the absolute best for someone and feeling sad and confused when they were sad and confused? Happy when they were happy? Ethan was the only guy Jenny had ever loved, but that love wasn't the only kind of love Jenny could feel. Maybe she didn't want to love anyone in *exactly* the same way she'd loved Ethan. And maybe that was impossible, anyway, since no two people or relationships were the same.

Jenny looked at Lydia and Selene and faked a smile only so Rain or Haru wouldn't ask what was wrong. Selene looked away. Jenny couldn't hear everything they said, but she did hear Lydia mention Santi's name and touch her cheek. Jenny wondered what had happened. The girls would also notice she and Haru were back on friendly terms, and she imagined them wondering what was going on. So much had happened in the couple of days they hadn't spoken, and Jenny was dying to apologize, tell them how much she loved them, that how much they loved one another was what got her to change her mind on Jeju.

But Lydia and Selene were ignoring her. She'd forgiven them for not coming to Jeju with her, but maybe they couldn't forgive her, even if they knew she didn't go through with it. Jenny sat there until she couldn't stand it any longer and excused herself to the bathroom. When she saw Haru waiting for her in the hallway afterwards, she walked directly into his outstretched arms.

18

Selene

Ignoring Jenny at dinner last night made Selene feel gross, but ignoring major things in her life until she was ready to deal with them had become a pattern lately. With the saved energy, she'd been texting back and forth with her parents, sending them photos of Seoul. She cherished the photos they passed along— selfies, the new bookcase her dad made, the stray marmalade cat her mom had gotten attached to on her evening walks.

Joon had been calling and texting, and both Bitna and Deiji had reached out, too, but Selene couldn't bring herself to respond to any of them until the morning Joon wrote her an email.

Hey Selene. I am continuing to look for your birth mother. I don't know exactly what you're feeling right now, but whatever it is, don't let that keep you from searching. I will let you know if I find anything, and I also want you to know how much I care about you. That's not dependent on whether you respond to my messages or want to see me.

Even after everything, he was helping her. Despite her embarrassment, she couldn't hold herself back any longer. She wrote:

Joon, I'm sorry I've been ignoring you. It's not what I WANT to be doing, I promise. I'm fucking *mortified*. You, your mom, Deiji . . . you all went out of your way to help me . . . to welcome me in as part of your family, and I let my imagination run wild. I'm so relieved we're not RELATED, obviously, but I'm too ashamed to see any of you right now. I can't believe I'm typing this all out and sending it to you, but . . . you've been the best. I care about you so much, Joon. I *really* do.

She hit send, surprised when she heard her email ping a few minutes later with his reply.

Ok. So, what if we meet up . . . just the two of us, and we don't talk at all? Just get coffee? NO pressure. Eventually we'll work up to getting my mom and Deiji involved? (They both love you so much, and neither one is angry with you, just so we can clear that up quickly.) Would you do that for me? Because I really *really* want to see you. 1pm this afternoon at the same café near Gwanghwamun Square we went to that time it rained? It may snow again today. Our precipitation café. I could pick you up?

She didn't hesitate this time.

I'll meet you there.

Neither did he, thirty seconds later.

See you very soon, Selene. It's cold. Please dress warmly.

After dropping Nabi off with Lydia so she could hang with Tae and Eun, Selene went down into the subway, exiting at Gwang-hwamun station to the view of Bugaksan Mountain through a froth of light snow. She got to the café before Joon and ordered a coffee, choosing a table by the window. Multicolored lights were strung from end to end, and speakers piped out peppy Christmas music. Selene got a text from Joon letting her know he was going to be five minutes late. When he got there, he came over to her and pulled the text up on his phone. Pointed to it, miming that he was sorry he got stuck in traffic. She mirrored him, nodding that she understood.

Joon looked alarmingly handsome as he took his coat off, revealing a thin black blazer over a white T-shirt and black pants. The blazer sleeves were rolled up, revealing white-gray plaid. He had his same black bag, same watch, same gray suede sneakers. It was such a relief knowing that no matter the chaos of the past couple weeks, Joon would still be wearing the same things he always wore, that his pretty eyes and eyelashes would be behind his glasses whether he was wearing his round ones or the black frames. The merciless angles of his beautiful cheekbones were the same; his face was the same. He was steadily and certifiably Joon, even when the rest of life baffled her.

Selene thought back to him taking his glasses off when they were together at Deiji's. She wanted to close her eyes and put her head down on the table, remembering Joon's slow, royal kisses, how he spread his legs so she could melt between them on Deiji's soft couch. His problem-solving skills were incredibly attractive, too; he'd gotten her to get over herself and meet him out for coffee. She had a hard time thinking of anyone else who could sweet-talk her into doing that so easily.

He ordered at the counter, and she knew he'd get a snack, too, because the boy loved to eat. He came back to the table with his cup and a small white cake covered in a cloud of red frosting, decorated with fondant Christmas trees and garlands. Joon put a bite on his fork and held it out for her. She shook her head no. He kept holding it, motioning for her to eat. She leaned forward, let him put the cake in her mouth—vanilla buttercream and sweet cranberry jam. He motioned for her to finish the whole bite on the fork, so she did. Only then did he take a bite for himself. They took turns eating until it was gone.

Selene went through her Instagram comments and responded to some, doing the same for the Sobok Sweet account. She scrolled through the photos Joon had taken of her.

Thinking of all the *before* made her sad.

Before Jenny undid the wishes and *before* Selene had gotten Bitna and Deiji so wrong.

She zoomed in on a photo, one Joon had taken as she'd pinned the back of a *hanbok* blouse during a model's fitting. Selene remembered how good she'd felt that day. How buoyant she was when she and Joon went to Bitna's afterwards for tea and cookies in the slanting autumn sun—the orange of it glowing Joon's dark brown eyes to amber.

She watched him tapping away on his laptop, wondering what he was doing. He stayed so busy as a freelancer, but he never seemed stressed or hurried, and although it'd been a year since he returned from his military service, he still carried an air of discipline left uneclipsed by his easygoing nature.

Selene loved him.

It hadn't happened all at once. That wasn't how love had ever worked for her. She could only say for certain that she'd been in love one other time, with her early college boyfriend, and it had happened slow then, too—that same incessant *drip-drip-drip*ping until she looked down and saw she was knee-deep in it. This Joon-love had swelled until it burst, and looking at him now, no part of her was unsure of what she felt.

Selene wanted to open her mouth and tell him, but they were committed to their weird, silent afternoon in the café, and Selene admitted to herself that sitting like this without the pressure of talking or explaining anything was making things easier. Like taking her time to get her body used to a hot bath—a toe, an ankle, the tickle of her stomach swooping down. She watched the snow swirl as it fell harder outside the window, watched the people walking by with their bags and long coats. A woman in a saffron puffer jacket pulled a cart of groceries from one end of the square to the other and disappeared.

Selene and Joon took breaks from people-watching and their devices, looking into each other's eyes.

I love you in the midst of all this craziness, she thought, hoping her thoughts were telepathically beaming into his brain.

After about an hour, Joon put his laptop away and motioned to the window, meaning maybe they should leave. She agreed. Once they were outside, she opened her mouth to speak. He shook his head no, put his finger to his lips. He mimed driving again and took her hand as they walked through the snow. When a speedy food-delivery guy on a scooter came near, Joon tucked Selene close to him, protecting her under his arm.

Joon opened the car door for her and turned up the heater as soon as he sat behind the wheel.

"I don't want you to be cold. Are you cold?" he asked. She shook her head no, so toasty already, so wholly thankful to hear his deep voice again.

He handed her a small bag of persimmons from the back seat, telling her Bitna wanted her to have them. Selene blinked in the bright of that dazzling, undeserved kindness. Joon's car smelled like his neck: rose petals and handsomeness. She unzipped her coat, lifted her sweater carefully to show him she was wearing the Tears for Fears kitten T-shirt he'd brought back from Japan. She took out one cold persimmon, cupped it like a fragile baby animal. Such an unreal, perfect fruit. She asked Joon to teach her how to say *persimmon* in Korean, and he told her the name of the kind she was holding, but that there were different names for them depending on their color and ripeness. He listed, she repeated. She breathed him in, looked at his sweet face, and dove in completely.

"Joon, I'm sorry. For everything. I'll go to your mom's tomorrow and apologize to her and Deiji. I'm so——" Selene was interrupted by his kiss.

She never wanted to stop kissing him; she wanted to greedily gulp him down like an effervescent vitamin. She *loved* him. She hadn't expected to come to Seoul to fall in love. She hadn't wanted it! What she'd wanted was to find her birth mother. Maybe that would never happen, and she had no choice but to accept it. But what Selene *had* found was a home with the Chois, with Lydia and Jenny, too, even though she and Jenny had making up to do. And she'd found a home with Bitna, Deiji, and Joon. They may not have been her "real" family—and she was *exceedingly* (!) thankful for that when it came to Joon—but they were still her family. She hadn't wished for them, but thanked God she got them anyway.

Selene was nervous again the next day in front of Bitna's door.

She'd talked to Joon on the way over and knew he was there, which was reassuring, but her hands still shook when she tapped on the wood. The smell of beef and garlic coming from inside made Selene hyperaware of her stomach. She whispered *I'm hungry* in Korean to no one.

Joon opened the door like he said he would and wrapped her in a hug, cradling her head gently. They lingered. Selene took off her boots and put on slippers; Joon was wearing a pair the same color.

"Mom is making *dduk mandu guk*."

She loved dumpling soup and had been craving its warmth so often now that the days were colder and darker. The longest night of the year would be coming soon, and Selene appreciated the familiar smells and tastes of a Korean kitchen——so dependable and so able to keep Selene's heart afloat. Being in Seoul made her realize that Korean food was a part of her life in a bigger way than just going to a Korean restaurant with her family back home. Every now and then, her mom had made a point of attempting Korean dishes in the kitchen Selene grew up in, and she was grateful for that. A couple times a year, they went to the Asian grocery store together, and Selene marveled at how different it was from the other grocery stores they went to. How the scallions and pears were bigger and there was a better assortment of seafood. Down every aisle, she'd hear a different language being spoken, see a new-to-her ingredient.

Selene's parents were busy and not particularly interested in food outside of basic sustenance, so neither of them ever spent hours and hours in the kitchen. She loved the stark difference she'd experienced in Seoul. Bitna was always in the kitchen, patiently chopping and boiling things, however long it took. The Chois and the other two families crowded in the kitchens on the nights they had dinner together, sharing space at the stove. Selene had always found comfort in the sight and smells of Korean food and grocery stores, no matter where she was. She wanted that comfort to remain inside her forever.

"Selene-*ah*, come here and help me make the *mandu*," Bitna said from the kitchen.

Selene felt small enough to sit underneath a mushroom when she saw Bitna's face. She said hello and bowed slightly, addressing Bitna in formal Korean. Selene apologized for accusing her of lying and for how she acted. Bitna held up her flour-covered hand.

"*Mandupi*," Bitna said, pointing at a small stack of the dumpling wrappers she'd made. "We'll make them extra big so plenty of yummy things will fit inside."

The dough was cut into disks, and Bitna rolled one until it was as thin as she wanted, explaining that they shouldn't be too thick in the middle. She instructed Selene to wash and dry her hands. When that was done, Bitna handed Selene the rolling pin.

Selene heard Joon's camera click behind her. She turned to see him standing back, taking pictures of both her and Bitna. He whirled his index finger.

"I never let men tell me what to do, but I listen to you. I can't explain it," Selene said, turning around like he'd asked.

"I'm honored," Joon said.

She rolled the dough thinly, ignoring the camera clicks. The pot of boiling beef and garlic bubbled with gusto on the stove, and Bitna reached over to turn the heat down.

"Shrimp, chives, tofu," Bitna continued. She pointed to the

bowl, poured in two tablespoons of sesame oil, and stirred. She waited patiently while Selene finished making the wrappers; then Bitna took one in her hand and scooped the mixture out of the bowl with the other, filling it and folding it over, crimping the ends until the dumpling was a perfect, puffed pouch. "That's one. We need about fifteen for *dduk mandu guk*, and we'll freeze the rest for New Year's Eve. We don't do much on that night, but the fireworks are pretty and our Joonie likes when we have *mandu*. This is probably the last New Year's Eve he'll be living with me," Bitna said, turning to look at her son.

"Why?" Selene asked as she scooped, filled, folded, and crimped. Her dumpling looked far from the beauty of Bitna's, but she was proud of it.

"He will probably get married and have his own home soon. He travels so much, and he is in love, but clearly you know that already," Bitna said, winking at her.

Selene set another dumpling on the plate with the others and waited for Joon to speak, but he was at the table on his laptop now, typing quietly.

"Oh." Selene smiled slowly, knowing her cheeks were glowing with warmth. "Well, I'm sure he'll be here all the time anyway. Sons always find a reason to come back to their mothers' tables."

"That is true," Bitna said, taking an extra-long look at Joon, who was still typing. He turned to both of them when he was done, smirking and pretending he hadn't been listening.

The door keypad beeped and Deiji announced herself. As soon as she stepped into the kitchen, Selene bowed slightly and said hello and apologized in formal Korean, the same way she had to Bitna. Deiji's bracelets jingled as she hugged Selene around the waist and kissed her cheek. She heard Deiji saying *I wish you were mine* again and started to cry.

"No crying, *gangaji*," Deiji said to her, holding her face. *Gangaji* was the Korean word for *puppy*, a sweet term of endearment coming from Deiji since Selene heard her call Joon *gangaji* often, too.

"I was wrong and I'm so very sorry," Selene said to Bitna, Deiji, and Joon, now that everyone was there. The lights went wobbly through Selene's tears.

"Selene-*ah*," Bitna said, motioning at her to move closer, "no more crying. You have more dumplings to make before we can eat."

Everyone ate their fill of *dduk mandu guk* at the table and complimented Selene on her *mandu*.

"I don't want to make my mom jealous by saying yours are as good as hers, but——" Joon said.

"It's okay because I taught her everything she knows!" Bitna said.

"I know you missed this sort of thing while you were growing up, but it's nice your parents tried to expose you to Korean culture as much as they could," Deiji said, standing. She kept her cigarettes in a silver case in the zipped pocket inside her bag. She got it out and grabbed her orange lighter, walked back to the table. She always smoked one cigarette after their meals, and her ritual was familiar and soothing to Selene. "Join me?" she asked Selene.

They put on their coats and stepped onto the balcony. It was nearing sundown and the sky had taken on a pink sorbet light.

"The sky makes me believe in God," Deiji said, sparking her

cigarette. "When my faith is cracked, there's still the sky." She held her arm up and out.

"It's hard to take in the glory of it."

Deiji made the same closed-mouth sound of acknowledgment that Joon sometimes did. Selene loved noticing the small similarities they had, and how all those tiny things combined with big things to make a family *feel* like a family. It wasn't until Selene was in middle school that she realized she couldn't ever look to her adoptive parents for traits that had been passed down to her.

Selene imagined Deiji was her real mother as she watched her smoke. Namsan Tower rose in the distance, a beacon of hope. A reminder that broadcasts could be beamed all over the world, that connection was possible. One thing absent in Selene's life growing up was the beauty of Seoul, so she never took views like this for granted. The street Bitna's apartment complex sat on was busy with Christmas shoppers and people bundled in their winter best, wandering, hunting for dinner. Selene and Deiji peered down, watching them. Selene looked towards the intersection where she was found, remembering how gentle Joon had been with her the first time she was there.

When Deiji was finished with her cigarette, she snuffed it out in the glass ashtray on the table. Her fingernails were painted the deepest red they could be and still be called red and not black. Deiji took her bottom lip between her thumb and index finger and squeezed. She sighed.

"I was forty years old when I realized how easy it is to love a person, if you just let yourself," Deiji said. "I hope you are letting yourself love our Joonie without thinking about it too much."

Selene took in a deep, intentional breath of cold air as Deiji continued.

"The moment I saw you, I knew he would fall in love with you. If you love him, love him, and let yourself be loved."

"I do. I will," Selene said, tearing up again.

"I know," Deiji said, hugging her.

"Thank you for forgiving me."

"Forgiveness is what family is for, *gangaji*."

Deiji was heading to Daegu for two days with her boyfriend so they could visit his siblings, so she left to meet him after one more cup of tea. Selene and Bitna were on the couch watching *Something in the Rain* in the Christmas tree light, waiting for Joon to return from the store with milk and eggs. Selene was reminded of Jenny since she'd mentioned the K-drama was next on her list. Again, she thought of how hard it was to ignore Jenny at dinner, how immaturely Selene had behaved, too, but all she wanted to do now was text Jenny and tell her that she'd been right about how much *blazing* chemistry the main couple in the show had, and how she was right about the male lead, too, because he was both handsome and sweetly cute enough to melt the TV.

Bitna pressed the mute button on the remote. "I still believe you'll find your birth mother, but our relationship is much bigger than that now."

"Deiji said earlier that the sky always makes her believe in God, and the two of you make me feel that way, too. How you open your home, feed me at your table, forgive me with an open heart. I want to be more like you."

And just like that, her body flooded with relief. She was ready to forgive Jenny and move on. It didn't have to be more complicated than that. Selene explained to Bitna that she was in an argument with a friend and was working on forgiving her unkind words. Hurt feelings, too. The two women on the screen were having an intense conversation, and for a moment, Selene imagined she and Bitna were in their own K-drama.

"You two will be just fine because you love each other. I can tell from how you talk about her. Love covers it," Bitna said, patting Selene's leg. "Focus on other things now. My son requires a lot of attention. You saw how he drank all the milk and I had to remind him to go get more. Soon that'll be your job."

Bitna sent Selene home with two boxes of *mandu* to freeze.

After calling Aera and making sure Nabi was taken care of and everything was fine, Selene let Aera know she would be spending the night out but would be at Sobok Sweet first thing in the morning. They were having a last-minute Christmas sale, and Selene had seen people say they were considering lining up before the doors opened. Nabi was spending the night with Arwen at the Kim-Crawfords', and tomorrow afternoon, Selene would talk to Jenny when she went to pick up Nabi.

But tonight.

Tonight, with Deiji's house to themselves, as soon as the door closed behind Selene and Joon (and the dumplings were in the freezer), Joon was kissing her against the kitchen counter, softly at first, then more insistently, taking breaks only to peel off all their clothes. From the kitchen to the living room to the hallway, where Joon turned her around so he could spread her legs with his, kiss the back of her neck, and slowly slip his finger inside her, to the spare bedroom, where Selene gasped when Joon used the filthiest words he could to tell her he'd been wanting her like this for months. "Do you like that?" he asked. She showed him how much.

They were both breathing hard, naked on the bed. Joon said something in Korean that she didn't understand, and she didn't ask him to translate. He was kissing his way down her body, stopping to lightly lick her stomach and stick his nose between her legs. He kissed her knees, the arches of her feet.

Everything was different with Joon. On the outside, he was the most introverted, reserved guy she'd ever been interested in. Everything about him was minimalist, from his clothes to his bag to his small black SUV.

But *inside*, Joon was wildly exhaustive, making sure every light in Selene's body was violently blinking.

"I'm so glad you're not my cousin," she said in a rush when she finally pushed him back and crawled on top of him. He flicked her nipple with his tongue and paused to look up at her.

"Please don't ever say that again. Promise?"

"I promise."

Her hips took over; he sat up straighter so he could tug at her hair.

Selene felt hungover at Sobok Sweet, but she and Joon hadn't drunk a drop. What they had done was push their bodies together in the dark, sleep a little, and wake up to snack before doing it all again. Then sleep and wake to scavenge whatever they could from Deiji's fridge, quickly shower, and—whoops— have sex on the couch with Joon's jeans around his ankles, him telling her again how good it felt to be inside her, how much he loved her. They'd said *I love you* at least five times last night, and Selene could still feel Joon's strong hands all over her, but what she had to focus on now was talking to customers about Sobok

Sweet's sizing, and making sure the *CAUTION WET FLOOR* sign
stayed upright because of the snow and slushy boots. The snow
had started falling as she and Joon spooned and slept; it was still
falling when they woke in the morning.

> I'm meeting with the guy from the Busan
> newspaper after I photograph the protest in
> Seoul Plaza this afternoon. He had to
> reschedule last week. He has in-depth
> knowledge of orphanages and the adoption
> process, especially around the late 90s, early
> 00s. Last minute, but join us if you'd like?

Selene read Joon's text as she was in Aera's office getting re-
ceipt paper, and she wrote him back quickly, letting him know
she couldn't make it because she needed to pick up Nabi.

> It's okay. I'll call you after. Make sure you stay
> warm and eat well today. I hated taking that
> shower this morning. I wanted to smell you on
> me all day, all night.

> We'll make sure that happens next time. I love
> you.

> I love you too, my Selene.

Another door, another nervous stomach.
    This time it was the Kim-Crawfords', as Selene stood in the

hallway. She was there right at four, like she'd said she would be, even though she was exhausted from not much sleep last night and working all morning and afternoon.

Selene waited to knock until Lydia stepped off the elevator with Tae and Eun; Selene and Lydia had decided to do this together.

Jenny answered the door with a green velvet ribbon in her hair. Tae and Eun were inside and up the stairs immediately after saying hey to Nabi as they ran past her.

"Selene *unnie!*" Nabi said, bounding into the foyer and grabbing her around the waist.

"Nabi-*yah!*" Selene singsonged back.

"I missed you," Nabi said.

"I missed you, too, Butterfly," Selene said, letting her know she needed to talk to Jenny in her bedroom, but that they'd go get Gureum and take him for a snowy walk in his ridiculously cute, tiny blue puffer jacket after. "So hang out with the kids some more until then, okay?"

"Okay. Can we have a fun drink, please?" Nabi asked, looking up with her big eyes. Aera had put her hair in two twisty knots that made Nabi resemble a gorgeous bug.

"Sure, if Jenny says it's okay."

Jenny let Nabi know exactly where the yogurt drinks were in the fridge.

Selene and Lydia traded their boots for slippers in the foyer, and once Nabi had disappeared with the other kids, the three girls went into Jenny's bedroom and closed the door.

"So, look, I *hate* not talking to you two and I hate that we're fighting. You're mad at me, and I guess I deserve that, but—" Jenny said after sitting on the bed.

"Jenny, I'm sorry," Lydia interrupted. "I'm sorry in general for the things that were said, but also, I'm sorry I didn't include you in my latest text." Lydia paused for dramatic effect, but then looked at them both, beaming. "I finally hooked up with Santi. He's *officially* my boyfriend, and I don't care how ridiculous I sound right now, I'm so stupidly happy."

"Seriously?! Ahh!" Jenny bounced on the bed like one of the kids—everything felt better instantly. They truly felt like sisters in this moment. The fight had been explosive, but all three were ready to forgive and forget. With the bond they shared, reconciliation had been inevitable.

"Oh! You need to know the *biggest* thing! Seriously, y'all, we can never stop talking ever again because there's too much for us to catch up on. A running group chat is mandatory for us. Jenny! Look at this," Lydia said, pulling out her phone and showing Jenny the picture of Santi next to her from 2014. Jenny was confused as Lydia explained they'd both been at the Museo del Prado at the same time, and although Selene knew the story and had already had her own freak-out about the impossibility of it, she enjoyed reliving it.

"And you and Joon?" Jenny asked Selene with wide eyes, still shocked from the Lydia and Santi reveal.

"We spent the night together last night and, yeah . . . that's my man. *Namjachingu,*" Selene said, using the Korean word for *boyfriend.* She flipped her hair and stuck out her hip, eliciting excited smiles from both of them.

"What?!" Lydia asked, and Selene remembered she hadn't told her the news yet, either.

She filled them in on everything—the confrontation with Bitna and Deiji, the dumpling making, the apologies.

"That's why I was so quick with the 'fuck you' that day, Jenny," Selene explained, wincing apologetically. "I'd just made a total fool of myself in front of them and was reeling from the epic ping-pong match in my head about whether or not I almost had sex with my *cousin*."

"I earned that 'fuck you' and I'm sorry. I never should've accused you of lying about Deiji not being your birth mother. I know you'd never do that. It was stupid. And I'm sorry for saying what I said about you having a crush on Haru—I never really thought that. I was just so mad I couldn't get you two on my side." Jenny looked down, shamefaced. "I was only thinking about myself, and it was hard, feeling like it was two against one." She then apologized profusely to Lydia for saying her wish wasn't as important as theirs, but Lydia was gracious and changed the subject quickly, telling her how well the lantern festival presentation had gone.

"Wait, don't you want to talk about what happened on Jeju?" Jenny asked, circling back to the wishes. Selene and Lydia looked at each other, an unspoken agreement passing between them. They shook their heads no.

"You two are *totally* satisfied with how things are right now? You feel good about how things are going?" Jenny asked them carefully. Selene and Lydia said yes. "Besides being able to find your birth mother, Selene, the two of you don't want anything to change?" Selene and Lydia shook their heads again. "If you're both completely sure then," Jenny said, a bit reluctantly, "let's move on."

Joon came to the Chois' the next evening in a sweater-vest to bring Selene a beautifully bound photo book he'd curated over the past few months. It included one of the photo booth strips they took together, everyone in their traditional clothing on

Chuseok, photos of Selene making dumplings in Bitna's kitchen, and a few pages of photos Selene hadn't known he was snapping. One of her and Deiji talking on Bitna's balcony, another of Selene through the window from outside their precipitation café on their quiet date, watching the snow.

"The last page is blank. I wanted you to have a place for when you have a photo of your birth mother."

Selene started to cry, touching the thick paper. "This is so precious. Thank you."

She gave him the cardigan she'd gotten for him and a small fluffy puppy charm she bought for his bag so he could match hers. He clipped it right on and ran his thumb over it, smiling.

Before he left, he let Selene know that the guy from the Busan newspaper had given him the name and number of someone else who might know more.

"Now isn't the time to lose hope," Joon said confidently as he was walking out the door. "I am dedicated to this search, and I am dedicated to you. I am a Selenophile. A lover of the moon, a lover of you." He kissed her again before he left.

19

Lydia

There was a gala for the lantern project a few days before Christmas. Lydia and Santi were one of two teams whose ideas had piqued the interest of Kim Chinmae. They were invited along with two other winning students they didn't know well—their project was vastly different from Lydia and Santi's, focusing more on repeated, traditional lanterns instead of an assortment. Lydia could see how Mr. Kim would be interested in both approaches.

Lydia had borrowed a black velvet dress from Hye with a sweetheart neckline and a high slit in the leg. Hye had a closet full of expensive dresses, and Lydia would've never dared ask to wear one, but Hye insisted. It was a tad small in the boob area, but Lydia made it work to her cleavage advantage.

She remembered slipping into it earlier. Hye had been sitting on Lydia's bed and leaned over. Lydia loved it when Hye got comfortable in her bedroom. It was like they were girlfriends having a sleepover, even if it hadn't stopped feeling surreal when Lydia went out in the world and saw Hye's coffee machine ads on the wall of a convenience store or saw her face scrolling across the gigantic screens in the subway.

"Have I ever told you that you remind me of myself?" Hye asked. Lydia was in her bathroom, checking her red lipstick in the mirror one last time.

"*I* remind *you* of *you*?" Lydia asked, stepping in front of Hye once what she'd said fully sank in.

"Yes."

"Me?" Lydia asked again, pointing to herself to be sure.

"Yes, Lydia. Do you know why?" Hye asked, unclipping her long hair and letting it fall over her shoulder.

Lydia shook her head no and, if she wasn't dreaming, waited for Hye to finish her thoughts.

"Because you're *ambitious*. I could tell by your résumé and letter. I could tell by how you painted without fully knowing that my friends would pay you so much money for your art. Now you've won this big thing and made yourself a professional artist in Korea. You never seem to worry about your competition or whether you're good enough—you just go for it anyway, and I'm the same way. I admire that about you. It's why you're the right au pair for Tae and Eun. I want them to be surrounded by that sort of energy."

Lydia tried to tamp down her shock, but it didn't work. "Really?"

"Rain, Aera, and I picked au pairs who had a spark of something that reminded us of ourselves. We thought it'd be obvious. Rain chose Jenny because she's romantic; Aera picked Selene because she's independent and chic."

Hearing Hye lay it out like that—it suddenly made a lot of sense.

"Well, that's one of the nicest compliments anyone has ever given me. Thank you, Hye." She added *thank you* again in formal Korean.

"Congratulations on everything. You look great! Have a lovely time tonight," Hye said, standing from the bed and moving closer. One of the satin hanging straps stuck out near the arm of the dress, and Hye tucked it in for Lydia. "*Now* you're perfect," she said, squeezing her shoulder.

Christmas music jeweled the air, adding a cheery, bright ambiance to the dark night. Lydia was wearing Hye's real pearl earrings and fiddled with one as she waited for Santi outside the front entrance of the museum. She had a wool camel coat on over her dress, and although only her stockings and heels were peeking out at the bottom, she was still a little cold. It wasn't snowing, but snow was still on the ground from the other day, and it felt like it could start back up again at any moment.

Line after line of fancily dressed people filed into the museum. A couple made eye contact with Lydia, smiling as they walked inside. She'd been noticing whether people smiled at her, wondering if she was imagining a difference. She was so happy about the lanterns and so happy about Santi, she didn't find herself thinking about the wish as much as she'd imagined she would. If things had completely crumbled at home, maybe she would've been more concerned, but everything seemed to have leveled out with Hye. She wasn't exactly praising Lydia for wearing a T-shirt and jeans anymore, but she wasn't side-eyeing her, either, and it'd been kind of her to go out of her way to encourage Lydia as much as she did.

Lydia felt lighter knowing things with Jenny were smoothed over now, too.

More cars pulled up and dropped people off. One of the taxis was Santi's chariot. He stepped out wearing a black velvet suit coat and black turtleneck with black pants, black shoes, black hair tucked behind his ears. She'd mentioned her dress was black velvet, and he said he'd try to find something that matched. She told him he looked princely once he was next to her.

"I don't think I've ever been called *princely* before," he said, roguish.

"Well, shame on everyone else, then."

She noticed he had the blue rose enamel pin she'd given him on the lapel of his jacket. She touched the cool of it.

"You look beautiful," he said after kissing her, and she thought about how grateful she was that he was her boyfriend now. She didn't have to try to figure out a way to win him over or get his attention. The picture of the two of them in Madrid had erased any fear she could ever have that they weren't meant to be, or that this love affair would be one-sided. The magic of the wish had nothing on the magic of finding Santi.

Penelope *seonsaengnim* beamed and used glowing words to describe the art students to the crowd as they listened and sipped their drinks. She alternated between Korean and English and praised the two winning teams from the class. Kim Chinmae— in a purple velvet suit and red eyeglasses—also said a few words. Lydia, Santi, and the other duo from their class were asked to come to the stage.

"Lydia Shelby, I recognized your name immediately from a friend of a friend who'd mentioned buying a piece from you. A wash of yellows and blues you said you based on Pissarro's *Chrysanthemums in a Chinese Vase*," Mr. Kim said, leaning into the mic as he looked over at Lydia.

Speechless that he'd recognized her name and her painting, Lydia smiled at him and waved with one hand as Santi squeezed the other. She'd expected Kim Chinmae to have an air of cold mysteriousness, but the warmth in his voice was endearing. He sounded like a proud father. "These four students we have chosen as the winners will be accompanying me to Florence and Paris in the spring to present the festival details to the boards of the Uffizi Galleries and the Louvre, before we make our way to Museo Nacional del Prado in Madrid to work together on my art installation. Our hope is that these young artists are more inspired than ever as they work side by side with artists from other countries, and watch their creations come to life," Mr. Kim said as everyone clapped.

The Museo Nacional del Prado. Lydia knew what Santi was going to whisper in her ear before he said it.

Inyeon.

Lydia and Santi drank champagne and slow-danced the night away to the string quartet. When they got into a taxi at the gala's end, Lydia didn't know if she'd ever been happier. Before going back to Santi's apartment, they stopped for hot noodles by the Han River and ate them in their coats sitting next to the cold water. Slurping, steam rising.

"So, we're really going to travel around the world together on someone else's dime?" Lydia asked him as she lay on his chest in the dark of his bedroom.

"We are. I want Seoul to be my base, though. What about you?"

Santi was playing with her hair, and it was giving Lydia goose bumps all over, the way he would lift as much as he could with one hand and let it fall before lightly massaging her scalp and doing it all over again.

"Same. I want to keep au pairing for the Parks, but I don't know how that'll work since I'll need to leave for a few months."

"They'll figure that part out—it sounds like Hye will be happy for you. Tae and Eun will miss you, though."

"You always know how to make me feel better," she said, looking up into his eyes before kissing him softly.

As soon as Lydia got to Santi's the day after Christmas, she plucked a melon milk from the fridge and laid her legs across his lap, sinking into his couch. He'd ordered bacon cheeseburgers and fries; they were in the bag on the table, making the room smell delicious.

"I missed you," she said, although it'd been only twenty-four hours since she'd seen him.

Hye and Minsu had suggested she invite him over for Christmas dinner and cocktail hour with the families before Lydia could even ask if it would be okay, and it felt so natural, having him in the condo with everyone. He played with Tae and Eun, talked to Minsu about food. The night was warm and comfortable, like Santi had been Lydia's boyfriend forever.

"Missed me enough to come to Tokyo with me?"

"What are you talking about?" Lydia asked. Santi kissed her before saying anything else.

"Sorry. I meant to ask you if you like surprises first." He made a new facial expression she'd never seen before; he widened his eyes and let his mouth hang open in an *oh*.

"Surprises like going to Tokyo with you?" Her heart started to spin like a top.

"Can we start over?"

"Yes, please."

"Lydia, do you like surprises?"

"Yes."

"Do you want to go to Tokyo with me tomorrow, to the Yayoi Kusama Museum? We could stay a few nights and be back in time for Haru's going-away party." He snuggled her closer underneath his arm.

She couldn't think of anything she wanted more. Minsu would be busy, but Hye's schedule was light until after next week. Lydia would ask Jenny and Selene to watch Tae and Eun to fill in the gaps.

"My friend is having a showing at a small gallery, and I'd like to take you to that. I know you want to see Tokyo, since you've never been." He explained he wasn't the best at deciding what gifts to give people, but this seemed like something she would love.

"I do love it. This is the *best* surprise!"

"I told my friends about you and they're excited to meet you. Do you want another surprise?" Santi asked after kissing her again, this time for longer. She was hungry for him *and* the food on the table. "I talked to Minsu last night and already made sure it was okay for you to be off au pair schedule for Tokyo. I also checked with Jenny and Selene to make sure you'd love something like this, and they said yes. They helped me decide between hotels," he admitted, explaining he'd talked to them in secret after she'd fallen asleep post–Christmas cocktail hour.

The Yayoi Kusama Museum in Tokyo was a polka-dotted dream; the building was five floors of wonder partially wrapped in glass, curving at the edges. Lydia and Santi walked through every inch of it, sometimes holding hands, sometimes wandering off alone to take closer looks at pieces that most interested them. They were inseparable in the infinity room—what seemed like a million dots of light in a dark room walled with mirrors. Being inside it felt like being on a distant planet. Neither said a word while they were in there together, just held hands in awe.

They went to Santi's friend's art opening and took long walks in the cold because Lydia didn't want to miss a moment in Tokyo. She'd always wanted to visit, and wanted to explore Japan's countryside one day, too, but being in Tokyo for three days during the blissful stretch between Christmas and New Year's felt like she was suspended in time. They walked through the busyness of winter foot traffic and bundled-up people on bikes, past *kawaii* shops and colorful, glowing restaurants that gave Lydia the same inside-a-pinball-machine feeling that Hongdae did. So many of Tokyo's streets reminded her of Seoul. It was a treasure to know a place she'd never been before could also feel like home. The sky began to shed wet shakes of snow, and upon spotting a chic candlelit eatery on the corner, they went inside to warm themselves with curry udon and sake.

Back in their hotel room, Lydia and Santi had decaffeinated tea and strawberry mochi cookies as they sat cozy and warm under the *kotatsu*. Lydia had started her period on the plane ride over, and when she came out of the hotel bathroom for the second time that hour, Santi was standing, holding her phone.

"Are you still texting Haru's friend?" He handed her phone to her, and she saw a message that read, Send pics soon? Please? I miss seeing your face/body/everything on my screen.

Shit.

"No, I'm not. I would never do that, Santi, now that we're together."

The night was perfect, the trip was perfect. It was snowing, and she'd read that it didn't even snow often in Tokyo in December! *He* was her fate, and no way would she let some stupid text from a guy she barely knew ruin that. She was used to trying to gauge Santi's moods when he said very little, but she couldn't tell how he was feeling right now. No angry energy poured from him, and his expression was calm, but the sound of his voice was detached, like he could've been asking her anything. Like he could've been asking *anyone* anything.

"I'm not trying to control you, Lydia. You can do whatever you want. I just want to be sure I know what we are, that we both want the same thing," he said, pushing his hair back. He was wearing the button-down pajamas Lydia had gotten for him as a last-minute Christmas gift——she was wearing a pair that matched. They were light-blue-and-brown plaid, and although Lydia was paranoid she'd bleed through the bottoms, she was wearing them anyway because being cute together in Tokyo right now was totally worth it.

"Do you think I would've gotten us matching couple pajamas if we didn't want the same thing? I'd just go ahead and tell you I want to be with you and *only* you forever if I didn't think you'd smash the window open and jump into the street to get away from me after I said it. I know how wild and scary that is to hear. I don't care about anyone texting me anything. I'll block his number right now and you can watch me. I can't even remember his name, Santi. That's why I never changed it from 'Haru's friend.'"

"Why would you send him pictures if you don't know him, though?"

"I told you, it's because I was feeling insecure, because I

craved the attention. I was bored, and it made me feel good when they told me I was beautiful."

"Do you really *not* know how beautiful you are? Do you not see how men turn to look at you? You don't remember how half the guys in class asked you out? I was jealous, but I didn't say anything. I hope you're completely satisfied with the attention you get from me now. Our relationship is just as important to me as it is to you. This isn't one-sided. I express my emotions differently than you, but mine aren't any less strong."

If only she could tell him about the wish and how much confidence it had given her. She didn't want to be having this conversation. She wanted him to forget about all of this, wanted Santi on top of her, touching her mouth. He always touched her mouth when he was inside of her. At first soft and sweet, and towards the end more aggressively, thumbing her bottom lip, rubbing it until she opened her mouth to let him in.

"I'm completely satisfied with the attention you give me. I wasn't as confident when I first came to Seoul, but the difference now is huge. You know the me *now*. The me who knows definitively you're all I want. I promise you never have to worry about anyone else. Ever," Lydia said. Santi sank into the couch, and she went over to him, curled up in his lap.

Santi pressed his mouth to hers. "I'm in love with you. The old you, the new you, I don't care. I love *you*."

Her heart beat *Santi, Santi, Santi* like it had the moment they were first together, the moment she laid eyes on him in the classroom. Her heart knew.

Her heart had always known.

Santi touched her bottom lip before he kissed her mouth again and again, as the snow whispered down, *sobok, sobok*, ice blue sparking the dark.

20

Jenny

Haru's going-away party was the night before New Year's Eve. Rain and Daniel took Fox and Arwen out to lunch, and the kids were excited to stop by Daiso and pick out party supplies.

Whenever Jenny and Haru were alone in the house together, she wanted to touch him, to kiss him, to see him with his shirt off and marvel at the body of this man who worked in a restaurant day and night and ate everything he saw, but still found time to go to the gym. She was sitting on his lap facing him and the door, slowly rocking her hips against him, knowing she would hear the keypad beeps if the Kim-Crawfords came home. He kissed her neck, lifted her shirt to kiss her breasts.

"You're so soft. You smell so good," he groaned as she pressed her cheek against his.

Even with all her clothes on, she knew she'd come quickly—she'd been fantasizing about this all morning. Every time he made eyes at her over the kitchen table, or anytime she moved to adjust herself across him as they watched TV.

"I love you," he said. Obstinate. Her mouth was open as she finished, but still, she didn't say it back.

~

Jenny, Lydia, and Selene were in Jenny's bathroom in the condo, and Lydia was peeing. Haru's going-away party was in full swing, and someone had turned up oldskool '90s hip-hop. The bass thumped the walls. They'd just calmed down after laughing so hard about Haru's friend bringing his girlfriend to the party, the same girlfriend he'd apparently had the whole time he was texting Lydia. Lydia was both annoyed and aghast that she'd unknowingly sent sexy pics to a guy with a girlfriend, but Jenny and Selene consoled her by saying she didn't have to think about any of it ever again.

"Are you okay with the *going-away* part of this party?" Selene asked Jenny.

She couldn't escape the thought of Haru leaving so soon. She thought about it every time she heard his name, every time she looked at him.

Who was Haru to her?

"I don't know. I can't make sense of anything in my head right this second, but I will soon," Jenny said.

"You probably need food," Lydia said as she washed her hands, adding the Korean for *let's eat*.

In the kitchen, they piled their plates with kimchi and sweet potato noodles, *tteokbokki* and fried chicken. The kids were playing a game of "don't let the balloons touch the floor" that occasionally got so loud, the au pairs had to intervene and remind them not to scream. Haru—in his white button-down and slim navy pants—was everywhere, chatting with everyone, sometimes women. Sometimes attractive women. Jenny couldn't help but wonder if he'd ever dated any of them. If he'd ever bought them a ribbon. She was wearing the ribbon he'd given her with a short black dress. He'd told her how good she looked at least seven times already.

After eating all she could, she followed Lydia and Selene into the crowded living room, and as they sat on the couch, peeking at a silly video on Selene's phone, Jenny stood behind them, watching Haru on the other side of the room. Despite their assurances, Jenny still wanted to talk about what happened at the waterfall, although at this point, she was worried telling Lydia and Selene the truth about *not* undoing the wishes would shake them up too much—*again*. Lydia had found new confidence in herself, thinking she had no choice but to go on without the wish, and now she and Santi were in love. Selene and Joon had found their way together, too, and he was still pursuing leads about her birth mother. Jenny didn't want to set them back with the truth since they'd already accepted they were on their own.

Maybe it didn't matter. Wasn't *this* love? The way Jenny felt when Haru walked in the room? *Was* the wish really protecting her like she thought it was? Had it ever, truly?

Dizzy, Jenny slowly got on her knees, put her arms on the back of the couch and her chin on her hands, watching Haru. Like always, he found her eyes. Her heart shimmered.

The way he listened when she spoke. The sickness she felt when he wasn't around. The way he looked for her in a crowd. The unbearable desire she had to smell him and touch him. The way their bodies knew each other's, even in the dark.

She *loved* him. She *loved* Haru.

Despite it all.

Despite her feelings about the wish and her healing broken heart, love had found a way.

Of course she loved him. She knew that now.

She tried to imagine making a life with Haru and *not* loving him. Wanting to be with him, wanting to hear from him, learning everything about him and *not* loving him. The thought was absurd. If this *wasn't* love, nothing was.

Of course she loved him. Her heartbreak had led her *five thousand nine hundred fifty-five miles* to Seoul, all the way to Haru. Jenny stood with the room spinning and went to him, took his hand without saying anything. He excused himself from his friends, and when they got to her bedroom, she closed the door.

"Are you okay?" he asked her in Korean.

She faced him, tears in her eyes. "I love you. I *love* you, Haru."

The adorable, puzzled look he wore was such a comfort before he pulled her into his arms. "What made you want to tell me that right now? What happened?"

"*Everything* happened. Us! I want this. I love you. I *know* it. I love you, and I'm sorry it took me so long to say——"

Haru took her face in his hands and kissed her. Every anxiety she had about them making this work while he was in New Zealand spilled out.

"We don't have to worry about any of that, Jennybelle. We'll figure everything out together," Haru said.

"Call me Jennybelle again, please."

"Jennybelle, Jennybelle, Jennybelle," he whispered into her neck, squeezing her tight.

Jenny had told Haru that she and her dad had a tradition of getting doughnuts and marathoning *The Twilight Zone* on New Year's Eve, but she was still surprised when Haru showed up in the morning with a dozen of the prettiest doughnuts she'd ever seen—long knots dusted with cinnamon and sugar, traditional cake covered in pink icing and pearlized fondant, mini baguette-sized ones dripping in thick chocolate. She and everyone else dug into them and couched it, watching the *Twilight Zone* DVDs

Haru had borrowed from one of his friends until they had to get ready for Rain and Daniel's recommitment ceremony.

The event was a small affair but important enough to warrant renting out a room at the hotel, complete with a dance floor and a DJ. The actual ceremony had been beautiful, full of tenderness and respect and admiration, and now it was time to celebrate. Jenny, Lydia, and Selene danced to K-pop for so long their dates had to take a much-needed break and were now sitting at a table with beers.

Haru rejoined Jenny when Sade came on and put his arms around her waist. They swayed together as the lights above them swept through a rainbow of colors, washing the room from violet to red. Red to orange. Orange to yellow. Yellow to green.

"Do you want to sneak off somewhere?" Haru said against her ear when the song was almost over. She was wearing the gold dress with a gold ribbon tied around her high ponytail. She was also wearing the diamond-bow earrings Haru had given her for Christmas. She'd gifted him a bottle of cologne—mossy, vespertine—and could smell it coming through the heat of him. On their way out of the room, the sequins of her dress flashed in the lights, dancing like water on the wall next to them.

They held hands down the hallway, and she didn't bother asking where they were going because she knew he wouldn't tell. They moved quickly. Haru's jacket flipped up, revealing gold and a frosted blue so elegant she wanted to cry. They kissed on the elevator all the way up to the twentieth floor. Haru led her to the room at the end of the hall, only then showing her the matte black key card in his pocket.

"I know a guy who knows a guy," he said as he beeped the door open to the most luxe hotel room Jenny had ever seen. They slipped off their shoes, slid into the slippers waiting for them. The curtains of the wide window were pulled back, and fireworks flashed and dripped across the sky. A pink bunny plushie with floppy ears was on the bed alongside matching couples T-shirts with teddy bears on them. "Bunny Haru for you," he said, picking the stuffed animal up and handing it to her. A bottle of champagne in ice sat on the bench, a dozen white roses on the dresser. "I know you have plans to meet up with Lydia and Selene right after midnight, but this room is ours for the night if you want to come back and stay. Rain and Daniel know about it. I've had this planned since October, and tomorrow I want to take you to Busan with me. A little trip before I leave. And in February, when I come back to visit, we can see the mountains and hot springs in Sokcho. I want to take you to a restaurant there so we can get *dakjuk*. It's the only place in the world where the *dakjuk* is better than mine. Does that all sound good to you?"

Jenny tugged his tie and pulled him closer, answering with a kiss.

Jenny had ordered a fresh cream friendship cake for the girls to share and decorated it with cutout photo booth pics of the three of them on top. She lit three candles in the Kim-Crawfords' kitchen, and they took turns blowing them out. They'd counted down the new year together at the hotel, and now everyone was where they belonged. The kids, sleeping in their bedrooms. Haru, waiting for Jenny in the hotel room. Jenny herself, waiting for all the adventures she was looking forward to having with him.

The girls wrapped themselves in their coats before heading out onto the balcony. Jenny had the Bunny Haru plushie in one arm and with the other raised her half-full champagne flute.

"To us, to the new year, and to these days in Seoul we will never forget! Most *importantly*, to the wishes I never undid. I couldn't bring myself to do it. To the wishes!" Jenny said, clinking their glasses one by one while Lydia and Selene stared at her incredulously.

21

Selene

"What do you mean, you didn't undo the wishes?" Lydia asked.

"I couldn't do it. I went to the waterfall and stood there, but I couldn't undo mine . . . *ours*. I decided not to go through with it," Jenny said.

"I don't understand, Jenny. Why'd you act like you did?" Selene asked. Part of her felt like she should be mad at Jenny for keeping this from them, but if she didn't undo the wishes, maybe Selene really would find her birth mother soon. She'd long accepted that it might not happen, but that didn't mean she wouldn't be completely filled with happiness if it *did*. She'd exhausted her social media reach by posting about her search on Instagram again, asking for any info about her birth parents without getting any leads. She'd been hopeful, since she had so many new Korean followers now because of Sobok Sweet, but so far . . . nothing. But! Joon had stepped out to take a phone call after Rain and Daniel's ceremony. Maybe he'd received breakthrough information this time. Maybe.

"Are you mad at me? Please," Jenny pleaded, "let me explain."

They stood in the cold as she told them about not wanting to risk shaking up their newfound peace by bringing up her trip to Jeju after they specifically told her they didn't want to hear about it.

"Aren't you happy?" Jenny asked them both.

Lydia and Selene hesitated, looking at each other before nodding slowly.

"So now you're happy *and* you still have your wishes, if you choose to believe. If you don't, that's fine, too. Don't worry about me. Mine ran its course. My wish proved to me that love was stronger than a wish, and I got what I *needed* out of this experience, not what I *thought* I wanted. Please don't be mad. Are you mad?" Jenny asked again.

"I'm not mad at you. It all worked out, right? I finally started thinking I didn't need the wish anymore anyway," Lydia said.

"I'm not mad, either," Selene said truthfully. "Is there any *other* enormous secret you're keeping from us, Jenny? I'm serious."

"Maybe? I'm in love with Haru and he knows that now. Is *that* an enormous secret?" Jenny said, smirking.

"You're unbelievable, Jenny, honestly," Selene said, laughing in complete exasperation. "*Yes*, that counts."

"Okay, I promise, no more secrets! Promise, promise," Jenny said. She linked pinkies and kissed thumbs with both of them to prove it.

"And since we're talking promises . . . do you both promise you really think something magical happened to us that night we made the wishes? I know we've all gone back and forth about it but, like, deep down in your bones now after everything . . . you undeniably, *truly* believe that?" Selene asked, looking back and forth between them, anticipating what they were going to say.

She listened with love as they gave their answers, her little fire of hope burning hot.

If Selene could see the future, she'd see Lydia and Santi interning together at the new modern art museum after their travels, and in another two years, still bursting with love, splitting their time between the United States, Spain, and Korea. She'd see Jenny and Haru getting married in three years, herself and Lydia draped in honorary ribbons and pink dresses, bridesmaids supporting the beaming bride. Selene saw herself working full-time at Sobok Sweet as a fashion consultant, sharing a quaint apartment in Seongsu-dong with Joon, the girls coming over for dinner once a week whenever they were in town, always ending up on the rooftop, becoming one with the sky and sparkling sprawl. She'd see a small wedding and a little girl called Saetbyeol she and Joon would have in four years, meaning *morning star* to match Selene's *moon*—a daughter with Selene's eyes and Joon's mouth, a splash of freckles across her nose.

If Selene could see the future, she'd see herself with Lydia and Jenny back on Jeju Island, the three of them going to the Waterfall of God on another full moon night in August, one year after they made their first wishes, wishing together again, keeping their innermost desires a secret this time.

She'd hear the voicemail Joon would leave her on the walk back to the villa that night, telling her he finally found someone in Pohang who recognized her birth father's face and knew who her birth mother was.

She'd hear Joon say her mother's name, and finally, Selene would say it aloud, too.

Ahn Sarang.

Sarang, meaning *love* in Korean. Her mother's name is *love*, and it feels like home.

She'd look at the photo Joon would send of Sarang with her father, both of them smiling. So young, so *before*. She'd see that she and her mother have the same eyes, the same constellation of freckles across their noses. Hear Joon tell her Sarang lives in

New York City. Selene would see herself with Joon next to her as she stands in front of Sarang's door, the red blanket gripped in her fist. How Sarang would cry and tell her she's always loved her, that her parents forced her to abandon Selene because she was young and unmarried, that she'd thought about her all the time but had been scared to look for her. How Selene will tell her in both Korean and English she is so glad she finally found her. She would hear her mother say *I have been waiting so long to see you* and feel her mother's arms come around her like the fulfillment of her own wish, with a newfound promise to never let go.

The New Year's Eve night sky was variegated with shades of deep and deeper blue holding firework light, blinking with scads of hidden stars. Sharing a blanket, the girls looked out at the city as bursts of twinkling amethyst, ruby, quartz, and citrine glowed inside the cerulean crystals of apartment buildings, offices, shops, churches. Seoul, a precious jewel.

A gem worthy of wishing upon.

Author's Note

Dear Reader,

I keep my deep, intense love for K-dramas in a very safe spot in my heart. Nothing and no one can touch it. That's how precious it is to me! I wanted to fill *As You Wish* with the same friendships, romance, comfort, and coziness I find in my favorites. I am providing a starter kit of my personal favorites (at this exact point in time!), broken down into categories of my own making. Whether you've never watched one before or, like me, you've (almost) lost track of how many you've seen, I hope it helps!

Thank you for reading. I hope this finds you warm and well. I hope all your wishes come true.

As ever,
Leesa

K-Drama Starter Kit

Sweet/Romantic/Cute: *Something in the Rain, One Spring Night, Yumi's Cells, King the Land, Encounter, Soundtrack #1, Suspicious Partner, Our Beloved Summer, Strongest Deliveryman, She Was Pretty, Witch's Romance, My First First Love*

Healing: *Rain or Shine/Just Between Lovers, Hometown Cha-Cha-Cha, Lovely Runner, It's Okay to Not Be Okay, My Liberation Notes, Doctor Slump, Welcome to Samdal-ri, If You Wish Upon Me, Melting Me Softly, Mad for Each Other, Because This Is My First Life, The Sound of Magic, I'll Go to You When the Weather Is Nice, A Piece of Your Mind, Little Forest* (movie)

Hilarious: *Business Proposal, Gaus Electronics, Welcome to Waikiki, Backstreet Rookie*

So Good, but Prepare Yourself for Lots and Lots of Crying (also file under "K-trauma"): *Snowdrop, The Red Sleeve*

So Good, but Dark/Heavy: *The Worst of Evil, Nevertheless, Burning* (movie)

Absolute Classics: *Goblin/Guardian: The Lonely and Great God, Crash Landing on You, The K2, Fight for My Way, Itaewon Class, What's Wrong with Secretary Kim, Healer, True Beauty, Reply 1988*

Acknowledgments

As always, thank you so much to my agent, Kerry D'Agostino, for everylittlebit of everything! I couldn't do this without you. And big thanks to everyone at Curtis Brown, Ltd. Huge thanks to Alli Dyer! I love the magic we make together. And big thanks to everyone at Temple Hill Entertainment.

Thank you so much to my editor, Rachael Kelly, and to Isabel DaSilva, Diamond Bridges, Hannah Poole, Maya Ziv, Alice Dalrymple, Grace J. Kim, Mary Beth Constant, LeeAnn Pemberton, and Lindsey Tulloch. Thank you so much to everysingleperson on my team at Dutton/Tiny Reparations who make books happen!

Thank you so much and my love to my dear, brilliant friend Alvin Park.

My love to my amazing and kind Korean teachers, 최경주 and 강정인. My love to my Korean class and my dear friends Erica Rucker, Shy Stalling, and Lindy Anne Almaguer Viamonte. My love to my beautiful K-pop girlies for life Alayna Giovannitti and Caro Ramirez.

Thank you to BTS: Kim Namjoon, Kim Seokjin, Min Yoongi, Jung Hoseok, Park Jimin, Kim Taehyung, and Jeon Jungkook for your music and hearts and inspiration and love. And thank you to GOT7: Lim Jaebeom, Mark Tuan, Jackson Wang, Park Jinyoung (and his Disney Prince walk), Choi Youngjae, Kunpimook Bhuwakul, and Kim Yugyeom, too.

Thank you to Ji Changwook, Jung Haein, Lee Junho, Park

Seojoon, Park Bogum, Wi Hajoon, Steven Yeun, Kim "Dimples" Minkyu, Byeon Wooseok, Son Sukku, and Gong Yoo. Thank you to Kim Goeun, Kim Jiwon, Kim Dami, Kim Taeri, Son Yejin, Jung Somin, Ra Miran, and Kim Sunyoung. (I have so many favorites, this is just a start!) Thank you to everyone in my K-dramas! Thank you to "Laundry," by Lee Juck, and the video I watch every night of Ji Changwook singing "Laundry," by Lee Juck. Thank you to 2PM, ATEEZ, EXO, TXT, BLACKPINK, TWICE, Stray Kids, LE SSERAFIM, BIBI, IU, NewJeans, and SEVENTEEN. Thank you to Kim Jongin and every Kai song. Thank you to Maangchi. Thank you to Banana Yoshimoto. Thank you to Rachael Yamagata. Thank you to toast with strawberry jam, tangerines, peppermint tea with lemon, cherry blossoms, kimchi, and the Asian market. Thank you, Seoul; I love you very much, Seoul. Thank you to room service at the Four Seasons Hotel Seoul. Thank you to Monster Pizza in Hongdae. Thank you to *Kiki's Delivery Service*, *Ponyo*, Studio Ghibli, and Hayao Miyazaki. Thank you to my very long list of watched, currently watching, and to-be-watched K-dramas. Thank you to my comforting K-drama OSTs and my emotional support K-pop/K-drama photocards and every K-pop song that finds my ears and every K-pop group that makes me smile. I love you!

Huge thanks to my parents and my brother for their support and love, always! I love you!

Huge thanks to my babies, R&A, who aren't even babies anymore, but will still always be my babies! Thank you for making my wishes come true! I love you!

Huge thanks to my lover, my husband, my best friend, and first reader, Loran, for everything all the time forever. Thank you for feeding and watering me like a little plant. Thank you for loving me like Jesus does. Thank you for making my wishes come true! I love you!

About the Author

Leesa Cross-Smith is a homemaker and the author of seven books. She was longlisted for the 2022 Mark Twain American Voice in Literature Award and the 2021 Joyce Carol Oates Prize. Her third novel, *Half-Blown Rose*, received the Coups de Cœur recognition from the American Library in Paris and was the Amazon Editors' Spotlight pick for June 2022. It was also the inaugural pick for Amazon editorial director Sarah Gelman's book club, Sarah Selects, and a Barnes & Noble Book Club pick. She lives in Kentucky with her husband and two children.